SAVAGE reign

MONICA KAYNE

Cover Design: Lori Jackson Design

Photographer: Wander Aguiar

Manuscript Critique: Romance Editor, Nina Fiegl s.p.

Beta Reader: Sierra Cassidy

Line editing: Ivy L. James

Proofreading: www.debpeachediting.com

ISBN 978-1-7782704-6-8

First edition 2025

For my readers,

The world might feel like a dumpster fire right now, but we can always escape into fiction—where a sexy, possessive bratva king with a filthy mouth will grab you by the throat and fuck you senseless.

AUTHOR NOTE

Savage Reign is a dark mafia romance with mature themes and profanity. Please check the FAQ section of my website for trigger and content warnings.

https://monicakayne.com/trigger-warnings

PROLOGUE

Five Years Earlier

SOFIYA

Your wedding day is supposed to be the happiest day of your life.

But not mine. Today feels more like a living nightmare than a dream.

A strangled sob rips from my throat as a guard shoves me into the backseat of the Jeep.

"Shut up, will you? It's a wedding, not a funeral."

I almost laugh at the bitter irony. I wish it were a funeral—my own. I'm being forced to marry a monster, and there's nothing I can do to stop it.

The vehicle lurches forward, and I press my hand against the window, my gaze locked on the farmhouse that's been our prison since yesterday. My older sister, Liza, just as helpless as I am, is still somewhere inside.

A day ago, everything was different. I was a typical seventeen-year-old in Moscow, attending boarding school, hanging out with friends, and acting in the school play. My world was predictable—boring, even.

I was living in a bubble, naively believing that nothing could touch me or the people I loved. Yesterday, that illusion shattered when my sister's fiancé, Anatoly Petrovich—the man I had believed to be her Prince Charming—abducted Liza and me and flew us here, to some foreign country.

While we were locked together in the farmhouse, Liza finally revealed the secret she'd been hiding. Anatoly isn't a prince; he's an abusive predator. The only reason she stayed with him was that our selfish parents forced her to. My father had gambled away our family fortune, and without Anatoly—heir to a shipping empire—covering our expenses, we would have been out on the streets.

But Anatoly isn't the clean-cut businessman he pretends to be. My sister said he secretly formed a partnership with the Zhukov Bratva, a small but brutal organized crime outfit from St. Petersburg. Along with its leader, Sergey Zhukov, they plan on uniting their business interests.

That's why we're here. I'm being forced to wed Sergey, a virtual stranger, while Liza is expected to marry Anatoly. They want to bind their empires together through our bloodlines. In this world, family connections mean everything.

My hands tremble as I grasp the white lace of the wedding dress, the fabric sticking to my back, damp with sweat. I choke back useless tears as we race along sun-soaked mountain roads. The Jeep jerks to a halt in front of a small, whitewashed chapel, its entrance patrolled by half a dozen armed guards.

One of them yanks my door open, and clamps his hand around my upper arm, wrenching me from the vehicle. For one desperate moment, I consider running. But where? I wouldn't get far surrounded by all these men.

Another man steps up, giving me a once-over like I'm an

object on display. "Cuff her. Then send her in." He smirks. "Her groom wants a taste before the ceremony."

Panic seizes my lungs as my hands are secured by zip ties in front of my body, and I'm pulled inside the chapel. For one merciful second, I think it's empty, but then I see him—a lone figure, seated in the front pew.

I stand stock-still. Small windows allow in little light, leaving only the soft glow of candles at the front to illuminate the space. The air is thick with incense, and it's not doing my already anxious gut any favors.

This place has probably hosted many happy celebrations, but this won't be one of them. It'll be the exact opposite.

When he stands and turns, the breath is stolen from my lungs. Because the man walking toward me is not Sergey Zhukov.

I know because I met him a few weeks ago when Anatoly took me out for dinner with some of his business associates. At the time, I had no idea who Sergey really was. He looked like a respectable businessman with pressed designer suits and neatly trimmed dark hair.

This man doesn't bother hiding his savagery: a shaved head, an eyebrow ring, and dark tattoos coiling out from under the crisp collar of his tux. One tattoo, a star encircled by thorny vines, catches my eye. His features are beautiful yet unforgiving, with a rugged jaw, sharp cheekbones, and piercing blue eyes.

With his every step toward me, I take an automatic step in the other direction.

"Stop," he commands, but I can't. It's only when my back hits the wall and there's nowhere else for me to go that I still.

"I see you don't follow orders very well," he purrs. "You don't need to be afraid of me. Guess you've figured out I'm not Sergey?"

I nod, slowly. About all I can do.

"I'm Nikolai Zhukov. Sergey's older brother. I'm working

with Roman and other members of the Belov Syndicate to free you and your sister."

I stare at him blankly, trying to process this information. The Belov Syndicate is the country's most powerful Bratva, and Roman Vasiliev is one of its leaders. He's also the man Liza's in love with. When we were taken, she was about to leave Anatoly for Roman. But he's dead—murdered by Anatoly's goons earlier today.

"Y-you think I'll believe that?" I stammer. "I know Roman is dead."

A muscle in his jaw ticks. "That's what we wanted Anatoly to believe. He's not dead—Sergey is. I killed him myself."

My face drains of color. What kind of man kills his own brother only to partner with a rival bratva? I shake my head. "Why would you be working with the Syndicate?"

"That's a long story, and we don't have time for it. The important piece is, I just got out of jail to find out Sergey had partnered with Anatoly. While I was locked up, they started a side business in sex trafficking." He frowns, his jaw tightening. "It was something we swore never to touch, but Sergey got real good at breaking his word."

Liza said they were into dark deeds, but sex trafficking? That's sickening.

"My brother was a piece of shit that didn't deserve to live," he continues. "That *mudak* was going to marry you today… a seventeen-year-old." His jaw hardens as he scans the chapel. "Roman and others are rescuing Liza from the farmhouse, which means we have to kill some time here before they can provide us with backup. There's one guard too many for me to take out on my own."

"Why should I trust a word you say?" I huff. He's a cold-blooded killer, not exactly a man of his word.

He tips my chin up so I can't look anywhere else but at him. "You don't have a choice. These guards are mercenaries.

Anatoly hired outside help for this job, which means they don't know what Sergey looks like, and they believe I'm him. In a few minutes, a priest is going to walk through those doors, and we will be expected to marry."

Anxiety claws at my throat. "We have to get… married?"

"We have to go through the motions so the guards believe everything's going according to plan. It also means I have to act the part—brutal and ruthless." He cocks his head, studying my reaction. "I'm here to protect you, but I can only do that if you play along. Do you understand?"

I understand what he's saying, but do I trust him? No. Except, like he said, I don't have a choice.

The door swings open, and a terrified-looking priest is marched toward us by one of the hulking mercenaries. In a blink, Nikolai's demeanor changes. His back snaps straight, his stare grows cold, and he wears a callous smile.

"I was playing with my bride-to-be. But if the priest is here, let's get this over with so I can enjoy the real prize." His eyes drink me in, flashing with hunger.

Dread snakes through me. Is this the real Nikolai, or is he only playing the part as he claimed? When the guard's attention turns toward the priest, Nikolai's gaze softens, and his thumb brushes over my cheekbone.

The rest of the men trail in, and Nikolai frowns. "She needs to be cut free. I'm not marrying a woman in zip ties."

One of them reaches for me, but Nikolai steps between us. "You don't get to touch what's mine," he growls. The guard produces a knife, which Nikolai snatches from him.

My hands tremble as Nikolai carefully slices through the heavy plastic, freeing me from the bonds. He pulls me against his body and announces, "Are you ready to get married, my little mouse? Don't look so scared. I promise to be gentle… at first."

Snickers fill the room, and my blood runs cold. I'm in the

company of predators—the kind who enjoy watching others suffer.

"Gentlemen," Nikolai addresses the guards. "I require everyone to witness this holy union. Sit and watch." He points to the pews.

They exchange looks as if this is the strangest thing anyone has ever asked of them.

"What's the fucking holdup?" Nikolai snaps. "All of you, sit the fuck down. This is my wedding, and we're doing it my way."

His authoritative voice has them scrambling into place. Half a dozen guards sink into the pews, our reluctant guests.

"Y-you sign marriage certificate first," the priest stammers in broken English, gesturing toward a small desk beside the altar.

Nikolai grabs me by the wrist, shoving me toward the desk. He doesn't read it, just adds his signature at the bottom.

"Sign it." He thrusts the pen at me and jabs his finger beside the line that requires my signature.

My hand freezes. Could this make our union real? The idea is so horrifying that the pen drops and clatters to the floor. I leave it there, my limbs frozen.

Nikolai reaches down to pick it up before forcing it back into my hand. "I said, fucking sign it. Are you stupid?"

Another round of harsh laughter fills the small space. Either Nikolai is a top-notch actor, or he actually has no soul. The jury is still out.

I draw my shoulders back and put pen to paper, adding my signature. The ink is barely dry on the paper when Nikolai hauls me back in front of the priest, and the ceremony starts. I don't understand a word of what the priest is saying because it's in another language, Greek, I'm pretty sure, although I can tell he's stuttering and losing his place more than he should. Like me, he's clearly not here willingly.

As the priest chants, the guards shuffle in their seats,

distracted, but Nikolai isn't. His attention locks on me, studying every detail of my face like he's committing it to memory.

As much as I'm scared for myself, my mind drifts back to Liza. Is she okay? Is Roman really alive, as Nikolai claims? Can he save her? Is Nikolai really who he says he is, or will this end with me in a worse situation than I'm already in?

And then it's the part where we say, "I do." Nikolai says it first—those two words carry more weight than they should. I have to say it now, but when I open my mouth, the words get stuck in my throat.

Say it, Sofiya, and be done with it.

What does it matter anyhow? Everything in my life has already gone up in flames. "I do."

Nikolai grasps my hand, his touch warmer than I expected, and slides a gold band onto my finger. He doesn't look at me as he picks up the second ring, slipping it onto his own finger, his attention shifting briefly to the guards.

My gaze drops to the ring. All of this feels like a dream. A bad one. If someone told me this was in my future a few days ago, I would have laughed, but there's nothing funny about it now.

The priest says something that I don't understand, though I get the insinuation—this is the "you may kiss the bride" part. As scary as that is, like everything else, I don't have a choice.

Nikolai moves toward me slowly. His attention drifts to the door, then back to me. What's he waiting for? Backup? The priest looks between us and says the words again clearly, that we need to kiss. Nikolai takes in the guards sitting in the front pew, stone-faced and bored.

As he closes the small gap between us, his demeanor softens. His mouth lingers inches from mine, giving me a moment to brace myself. I wet my lips and look up at him. A shiver skates down my spine. It's not quite fear but something else that pulses under my skin.

I tip my head up, my eyes fluttering closed as his lips press softly against mine, the gentleness unexpected. His fingers graze my cheek, and almost instinctively, my hand rests on his chest, sending a warmth through me that I wasn't prepared for.

POW POW POW.

A series of explosions echo in the distance, and Nikolai breaks away sharply, his head snapping up as he locks onto the guards seated in front of us.

It all happens so fast. Nikolai shoves me down behind the altar, yanks a pistol from the back of his waistband, and fires toward the pews.

Holy shit! My heart pounds furiously in my ears. I can't help but peek out from behind the altar, my stomach twisting as I take in the guards, each one slumped forward, a bullet hole in their heads.

Nikolai waves off the priest, who scrambles out the back without a second glance. Then he kneels in front of me, his hands cupping my face as he murmurs something I can barely make out. Whatever it is, it doesn't penetrate the horror of what I just witnessed.

"Breathe, just breathe. It was kill or be killed, *moya sladost.*"

Sweetheart.

He brushes the hair off my face. "Those explosions you heard were Roman and his men attacking Anatoly and the other guards. These guys here would've figured out what was happening pretty quickly. I said I would keep you safe, and I did, but now we have to get out of here."

I nod, numb and heavy with shock. Despite everything, a strange calm roots itself in me. He's a cold-blooded killer, but he risked his life to protect me.

When he lifts me into his arms, I don't fight or struggle. I lean into his chest and let him take me away.

CHAPTER ONE

Present Day

SOFIYA

There's a knock at the door, and I hurry to answer, knowing it's my sister, Liza. Before I can get a word out, she wraps me in a hug, squeezing me like her life depends on it.

I pull back with a laugh. "You're acting like we've been separated for months. I saw you and Roman last week for dinner."

"Well, it feels like longer," she pouts, stepping into my apartment. The apartment she and her husband, Roman Vasiliev, pay for to ensure I live somewhere with top-notch security in one of Moscow's safest neighborhoods. With Roman being one of the heads of the Belov Syndicate, it's a necessity, not a luxury. Same goes for the ever-present bodyguard, something I resent but understand. "You've been so busy getting ready for the final recital that I almost considered enrolling in your classes just to spend time with you."

I snort. "I'd love to see you dancing *barynya* in Madame Orlova's folk dancing class."

"Folk dancing, seriously?"

"It was an elective. I don't know why I thought it was a good idea." I shrug.

Liza presents me with an overflowing bouquet of flowers.

"These are gorgeous, thank you," I say, taking them from her. "Better put them in water." I lead her into the kitchen.

For the last four years, I've attended Moscow's premier performing arts college, pouring everything I have into the contemporary dance program. This is my final week before graduation, and I've been laser-focused on the recital, where I'll be performing the night's closing solo—a piece I choreographed myself. It's an honor to end the show, but it's also nerve-wracking as hell.

Still, I'm more excited about what comes next. I plan to move to Berlin to launch my dance career. Not only is it one of the best cities for live performance, but it's far from Moscow. Here, I'll always be Roman Vasiliev's sister-in-law, tied to the powerful Syndicate.

Moving to Berlin is my chance to make a name for myself on my own merits. I've avoided telling Liza my plans since I know she'll be upset I'm relocating so far away. A wave of guilt washes over me as I imagine her reaction, but there's no more time to wait.

"Where do you keep your vases?" Liza asks, rummaging through the cupboard.

I laugh and pull out an old spaghetti jar. "This will have to do. I don't own anything else."

"You don't own a vase? Seriously? What kind of adult are you?" she teases, rinsing the jar and filling it with water.

"One who likes her independence," I quip. "Roman and you spoil me enough. I don't need anything else."

"Guess I know what I'm getting you for Christmas," she says, arranging the flowers and setting them on the table.

In the sunlight, Liza looks as stunning as ever. Her dark

auburn hair, nearly identical to mine, falls in soft waves, framing her delicate face.

People always say we look alike, and they're not wrong. We have the same full lips, high cheekbones, and tall frames. But where Liza is willowy, I'm curvier, my body strong from years of training. My hazel eyes, flecked with green, also set us apart.

"These flowers are beautiful. Thank you again," I say, smelling the bouquet of lilies and peonies. "You really didn't have to."

Liza curls into a chair, tucking her feet underneath her. "Roman and I feel terrible we can't make it to your recital. If I could move the appointment, I would."

After everything we went through five years ago—being abducted and nearly forced into marriage—Liza has finally found her happiness. Six months after we were rescued, she and Roman married, and years later, they're still blissfully in love. Recently, she earned a degree in finance and is working as an analyst for one of the Syndicate's legitimate businesses.

The only cloud hanging over them is their struggle to get pregnant. For two years, they've tried without success. I know how much it's weighed on them—Liza especially. After a long wait, they've finally secured an appointment with one of the world's top fertility specialists in New York City. It means she'll miss my recital, but there's no way I'd let her cancel.

"Don't worry about it for a second," I say, waving off her guilt as I pour us each a cup of tea. "This appointment is way more important. The recital's being filmed, and I'll make sure you get a copy."

I can't deny a small part of me feels relieved. Liza and Roman never go anywhere without their full security detail, and the last thing I need is to draw more attention to my Syndicate ties. It's bad enough hearing whispers from classmates who think I only got the solo because of my connection to the Belov Syndicate.

They're wrong. I've worked my ass off for this, clawed my way through sleepless nights, injuries, and grueling practices to earn that solo. But even so, a part of me still feels like I have to prove myself.

I've spent enough time in therapy to know why. When your own parents treat you like a pawn, a bargaining chip, it leaves scars. If they couldn't see my worth, what does that say about me?

Liza smiles softly, but guilt flickers in her eyes. "I hate that you won't have any family at the concert."

"It's fine. I'll have Daria and Alex," I reassure her. They are my two best friends at school, and we've been inseparable for the past four years. "Seriously, I want this baby for you and Roman almost as much as you do. If this doctor can help, you need to go. You're going to be an amazing mom—the polar opposite of ours."

Liza's mouth twists into a grimace, and I immediately regret my words. Mentioning our parents is always a delicate subject. Eight years older than me, she still carries guilt over the fact that she couldn't protect me when our parents sold me off to Sergey to cover my father's mounting debts. None of it was her fault, but guilt doesn't play by logic.

She recovers quickly, her expression softening. "God, I hope so. Do you remember that summer when our parents ditched us for France? At least the au pair they left us with didn't care what we did."

"It was the best," I say, my thoughts drifting back. "Don't you remember? We camped out in the backyard, sleeping under the stars, and we lived off junk food in the pantry. I'm pretty sure I didn't wear shoes that entire summer. It was heaven."

"Some of my best memories," she agrees, a soft smile

touching her lips. She takes a sip of her tea before her gaze settles back on me. "So, how are you feeling about graduating? You'll be taking the Moscow dance world by storm soon."

I swallow hard. It's time to tell her my plan to move. I know she pictures her future kids growing up with their "cool aunt" close by, and she imagines a big, tight-knit family with me as an important part of it. Telling her I'm leaving the country feels like ripping that dream apart, especially with everything she's doing to have a baby. But I have to do this for myself.

"A little nervous, but good," I say, keeping my hands busy, stirring sugar into my tea. "I need to tell you something, but first, you need to know I'm okay. I really am."

Her eyebrows pull together. "Of course you are. You've come so far. Roman and I are so proud of you."

Her words hit me harder than I'd expected, and I don't know how to respond. "Thank you," I say, my voice thick. "You don't know what that means to me. I felt so ashamed for so long because of… everything."

After Liza and I were rescued from Greece, I was like a ghost for a year, wandering Roman's penthouse, numb and detached from the world. I didn't return to school; instead, I took the high school equivalency test and avoided everyone from my old life. All my friends still lived in their bubble of privilege with their loving parents, and I knew I could never go back to being the person I was before my world was turned upside down.

In my darkest moment, I didn't think I'd ever find happiness again. Ten sleeping pills and a pint of vodka later, I woke up with my stomach pumped and a crushing headache. Killing myself was never my intention—I only wanted to numb the pain. It was my lowest point, but it became a turning point. Waking up to Liza's tear-streaked face and Roman's terrified expression, I knew I had to make a change.

Finding something I love—dancing—has been a huge part of that.

Liza places a hand on my knee, giving a gentle squeeze. "I wish you didn't feel that way."

"I don't so much anymore," I assure her. "But I'm ready for a change. Which is why…" I take a breath. "I've decided to move to Berlin after I graduate."

Her face falls. "You're leaving Moscow?"

"I am."

She swallows, working to keep her emotions in check. "Why? I thought you were happy with your life."

I shake my head. "I am. It's just… I haven't found my place yet. Lizka, I need this. A fresh start somewhere new."

Liza's expression tightens as she blinks back tears. "Of course, I want you to be happy. You're a grown woman who can make her own choices. But are you sure moving to a city where you don't know anyone is the right call?"

"I like the idea of starting over where no one knows me. No whispers about who I am or the family I'm tied to."

"I get it. Living under the shadow of the Syndicate is… a lot."

"That's not why I'm moving," I promise. "But Berlin isn't that far. And you're married to a man who owns a jet, remember?"

Liza laughs, even as a tear slides down her face. She wipes it away quickly. "Not gonna lie, I need a moment to wrap my head around this. But you've worked your ass off to get where you are, to leave the mess of our past behind. If this is what you want, I'm here for it. Promise me you'll take care of yourself."

I nod, squeezing her hand. "I will."

"And maybe you'll meet a hot German dancer and, I don't know, pirouette into the sunset or something." She winks.

Groaning, I cover my face. "That is so wrong on so many levels."

"Oh, come on. You're single and deserve to have some fun. Play the field." She holds up a hand. "Safely, of course."

"Not easy with a bodyguard watching my every move."

Her mouth curls at the corners. "Are your guards cramping your style?"

"I mean, they would if there was someone I was into."

The truth is, I'm not sure what I want from a relationship. I'm not even convinced there's a man out there for me.

Except… in the dark of night, when I'm alone, one man invades my fantasies: Nikolai Zhukov.

It's messed up, and I'd never admit to my sister that I think of him like that. I haven't seen Nikolai since the night he saved me from Anatoly's goons. There was no need to annul our marriage because, according to the lawyers, it was never legal in the first place.

Nikolai may have been part of my rescue, but I know he's no hero. From what I've overheard between Liza and Roman, the Zhukov Bratva controls all of St. Petersburg. He's a hard, dangerous man, and yet…

Something must have snapped in my brain that day. I was young, terrified out of my mind, and he protected me—saved me from what would have been the worst experience of my life, hands down. So maybe it's a savior complex that I've somehow twisted into some kind of misplaced desire.

I haven't even told my therapist about these fantasies. Not because she'd judge me but because some things are better left buried in the past.

"Maybe you can have a signal with your guards to get lost when you want to get laid."

"Huh!" My cheeks redden, having been lost in thoughts of Nikolai.

"Calm down. I'm kidding." Liza laughs, her voice light.

I shake my head. "I am officially horrified by this conversation. And for the record, there's no way any of them would leave me alone with a stranger."

Liza sighs dramatically, tipping her head back against the chair. "True, but if he were a guy you were seeing, not a stranger, that would be different. Assuming he passed the rigorous background check required by—"

I toss a dish towel at her. "Please stop talking!"

She laughs and tosses it back, her expression softening. "Kidding! Kind of. You know I only want you to be safe. But I get it. Maybe getting out of the city will help. And if Berlin gives you a shot at a normal life, well… I'll try to be happy for you."

Grinning, I lean over and hug her tightly. "Thanks. And just think, Berlin has amazing shopping. And their Christmas market is legendary."

Her face falls. "But you'll come home for Christmas, right?"

Christmas has always been something we celebrated together. Staying up late with hot chocolate and bad movies, decorating a lopsided tree, and sneaking bites of cookie dough before baking. It started because our parents were too wrapped up in their own lives to bother with us during the holidays, but Liza stepped up and made it special.

"I'll definitely try," I promise. Silence stretches between us as my mind drifts to the past. "Do you ever think about them? About our parents?" The question tastes bitter, but I have to ask. Roman exiled them to some godforsaken village near the border. I don't even know if they're still alive.

"Sometimes," she admits. "I've sent them some money here and there. Roman doesn't know. I just... couldn't let them starve."

Surprise flickers through me. "You're a good person, Lizka."

"I don't know if it's kindness or me not wanting to carry that bitterness forever."

I exhale, some tension easing. "Agreed," I say.

Maybe it's time we both move forward.

CHAPTER TWO

NIKOLAI

Roman Vasiliev is still one tough motherfucker.

Some say love and marriage soften your edges and tame you, but Roman's an exception. Even happily married to Liza Ivanova, when it comes to business, he remains the same cold, calculating force he's always been. And as much as I respect that about him, right now, I'm finding it irritating as fuck.

"We're not looking for a new business partner," Roman says, running a hand through his dark hair. "If anything, we're consolidating our power, tightening up now that Maxim is fully retired."

Maxim Belov remains the figurehead of the Syndicate, but he has stepped back from day-to-day operations to focus on raising his children with his wife, Kira. Roman and his partner, Pavel Federov, sitting directly across from me, now handle most of the Syndicate's operations.

With a flick of his wrist, Roman signals the waitress. She nods, slipping away to grab another round of vodka. We're in the back room of one of the Syndicate's clubs. The kind of place where men like us can speak freely.

I run my knuckles over my jaw. "I'm not a fucking new partner. I've proven myself to be loyal. You see what I've done with the Zhukov Bratva. You know what I'm capable of."

I let that statement sit as the waitress delivers an ice bucket of premium vodka, sliding fresh shot glasses across the table. She throws me a flirty smile before stepping away, but I barely glance her way.

I'm not here to get laid. I'm here to secure a deal.

The minister of finance is close to awarding my legal business a contract to operate casinos across Russia. For the Zhukov Bratva, it's the perfect setup.

I'm involved in everything from drugs to arms to counterfeits, and business is booming. Those illegal profits mean I need better, more efficient ways to clean the cash. That's where casinos come in—an industrial-sized laundromat for dirty money.

Not only that, but it will give me access to power players —politicians, oligarchs, and billionaires who shape economies and governments.

Our contact in the government guarantees the contract is ours on one condition. We have to build the largest casino in Moscow. It's the capital of the country and the seat of money and power.

The catch? Moscow is Belov Syndicate territory. It's a death sentence and a violation of bratva code to operate on their domain without their permission and cutting them in on the deal.

Roman leans back, spinning a shot glass between his fingers. He exchanges a look with Pavel, that says everything without uttering a word. They've always been like that, able to communicate in silence.

"You know we value your partnership," Roman says, gaze

drifting around the dark room. "But we have to protect our business interests. We're not looking for any new ventures."

I glance beside me at my second-in-command, Vadim Lazarev. We're both very fucking aware that without the Syndicate's approval, we will not be granted the casino contract.

Vadim runs a palm over his jaw. "We're offering to cut you in on the deal as a silent partner—no further investment from you, manpower or otherwise. It benefits us both."

Vadim pushes the stack of paperwork across the table, each page filled with financial breakdowns and projections ready for review. But neither man so much as glances at the documents.

Roman's jaw hardens. "The Zhukov Bratva runs St. Petersburg; the Syndicate runs Moscow. That's all there is to it. We don't allow anyone else to operate in our territory."

That's what he says, but there's more to it. Running casinos across the country will make me as powerful, wealthy, and influential as the Syndicate, and they're not about to let that balance shift in my favor.

But I've clawed my way back from the depths of hell to regain my seat, and I won't let anyone stand in my way—not Roman, not the Syndicate, not even my own fucking demons.

It's time for me to remind them precisely what they owe me.

I press both palms against the table, locking gazes with Roman. "I saved your life, Vasiliev, and now it's payback."

Roman's dark eyes flash with fury. Maybe he doesn't appreciate the reminder, but it's the truth, and he knows it. That moment and everything that led up to it is etched in my memory forever.

My head hangs low, hands braced against the wall of our basement office, the weight of Sergey's admission pressing down on me. I've only been out of prison for a few weeks, but it didn't take long to realize something was off. After two years locked up on trumped-up drug charges, taking the fall so Sergey didn't have to, I found myself questioning whether the sacrifices I made were worth it.

I was supposed to be the brains on the inside, Sergey the muscle on the outside. But from the moment I stepped back in, everything felt different. He was secretive, had cut my loyal men and replaced them with thugs who looked more like they couldn't rub two brain cells together.

Sergey swore to me it was business as usual, that nothing had changed. But the deeper I looked, the clearer it was that he'd entangled the Zhukov Bratva, a bratva I started from nothing, in a realm of business we agreed never to touch.

I can feel Sergey looking at me, waiting for my reaction to his confession.

"You're trafficking girls?" I grit out, meeting his gaze. "I spent two years locked up, and this is what you do behind my back? I told you we'd never go near that filth—not after we lived it every single day of our childhood."

Our mother was a prostitute, dragged into the life by a boyfriend who got her hooked on drugs and then forced her to sell her body. We went through hell and agreed never to touch that shit.

"Power at any cost, Nikolai. You taught me that!" Sergey sneers, pacing the room.

My hand curls into a fist, and I thump my chest. "I lead this bratva. I make the deals, not you. If you've got a problem with that, I suggest you rethink your position, or you'll find yourself on the wrong side of my mercy."

"Why don't you see which of our men are still loyal to you? I have a feeling you'll be disappointed, pakhan.*"* Boss.

His final word is delivered with a mocking lilt.

He's trying to cut me out of my own bratva. Taking my place with no remorse.

My heart drops like a stone. The little brother I stole for, the one I went hungry for to make sure he ate a proper meal, the kid I shielded from our mother's fits when she couldn't score… that

Sergey is gone. All that's left is a hollow stranger, willing to betray his own blood.

Gunfire erupts from the other room, cutting our standoff short. Instinctively, I drop to the ground, taking cover and pulling out my own pistol. I prepare for an attack, but that's not what this is. As the fighting dies down, a tall man who's vaguely familiar strolls into the center of the room, arms raised.

The guards take their positions around the room, but Sergey instructs them to stand down. Instead, he raises a gun in the stranger's direction.

"Morning, gentlemen," the man announces. "I believe we have some business to discuss."

Sergey's smile turns predatory. "Roman Vasiliev. I was wondering when you'd show your face."

I know Roman by reputation—the feared right hand to Maxim Belov. But the fact that he's here in person? That's not exactly a comforting sign.

"I've been looking for you, Sergey. Do you know why?" Roman asks, his tone dangerously calm.

My brother smirks, a smug expression I'd like to punch off his face. "I may have an idea. We're overdue for a talk."

"What the hell is this about?" I demand, stepping forward. I'm done being kept in the dark. That ends now.

Roman's eyes flick to me. "This is about your brother and Anatoly abducting women from the US to be sold in Europe, sneaking them onto Syndicate-chartered ships. For the record, that really fucking pissed me off."

Seems Roman and I are on the same page—at least on this.

The conversation veers into darker territory as Sergey lays out his plan to marry a girl named Sofiya Ivanova, while Anatoly will marry her sister, Liza. I've never heard of either, but I understand what Sergey's after—an alliance cemented by family ties with Anatoly Petrovich, and he'll destroy anyone in his way.

"Your marriage isn't happening," Roman snarls. "Liza and Sofiya are in hiding, and Anatoly is as good as dead."

"I think you'll find that's not the case at all. Have you spoken to your beloved Liza recently?" Sergey's voice drips with venom, and a cruel laugh escapes him as Roman's face goes stone-cold. "That's right—you haven't," Sergey taunts. "And you won't be speaking to her ever again. Because you're not walking out of here alive."

Roman roars and charges forward. Time seems to slow, each second stretching out as Sergey's arm rises, the barrel aimed squarely at Roman's heart.

My thoughts collide, but I know there's only one way forward. I raise my pistol and fire.

The shot is deafening—Sergey stumbles back, eyes wide as he hits the ground. His blood pools like ink across the floor.

And though I know he would've turned that gun on me, something heavy and painful settles in my gut, and a part of me dies with my brother.

My concentration snaps back to the present as Roman's focus locks onto me.

"Don't fucking kid yourself, Nikolai. You had your reasons for saving my life—you did it because it served you."

Not untrue, but it's beside the point. My steely voice drops. "I helped pull the woman you love out of hell. I put my own life on the line for her and Sofiya. Now, I expect some consideration in return. Not a big ask, given what I'm offering."

"You called in your favor when you needed my help to negotiate a truce with the Volkov Bratva. I'm not in the business of gratitude, and as much as I've appreciated our alliance through the years, you are not connected to us by blood or marriage, which means you aren't running a business in our territory. End of the fucking story." He slams his hands down on the table with a force that rattles the glasses.

"Actually, I don't believe it is," I say through clenched teeth. Behind me, Vadim shifts. We left our weapons at the door, and he's on edge. But I'm not looking for a fight. At least not yet.

Pavel raises his glass, giving it a slow spin. "What exactly are you saying?"

I crack my knuckles, shrugging. "I guess you'll see."

As Vadim and I head for the exit, Roman's voice follows me. "Don't do anything stupid, Zhukov. Consider that a warning."

"Appreciate it, but I'd save my breath if I were you."

I walk out without looking back. Their position is clear, and soon mine will be, too, because I have an ace up my sleeve. One I've been sitting on for a very long time.

Our driver waits for us in front of the club. Vadim and I slip into the back seat, and we pull away into the warm night. I loosen my tie and take in the sight of Moscow, whipping by beyond the window. Even in the early days of summer, this city can be so gray and uninspiring.

A city, it seems, where I'll never be welcome to do business.

Unless, of course, I'm connected by *blood or marriage.*

An interesting choice.

Over the years, I've done plenty of business with the Syndicate, but always from our own territories. They sit firmly at the top of the underworld food chain, with no intention of sharing.

But I'm not here to ask. I'm here to *take.*

That's what I did five years ago. With Sergey dead, and too many of my men turned against me, I rebuilt from scratch. I took back my city.

Vadim was one of the first people I recruited as my right hand. We met in prison a few years back, when he saved my life. Word had spread fast that a bratva boss had landed in high security, and it didn't take long for a few punks to decide they'd make a name for themselves by coming after me. They didn't have the brains to be subtle—they went for me in the shower.

A blade sank into my shoulder before I realized what was happening. I fought with everything I had, but fighting in a shower is a losing game, especially when blood's involved. Three against one, and I was barely standing upright when Vadim stepped in. I didn't even get a good look at him before he ripped through them—cold, precise, and brutal.

The fuckers got exactly what they deserved. I was battered, but I'd lived through worse. His parting advice to me had been, "Shower with a blade next time."

A few weeks later, I got my chance to return the favor. The guards had a hard-on for Vadim because he was former special forces, and somehow, a baseless rumor had started that he'd deserted his unit in Crimea.

One night, they dragged him out of his cell and started kicking the shit out of him in some dark corner of the block. I couldn't see it, but the sounds were enough to know it wasn't a fair fight, and I sure as hell had no loyalty to the guards.

I found the main power switch to our block and cut it, plunging all the cells into pitch black. In the chaos, with prisoners shouting and guards scrambling, Vadim was left lying in a heap on the cement floor. I couldn't offer much, but I helped him back to his cell and called for the nurse.

After that, we didn't exchange many words, but it was known we had each other's backs. After I got out of that shithole of a prison and started to take my bratva back, he was the first person I called.

Best decision I ever made. To this day, he's saved my ass more times than I'd like to count.

"Well, that was a clusterfuck," Vadim mutters, running a hand through his close-cropped brown hair as he leans back, exhaling slowly. "I figured they'd counter, maybe ask for a bigger slice, even some control over the terms. But a flat-out fuck you?"

I shake my head. "Didn't see that coming, but it doesn't mean I'm not prepared."

"Prepared?"

I pour us both a generous shot of whiskey into the glass tumblers. I take a long sip, appreciating the smoky flavor. I hate vodka, but in a meeting like that, it's more of a courtesy. Not that anything that went down was courteous.

I shrug. "Roman was very clear. They only do business with people related by blood or marriage. If that's what he requires, that's what he'll get."

His eyebrows pull together in confusion. "I feel like I'm missing something here."

"Because you are." I chuckle, leaning forward to catch the driver's eye in the rearview mirror. "Take us to my Moscow residence. We're not flying back to St. Petersburg tonight." I turn back to Vadim. "When I helped Roman rescue Sofiya in Greece, I walked away with a little insurance policy."

"The fuck you did," Vadim mutters, crossing his arms, waiting for the punchline.

"I grabbed the marriage certificate we both signed before leaving the chapel. Once we were back in Russia, I pulled some strings, greased some palms, and made the marriage legal… using highly illegal means."

"Are you serious? You're… married to Sofiya?"

"Technically speaking. The marriage was a contingency in case I needed leverage over the Syndicate." I run a hand over the back of my neck, my mouth twisting into a smile. "Seems that day has come."

Vadim leans back, huffing out a laugh. "You're fucking crazy if you think Roman's going to welcome you into the family with open arms."

"He will if I apply the right kind of pressure." I lift an

eyebrow. "It's time I claimed my wife and brought her back to my world. And I know Igor would agree."

Igor Bocharov is my silent partner in the casino deal. He's also the senior advisor to the minister of finance, which gives him political sway that he uses to favor the Zhukov Bratva. And like me, he's a man who believes the end justifies the means, no matter what.

"You've suggested some fucked-up things before, but this..." He makes a mind-blown gesture with his hand. "The Syndicate is going to come at us with some serious firepower."

I down the rest of my whiskey. "Roman doesn't know where my estate is, and if by some miracle he figures it out and attempts an attack, he risks Sofiya's life. If they want to see her again, they'll agree to our terms."

"Is this worth it?" he asks, voice low. "Making an enemy out of them?"

My hands curl into fists in my lap. "Yes, it's fucking worth it."

If life has taught me anything, it's that power doesn't betray you like people do. My brother proved that. Power doesn't lie. It doesn't pretend to care, only to leave you bleeding. Power is absolute.

For the past five years, I've worked to make myself untouchable, and I'll crush anyone who stands in my way.

"In that case, please tell me you have a plan, because Sofiya won't be easy to get to."

He's right. She has a guard with her at all times, but even the best protection has weak spots.

Because of Sofiya's strategic importance, I've kept her under surveillance over the years. I know she's studying dance in school and about to graduate. She's a dedicated student, with a few close friends but mostly keeps to herself. She's only had one boyfriend, and he's damn lucky she dumped him before I got the chance to take care of him.

She was beautiful at seventeen, but at twenty-two, she's dangerously alluring. She's still too young for my thirty-four years, but my dick doesn't seem to care. I've only seen her from afar—video clips and photos that my man sends me. But that's been enough to awaken a possessive hunger.

I clear my throat, staring out at the city lights. "She's performing in a dance recital two days from now. Roman mentioned earlier that he and Liza can't make it. They'll be in New York. Seems like a shame to miss such a… cultural event, don't you think?"

He releases a low whistle. "What are you suggesting?"

"A little reconnaissance," I say, rolling my shoulders. "We'll go to the performance, check things out. If we see an opening, we take it. The chaos of a live show could work to our advantage."

"If you say so," he drawls.

But my mind's already miles away, fixated on the chance to finally see her dance in person. Over the years, I've caught glimpses of her talent, but they've been nothing more than fucking breadcrumbs, leaving me starving for more.

I know Sofiya is leverage, a pawn… and a dangerous addiction I need to shake. Letting her become anything more would mean losing focus, and after putting a bullet in my brother's head and clawing my way close to the top of Russia's criminal underworld, I'm sure as hell not about to lose it all now.

CHAPTER THREE

SOFIYA

THE OPENING NOTES OF THE SONG FILL THE EMPTY STUDIO, AND I catch my reflection in the mirror. My black leotard clings to me like a second skin. Every muscle is taut with energy, ready to spring into action. For a moment, I close my eyes, imagining the crowd's buzz and the rush of anticipation I'll feel in a couple of days when I'm onstage.

I take a deep breath and launch into a sharp turn that flows into a powerful leap. The mirrors echo my every action, each sweep of my arms and kick of my legs deliberate and precise. Months of relentless practice have made this routine second nature, and with each movement, I sink into the rhythm and let the story take over.

A smattering of applause takes me out of my bubble and pulls me back into the present.

"Knew we'd find you here," Daria announces. She and Alex stand at the room's entrance with my bodyguard, Samuil. He makes eye contact with me and nods before turning around to stand guard outside the studio.

"My home away from home," I quip. "Where else would you find me?"

I reach for a towel to wipe my brow as Alex hands me a bottle of water, which I take gratefully, downing half of it in one go.

Daria and Alex are not only my best friends but also fellow students at the performing arts college. We met in our first year, stuck in a ballet class we all despised.

Alex narrows his eyes. "Have you eaten dinner yet?" When I freeze and an *oh shit* look flickers over my face, he sighs. "Sofi, it's nearly nine."

I slump back against the wall. "I know, I know. Time got away from me."

"I see we need to take over the situation." Daria rests a hand on her curvy hip. Her stark black bob sways in front of her face, and she gives me a hard stare that nobody in their right mind would argue with. Daria looks like an emo dominatrix, with a septum piercing and a wardrobe of leather and lace—but she's actually sweet once you get past her hardened, no BS outer layer.

Alex, on the other hand, is a human golden retriever, loyal to a fault and always looking out for his friends.

"Shower, and get dressed. We're taking you out for food," Alex insists. His stern tone would be more effective if he weren't so damn boyish with shaggy, sandy blond hair and big pouty lips that make him especially popular with the other guys at our school.

I wouldn't bother arguing even if I weren't starving; when these two get something in their minds, there's no dissuading them.

An hour later, we're cozied up in our favorite diner across from the college, waiting on the meals we ordered.

I'm hoping to steer clear of any comments about my tireless rehearsing, but my stomach's loud growl betrays me. All students put in extra hours leading up to graduation, but admittedly, I've been a little hyperfocused, practicing up to twelve hours a day, losing myself so completely that I forget basic things like eating.

Daria frowns, spreading a napkin on her lap. "What's going on? You don't need to practice like you're a first-year student, running yourself ragged. Save some energy for the actual recital."

The waitress drops off our food, and I have to stop myself from tearing into my sandwich like a wild beast, even though I have the appetite of one. "Word is scouts from the major European dance companies will be at the recital, including one from the Berlin Contemporary Dance Company. I want it to go perfectly."

Daria and Alex know that the Berlin dance company is my dream. Their performances are innovative and bold but always beautifully performed.

Alex frowns. "It *will* go perfectly. You've put your heart and soul into this dance, and the teachers picked you for a reason—because you're the best." He lays his hand over mine. "Don't let anyone make you doubt that."

"I know. It must be nerves," I acknowledge.

"Have you told Liza about Berlin yet?" Daria asks, taking a sip of her drink.

"A few days ago. She took it better than I thought. I mean, she was surprised and a little sad about me leaving, but I think she gets it. Now, I need to land a job in Berlin so I can support myself."

"You will." Alex wraps an arm around me. "Come on, you need a little motivation. Let's play the game."

"Again? Aren't you guys sick of hearing about my dream life?"

"Absolutely not!" Daria rests her elbows on the table and leans her chin in her hand. "Because then I get to tell you mine."

I sigh, but a smile creeps onto my face. "Fine. I'll live in a small, sunlit apartment above a café in Berlin. I'll be part of an amazing dance company, spending my nights and weekends performing. In my spare time, I'll bike through the city, exploring and wandering through art galleries and quaint little bookstores. All without a bodyguard," I add because, hell, this is my dream life scenario.

I turn to Alex. "Your turn."

He sits back, a thoughtful expression settling over his face. "I'm going to live in a beautiful flat in London's Soho, close enough to walk to the theatre district. I'll land a leading role in something big—a musical or maybe one of those classic dramas. My nights will be spent at the pubs with the rest of the cast and making out with all the cute boys."

Daria snorts. "And how is that different from your life now… minus the very expensive real estate?"

Alex elbows her, but she just grins. "All right, your turn, Miss Hollywood."

"I'll find a little place in the Hollywood Hills, one of those old art deco apartments with a view of the city. I'll land a role on the next big Netflix series opposite some super famous and hunky actor, who I'll also be fucking on the side."

"I love that for you," I deadpan.

We're all quiet for a minute before Alex speaks up. "I'm going to miss you two."

I swipe a napkin across my mouth, setting my sandwich down. "I can't believe that after this week, we go our separate ways."

Daria and Alex exchange a look. "And that's why we have something planned for after the final performance," Daria says, leaning toward me.

Alex rubs his hands together. Okay, they definitely have something up their sleeves.

"And that is?"

"I got us VIP tickets to Soundsystem." When I stare

blankly at Daria, she rolls her eyes. "It's *the* hottest nightclub in Moscow right now. How do you not know this?"

"Because I don't go to clubs." It's not like I don't want to go out and have a good time, but constantly being trailed by a bodyguard puts a damper on that kind of fun.

"Well, get ready for a legendary night. Without him." Alex nods toward Sam, seated across the room, his attention on the door like he's expecting an ambush.

I snicker. "Good luck with that. Wherever I go, he goes. That's kind of the point."

"Oh, come on." Daria pouts. "I get that a bodyguard is part of your life, but you deserve one night of freedom. I can't imagine you're a high-profile target."

"And he's a total killjoy." Alex wrinkles his nose. "Always giving you a dirty look if you dare to have a second drink."

They're not wrong, but Liza and Roman have drilled into me that I could be a target if someone wanted revenge on the Syndicate. It's unlikely, but not impossible.

"I don't know, guys. Liza would kill me if something bad happened."

"Well, you'd already be dead, so who cares?" Alex bats his baby blues at me, fully aware of how persuasive he can be. "Come on. It's our last night to have fun before we all go our separate ways."

"It's a bad idea," I murmur, but with less conviction.

"Bad ideas are the best ones," Daria adds. They both stare at me expectantly.

I know it's reckless, that I shouldn't take a chance, but it's my grad night, and I refuse to miss out on a night to remember with my friends before everything changes. "Screw it. I'm in."

They both squeal and clap their hands, but I shush them, motioning with my head toward Sam.

Alex blows out a breath. "Speaking of which, how are you going to get rid of broody Sam over there?"

I drum my fingers on the table in thought. "The fire escape is the only way." I've never climbed down the narrow ladder before—it's four stories, after all—but with a guard stationed out front of my building, I don't have a choice. "It'll drop me straight into the alley."

"Then it's settled. We'll pick you up around the back of your building. Get slutted up and prepare to have some fun." Daria grins. "Maybe you'll even meet a sexy guy and do something crazy like, I don't know, have a one-night stand?"

"One thing at a time," I joke. "I'm sneaking out—let's not jump to sleeping with someone whose last name I don't even know."

My friends love to tease me about the fact that I've never had a one-night stand. Yeah, I've gone on dates. I even managed to lose my virginity to a guy I briefly dated last year, a rigger on the backstage crew. I was attracted to him; he was cute and funny, but... I don't know. The chemistry wasn't there.

What does that even mean, chemistry? I'm not sure myself.

Liar.

Nikolai's brutal but handsome face flashes in my mind. My friends don't know about that part of my life—the kidnapping, the nearly forced marriage, and how the man who saved me is just as dangerous as the monsters he protected me from.

But somehow, he still plays a starring role in my fantasies.

Alex smirks, pulling me out of my thoughts. "Last names are overrated."

Daria balls up her napkin and drops it on her empty plate. "Sex isn't always about love and romance. Sometimes, it's about getting a hardcore f—"

I clear my throat. Sam's attention is on me, and a blush stains my cheeks. Not that I have any reason to feel embarrassed—my sex life, or lack thereof, is none of his business.

But considering it's his job to keep me safe, bringing a stranger back to my apartment for the night would probably be out of the question.

I meet his gaze with a broad smile that he doesn't return. Instead, he shifts his focus back to the diner's front door.

"And that's why he's not invited," Alex says with an evil grin.

CHAPTER FOUR

NIKOLAI

Families swarm the theater lobby, buzzing with excitement, ready to watch their loved ones take the stage for the last time as students.

Vadim and I blend in surprisingly well, camouflaged among the proud parents. We've swapped our Brioni suits and Patek Philippe watches for merino wool sweaters and brown loafers—shoes I plan to burn at the first possible opportunity.

Our tattoos are covered with makeup, and I'm wearing black wire-rimmed glasses to round out the history teacher look. Long ago, I ditched the eyebrow ring and the shaved head I sported right after prison. To be taken seriously, I had to look the part of pakhan.

Vadim has an enormous bouquet of white roses in his arms, like some doting father ready to surprise his kid after the performance.

"I feel like a fucking chump," I mutter under my breath. "How did you talk me into dressing like a—"

"Normal person?" Vadim interrupts. "I should take a

picture to commemorate this moment. You look civilized for once."

"I could say the same to you."

With his tattooed knuckles concealed and his unruly dark curls slicked back, Vadim looks less like a man who could kill with his bare hands and more like someone ready for an afternoon on the golf course, which is exactly the point.

"Take a look at this," he says, sliding a program into my hands as we linger off to the side, watching the crowd.

I take the program and flip through it until I find her name. Sofiya Ivanova. She's scheduled to dance the final performance of the evening—a solo that she choreographed.

A Hades and Persephone retelling.

I bite back a laugh. If I remember my Greek myths right, Hades, the god of the Underworld, sees Persephone picking flowers one day, and he's so captivated by her beauty that he takes her by force to the underworld and eventually forces her to marry him.

Well, shit. The irony is almost too much.

Vadim grabs a champagne flute from a passing waiter. "Looks like there are a few undercover guys. That one by the exit—" he angles his head in the man's direction, "—and another by the staircase."

I glance over, following his line of sight. Their suits may help them blend in, but the way they stand—feet slightly apart, hands clasped in front, scanning the room—gives them away. It's a stance I've seen countless times in my own men.

Considering this is a public event, I'm not surprised. Still, I'm a patient man, and if I've learned one thing over the years, it's to bide my time and wait for the right moment to strike.

A dramatic kidnapping would alert Roman and his men. We want to get her out of Moscow as quietly as possible. No one will realize she's gone until it's too late.

The auditorium lights flicker, signaling that the show will

start soon. I join the crowd, filing into their seats, while Vadim disappears backstage to scope things out. Even though he's striking, he's very adept at blending in when he needs to be.

I take a seat among the smiling faces of families gathered to watch their friends and relatives take the stage. Sofiya is graduating from Moscow's elite performing arts school, but she has no one here to celebrate her. Her parents sold her to my brother to cover their debts. The realization settles over me—I'm her husband, her family now, even if she doesn't know it yet.

The lights dim, and the show begins, one performance blurring into the next. I barely register what's happening onstage. Every nerve in my body is primed, waiting for Sofiya. I want to watch her move, to see the way her body commands the stage.

After what feels like fucking forever, it's finally time for her solo. The music shifts to something dark and ominous, and Sofiya steps onto the stage. The pictures I've seen didn't come close to doing her justice. Her pale skin glows under the lights, her auburn hair swept up to reveal the graceful line of her neck. Her costume clings to her skin, revealing full breasts and solid muscle built over the years.

Sofiya begins to dance, and she's mesmerizing, gliding across the stage with effortless grace. The flowing fabric of her costume swirls around her as she spins, her silhouette softening, then snapping into sharp, controlled movements. She exudes confidence now—a far cry from the scared little girl I found in that chapel.

I don't know if Persephone fought Hades when he dragged her from the field, but I have no doubt Sofiya will put up more of a fight when I drag her back to my city. Not that it will stop me.

When her performance ends, the audience erupts in applause, rising to their feet. She's breathing hard, but her eyes shine as a smile spreads across her lips. I've never seen a woman look as exquisite.

The rest of the students join her, and they all take their final bows, soaking in the crowd's energy.

My phone vibrates in my pocket, revealing a text from Vadim instructing me to meet him in the car out front. I let out a quiet breath, my attention still on Sofiya as she basks in the moment. With one last look her way, I turn and head for the exit.

I'll be seeing her again soon. And when I do, I won't just be watching. I'll be taking her with me.

Entering the car, I pull the door shut, the cool leather pressing against my back as I settle in. Vadim glances over, a smug smile tugging at his mouth.

"I'm guessing everything went well?" I note.

He cracks his neck. "Almost too well, if I'm being honest. Was looking forward to a little more challenge."

I raise a brow, turning to face him.

"I overheard Sofiya and her friends talking. They're planning to hit up a club in the city called Soundsystem tonight." His smirk widens. "Without her bodyguard."

My fists clench. A packed, loud nightclub with no bodyguard is the perfect setup for someone to take her. Someone like me. I should be grateful she's making this so damn easy, but what the hell is she thinking, being so careless with her safety? It makes me want to bend her over my knee and teach her a lesson.

"Soundsystem," I mutter, running a hand through my overly gelled hair. "One of the Syndicate's clubs?"

"Nope. Owned by a couple of tech billionaires with no bratva ties."

I nod, clearing my throat. "Looks like it's our lucky day."

"And just in time. I overheard one of her friends talking about Sofiya's plans to move to Berlin after graduation."

My eyebrows lift. "What for?"

Vadim guides the car into Moscow traffic. "Who the hell knows? Probably for a job."

I take off the fake glasses and rub my temples, the wool sweater suddenly itchy against my skin. Whatever plans Sofiya had don't matter anymore. Everything's about to change. Someone with a heart might feel bad about that, but I'm not that guy.

Leaning back in the seat, a grin tugs at my lips. "Tonight should be interesting."

CHAPTER FIVE

SOFIYA

"DAMN, YOU LOOK HOT!" ALEX EXCLAIMS AS I SLIDE INTO THE taxi, squeezing in beside him and Daria in the back seat.

I blow out a nervous breath, tugging at the hem of the miniature sequin dress that reveals way more thigh and cleavage than I'm used to. I bought it yesterday on a whim, figuring if I'm sneaking out to Moscow's hottest club, I might as well dress the part.

"Probably wasn't the best choice for shimmying down the fire escape, but here I am." Earlier, I said a brief goodnight to Sam in the lobby, letting him think I was in for the night, and then snuck out through my bedroom window.

Daria and Alex exchange broad smiles, like proud parents.

"We thought you'd chicken out," Daria admits, "but we're glad you didn't."

I push down the flicker of guilt threatening to rise up. The reason Sam and the rest of my guards trust me is that I've never pulled a stunt like this. It crossed my mind, but it always seemed like too big of a risk. And if anything ever happened to me, Liza would be distraught.

Alex leans forward in his seat, his eyes bright. "And tonight, we have even more reason to celebrate."

A grin spreads across my face. The rush from my performance and the standing ovation still hum through me. I've done plenty of live shows, but tonight was electric. I felt powerful, confident—like everything finally clicked. The audience was with me every step of the way, and I was already craving that high again.

The best part was after the recital, a scout from the Berlin Contemporary Dance Company came backstage, and offered me an audition with their artistic director in a few days. It's a rare opportunity for a new grad, and I'll be there, come hell or high water.

But it also means a lot of hard work in my future. After four years of busting my ass, tonight might be my last chance for me to let go, to be reckless and wild before I'm consumed by the demands of my passion once more.

I turn to my friends, excitement buzzing through me. "Tonight, I'm all in. Let's make it count."

The lineup in front of Soundsystem stretches a full city block —not surprising if it's the place to be, as Alex claims. Despite a flicker of nerves, I'm doing my best to look like I fit in as we approach the massive bouncer guarding the door. Daria shows him something on her phone, probably our passes, and after a few flirty words from her, he nods and lets us through.

I follow my friends down a hallway into the cavernous, warehouse-style space already packed with hundreds of young partygoers, here to cut loose and forget everything outside these walls. The air in the club is thick, and the electronic music is loud—the perfect setting to disappear into the crowd, as anonymous as anyone else in here.

"Should we hit the dance floor?" I have to shout to my friends, even though they're right beside me.

"We need a few shots first," Daria yells back, motioning to a roped-off area on the other side of the room. "VIP is over there."

Alex and I follow her. I have no intention of getting wasted, but a few drinks won't hurt.

The VIP section is almost as busy as the main club, but at least you can get to the bar without being trampled.

"First round's on me," I announce. "Any requests?"

"How about a Blow Job?" Daria asks with a wicked smirk.

I laugh. "Really? Is that an actual shot?"

"Yes, and it's delicious," she assures me, "but if you'd rather not ask for something so scandalous, ask for a Kamikaze."

"Oh, I like those," Alex adds, but he's barely listening, his stare glued to a sexy guy across the room who's definitely eye-fucking him back.

I head over to the bar, catching the attention of a bartender who looks me up and down, not bothering to hide his appreciative stare.

"What can I get for the most beautiful woman in the club?" he asks, leaning on the bar and taking a not-so-subtle glance at my chest before flashing a grin.

He's good-looking, with tousled dirty blond hair and sharp features, but he has major fuck-boy energy.

I brush off his flirty opening. "Three Kamikaze shots, please… on second thought, make it six."

What the hell. We're celebrating. The faster we get a few drinks in us, the faster I can hit the dance floor and shake off all this pent-up adrenaline.

"Anything else I can get you?" His tone drips with suggestion, and I fight back an eye roll.

"Nope."

He winks as he turns to make my order. Daria and Alex's

teasing about my lack of one-night stands echoes in my mind. This guy would be an easy option, sure, but if I'm going to take a risk tonight, it won't be with him.

"Think that line actually works for him?"

A deep, amused voice catches me off guard. The scent of musky cologne fills my senses, and a shiver traces down my spine before I even turn. But when I do… *damn*. The man beside me is the embodiment of tall, dark, and handsome, with thick dark hair and black-framed glasses giving him a Clark Kent vibe. Masculine energy radiates off him, and I take a slow, deep breath, trying to stop myself from staring.

Under the dim lights, I can make out strong cheekbones, full lips, and a chin with an enticing indent—enough to send a spark of heat through me. Jesus, I'm a sucker for a chiseled jaw, and his is nothing short of perfect.

"I'm sure he flirts with all his customers," I manage, trying to keep my voice steady. "He must be working for those tips."

He chuckles, a low, gravelly sound that I feel between my legs. It's been a long while since anyone's made me weak in the knees, and it's a welcome feeling.

"Maybe," he says, leaning in so I feel his warm breath fan over my ear. "But in this case, he's right. You really are the most beautiful woman here."

A flush creeps up my neck, warmth spreading through me despite my best attempt to play it cool.

"Now who's the one with the cheesy lines? Tell me—does that line ever work for *you*?"

He smiles, resting his muscular arms on the bar top, his thumb tracing down the center of his lips. I follow the movement, transfixed. "Don't know. Never used it before. I don't bother with flattery unless it's true."

I glance away, fighting a small smile. "Everyone resorts to flattery once in a while," I challenge.

He raises a brow. "Luckily, I'm not everyone."

Something about his expression seems familiar—he

reminds me of someone, but I can't figure out who. "Have we met before?"

"I don't think so." He tilts his head to the side. "I'd definitely remember meeting you if I had."

My heart races, and for a second, I can't think of a single word to say. But I'm saved by the bartender when he reappears.

"Here you go, gorgeous," he says, sliding a tray of shots toward me with a wink. There are way more shots than I ordered. "Drinks on me tonight. And if you're interested in a little company later—"

"She's not." The sexy stranger cuts in, his tone icy. In one smooth motion, he picks up the entire tray and dumps it behind the bar.

My jaw drops. This man might be insanely hot, but he also might be straight-up *insane*. "Make them again," he snaps at the bartender, who looks rattled. "This time, in front of me."

I blink, frozen, as the bartender nods silently, the tendons in his neck working hard to swallow. He starts remaking the shots in clear view, his hands a little unsteady.

"What the hell was that?" I hiss.

With one eye on the bartender, he turns to me. "You need to pay better attention when a stranger's making you a drink."

I shake my head. "He's the bartender. It's literally his job."

His gaze drops to my lips. "A terrifying thought, isn't it?"

Heat pools low in my belly. What the hell is wrong with me? His over-the-top alpha vibe shouldn't be a turn-on, but damn, it kind of is. Maybe my friends were right—I need to get laid.

He slaps a stack of bills on the bar. "This'll cover your drinks for the night. Under no circumstances is that mudak paying for you. Got it?"

I straighten, trying to reclaim some self-respect. "I can pay for my own drinks, thanks."

He slides a finger under my chin, lifting my face to his, and a rush of warmth spreads through me. "I know you can, but I want to. I'll be watching you all night, moya sladost. Keep that in mind."

Goosebumps prickle along my arms at the term of endearment, one that's oddly familiar. My brain must be scrambled. I'm not used to feeling this kind of pull, like every nerve in my body is suddenly tuned to him, crackling with energy.

"Your drinks." The bartender sets down the shots, keeping his head down as if he'd rather be anywhere else. When I glance up, my mysterious protector has vanished like smoke.

"Who was that guy?" I ask the bartender.

His eyes flick up briefly before darting away. "I-I don't know, but I really don't want to find out." He hurries off to serve someone else.

Alex and Daria's faces light up as I approach with a tray full of shots.

"So, who was the hot as fuck guy you were chatting with at the bar?" Alex asks, nudging me with his shoulder.

I shrug, trying to play it off. "Don't know. We were just chatting while we waited on our drinks."

Daria finishes applying her lipstick, closing the compact mirror with a click. "The way he looked at you was anything but casual."

"Forget him. Tonight's about us." But I'm not sure I can. Something electric hums under my skin from our brief exchange.

I raise a shot and toss it back, savoring the citrusy taste. My friends are watching me as I slam the glass on the table.

"What?" I ask, feigning innocence.

"You might have forgotten about him, but he hasn't forgotten about you," Alex says, nodding toward the upper level.

I glance up. My sexy stranger is there, leaning on the railing, watching me. When our eyes meet, he lifts his drink in a silent toast. A rush of heat floods my cheeks, and I look away quickly, my pulse racing.

Daria whistles. "If a man that fine was staring at me, I wouldn't be down here. I'd be up there so fast, he wouldn't know what hit him."

"I'm playing it cool," I say, shrugging. His promise to watch me all night lingers in my mind, and I can't deny the thrill that runs through me. "But I want to dance, not flirt with a random dude. So, are we hitting the dance floor or what?"

"Oh, Sofi, I wasn't talking about flirting," Daria says with a wink. "I was talking about getting a lot more up close and personal."

"Leave her alone," Alex says, giving Daria a light shove. "Sofiya just wants to have a good time with us."

"Exactly," I agree, although I'm not sure that's the entire truth.

CHAPTER SIX

NIKOLAI

Tonight wasn't supposed to play out like this. I wasn't supposed to approach Sofiya, talk to her, or even let her see my face. I was supposed to stay in the shadows, watching from a distance, waiting for the right moment to strike, but I'm all for a quick pivot when it needs to happen.

The second that sleazy bartender eyed her in that dress like she was fair game, everything changed. And then changed again when he tried to drug her damn drinks.

When I stepped up to the bar, Vadim's disapproval practically drilled into the side of my skull, but I didn't care. Being that close—close enough to catch her floral scent, hear her sweet, melodic voice—was a thrill.

Sofiya looks unbelievable, wearing a short, sparkly number that almost made my head explode and my dick rigid the second she walked into the club. Her hair is down, loose around her shoulders, and she's wearing heels that add a few extra inches, bringing her up to my chest. Smoky makeup enhances her hazel eyes, making them flash a deeper green.

She didn't recognize me, but I was familiar. Either way, I look different enough from the man she met five years ago that she can't quite place me. *Yet*.

From my vantage point on the balcony, I scan the dance floor until I find Sofiya.

She looks up and meets my gaze with a challenge. She wants me to watch her, and I'm more than happy to oblige.

She moves to the bass-heavy beat, her body in perfect rhythm, giving me a private show in the middle of a packed dance floor. I raise my glass, the warmth of the amber liquid sliding down my throat as I devour the sight of her. She's so damn sexy like this—loose and uninhibited.

A carefree smile spreads across her face as she stretches her arms toward the ceiling, the hem of her dress creeping up her thighs. The thought of another man watching her like this makes me tense. She's mine. And soon, she'll have no doubt about what that means.

"Someone caught your eye?" Vadim's dry tone cuts through my thoughts, his arms folded as he leans against the railing beside me.

"You could say that," I acknowledge, not looking away from Sofiya. "Did you deal with the bartender?"

"Taken care of. His bartending days are over. Hard to mix drinks with two broken hands."

I shake my head in disgust. "Some assholes have to learn the hard way."

Vadim sighs and shoots me a sideways glance. "You think she recognized you?"

"Not exactly."

He arches an eyebrow in a *what the fuck does that mean* way.

"She thought I looked familiar, but I assured her we had never met before."

"I realize you're enjoying the show, but our jet's ready and prepared for takeoff. I'd like to get out of here in case her guards realize she's not home."

I finish my whiskey, savoring the burn before setting the glass down. "Doubt it. They won't realize she's missing until morning." I glance back at the dance floor. "We can't drag her away, not with a crowd this size. We wait for the right moment."

He checks his watch. "Eventually, they'll need a bathroom break or to get more drinks. I'll handle her friends; you focus on your… bride." His lips twitch.

"Why don't you make a new friend to pass the time." With my head, I gesture to the blonde in the corner who hasn't looked away from Vadim once.

He huffs a laugh and then wanders off, leaving me alone with my thoughts. I'm not ready to break the spell yet. I want to watch her some more, to savor the chemistry between us. Because after tonight, she's going to hate me. I'd hate me, too. What I'm about to do is nothing short of ruthless—but that's the price of my endgame, and it's one I'm willing to pay.

When I catch sight of Sofiya again, she's talking with her friends. The woman with the dark bob whispers something in her ear, and Sofiya shakes her head in response. Her friend nods, and the two of them turn around, leaving her alone in the crowd.

For a second time tonight, I want to take her over my knee. What the hell is she thinking, splitting off from her friends? She has no idea how vulnerable she is. She'll learn soon enough.

The DJ drops a popular track, and half the club surges onto the dance floor as a laser show flickers overhead. Sofiya slips from view, swallowed up in the sea of bodies.

I scan the floor again and again, but I can't find her. My pulse kicks up, and pressure builds beneath my ribs. Damn it. A club like this is full of trouble, and the last thing I need is something happening to her. Against all logic, a fierce urge to protect her flares up, and I'm about to go down there myself to find her when I feel a tap on my shoulder.

Acting on pure instinct, I spin around, seizing the person by the throat and pinning them to the wall. It takes me a second to register who it is. Sofiya. My grip on her throat loosens instantly, her pulse thumping beneath my fingers. Her chest rises and falls, her eyes wide and locked on mine.

Fuck, did I hurt her? But she doesn't look hurt. She looks… turned on. The air between us is charged, our bodies nearly touching. I try to decipher what she wants from me, but she makes it easy when she wraps her hand around the front of my shirt and pulls me toward her.

Our lips meet in a searing kiss. For a second, I hold back. Is she drunk? Considering I haven't let her out of my sight, I don't think that's it. She hasn't had anything more to drink.

No, this is something else. The girl who danced her heart out tonight just wants to let loose—with me. And damn if I'll be the one to stop her.

My tongue plunges into her mouth, tangling with hers, and I can't help but groan against her lips. She tastes like forbidden fruit, sweet and tempting, with a hint of the shot she had earlier.

A moan releases from her lips, and her palm flattens against my chest, her fingers splaying over my racing heart. I keep my hand loosely clasped around her throat, my thumb caressing the delicate hollow at the base of her neck. My other hand drifts to her waist, hauling her body against mine as I deepen the kiss.

The sharp pop of a champagne bottle, followed by the rowdy cheers of a nearby group, breaks the spell. Fuck. It takes everything in me to pull away because if we continue like this, we're going to attract some unwanted attention.

"Well, that was unexpected but very fucking welcome," I grit out, still catching my breath.

Her eyes flicker. "Is there a place where we can be alone?"

I scan her face. She seems fiercer now, bolder than she used to be.

I shouldn't even be considering it. I should take her and be done with it. Because if I fuck her, even this once, it's only going to mess with my head. A taste of something I'll never have again. She rises on her tiptoes and presses her lips to mine again. I swear, the way her mouth moves against mine makes my brain short-circuit.

Fuck… this is a terrible idea, but I don't have the willpower to say no.

"Is that what you want? For us to be alone?" I ask when I pull away.

She nods and bites her full bottom lip. My pulse kicks up a notch. I'll give her what she wants, but afterward, she won't go back to her friends and her neatly laid-out life. She's coming with me.

I push down the contesting voices in my head telling me how fucked-up I am, and I silently grab her hand, moving through the crowd. I spot Vadim at the bar, watching us. He doesn't move a muscle, his face unreadable, but I know he's questioning my decision. Hell, I'm questioning myself, but that won't stop me.

We make our way down a narrow, dimly lit hallway meant for staff that I scoped out earlier. It's grimy, nothing like the main club, but it leads to the back alley where our car is waiting. I'll fuck her in the back seat, make her come as many times as she'd like in many different ways before I take her.

But before the exit, she hesitates, stopping us both.

"Where are you taking me?" she demands.

"My car is parked out back."

Her hands land on her hips. "I can't leave the club… My friends are here." She looks away, fidgeting with the strap of her purse. "Isn't there a bathroom or something?"

I smile, tracing my finger along her jawline. "A nice girl like you doesn't deserve to be fucked in a bathroom."

"How do you know I'm a nice girl?"

I smile. "Just a hunch."

She exhales slowly, her lips pressed together. "I don't want to be a nice girl tonight," she murmurs. "I don't want to know your name, I don't want to know who you are, I don't want to exchange phone numbers. I want somewhere we can be alone so you can blow my mind. You're up for the challenge, aren't you?"

I pull her against me, enjoying this newfound confidence. "I see. So you only want me for my body?"

"Absolutely."

I bend forward, whispering in her ear, "In that case, do you want me to make you come with my fingers, my tongue, or my cock? I'm happy to oblige with all three, but that means going somewhere more private."

She reaches down and cups my package. Holy hell, this is not the Sofiya from five years ago. This creature is someone entirely different. She knows what she wants, and what she wants is growing by the minute, hardening at her touch.

"Let's not make this complicated. Take me somewhere with a lock on the door and fuck me senseless. And then… we say goodbye. Got it, stranger?"

I'll gladly grant her the first part of her request, but saying goodbye after, definitely not happening.

"Got it."

CHAPTER SEVEN

SOFIYA

EVEN AS HE PUSHES OPEN THE BATHROOM DOOR, I KNOW THIS IS insane.

My friends know I went to talk to the sexy stranger—I told them that was my plan. I'm sure they think we're making out in some dark corner, but they have no idea I am in this out-of-the-way bathroom, about to have sex with a man I don't know. A man with rough edges and a dark intensity that should feel scary but doesn't. Instead of panic, I feel a heady rush as the lock clicks into place.

Just for tonight, I want to lose myself in the arms of this stranger who sets my blood on fire. I craved freedom, and now I have it for a short while. This is as free as it gets. Maybe Daria and Alex are right—last names are overrated.

The bathroom is private. Fancy-looking, with marble countertops and a sleek gold backsplash. The low lighting casts enough of a glow for me to meet his eyes in the mirror above the sink. His stare is intense, but that's his entire vibe.

My heart pounds, anticipation curling tight inside me as he spins me around so I am facing him and my ass is pressed against the counter. His hands glide down my body, skimming the curves of my breasts, pausing as they reach the hem of my dress.

"You sure you know what you're getting into?" he growls against my neck.

"I'm sure," I insist. He's giving me an out, a chance to run, but I won't.

There's something about the way he moves, smooth and predatory. Like a man who always gets what he wants. That kind of swagger reminds me of Roman, of the Syndicate men, but he's not from that world, as far as I can tell. No tattoos, just a sharp jawline, and that calm, lethal confidence.

"I won't ask again," he says, threading his fingers through my hair and pulling my head back. I've never been handled like this, and I fucking love it. When he grabbed my neck earlier, not knowing it was me, it was shocking—but it awakened something inside me.

Our lips hover inches apart, but he doesn't close the distance. Instead, he lets his breath brush against my mouth and meets my gaze like he's savoring every moment of our exchange.

"Fuck," he growls before claiming my lips. His kiss starts soft but quickly turns hungry. Possessive. Almost angry.

His tongue teases mine, tasting me with a confidence that makes my head spin. It feels like he's claiming my mouth, and I grab the back of his head, pulling him closer. He makes a rough sound, his hand on my ass tugging me close, every inch of my body flush against him.

He tastes smoky, with a hint of heat, and I let myself drown in it. I don't know him, and I never will, but right now, I'm counting on him to fulfill every unspoken promise between us.

His palms glide down my thighs, fingers digging into my flesh as he lifts me onto the sink's edge. His hard length presses against me as he hikes my dress around my hips. A whimper escapes my lips when he slips my panties aside and traces a knuckle over my soaked entrance.

"Oh, baby, you're so fucking wet. Is this all for me?"

His lips move down my neck, and I arch into him, my core pulsing with need. "Yes," I breathe, unable to deny how badly I need him.

"Do you want me to fuck you?"

"Obviously," I choke out. What's with all the talking?

"Then say it," he demands.

This is so far outside my comfort zone, and even after the shot, I'm far from drunk. Barely tipsy. But damn it, I've never felt this drawn to someone. Never felt tempted to do something this wild, and I'm not backing down.

His gaze searches mine, unflinching as wetness pools with each slow stroke of his knuckles between my legs.

"Yes, I want you to fuck me… please."

He groans. "Hold that thought. There's something I need to do first."

Before I have a chance to question what the hell he means, he releases my legs. I expect him to reach for a condom, but instead, he takes off his glasses and sinks to his knees, looking up at me with hooded eyes.

Without breaking eye contact, he reaches for my panties, peeling them down in one fluid motion before tossing them aside and hooking my leg over his shoulder. His tongue drags along my slit, and pleasure slams into me, stealing my breath.

Oh. My. God.

I shudder as his tongue sweeps through my folds again, then settles on my clit, swirling it in hot, deliberate circles. The part of his face I can see is consumed with desire, his stare locked onto mine with a need that sets my skin ablaze.

He slides a finger inside me, then a second, curling them perfectly in time with the flick of his tongue on my clit. The orgasm builds fast, tightening low in my belly. My mouth falls open, my breaths ragged as my head falls back, legs trembling under the onslaught.

Only one man, the rigger I dated, ever went down on me, and it was nothing like this. This is pure heat and electric need.

"Soak me," he growls. "Come all over my face like a good girl. I want every drop."

That's all it takes for me to come undone. A cry slips from my lips as my entire body shakes with release. He doesn't stop, coaxing each tremor out of me until I'm completely spent, my fingers still tangled in his hair.

He barely gives me time to float back to earth before he rises, unbuckles his jeans, and pushes them, along with his briefs, to the floor. Then he tears open a condom and rolls it over his impressive length.

Oh, Jesus. How the hell is that going to fit? But he doesn't give me a second to dwell on that question before his hand grips my thigh, and he positions his dick at my soaked entrance.

With one firm thrust, he pushes all the way in, filling me completely.

This should be way more uncomfortable, considering how rarely I have sex, but it's not. It feels perfect—especially after that earth-shattering orgasm minutes ago.

He holds still, his breaths coming in quick, shallow pants, watching my expressions to see when I've adjusted to his size. I'm so wet and relaxed, the stretch is more pleasure than pain.

"I can take you," I whisper, breathless.

That's all the encouragement he needs. He buries his face in my neck and rocks into me with a hard, steady rhythm.

I tilt my hips to meet each of his thrusts. He lets out a low growl, pushing deeper, his mouth capturing mine. He teases me, his tongue mimicking the movements of his cock. When his hand dips down, finding my clit and stroking it with expert precision, my eyes fall shut, and I give in to the sensation.

The club noise falls away, my focus narrowing on how good this feels. Each stroke is deeper than the last, and his fingers continue to work my clit in circles.

"That's right. Are you going to give me what I want?"

All I can do is nod. My legs tremble as the tension builds, pushing me to the edge. I gasp and throw my head back, my arms wrapped tightly around his neck.

"Come for me—I want to feel you milk me dry." His voice is rough. He pinches my clit, his cock driving deep, again and again, until I shatter. He doesn't stop until I feel like I'm going to melt.

Then he grabs my hips and drives inside, holding himself deep—so deep I feel like I might split apart. His groans fill the space, the tremors of his release coursing through me.

I've never felt anything that intense before, and it leaves me shaken, like I've crossed into a whole new world. But slowly, reality settles back in.

He lowers my shaking legs, his fingers brushing up my thighs, leaving a warm trail before he pulls away. His large hand lifts to cup my face, and he studies me as if he's committing every detail to memory. This close, I spot a faint scar near his temple I hadn't noticed before and a dimple in his chin.

With a quiet sigh, he pulls out, ties up the condom, and tosses it away before fastening his pants. I pick up my discarded panties and slide them back on, smoothing out my dress. I run my fingers through my hair in the mirror, noticing the light sheen of sweat that makes my skin glow.

He steps up behind me, wrapping his arms around my waist. For a moment, I think of asking his name, just out of curiosity, but I resist to prove to myself that I can.

"Thanks. That was exactly what I needed." I smile, but he doesn't respond, his expression unreadable. "My friends are waiting for me downstairs, so…" I turn my head to look directly at him, a clear signal that this is goodbye.

He clears his throat, his lips pressed into a firm line. "I have something to tell you, and you're not going to like it."

My stomach drops. Is he going to tell me he's married? Daria warned me about this before. Men who confess they're cheaters only after the deed is done. He wasn't wearing a wedding ring—I checked—but I know that doesn't always mean anything.

I'm well aware not all marriages are built on love, but being with a married man feels gross. No matter how casual, I don't want to be part of something that could hurt someone else, especially another woman.

"You're married," I say, my voice laced with disgust.

"I am," he confirms, but he doesn't seem all that torn up about it. Does he really think confessing will absolve him? Sorry, but it won't.

"Congratulations. You're a terrible husband." This was supposed to be a fun, wild night, something I'd remember forever, and he ruined it.

He regards me with cool detachment, unaffected by my accusation. Running a hand along his stubbled jaw, he smirks. "I don't think she's under any illusion that I'm a good man. Tonight won't change that."

I break away from him, bending to grab my clutch from the floor so I can get the fuck out of there. "I'd say it was nice meeting you, but it wasn't." I straighten and turn toward the door. "I hope you have a nice li—"

The words catch in my throat. He's standing in front of me, blocking the exit with his large frame.

A chill runs down my spine, and my hands grow clammy. This is bad. If I bang on this door, yell, and scream, will anyone hear me over the thumping bass of the club?

"Do you recognize me yet?" His voice is quiet but loaded, sending my pulse skittering.

Recognize him? Something pulls at the edges of my memory, just out of reach.

I step forward cautiously. My breath catches as I stare into his eyes—blue, piercing, unforgettable. My gaze drops lower, scanning his mouth and jawline, trying to figure out what it is that's so familiar about him. Then I see it—the faint outline of ink on his neck.

I lick my thumb and swipe it over his skin. He doesn't stop me as I rub, the makeup smearing away to reveal a tattoo. Bold ink emerges—a star encircled by thorny vines, a mark impossible to forget.

Everything in me goes cold as I uncover more of the tattoos he's kept hidden. Piece by piece, the puzzle clicks together. The thick, dark hair, neatly styled now, once shaved to the scalp. He no longer has an eyebrow ring or the same raw edge, but the man underneath is unmistakable. My knees nearly give out.

He tilts his head, daring me to say his name out loud. "Do you recognize me now, wife?"

CHAPTER EIGHT

SOFIYA

The room spins, and my chest constricts as if the air has been stolen from my lungs. I flatten my back against the wall to steady myself. He doesn't react. His face remains calm, unnervingly composed.

"Nikolai." My voice trembles as his name passes between my lips.

"That's right." A flicker of satisfaction crosses his expression.

I shake my head so hard I feel my brain rattle around. What the hell is happening? I went out tonight to celebrate and allowed myself one impulsive decision. And somehow, that choice led me straight to *him*.

Nikolai Zhukov.

The man who saved me. The man I've fantasized about. The man I just had sex with in a bathroom. Who somehow thinks we're married.

"I'm not your wife," I insist. It's the only thing I can think of to say.

His gaze darkens, the shadows in his expression growing deeper. "Can you be sure of that?"

Can I?

My mind spins, sifting through all the information I've stored away over the years. "Th-there was no marriage to annul. The lawyers said it wasn't legal, that the certificate was never submitted."

"I'll ask you again. Are you sure about that?"

I'm not sure of anything right now, but I refuse to accept what he's saying. "You're lying. Why would you marry me? I'm useless to you."

He adjusts the cuff of his sleeve as if we're simply having a chat. "I married you for leverage over the Syndicate. As sister-in-law to one of the most powerful men in the Russian underworld, you're quite valuable."

I notch my chin up. "It doesn't matter. I was tricked into this… forced. It can't be legal."

He shrugs. "True, but I made it happen anyway. That's what men like me do: force our will on others." He trails a finger down my arm, leaving goosebumps in their wake. "And the best part is, after five long years, we finally consummated our marriage."

Heat rushes to my cheeks at the reminder. It's a mistake I'll take to the grave but I can't focus on that right now. I need to keep my wits about me because he's obviously unhinged.

"Why do this?" I ask. "What is it you want from the Syndicate?"

Shadows cross his face, his jaw taut. "Roman and I are at an impasse over a deal. He needs a little incentive to see things my way. Taking you to live with me and making our marriage known to the Syndicate will help him come around."

A sick feeling settles in my gut. Does he seriously believe that taking me will make a difference? Yes, Roman cares about me and would do anything for Liza, but the Syndicate's a massive machine. I'm not the bargaining chip Nikolai thinks I am. And there's no way in hell I'll allow him to use me more than he already has.

I lift my chin. "I don't care what you say. I won't go anywhere with you willingly. My… my guards are downstairs, and if they don't find me soon, they'll rip apart this place looking for me."

He gives me a *nice try* smile. "I think we both know that's not true."

I swallow hard. I could tell him my friends will start to worry, but I don't think he'll care. This situation has gone from bad to worse. My panic sharpens into resolve. I came out tonight to celebrate, and now my future is about to be yanked away. Well, fuck that.

I lift my foot and slam my heel down hard on his toes. The impact is followed by a hiss of pain. He swears a blue streak, and I take the opportunity to spin around and unlock the door. Before I can go anywhere, his arms wrap around me from behind, locking me in place.

"Don't even think ab—"

I throw my head back, my skull colliding with his nose. Pain explodes through my head, but it's worth it. He grunts, loosening his grip enough for me to twist free.

I dart through the door, heading straight for the nearest staircase. Behind me, the bathroom door slams open, and Nikolai's footsteps echo like gunfire, chasing after me.

Adrenaline floods my body, and I take the stairs two at a time. At the bottom, I veer into the main club, throwing myself headfirst into the chaos of the dance floor. The DJ has the crowd at its peak, the bass pounding so hard I feel it in my bones. Everyone's drunk, making it easier to slip through the crowd.

I pray like hell Nikolai won't spot me in this sea of people. I keep moving and don't stop until I find a dark corner to hide in. Pressing myself against the wall, I try to steady my breathing, my heart hammering in my ears. I may have lost him for now, but I'm sure he's relentless. A man like him probably has men swarming this place.

And then, a realization slams into me like a freight train—my clutch is gone, left behind in the bathroom. My phone, my money, everything I need is in there. Forcing down the rising panic, I focus on what to do next. Getting out of here is priority number one. Finding somewhere safe to call Roman or Samuil is priority two. Somehow, I'll also have to let my friends know I'm okay.

At least I don't see Nikolai or anyone who looks like his crew lurking nearby. And the club's exit isn't far from where I am. I can dash out of here unnoticed.

One more glance over my shoulder, and then—

An arm snakes around my waist, yanking me flush against a hard body.

"So you fuck me and run? Is that how it's going to be?" Nikolai's breath warms my ear, tightening the knot of fear coiled between my ribs.

"Let me go," I demand, my voice barely audible over the music. "I don't deserve this."

"Deserve? No, you don't deserve it. But it isn't personal."

His grip tightens like a python coiling around its prey. One arm pins me in place while the other extends in front of me, holding up a phone. Horror fills me when I see what's on the screen. Daria and Alex. They're standing in the VIP section, talking. Alex glances at his watch, his face tense.

"Your friends are worried about you," Nikolai taunts. "And they should be. But they should also worry about themselves. I've got a man trailing them, and if you don't do as I say, they'll pay the price."

The blood drains from my face, and tears blur my vision. I stare at the screen, horrified. I've heard Roman talk about Nikolai—how he's only become more dangerous—more ruthless, calculating, willing to burn the world down to get what he wants.

My knees wobble, and I curl forward. If he weren't holding me up, I'd collapse.

All my future plans of living in Berlin, dancing, and my freedom—it all evaporates in an instant.

"Are you going to glare at me the whole flight? Because it's another half hour until we land in St. Petersburg. You might want to give that beautiful face of yours a break."

Nikolai looks up briefly from his phone, where he's been typing away since I was forced onto his private jet. He didn't need a gun to my back to get me here, only the threat of harm to my friends.

He must have been watching me for long enough to know where I'd be tonight and that my friends are important to me. And he's right—I won't put them in danger. I believe him when he says he'll hurt them. He's demonstrated precisely what he's capable of.

I can't believe I once thought he was a decent person. My savior. I was so very wrong.

"I'll glare at you if I want to," I bite out, clutching the blanket tighter around my body.

I lean back, studying him.

He's no longer wearing glasses. I guess they were for show. Without them, there's nothing to soften his features. He looks savage. Harder than the man I met five years ago. Faint lines frame his eyes, and his near-black hair is grown out, just brushing his collar. His appearance might be more polished, but instead of dulling him, it only sharpens his edge.

"Suit yourself," Nikolai rumbles, his voice calm. "Dirty looks don't bother me, Sofiya. I've dealt with much worse in my life."

I scoot forward in my seat, narrowing my gaze. Now that the initial shock is fading, I have so many questions. "How long were you watching me?"

He sets his phone down slowly and leans back in his seat, resting an ankle casually on the opposite knee. "Long enough."

"That's not an answer," I snap. "Did you plan this all along? The bartender, the flirting… th-the sex." A bitter taste rises in my throat. I'll hate myself forever for falling into his trap so easily.

He takes me in, a slow, sexy grin curving his lips. It pisses me off how attractive he is. I try to ignore it, but it's like trying to block out the sun. Impossible. But hot doesn't cancel out evil.

"My only agenda tonight was taking you. The sex…" He leans forward so I can't miss a word he says. "Was a nice bonus. As was watching you dance for me at the club. I admit, I didn't think you had it in you."

Blood rushes to my face, anger tightening my throat. "I thought you were the Zhukov brother with a shred of decency. But you're not. You're just as sick and twisted as Sergey was."

His mouth flattens into a thin line, and the slightest flicker of something raw crosses his expression. It seems Sergey is a sensitive subject, something I file away for later.

He rests his elbows on his knees, eating up the space between us with his large frame. "You're right. Sergey and I were not so different. Maybe the biggest difference between us is that I was willing to kill him before he killed me. That makes me worse than him, don't you think?"

I don't respond. Instead, I turn my attention out the window, where the first streaks of pale light creep across the horizon. Dawn is near. Has anyone noticed my absence yet? Probably not.

Before takeoff, Nikolai used my phone to text my friends,

telling them I'd gone home with my hookup and not to worry. It's out of character for me, but so was everything else I did tonight, so it may not throw up red flags.

A flight attendant glides into the cabin, wheeling a cart of food before stopping in front of us. "Breakfast," she announces with a bright smile as if this scene is perfectly ordinary. Like I don't have raccoon eyes, and I'm not curled into myself miserably.

"I'm not hungry," I reply flatly, still looking out the window.

Nikolai straightens in his seat, a slow, deliberate movement that feels like a warning. "It wasn't a question," he says quietly.

I frown at him. "I said I'm not hungry."

His voice is calm, but it carries an edge. "You'll eat, Sofiya. Hungry or not. Or I'll drag you into my lap and feed you myself. Is that what you want?"

The way he says it, low and full of intent, sends a shiver through me. My stomach tightens, and I know he's not bluffing. I grab the tray the flight attendant hands me, glaring at him as I set it on the table.

"There," I say, picking up a fork. "Happy now?"

"Ecstatic."

I shovel a forkful of eggs into my mouth, holding his stare as I chew. He doesn't touch his food, just sips at the orange juice she poured for us… and continues to watch me. "You're my wife, Sofiya. That means you're my responsibility. Whether you want it or not, I'm going to take care of you… in every way."

His focus drifts to my lips, lingering long enough to make my pulse spike. What does he want from me? What will he expect? Will he make me submit, bend to his will? Will he keep me locked away or expect me to play the part of a doting wife? The way he looks at me, like he already owns me, makes my skin prickle with unease.

I don't voice any of these questions out loud, too fearful of his response. "I don't care what you say. Our marriage will never be real to me. I'll never touch you again. You make me sick."

His jaw flexes, his expression darkening. "I don't force myself on women. I don't need to. But considering how fast and hard you came in that bathroom, maybe you should think about making yourself available for conjugal visits."

Heat floods my face as I lift my middle finger at him. It's immature, but I don't care.

His body shakes with quiet laughter. "Good to see how deeply I affect you."

"If I could take back those five minutes, trust me, I would."

"Oh, I could've gone all night. It was you who came all over my cock in record time." His tone shifts, the teasing edge replaced by something heavier. "If you require a repeat performance, just say so, wife."

I force myself to hold his stare, but something inside me breaks wide open. The same cracks I thought I'd sealed long ago. He's doing what my parents did to me. He's reduced me to a pawn, a means to an end.

"You act like my life doesn't matter. You robbed me of my future. I was about to move to Berlin and live like a normal person. You stole that from me, and you couldn't care less."

His face hardens, the teasing edge gone. "I know this, moya sladost," he says, his voice low and cutting. "And it still doesn't matter to me. I don't prioritize anyone's life or well-being above my own, and you shouldn't either."

I shake my head, glaring at him. "What is it you want? What is this actually about?" When he doesn't respond, I continue. "I have a right to know, don't I? You're ruining my life for your gain."

He rubs a hand over his chin, his expression cool. "The minister of finance is about to hand me a string of casinos to run across Russia, but I won't get the contract unless I secure Moscow."

"Let me guess. The Syndicate doesn't want you in their territory."

He shrugs. "It's a fair deal, but Roman and Pavel don't see it that way. And quite honestly, it pisses me off that after everything, they have so little faith in me. It's a slap in the face." He leans back, his gaze steady. "So here we are. If they want you back, they'll have to agree to my terms."

Dread pools in my gut. It sounds like this situation is far more complicated than I'd hoped. "You're wasting your time using me to get to Roman—or anyone, for that matter. The only thing you're going to accomplish is getting yourself killed when the Belov Syndicate comes for you."

He folds his arms in front of him, his broad shoulders pulling taut beneath his shirt. "The Syndicate won't find you. The location of my estate is a well-guarded secret. And even if they did, your sister would never let Roman risk your safety in an attack." His eyes bore into mine. "Follow my orders, and you'll have nothing to worry about. If that's a problem..." His lips curve into something wicked. "I'll teach you how to follow orders. And believe me, I'll enjoy every moment of it."

A chill runs through me, but I'm too tired to continue this conversation. I doubt there's anything I could say to change his mind. I pull the blanket tighter around me, wrapping it like armor, and lean my head against the window.

CHAPTER NINE

NIKOLAI

THE SUN IS JUST BREAKING THROUGH THE HORIZON WHEN WE touch down in St. Petersburg. My city.

Sofiya is out cold, unsurprisingly, after everything I put her through.

I sit nursing a whiskey, my eyes fixed on her as the plane taxis down the runway. I angle my head, studying the strands of her silky hair, dark with a hint of auburn, like the embers of a dying fire. They frame her delicate face, and I have the sudden urge to brush them aside so I can feel the softness of her skin. But I know better. My touch would be as welcome as a slap.

I have to get these urges under control. She's my wife in name only. On paper. But fuck me if being around her doesn't stir something inside me. I told her I'm an unfeeling monster, and ninety-nine percent of the time, that's true. Turns out, she's the one percent exception.

I felt it watching her dance on stage. And I definitely felt it when she cried in my arms as I dragged her onto the plane. I did what I had to, but seeing her miserable stirs something I'm not willing to explore.

The jet comes to a stop, and a few minutes later, the door opens. One of my soldiers, Emil Merinov, bounds up the stairs, a grin stretching his face. "Welcome home, pakhan." He claps me on the back, his eyes flicking to the sleeping woman across from me. His head tilts with curiosity. "You brought a friend with you."

I grit my teeth. Turns out I don't like others looking at Sofiya when she's sleeping and vulnerable. But Emil doesn't know who Sofiya is to me, so I'll give him a pass. Along with the rest of my crew, he'll find out soon.

"You could say that."

He raises an eyebrow but doesn't press further. Emil and I have a long history. Along with Eva, one of my top lieutenants, we grew up in the same crappy apartment complex. Now, they're both trusted members of my bratva.

Guarding Sofiya will be his first major responsibility. He won't see it that way. He'll see it as babysitting duty, but that's too fucking bad. In my organization, the only way up is to earn it.

I don't bother waking Sofiya. I scoop her into my arms. The blanket she had over her falls, but I keep on going. She's soft and warm pressed against me, her head falling against my shoulder like it belongs there.

And it does. We fit together perfectly. The memory of fucking her will haunt me for the rest of my days. The way her body trembled against mine, the feel of her nails biting into my scalp, the way she clenched around my cock, milking the hardest orgasm of my life from me.

I knew what it would cost me to fuck her, but it was well worth it.

Her eyes flutter open, confusion clouding her expression. "Wh—what's going on?"

"We've landed," I inform her.

"Put me down." She struggles, but it's no use. I hold her tighter, refusing to let her go as I carry her down the steps to the car waiting on the tarmac.

"It's either in my arms or in cuffs. Which do you prefer?"

The cuffs are an empty threat. She wouldn't run with armed guards around and her friends' lives at risk. Vadim's idea to use them as leverage was genius. He's still in Moscow setting up surveillance on her friends.

Her cheeks flush, and she turns her head away, refusing to meet my eyes. But she stops resisting.

My driver, Matvey, jolts in surprise when he sees us, hurrying to open the car door. I place her gently inside the back seat, her gaze flitting around the interior, trying to make sense of what's happening.

"Emil and Matvey will take you back to my estate. I have other matters to deal with."

Her expression fills with panic. "Y-you can't leave me. Where are you going?"

My jaw tightens. I don't like seeing her scared, and I have a strange impulse to get in the car and soothe her anxiety, but I stop myself. I can't show her softness. It's not who I am, and it's not why she's here. The sooner she understands that, the better.

Irritation spikes when I catch Matvey and Emil eyeing her in the rearview mirror. Without the blanket, her club dress leaves too much exposed—her toned legs, her mussed hair, the smudged makeup around her eyes. The thought of any other man looking at her sends a murderous heat through me.

I shrug off my jacket and drape it over her shoulders. Her eyes snap to mine. "Keep that on," I say flatly, my tone leaving no room for argument. "You'll be fine."

I slap my hand against the roof of the car, and Matvey and Emil turn their attention toward me, their bodies straightening.

"This is Sofiya Ivanova, Roman Vasiliev's sister-in-law,

and my new wife." I let that sink in for a second. Their surprise is clear, but neither dares to speak. I look straight at Emil. "Let Yelena know she needs a room, and for fuck's sake, have Eva find her something decent to wear. I'll need you to keep an eye on her. The marriage wasn't what you'd call a mutual decision."

"You got it," Emil says, while Matvey, a man of few words, nods. The look they give her this time around holds more respect. Good.

I've never brought a woman to my home, let alone mentioned marriage. The women I fuck know the deal—no strings, no questions. My life doesn't leave room for anything more. It never has. My entire existence has been about clawing out of the gutter I was born into.

I started small, stealing cars for chop shops, learning how to strip them for parts or resell them clean. It wasn't glamorous, but it kept Sergey and me off the streets. From there, I moved to robberies—small stores, cash-heavy businesses, anything that wasn't too risky but paid well enough to survive. By my early twenties, I was hitting armored trucks. The adrenaline rush was addictive, and the payouts were life-changing.

The next step was controlling territory—smuggling high-value goods like stolen jewelry, rare artifacts, or anything that moved through the underground. It made me both rich and respected. By twenty-five, I had built the Zhukov Bratva into a force to be reckoned with.

After a childhood spent feeling powerless, I finally understood the value of power and money. They were a shield and a sword, ensuring no one could ever hurt me again.

A wife is a distraction I've never had any interest in. Whatever protective instinct I feel toward Sofiya is only that—an instinct. It doesn't mean anything.

I leave her with a final warning. "Your friends are being

tailed from now on. Don't make me do something you'll regret."

Her shoulders tense, her gaze flicking away as if she can't bear to look at me. I slam the door shut and step back, giving Matvey the signal to drive off.

Despite the exhaustion tugging at my body, energy courses through me. The kind that comes with knowing you've won. Sofiya is more than leverage—she's the turning point I've been waiting for.

My Bugatti Chiron waits at the edge of the airstrip, where Emil left it. Triumph courses through my veins as I stride toward the sleek machine, the symbol of everything I've worked for. With a press of my thumb on the keypad, the car unlocks, and I sink into the driver's seat, the engine humming beneath me.

Taking Sofiya was a gamble, but it went off without a hitch. Now, the real game begins. And I can't fucking wait to throw this victory in the Syndicate's face.

The heavy iron gate swings open, and I nod to the guard at the entrance before following the winding lane that leads to the opulent French colonial-style mansion ahead.

As I pull into the driveway, two guards instinctively rest their hands on their holstered weapons. But the tension melts away as I step out of the car, and recognition flashes across their faces. They lift their hands in greeting. I'm a regular at Igor Bocharov's estate.

Igor is a high-ranking politician, serving as the senior advisor to the minister of finance. But the real reason he can afford such a beautiful home and lavish estate is his criminal ties to me.

He approached me not long after I put a bullet in Sergey's head. Back then, he wasn't the big-time player he is now—

just another mid-level politician Sergey kept close for leverage. But when I took out my brother and the power shifted back to me, Igor proposed an alliance: he'd use his political connections to help me rebuild and grow the Zhukov Bratva in exchange for a cut of our deals.

It was mutually beneficial. As a politician, Igor had access to sensitive information, influence over law enforcement, and the ability to sway political favor.

With his help, I expanded my operations without worrying about the cops or the government getting in my way. In return, I made Igor a very rich man.

A corrupt politician and an organized crime leader turned out to be a match made in underworld heaven.

Igor's connection to the minister all but guarantees my legitimate company will be awarded the deal.

Here is how we both benefit: casinos attract billionaires, foreign investors, and oligarchs—people we can sway, buy, or blackmail. This means power, legitimacy, and influence.

For Igor, it's his ticket to climbing higher on the political ladder.

With the power and influence the casinos bring me, the Zhukov Bratva will finally put me on equal footing with the Belov Syndicate. They've ruled Russia for far too long, their reach stretching far beyond their territory. I'm sick of it.

After today, the Syndicate will understand one thing: I'm done playing second to anyone.

As I step up to the entrance, one of the guards points me toward the back gardens, where Igor likes to spend time when the weather's good. I cut through the sprawling home, as luxurious on the inside as it is on the outside.

Stained glass doors imported from France open to an impeccable garden where Igor is tending to his prized roses, pruning them with care.

"Nikolai." He greets me without looking up, his back still to me. "What brings you here so early?"

Sliding on my sunglasses, I make my way toward Igor. He's in his late fifties, heavy-set, balding, and shorter than my six-foot-three frame, but his presence demands respect. "I've got news. Thought you'd want to hear it right away."

"First, come and admire my flowers." He waves me closer without stopping his pruning. He once told me that tending his garden clears his mind—a bit of peace in a chaotic world. Ironic, considering the man might wear the mask of a respectable government official, but there's a ruthless criminal beneath his polished veneer.

Igor gestures to a cluster of roses, their petals a soft ivory. "Beautiful, aren't they? Reminds me of the ones my mother used to grow."

I raise an eyebrow but stay silent. Sentimentality isn't my thing, but I let him have his moment. Igor finally steps back from his flowers, brushing a speck of dirt from his fingers. "Now, what's this news you've brought me?"

"I dealt with the Belov Syndicate problem. They'll soon agree to the casino deal."

Igor pauses, his shears hovering over a stem. He shoots a curious look my way. "How did you convince them? I thought they only allowed family to operate in their territory."

I shrug, a hint of a smirk growing on my face. "I made myself family. Sofiya Ivanova, Roman's sister-in-law, is my wife."

He raises an eyebrow. "How the fuck did you do that? I'm assuming Roman didn't hand her over to you on a silver platter."

If I've learned one thing dealing with Roman over the years, it's that he's fiercely protective of his wife and sister-in-law, especially after all the shit they've been through. He'd do anything for them. And in this case, his devotion is his weakness.

"Not at all. Roman doesn't even know yet." I let out a

dark laugh. "I'll spare you the sordid details. For now, what's important is we have something over the Syndicate. If Roman wants Sofiya back, he'll agree to our terms."

Later today, Vadim will send Roman a package containing a copy of our marriage certificate, video footage of her on my jet, and a picture of the ring I'll soon require her to wear. I'm sure I'll be able to hear Roman cursing me out all the way from New York.

His fucking problem. He reaped what he sowed. If the Syndicate doesn't want to share power with me, I'll have to take it from them. I haven't worked this hard and sacrificed this much to stand down.

Igor whistles between his teeth as he clips a flower and hands it to a gardener he has standing by. "She's a very beautiful young woman if I recall. Met her once, a little while ago. A dancer, is that right?"

"That's right." I choose my next words carefully. Igor sees women as things to own and sometimes as things to break. Sofiya may mean nothing to me, but I don't like the idea of him playing with what's mine. It's why I plan on keeping Sofiya far from him. "It's a marriage on paper, nothing more. I don't care what she does, only that she's useful to me."

His grin is wolflike. "Come on now. I'm sure you'll enjoy the benefits of possessing such a young and innocent creature."

My fists tighten at my sides, and I do my best to keep my voice even. "Like I said, a wife on paper. If I need to fuck, I have plenty of women on speed dial more than willing to do the job."

"But breaking her in is part of the fun, Nikolai. If you want to light a fire under Roman, a picture of his sister-in-law bound and gagged with your dick up her ass would do the trick."

Anger blazes up my spine. He has a point, but I don't much like that idea.

He snips a dead leaf with more force than necessary, his expression hardening. "But I'm glad you know better than to let her get close. Women make you weak. Roman is proof of that."

I clear my throat. "I'll keep you updated once the Syndicate responds to my happy news."

"The minister wants to award the casino contract in the next six weeks. Not much time. You'll need to show the Syndicate how serious you are—what you're willing to do to get your way."

"I'll do what I have to. I always do," I say through clenched teeth.

"Good. Everything should fall into place perfectly." With a deceptively calm smile, Igor hands me a single blood-red rose, full and healthy. There's a good reason for that. Igor claims human remains make excellent fertilizer. "A blooming rose for your wife."

My hand wraps around the stem as a sharp pain shoots through my finger. A thorn has pierced my skin, a small rivulet of blood trickling down my hand.

I meet Igor's gaze, his eyes glinting with intensity. "Be careful, Nikolai. Even the most beautiful things can be dangerous."

My molars press together. "I'll keep that in mind."

CHAPTER TEN

SOFIYA

THE SOUND OF KNUCKLES RAPPING AGAINST THE WINDOW startles me awake. I'd drifted off again, my head pressed against the cool glass. I didn't mean to. I tried to stay awake and pay attention to my surroundings and anything that could be useful later on. But physical exhaustion won out.

The light-haired guard with the steel-gray eyes, Emil, announces, "We're here," and opens the passenger-side door.

Crisp morning air rushes in, but it does nothing to ease the sense of dread coiling in my stomach. It's the fact that I have no idea what awaits me. If I'll be thrown in the dungeon or treated like... well, the pakhan's wife. That thought is too bizarre to contemplate.

My legs are shaky as I step out of the car, and I brace myself for the worst—rough hands, cuffs, something to remind me I don't belong here. Instead, Emil reaches out, steadying me with an easy grip.

The house looms before us. Actually, mansion is probably a better term. The exterior is a mix of pale stone and dark wood, with thick columns flanking the entrance. Tall windows reflect the morning light, giving the place an almost magical quality. It's beautiful, in a cold, intimidating way. Like Nikolai himself.

"In case you're thinking about running," Emil says, "I'll warn you now—there are cameras and security guards everywhere. You wouldn't get very far."

I glance around, my heart sinking. Rolling green lawns stretch out, bordered by thick woods. The air is fresh, crisp, too clean to be anywhere near a city. It dawns on me that this isn't simply a house. It's a fortress.

"Don't worry. You'll have plenty of time to look around later," Emil adds, tugging me toward the entrance.

The inside catches me off guard. I imagined Dracula's castle—everything dusty and old—but this is not that. Massive windows allow in plenty of natural light, making it feel open and welcoming. The dark wood floors are stately, and Persian rugs are thrown about the place. The art is tasteful and looks carefully chosen. It's… nice. Cozy, for such a big space.

I clutch Nikolai's jacket tighter around me, the scent of cedar and smoke filling my lungs. Nikolai's space is a reflection of who he is, how he controls his world down to the finest detail. And now I'm part of his world.

My stomach swoops as we pass members of Nikolai's house staff. Their surprised stares dart between me and Emil, but no one says a word.

"Where are you taking me?" I ask.

Emil spares me a quick glance. "You look like you need some coffee."

We enter a room that is clearly the kitchen. It's more rustic than the main area of the house, with exposed wooden beams that stretch across the ceiling and a long farm table in the center of the room.

The smell of fresh coffee and baked bread wraps around me, and my stomach betrays me with a low growl, a reminder of how little I'd eaten earlier. My nerves wouldn't let me.

Emil gestures toward a stool at the counter, and I sit hesitantly, watching as he presses a button on a shiny, state-of-the-art machine. Less than a minute later, he slides an espresso in front of me.

"Aren't you going to offer her something to eat?" I turn in my seat, surprised as a gorgeous woman walks into the room. She looks to be in her early thirties, dressed in sleek workout leggings and a matching sports bra, her blonde hair pulled into a ponytail that swings with each step. Her flushed cheeks and glowing skin suggest she's just come from a workout, as does the horrible-looking green drink she's sipping. "Excuse Emil. He seems to have forgotten his manners."

Emil mutters under his breath about not being a damn maid before grabbing his own coffee and sitting at the farm table.

"I'm Eva. And you must be Sofiya," she says as she holds out her hand in greeting.

I shake it somewhat reluctantly, not knowing what else to do. Am I supposed to be friendly with these people? Do they know I'm here against my will? That I'm not Nikolai's wife by choice?

I have no idea who this Eva is, but since she's not a gun-toting guard, maybe she'll take pity on me. "You need to know that Nikolai abducted me. If you have any shred of decency, you'll help me. I need to call my sister an—"

"A word of advice," she says, cutting me off with a raised hand. "Save your breath. Everyone in this house is loyal to Niko."

"Then you're loyal to a bad man," I snap.

"Good, bad… all that's subjective," she responds, taking a sip from her juice.

"It's really not," I mutter, disheartened. What did I really expect, though?

"You must be hungry," Eva says, like I didn't just tell her I'm a prisoner. She opens a drawer and pulls out a container of baked goods, setting it in front of me. "Muffin? They're oatmeal flax blueberry muffins. Gluten-free, dairy-free, made them myself."

Not quite a selling point, but hunger wins out. "Sure."

She sets one on a plate and slides it across to me. I stare at the sad little thing before reluctantly taking a bite. It's not as bad as I expected, but it's definitely not good. Eva beams at me anyway, clearly thrilled that someone is eating her creation.

"So, are you the… cook?" I ask, hoping for a better read on her.

"Oh god, no." She laughs. "Niko would fire me in a hot second if I tried to feed him anything this healthy. Yelena's the cook. And the housekeeper. And the boss of all house staff. You'll see when she's back from the market."

Yeah, I guess I will see. I'm stuck here for now.

I was so close—so close to living my life on my terms before Nikolai fucking Zhukov barged in and dragged me into his world like Hades himself. A shiver coasts over my skin. The irony of my dance comes to mind. Did I somehow curse myself?

But I'm not going to accept this fate. I'll find a way out. I don't know how yet, but I will. And I'll do it without putting my friends at risk.

I drain the last of the coffee, the caffeine taking the edge off my exhaustion. It's not an actual plan, but I'm determined to figure something out. My first step is learning who works and lives in this house—starting with the woman in front of me, still nursing her green sludge.

"So," I ask casually, "what is it you do here?"

She pauses with her drink halfway to her lips. "Oh, I don't work here."

Right. She doesn't work here, but she recently finished a workout, seems to know her way around the kitchen, is obviously loyal, calls him Niko...

God, I'm such an idiot. She's his lover.

Of course. What did I expect? He might be evil, but he's hot as all get out, and she's also stunningly beautiful. I shouldn't be surprised someone is warming his sheets, yet I feel the tiniest pang of… I don't know what. Definitely not jealousy. Irritation?

Would she be as friendly if she found out I had sex with her boyfriend less than twelve hours ago? Maybe. Maybe not. Who knows what kind of open arrangement they have. Whatever it is between them, I don't care. I want nothing to do with Nikolai, in or out of the bedroom.

But none of this is on her, and if I'm going to be stuck here with her, even for a little while, it's smart to keep things civil between us. Maybe, if we become friendly and I gain her trust, she'll let something slip that will be helpful in my escape.

Her eyes trail down my body, taking in my disheveled state. At least I still have Nikolai's jacket over my shoulders. The one kindness he paid me today, if you can call it that. "Looks like you've had quite a night. How about I show you to your room?"

My room. When Nikolai put me in the car, he told his men to find me a room. And on the plane, he said he didn't force himself on women, but now I get it. He has this supermodel to share a bed with every night. I should be relieved, but for whatever reason, I'm annoyed. It's probably heartburn from the muffin. It sits in my belly like a stone.

"I'd love nothing more than to get out of this disaster of a dress."

She gives me a quick up-and-down look. "I have a few things that might fit you. I'll drop them off in the morning."

I nod and rise from the stool, the buzz from the coffee already wearing off. A shower and sleep will probably do me a world of good. And some answers, but I have a feeling I won't be getting those anytime soon.

CHAPTER ELEVEN

SOFIYA

My eyes fly open, and my heart pounds as something cold and hard snaps around my ankle. I jerk upright, tangled in sheets, unsure of where I am or what is happening.

"Rise and shine, princess." Nikolai's voice.

Sunlight stabs through the curtains as the world comes into view. Nikolai is at the foot of my bed, his hand covering whatever is locked around my ankle.

"What are you doing?" I rasp, my voice heavy with panic. "Are you… are you chaining me to the bed?"

"Good morning to you, too," he says, looking up at me with a small smile. "It's an ankle monitor to keep track of your location. Just taking precautions. Can't have my wife wandering off, can I?"

An ankle monitor to track my movements? It takes my morning brain a minute to process. Is he giving me an electronic leash?

The moment I look down, my confusion only grows. I expected something clunky and shackle-like around my ankle, but instead, a thick gold cuff rests against my skin.

Small, sparkling diamonds are scattered across its surface, making it appear as if it glows.

"It's real if you're wondering." Nikolai's fingertips brush over my sensitive skin above the device, and heat rushes up my leg. I bite the inside of my cheek, refusing to let him see the way his touch sends an unwelcome shiver through me. "Fourteen karat gold and hand-set diamonds. Only the best for my wife."

I want to rip it off and throw it in his smug face. "Stop calling me that," I insist. "And covering it in gold and diamonds doesn't make it any better. Might as well throw me in the dungeon if you're going to treat me like a prisoner."

"If sleeping in the dungeon is more in line with your expectations, it can be arranged."

I roll my eyes and hug the blankets tighter around me. "I'll keep my gilded cage, thanks."

Gilded isn't an exaggeration. The room is lovely, with pale green walls and elegant mid-century furniture. The highlight is a large window overlooking the lush back garden—not that I imagine I'll be allowed outside. At least, not alone.

Nikolai pulls up a chair and sits beside me while I watch him warily. He's fresh from a workout, his black athletic tank clinging to his skin, every muscle defined. A faint sheen of sweat clings to his skin. His forearms rest on his knees, the veins running up his arms so prominent they're distracting. I force my gaze upward because letting my eyes wander would only spark uninvited memories.

I don't need any more reminders of what happened between us. The slight soreness between my legs is reminder enough.

Nope. Not going there. I shake the thoughts away, combing my fingers through my messy hair. "With all your security, don't you think a tracker is a little excessive?"

"Take it as a compliment. I have faith you can do anything you put your mind to." His tone is infuriatingly calm. "Other than the basement, my office, and the east wing where my guards are housed, you're free to go wherever you like. But remember…" His fingers trail a deliberate line over my calf, brushing the monitor, and goosebumps rise unbidden in its wake. "This will alert me the second you step off my property. Day or night, it goes straight to my phone. And trust me, you won't like the consequences."

I grit my teeth, swallowing back a growl of frustration. This stupid monitor kills any hope of escape. It was already a long shot, but now it feels impossible. My mind goes to Roman and Liza. If they know I've been taken, maybe they're already working on a plan to get me back. I swallow before meeting his stare. "Do Roman and Liza know yet… about me being here?"

I expect Nikolai to dismiss my question, but he doesn't. He leans forward, studying my face as he slowly nods. "They've received my message. I imagine I'll hear back from them soon. But don't hold out hope of a big dramatic rescue. I covered my tracks well."

Helplessness wraps around me, and despite myself, my eyes burn with the threat of tears.

His mouth tightens. "Don't blame yourself, moya sladost. There was nothing you could have done to stop me."

"I don't blame myself," I hiss. "I blame you."

Except that's not entirely true. I barely slept last night, replaying every bad decision that led me here. Ditching my bodyguards was the first. Sleeping with Nikolai was the second and, by far, the worst.

This news is going to crush Liza. She'll blame herself somehow, and she doesn't need that guilt right now, not when her focus should be on getting pregnant and building the family she's always wanted. Once again, I feel like a burden to her and Roman.

I reach for a tissue on the nightstand, and as I shift, the

blankets slip, cool air brushing against my bare skin. Damn it! I'm practically naked in a bra and underwear.

Nikolai doesn't move, his dark gaze traveling slowly over my exposed skin, drinking me in with the kind of intensity that makes my pulse stumble. I yank the sheets up, clutching them tightly to my chest, and shoot him a glare. "Mind your own business."

"Don't be so modest." His gravelly voice is loaded with suggestion. "It's nothing I haven't seen before."

"And it's nothing you'll ever see again," I snap. "You ripped me from my life. My family, my friends, my future—they were everything to me, and you took it all without a second thought."

He exhales slowly, standing with deliberate calm. "I'm not looking to complicate my life, Sofiya. You're my wife in name only. I won't ask for more. You'll live here and follow my rules. Beyond that, you're free to do as you like."

That's hardly freedom, but I'm done arguing. I want him to leave. On his way out of the room, he gestures toward a neatly folded stack of clothes at the foot of the bed. "Eva lent you a few things for now."

The mention of Eva's name sets my teeth on edge. "Making me wear your girlfriend's clothes—real classy."

His brows knit together. "My girlfriend?"

"I'm not stupid, Nikolai."

A smirk plays at the corner of his lips as if he's somehow enjoying this. "Of course not." He's about to leave my room when he stops and turns in the open doorway. "If you don't want to wear Eva's clothes, you can always wear mine. I'd rather enjoy seeing you in my shirt and nothing else."

"In your dreams!" I yell out as the door shuts with a hard click.

My eyes flutter shut as I sink back into the pillows. The interaction with Nikolai drained every ounce of my energy, and for a moment, I was tempted to let the mattress swallow me whole. But I can't. Hiding in this room won't solve my problems.

Along with the stack of clothes, I find basic toiletries and makeup. Eva's doing, no doubt. I can't figure out why she's being kind to me. Maybe she's lonely living here, or more likely, Nikolai told her she had to play nice.

After I brush my teeth and take a hot shower, I slip into a red summer dress that's a little too tight across the chest—one of the many joys of being well-endowed. As a dancer, I'm strong and lean, but I certainly don't have the body of a workout queen like Eva, not to mention she's an Amazon, and I'm the height of a mere mortal.

For now, this dress will have to do because I'd rather wear a trash bag than put on anything belonging to that mudak. I refuse to think about everything he's taken from me.

The only thing I need to focus on is figuring out a way out of here.

The house is quiet as I head downstairs, retracing my steps to the kitchen, where I find an older woman with short, graying hair pulling something from the oven. She spots me and smiles, as if she knows who I am.

"Good morning," I say, unsure of how I'll be received.

Any uncertainty I have dissolves when all five feet of her come hurtling toward me. She hugs me more fiercely than I imagined someone of her size could.

"Look at you, so beautiful," she says and steps back to squish my cheeks between her hands.

"I… thank you." I have no idea what's happening or why she still hasn't let me go. "Uh, nice to meet you. I'm Sofiya."

"I know who you are: Nikolai's wife." She beams. "I'm Yelena," she says, releasing me from her grasp before thrusting a steaming cup of coffee into my hands. "Cook, housekeeper, and the one who keeps everyone in line. Even Niko."

Her words make my stomach drop. Nikolai's wife. She

says it so casually, like it's something to celebrate. Does she think this marriage is something it's not? Like a love match. I don't want to be the one to burst her bubble, but she needs to know the truth.

"Listen, Yelena, you seem very nice, but let me be clear. This marriage wasn't my choice. I don't want Nikolai as a husband, and I don't want to be here."

She pats my hand. "You just need to get used to him. His bark is worse than his bite."

This is definitely not going as intended. "I don't want to get used to him. I want to be free of him."

She studies me, her eyes narrowed. "I think you need something to eat."

I almost laugh. She's not wrong about that, at least. I sink onto one of the stools at the counter as she sets a platter of fruit and a basket of warm vatrushka in front of me. The cheese Danish is my weakness, and I don't even try to resist. I usually overthink everything I eat, but it's not like I'll be onstage anytime soon.

God, maybe ever.

An ache cuts through me like a knife. In a few days, I'll miss the audition with the Berlin Contemporary Dance Company. They'll assume I stood them up, that I'm not serious, when that's not the truth at all.

My dream life—my sunny apartment, my career, my lazy weekends—vanishes like smoke over water. In its place is an ankle monitor that costs more than my flat in Moscow and a husband I never wanted.

My shoulders sag as I take another bite of the Danish, which is absurdly good, and let my eyes drift around the room. No matter how civilized Nikolai's home appears, it will never feel that way to me. It will always be a prison with lavish cells.

"You don't like my vatrushka?" Yelena's frown pulls me back to the present.

My face must have betrayed my spiraling thoughts. "No, that's not it at all. They're amazing. I'm just… tired."

"More coffee," she declares, refilling my mug.

"Thanks."

As soon as I polish off the last bite, Yelena gives a satisfied nod and drops another Danish onto my plate. Might as well take enjoyment where I can.

Before either of us can say more, Eva saunters into the kitchen. Her eyes light up when she sees me. Once again, she's in skintight leggings and a sports bra that shows off her toned stomach. Her blonde hair is pulled into a messy bun, wisps framing her flushed face. Like Nikolai earlier, she looks like she just stepped out of a Peloton commercial.

They probably woke up together, tangled in silk sheets after a night of marathon sex, before deciding to hit the gym like any loved-up couple.

Gross.

"Oh, I'll take some of that vatrushka," Eva chirps, sliding onto the seat next to me.

Yelena responds with a disapproving sniff. Before I can blink, she lobs one of Eva's weird flax muffins at her head with surprising accuracy.

"You made, you eat," she declares.

Eva's face crumples like a kid denied candy. "But…" she starts to protest, her lower lip jutting out in a pout that probably works wonders on Nikolai.

I bite back a smirk as Eva shoots Yelena a grumpy look before shrugging and biting into her muffin. "She hates when I cook in her kitchen. This is punishment," she whispers.

I feel a little irrational thrill at Yelena's disapproval. Not that I have anything against Eva personally. She seems like an okay person. I just don't like the man she sleeps with.

"How are you feeling?" Eva asks, chewing on a bite of muffin. "You must've been totally exhausted."

"Feeling better, other than the being-held-against-my-will part," I acknowledge.

She ignores the jab and keeps on eating.

"By the way, thanks for the dress and toiletries," I offer in a gentler tone.

She gives me a once-over. "Looks good on you. Well, maybe a little tight in the boob area."

"We're not quite the same size."

"But if I had tits like yours..."

Her voice trails off as Nikolai enters the kitchen with Emil right behind him. My mouth goes dry. Nikolai is freshly showered, his dark hair slicked back, dressed in a tailored suit that clings perfectly to his broad shoulders and muscular frame. He looks annoyingly good in a suit.

His gaze meets mine and then drifts lower, his expression darkening with every inch his eyes take in.

"No." The single word falls from his lips like a command.

"No, what?" I glare at him.

"No to that dress," he says, smoldering with intensity. Emil immediately turns away, busying himself with the coffee machine. Nikolai's attention shifts to Eva. "Get her something else to wear."

Rude.

"Sorry," Eva chirps, though she doesn't sound remotely sorry. "That's the only thing I have here that'll fit Sofiya." She picks at a strawberry from the fruit platter. "Take your wife shopping if you want her to dress like a nun."

The muscles in his body go rigid as his glare locks onto my chest. I've never seen a man so offended by cleavage. "You must have a shirt or something else she can wear over that dress."

"Nope," Eva replies, looking far too amused.

"Excuse me," I interject, lifting my chin. "I'm right here. Don't talk about me like I'm not in the room. And I don't need to cover up. I'm perfectly fine the way I am."

In truth, I don't love having my girls on full display, but if it gets under Nikolai's skin, I'll make an exception.

A menacing growl leaves his throat. "You are not fine the way you are. No wife of mine is going to walk around this house, around my men, showing that much skin."

"Luckily, I don't consider myself your wi—" The words evaporate as Nikolai peels off his suit jacket and starts unbuttoning his dress shirt. Holy shit, what is he doing?

"Since we're out of options, you'll wear my shirt over that excuse for a dress."

My jaw goes slack as the shirt falls from his shoulders with an ease that makes my stomach tighten. I should look away, but I can't. Olive skin stretches tight over hard muscles, his torso and arms covered in tattoos. My eyes trail down the defined ridges of his abs, snagging on the V that disappears below his belt. He looks like he's stepped straight off the cover of a romance novel, and the sight causes my core to tighten.

He dangles the fabric in front of me to take, but I'm frozen in place. Is he for real? As if I'd ever willingly wear his clothes. Nope. Not happening.

"Did I not make myself clear?" he grits out.

I gulp. "I won't put on your shirt."

"In that case, I'll have to do it for you."

As he strides toward me, I instinctively stand and back up, but the wall stops my retreat.

The kitchen falls silent as he cages me in, one arm braced above my head. His bare form is inches from me, his broad shoulders blocking out everything else.

Without warning, he spins me around to face the wall. Heat radiates from his body as he holds the shirt open, making it clear I have no choice but to slip my arms through the sleeves. His hands slide down my sides as he turns me back around to face him.

My breath stutters as he starts buttoning the shirt himself.

Each brush of his fingers against my body feels electric, and I silently curse the woman who brought him into this world. As he fastens the last button, his eyes lock on mine. The air between us is charged, neither of us willing to look away first.

"There. Was that so bad?" His eyes glint with victory.

It's worse than bad. Because now, there's no way I'll be able to get him out of my head all damn day.

With a final glare in my direction, he steps back and turns to Eva. "Find better-fitting clothes for tomorrow," he growls before leaving the room.

Emil keeps his focus firmly on his coffee, while Yelena hums a tune as she tidies up, seeming unfazed. Eva, however, flashes a wicked grin, clearly enjoying herself. "I think you get under his skin."

"Yay for me," I grumble, feeling like a kid in his giant shirt.

"It's good for him to have someone who doesn't just roll over," she says with a wink. "He's not used to it."

"Yeah, well, he's pakhan. His word is law."

She shrugs like the title means nothing.

I don't understand their relationship. It seems strange to me that she's totally fine with this setup. Maybe she's used to him keeping other women. Men like him get to do whatever they want after all.

Eva straightens and glances at her watch. "Oh, damn, I have to run."

"You're leaving?" I blurt. "What am I supposed to do?"

She pats my arm. "This is where you live now, so make yourself at home. Explore. Watch TV. Go for a swim. There's a stack of magazines down in the gym if you're bored. Emil can show you the way."

This will never be home, but I hold my tongue. Under the guise of "exploring," I plan to spend the day hunting for a phone, computer, or any digital device with Wi-Fi to contact Liza and Roman.

I don't have high hopes. Nikolai isn't an idiot. He's likely locked up every means of communication. But that won't stop me from looking.

Eva points a playful finger at me as she backs out of the room. "Have fun! Don't get into trouble."

I throw my hands in the air. "What trouble could I possibly get into?"

CHAPTER TWELVE

NIKOLAI

"You're a fucking dead man, Zhukov." Roman's voice cuts through the line, sharp with fury. "If you've hurt her—"

"Is that any way to talk to your brother-in-law?" I lean back in my office chair, boots propped on the desk. A slow grin spreads across my face as I savor every second of his reaction.

The package I sent with the marriage license and pictures of Sofiya on my plane hit its mark. Instead of keeping his cool and having a rational conversation, he's frothing at the mouth. He's showing his hand that he'll do whatever it takes to get Sofiya back.

"Sofiya's safe—for now," I continue. "But you need to understand you don't have a choice. You try to attack me, you put her in danger. I don't think you want to take that chance."

"You don't know what I'm willing to do. And if you think you can force me into this deal, you're dead wrong."

Roman's breaths are ragged, like he's fighting to stay in control. I can picture him pacing, fists clenching and unclenching, wishing he could reach through the phone and rip me apart.

Too bad he underestimated me. Now, he has to live with the fallout.

"This is all on you. You claim you only allow family to do business on your territory. Well, look at that, we're fucking family. Sofiya is my wife and has been for a long time. I granted her freedom, but that ended the moment you tried to keep me under your thumb."

"You motherfucker," he snarls. "All this time we worked together, you were a snake. You knew exactly what you were doing, biding your time until you could bury the knife in my back." The line crackles with his harsh, humorless laugh. "You've messed with the wrong family. There's no world where this ends well for you."

"Enough." My hands slam onto the desk. "I've tolerated more than enough of this bullshit. The clock is ticking, Vasiliev. This is a simple proposition. I want access to your territory. That's it. Make this easy, and I'll even cut you in on the profits. As I said, Sofiya is bound to me for life. I'm sure your wife would be devastated if she never saw her sister again. So make the smart choice."

Mentioning Liza is deliberate. Roman would carve out his own heart for his wife, and I'm sure she would do anything to get her younger sister back. They don't trust me with her, and they shouldn't. My control is hanging on by a thread.

She looked fucking edible in Eva's dress this morning, but seeing her in my shirt, knowing my scent and heat surrounded her, was nearly my undoing. It took everything in me not to order everyone out of the room, hike up her dress, rip off her panties, and fuck her with my tongue until she came all over my face.

She felt it, too. I could tell in the way her body tensed. She might hate me, but she sure doesn't mind how I look without a shirt on.

"What are you saying?" Roman snaps, his voice raw.

"I believe I was crystal fucking clear. I'm done with this conversation. The next time we talk, it had better be because you're agreeing to my terms."

"Wait." Roman's breath hisses from his lungs. "I need proof of life." His voice stays strong, but I can hear the desperation bleeding through his tone.

He's in no position to be making demands, but in this case, it suits me to show him my bargaining chip is alive and well.

"Since you asked so nicely, I'll think about it." I hang up, satisfied I've made my point.

The leather chair creaks as I push to my feet, crossing to the bar cart stationed near the window of my office. From here, on the second floor of a nightclub I own, I can see the faint morning glow of the city filtering in.

I grab the whiskey decanter and pour a double shot into a crystal tumbler. In one fluid motion, I toss it back, the burn sharp and welcome. It's early for a drink, but after Roman's call, I need it.

Roman and Liza are still in New York, but I imagine they will be racing back to Moscow to manage the situation. He'll want to loop in Pavel and Maxim Belov. Belov might've stepped away from daily business, but the Syndicate still runs on his authority.

Footsteps sound through the hallway, announcing Vadim and Eva before they step in—my two right hands. Eva oversees all financial operations, from laundering to investments, keeping the books airtight and the authorities blind. Vadim runs the syndicate's day-to-day logistics, managing shipments, crews, and making sure everyone falls in line—or faces the consequences.

While Eva and I share a history shaped by survival, Vadim's story is different. He came from a working-class family, joined the army young, and climbed his way into the special forces. For a while, he thrived in that structure. But stability has its breaking point, even for someone like him. When his sister's bastard husband laid a hand on her while she was pregnant, Vadim made sure it was the last time. Beat the man within an inch of his life. It cost him years behind bars. That's where we met. And when I walked out, I walked out with him.

After everything, Sergey's betrayal had left me raw. I didn't trust anyone, and I needed people I could count on to rebuild the Zhukov Bratva from the ground up. Eva had always had my back. She was sharp, unyielding, and knew how to handle herself in a fight. After what Sergey pulled, loyalty wasn't just important, it was everything.

At the time, Eva was scraping by as a cocktail waitress. She agreed to join my bratva and suggested we look up Emil. We'd lost touch with him over the years, but word was that he'd been hanging with the wrong crowd, heading nowhere fast. I hoped the discipline of the bratva could keep him in line.

That was five years ago. We've had our share of fights, but we've built something solid. They're as close to family as I'll ever have again.

Vadim steps in ahead of Eva, nodding at me as he loosens his tie and undoes the top button of his shirt. His dark hair is slightly disheveled, and faint shadows circle his eyes. He's just back from Moscow, where he set up a team to monitor Sofiya's friends. He looks like he's been running on too little sleep.

I gesture to the lowball of whiskey in my hand. "Breakfast?"

"What the hell, I could use it." Vadim shrugs and sinks into the office's leather couch. Eva drops down beside him but waves off my offer of a drink. She's more the green juice type than whiskey.

Since joining the bratva, she's earned respect the hard way

—by becoming a ruthless fighter, proving she can take on any man and win. She looks every bit as kick-ass as she is. Today, she's wearing black leather pants, high-heeled boots, and a fitted tank top. The only pop of color is her bright red lips.

I know many consider her gorgeous, but to me, she's family.

I could've set Sofiya straight earlier, told her who Eva really is to me. But I didn't. I liked the way jealousy sparked in her eyes. She can act like she hates me, say she regrets spreading her legs for me, but her true feelings—the ones she might not even admit to herself—were written all over her face when she brought up my "girlfriend."

"Just got off the phone with Roman," I say, lowering into my office chair. "As expected, he was furious, but he got the message loud and clear. We have him by the balls, and the sooner he comes to terms with that, the better."

Vadim grins, tearing into a box of Lucky Charms. He has it imported straight from America on our ships, moving product. He's got a weakness for American sugary cereal—something I'll never understand.

Eva's nose wrinkles as Vadim shoves another handful into his mouth. She brushes off her disgust and turns toward me. "What's the timeline for him accepting the deal?"

"Igor says the contract will be awarded in six weeks. We need the Syndicate's buy-in before then."

The Syndicate is too powerful and well-connected to go to war with. That's why this plan works. With Sofiya as my wife, I have leverage. The Syndicate will fall in line on my terms, not theirs.

Vadim runs a hand over his two-day stubble. "If Roman values his sister-in-law's well-being, he'll come around before then."

Eva frowns with displeasure. "Why would we hurt Sofiya? She's innocent in all of this."

Hurting a woman—any woman—isn't something I take

pleasure in, but the thought of hurting Sofiya stirs something inside me. It's a feeling I can't afford. I swirl the whiskey in my glass and knock it back in one go.

"As long as the Syndicate comes around, no one will get hurt." Eva's about to argue, but I hold up a hand. She's tough as shit when it's required, but she hasn't lost her humanity—a rare thing in this world and something I usually appreciate. Except right now, it's pissing me off.

Vadim tosses another handful of dry Lucky Charms into his mouth. Eva snatches the box from him and does the same. The moment she tastes it, her face crumples in disgust. "This is nasty. Why do you eat this shit?"

"Because it's delicious." His eyes narrow. "So cereal is a problem, but you have no issue that I'm nursing a whiskey before ten in the morning?"

Eva shrugs. "Whiskey is what adults consume. Only children eat this crap."

"I beg to differ." Vadim shoots back, a wry smile on his lips.

I stand and button up my jacket. "If you two are done bickering, I believe we have some real business to take care of."

A container ship full of cocaine from Colombia is arriving this afternoon. Normally, this would be handled by my men, but I want to oversee the transfer myself. This deal has been months in the making, and it's the largest shipment I've handled this year. With so much at stake, we need to be there.

Vadim stands, adjusting the holster strapped under his suit, while Eva grabs her leather motorcycle jacket off the back of the chair, slinging it over her shoulders.

I pause at the door, and a nagging thought pulls at me. I turn to Eva. "Was Sofiya still wearing my shirt when you left the house?"

The moment the words leave my mouth, I regret them. Eva stops, a slow grin spreading across her face. "She was, but if you're so worried, check in with Emil. I'm sure he hasn't taken his eyes off your wife all day. As per your orders, of course."

My hands clench into fists. The idea of any man who's not me watching Sofiya burns under my skin. I don't want Emil noticing all the sexy little things about her. The way she bites her full bottom lip when she's thinking, or the soft curve of her neck when she tilts her head. That's for me, and me alone.

"Go ahead of me," I instruct them. "I'll meet you there."

Eva can barely hide her smirk as she and Vadim file out the door.

The moment they leave, I text Emil, telling him he doesn't need to shadow Sofiya around the estate. Between the ankle monitor and my guards, she isn't going anywhere, and there's no chance of her contacting the outside world. All communication devices are locked down tight.

But I need to know if she's still wearing my shirt or if she defied me. Part of me hopes she did, just so I have an excuse to go home and teach her a lesson.

I pull out my phone and scroll through the camera feeds from nearly every room. I finally find her in the old music room—the one part of the house I didn't renovate when I bought this former imperial estate. I like how untouched it feels with its worn rugs and antique instruments.

Sunlight pours in through the arched windows, catching the polished surface of the piano in the center of the room. Sofiya stands beside it, her hand drifting along the edge before pulling out a worn piece of sheet music. She studies it for a moment, a faint smile tugging at her lips, and then grazes her fingers over the keys, testing their sound.

Satisfaction stirs within me as she adjusts the hem of my shirt and lowers herself onto the piano bench.

Her hands hover over the keys like she's trying to remember something she lost. When she starts to play, the notes are rusty, her fingers uncertain. But she keeps going.

Her forehead tightens with concentration, and soon, a sorrowful song emerges.

The longer she plays, the deeper she sinks into it, like the music is pulling her under. It reminds me of how she was onstage, completely lost in her own world, unreachable.

When the last note fades, she stays right where she is, her hands resting on the keys as her head drops forward and her shoulders tremble. Something I don't want to name twists in my gut.

Fuck this. I turn off my phone and shove it back into my pocket.

Sofiya has her demons, just like I have mine, but that's not my concern.

She's a chess piece in this game, one I'll move however I need to.

CHAPTER THIRTEEN

NIKOLAI

The port worker slumps in a chair, his wrists zip-tied behind him. Sweat beads on his brow, even though we're in one of the port's cold storage rooms.

Metal racks filled with crates of goods line the walls, the faint smell of fish and damp concrete lingering in the air.

I circle him slowly, the sound of my boots scraping against the concrete. He shivers, his teeth chattering, though I doubt it's just from the cold.

"You took something that didn't belong to you," I say, my tone deceptively calm. "Tell me why I shouldn't gut you alive right here?"

The man's eyes dart around, his panic growing. "I—I had nothing to—"

I cut him off with a sharp punch to the stomach, my fist driving into his gut with enough force to make the chair rattle against the floor. He groans, his body jerking forward, but the ropes keep him upright.

"Let's try this again," I snarl, stepping closer. Vadim

places a firm hand on the guy's shoulder, shoving him back against the chair to steady him. "Who the fuck are you working for? Because I don't believe for one second that you masterminded the theft on your own."

Three million dollars of my coke vanished between the port and our warehouses, replaced with fucking baby laxative. It looks the same, weighs the same, and was even packaged the same. But one of my guys noticed a tear in a bag during the inventory check. The powder didn't dissolve properly, and that's when alarm bells went off.

After days of asking questions and beating down leads, all signs point to this motherfucker in front of me.

"No one!" he cries, his voice cracking. "It was just me, I swear! I needed the money—my kid's sick, and the hospital bills—"

I glance at Vadim, leaning casually against the wall, eating an apple like it's his lunch break. When I catch his eye, he shakes his head, silently confirming what I already suspected—this mudak doesn't have kids.

I grip his throat and squeeze, cutting off his air. His eyes bulge, his face turning a deep shade of red as his legs jerk wildly. I hold him there, watching as the panic sets in. When he's seconds from passing out, I let go, and he slumps back against the chair, gasping for air.

"You're not walking out of here alive. So you can make it easy on yourself and tell me the fucking truth, or you can make it hard, and I'll carve it out of you. Either way, you'll squeal. They always do."

His eyes dart to Vadim, who's polishing a machete with a rag. The man whimpers, his pants darkening as he pisses himself. Vadim raises an eyebrow. "You might want to hurry up. I'm feeling generous today, but it won't last for long."

"Alright, alright! I'll tell you what you want to know!" he cries, his voice hoarse.

"Smart choice," I say, gripping the machete Vadim hands me. The knife's tip presses under his ribs, enough to make him wince. "Lie to me, and I'll bury this in your kidneys. Now start talking."

It's past midnight when I finally return to the estate. The house is silent, just as I'd expect.

Shrugging off my blazer, I head for my office, the weight of the past three days pressing down on my shoulders.

The port worker talked, just as I knew he would. Turns out, he'd met a couple of guys at a bar not too long ago. A few drinks in, the idiot got chatty—told them where he worked, even bragged about my product coming through the port.

Dumber still, he let them convince him it'd be easy to pull a heist and rip me off. They promised him a cut, but what he didn't realize was that these clowns belonged to a low-level street gang with delusions of grandeur. They thought they could take me down.

They won't get the chance. By the end of the night, not one of them will be alive.

I grab a glass from the bar cart and pour a shot of whiskey, tossing it back in one go. The alcohol soothes my frayed nerves, but it doesn't clear my head.

I've barely been home over the last few days. I'd hoped the distance from Sofiya would erase her from my mind, but it hasn't. She lingers like an ember that refuses to burn out.

It doesn't help that I watch her on the cameras every chance I get. I didn't need Emil's regular updates to know everything she's been up to: wandering around, playing piano in the music room, reading in the library, and chatting with Yelena, though she mostly stays in her room. It's taken all my willpower not to watch her in that private space, because if my obsession is already spiraling, seeing her in her most unguarded moments would ruin me entirely.

I pour another shot, the alcohol sliding down smoothly as bad intentions fizz hot and heavy through my veins. I want to see her, feel the warmth of her skin, and hear the soft catch of her breath. But I also want to remind the Syndicate that I'm not a man who tolerates being put on ice.

From my desk drawer, I take out the ring—the one I had designed specifically to match her auburn-streaked hair and the ivory tone of her skin.

A better man would wait until morning, but I've never claimed to be a good man.

Her room is dark except for the moonlight spilling through the curtains. Sofiya is a vision when she sleeps, her dark hair spread across the pillow, her plush lips slightly parted, begging for my cock to slide between them.

I drag a chair from the corner and sit, the quiet of the night pressing in around me as I watch her. My eyes follow the slow, steady rise and fall of her chest, her features relaxed, her brow smooth, like she's finally found some peace in sleep. She looks so damn serene, untouched by the chaos I've pulled her into.

I should feel guilt for what I've done, and for what I'm about to do, but guilt isn't in my nature.

Instead, a dark satisfaction and a possessive thrill pulse through me, knowing she's mine now. Sergey wanted her as his bride, but that bastard is rotting in the ground while she lives in my house, soon to wear my ring. I hope he's watching from whatever pit of hell he landed in, confronted with everything he lost.

I rise and lean over her, brushing a strand of hair from her cheek before my hand finds her shoulder, and I give it a small shake. "Wake up, Sofiya."

Her eyes flutter open, hazy with sleep. But the moment she registers me standing so close, she bolts upright, dragging the blanket underneath her chin. "What's going on?" she gasps. "Why are you in my room?"

"Technically, every room in this house is mine. So, really, you're in my room."

I flick on the reading lamp on the bedside table, warm light flooding the space, and give her eyes a moment to adjust.

She blinks rapidly, glancing at the clock beside her before releasing a growl of irritation. "It's the middle of the night, Nikolai. What do you want?"

The wariness in her voice unsettles me. "Relax. I'm not here to hurt you," I say, my fingers grazing her cheek. "But you're the pakhan's wife, and it's time everyone knows it."

Her brows draw together. "You know as well as I do that this marriage is only temporary. Once Roman makes you a deal—"

I cut her off, tracing the curve of her jaw with my thumb. "Roman needs to be reminded that I'm not a man to play with."

She swallows hard, her voice dropping to a whisper. "What does this have to do with me?"

"Everything." The word lands heavy between us. "Now, get up. You're coming to my office."

She shakes her head and burrows further under the covers. "I'm not going anywhere with you."

"Then I'll carry you."

"Don't you fucking da—"

Her protest dies as I rip the covers off and haul her over my shoulder. She kicks and pounds at my back, but it's no use. My hand grips her perfect ass firmly to hold her in place.

She's wearing more of Eva's clothes—barely-there sleep shorts with a flimsy tank top, and my cock twitches at the sight, threatening to derail my focus. I force down the primal urge to throw her on the bed and claim her, and I keep walking.

"I can't believe you," she hisses, fists hammering uselessly against my back. "This is humiliating! Put me down!"

"I warned you," I remind her calmly, a small smile playing on my lips. Even at a time like this, I enjoy her fire.

Inside my office, I lower her onto the suede couch and lock the door behind me, just in case she gets the brilliant idea to make a run for it.

Sofiya wraps her arms around herself, glaring at me with venom in her eyes. "Stop playing games and tell me what this is about."

Instead of answering, I unlock my desk drawer and pull out what I need. "You have a choice to make, Sofiya."

Unease flickers in her eyes as she scans the room. "What choice?"

I sit beside her on the couch, laying the items on the coffee table between us. Her gaze shifts nervously between me and the box. "What is that?"

"Isn't it obvious?" I snap open the jewelry box, revealing a princess-cut ruby ring set on a platinum band, surrounded by a halo of diamonds that shimmer like fire. "Will you wear my ring, Sofiya Zhukova?"

Her eyes widen at the sound of my surname, twisted into its feminine form. Before I've even explained the alternative, she's already shaking her head.

"You're sure?" I ask, my voice dropping as I bring my lips inches from hers.

Her eyes narrow with spite. "I'm damn sure I'll never wear your ring."

"In that case..." I reach for the cloth, pulling it away to reveal what's beneath. Her eyes lower to the device in my hand. She blinks, her brow furrowing as confusion flickers across her face.

"What is that?"

I hold it up for her to see. "A tattoo machine."

Her voice is quieter now, more cautious. "What are you planning to do with that?"

I capture her chin, forcing her gaze to mine. "If you won't wear my ring, I'll tattoo one onto your finger. It's your choice, Sofiya. But one way or another, no one will question who you belong to."

CHAPTER FOURTEEN

SOFIYA

After days of not seeing or hearing from Nikolai, he storms into my room in the middle of the night, throws me over his shoulder like some barbarian, and carries me down to his office. Then he gives me an impossible choice: wear his wedding ring or let him tattoo my finger.

He can't be serious, can he?

But the way his eyes blaze into mine, and the tattoo machine in his hand, tell me he is.

A cold wave of panic crashes over me. If he thinks I'll let him tattoo me, he's out of his damn mind.

On instinct, I run. My hands fly to the door, shaking as I twist the knob and tug, but it doesn't budge. It's locked, and no matter how I twist or pull, it won't open.

Behind me, his footsteps are slow and deliberate. "Where do you think you're going, wife?"

I whip around, hands planted on my hips. "Get away from me!"

His head tilts, a dangerous smile playing at the corners of his mouth. "I can't do that, but I'm giving you a choice. If you don't like the idea of a tattoo, there's a half-million-dollar rock that many women would kill to wear."

"It's not the ring!" My voice rises, frustration spilling over. "It's what it represents. That I'm yours… and I will never be yours." I pause, shaking my head. "You can't force this on me. I'm not your wife. Not really. I don't care what the bullshit marriage contract says."

He shrugs, and the casualness of it sets my blood boiling. His indifference is a slap in the face. While he's been away on business, I've been here, wandering the halls like a ghost. Three days with nothing but time on my hands. Time to feel the weight of how nothing ever goes right for me. To know that no matter how hard I try, things always end up in ruins. And this time, I've managed to pull my friends and family down with me.

I wish I could roll back time to undo everything, but I can't, and I'll have to wear that shame forever. I've searched this entire house for a way out—a phone, a computer, anything to communicate with the outside world—but there's no sign of where we are, and I'm no closer to finding a way to escape.

And in the quiet moments, when my anger isn't enough to drown everything else out, my mind drifts to Nikolai and the maddening way he makes me feel. Like my body has a mind of its own.

My frustration boils over, and I grab a stack of files from the desk and fling them at him. Papers scatter in the air like snowflakes. He steps aside easily, his posture relaxed as they float to the floor.

"I see. This is how you want to play."

Nikolai's steps are steady and measured as he stalks toward me. I know there's no way out, but I scramble around his desk anyway, grabbing anything I can find. My hand closes on a stapler, and I fling it at his head. He swats it away with barely any effort.

This is so not good.

My fingers curl around a large book on the corner of his desk, my last hope, and I swing it at him as hard as I can. His hand shoots out, catching my wrist mid-swing. His grip is like iron, unyielding, as he pries the book from my grasp and tosses it to the floor. The sound of it hitting the ground echoes in the tense silence.

In two strides, he's on me, his arms wrapping around me as he throws me down onto the couch. His fingers press into my jaw, tilting my head up so I can't look anywhere but at him. His face is so close I can feel the warmth of his breath. "I like that my wife is fierce, but you pull this shit again, and you'll see a side of me you won't like. Am I clear?"

"I've only ever seen a side of you I don't like," I fire back, my voice sharp despite the hammering of my heart.

"Oh, moya sladost, your hate only turns me on more." His words shouldn't have this effect on me, but my pussy clenches with need, and a blush burns its way up my neck.

His smirk deepens, his hooded eyes dragging over my face, lingering on my lips before dropping lower to the rise and fall of my chest. My nipples tighten beneath the flimsy sleep tank, and when his gaze lifts again, it's lit with a spark of satisfaction.

Before I can blink, he hauls me up by the waist, takes my seat on the couch, and then drops me onto his lap. My thighs settle on either side of his hips, his grip firm even as I push against him, my nails biting into his forearms as I wriggle to get free, but for some reason, this doesn't feel like a fight—it feels a lot more like foreplay.

"Stop struggling," he growls, pinning my wrists behind me with one massive hand. His lips brush my ear. "The only thing you've accomplished is making my dick very hard."

My chest constricts, my breathing uneven. He's not exaggerating. His arousal presses into me, firm and insistent, setting every nerve ablaze.

“Trust me, that's not my intention,” I whisper back, breathlessly. Way too breathlessly.

I should shove him away, tell him how much he disgusts me, but that’s not what I do. Instead, I roll my hips against his hard length, a reflex that feels beyond my control. The friction against my clit has me swallowing back a gasp.

"Are you trying to get yourself off on me, wife?" he asks, his voice all sexy and gravelly.

I shake my head, trying to ignore the desire pooling low in my belly. Despite how fucking good it feels to have him hard between my legs, I know better than to invite trouble into my life. Except every time I try to push him away or tell him to back off, I can’t.

A shaky sigh leaves me. I close my eyes and tilt my hips, the pressure between my thighs growing. This wasn’t how it was supposed to happen, but his hard, warm body beneath mine was more than any mere mortal could resist.

His hand slides up my spine, his fingers threading into my hair as he tugs sharply, forcing my head back and exposing my throat. His mouth follows instantly, teeth scraping against my skin, his tongue leaving trails of warmth and wicked promises.

I arch into him, my defenses crumbling as his lips move over me. By the time he pulls back, his dark, hungry gaze locks on mine, and I can’t find the strength to look away. He’s unraveling me, piece by piece, and I’m letting him.

Nikolai groans, his breath heavy. “Tell me what you want. Use your words.”

“I want you to let me go,” I whisper, though my voice doesn’t sound all that convincing.

“Mmmm, I don’t think that’s true.”

“You’ve lost your mind if you think I’d let you tattoo my finger,” I manage to get out, even as his lips brush the curve of my ear.

"Does that mean you'll wear the ring?" he asks, his voice thick.

I let out a shaky breath, tension settling low in my belly. "You're insane, you know that?"

His chuckle vibrates through me. "If you're so against the tattoo..." He doesn't finish that thought before his mouth descends, capturing my nipple through the thin fabric of my shirt. His tongue and teeth work the sensitive peak, and I whimper, arching to give him better access. Just when I think I can't take anymore, he pulls back sharply. "Then wear my ring."

My jaw tightens, and I fight the desperate ache in my core. "I-I don't like either option."

"It seems we're at an impasse." He leans in again, capturing my other nipple with his mouth, working magic that is very hard to resist. My thighs clench as he drags out every ounce of control I thought I had.

When he pulls back, his intense gaze pins me in place. "Let's make a deal. If I can make you come in under a minute, I get to tattoo the Zhukov Bratva symbol on your ring finger."

"Nope. Not happening. And for the record, you wouldn't even get close in under a minute."

"If you're so certain it's impossible, then prove it."

I'm ready to tell him to go to hell when an idea occurs to me. It's a dangerous one. Reckless even, but I'm confident I'll be the winner. "I'll agree to the deal on one condition. If you lose, I don't have to wear your ring... ever. You drop the issue. Throw the half-million-dollar rock into the sea for all I care."

He drags his tongue over his teeth, his eyes narrowing. The air feels heavy as I hold my breath, daring him to take the bait.

Though my body aches for him, there's no way in hell a man can get me off in less than a minute. I can't do it myself that quickly—unless I'm armed with a vibrator, and even then, I can resist anything for a minute.

He gives me a slow, wicked smile, his hand gripping my chin as he pulls me closer, our lips a whisper apart. "Fine," he says, his voice a low purr. "One minute. But the clock doesn't start until I'm touching your pussy. Everything before that is a warm-up."

Wait, what?

I barely have time to process what's happening before his mouth crashes against mine. His tongue demands entrance, and I can't stop myself from letting him in. There's nothing gentle about this kiss—it's all heat and possession, breaking down my defenses with each stroke of his tongue against mine, devouring me like I'm his last meal.

When his mouth breaks away to trail down my throat, I barely have time to drag air into my lungs before he captures my nipple with his lips again. The hot suction sends lightning through my veins, every nerve ending firing at once. My hands fly to his shoulders, nails digging in as his tongue continues to work me. Each lap and stroke builds the ache between my legs until I'm dripping for him.

"So fucking sweet," he growls against my skin, his teeth grazing the sensitive peak before moving to my other breast. The warm slide of his mouth against my skin pulls a broken cry from my throat as I arch closer to him. His answering groan vibrates through my flesh as he sucks harder, stealing whimpers I can't hold back.

Ignore him, I tell myself. *Block out his touch.*

But that's impossible because when his eyes meet mine, my breath falters. He's looking at me with such fierce desire and something else. Like he's making sure I'm enjoying this, even though it's all part of a ridiculous bet—one I refuse to lose.

And evidently, so does he.

A whimper escapes me as he pinches my nipple, his groan

rumbling against my lips. His hands tangle in my hair, pulling me closer, his tongue claiming mine again. A sound vibrates from his chest, deep and rough. It reverberates through me as his hands drift lower, igniting every nerve.

This is it. I know what's coming next, and I need to clear my head and focus. He showed me what he was capable of in the club's bathroom, and this would be a bad time to lose my head.

His hand slides into my shorts, slipping lower until his knuckles brush my already damp inner thighs.

"There's a clock behind me," he says, his lips grazing my ear. "Tell me when my minute's up." Before I can respond, his mouth is on my neck, igniting a shiver as he kisses down to my collarbone. "Ready?"

I don't answer. I can't. His fingers drag over my slit, teasing, and my head falls back.

"Ohmygawd." The words spill out involuntarily as his fingers work my clit, each circle sending waves of ecstasy spiraling through me.

"You're dripping already," he says, his tone full of smug satisfaction.

Stars burst in my vision, and I can't think of a defense when he thrusts two fingers into my pussy, the tension building faster than I ever thought possible. All I can do is grit my teeth and focus on resisting the pleasure that's consuming every rational thought I have left.

"You're insufferable," I groan, my nails digging into his scalp as my hips rock against his hand.

He chuckles, the sound dark and sinful. "Admit it—you love how I make you feel." His fingers thrust deeper as his palm grinds against my clit. My legs shake in response. "Maybe it turns you on to be at my mercy."

I want to deny it, but the words won't come. His fingers curl, hitting that devastating spot that steals the air from my lungs. A broken moan slips from my lips, and his smirk only deepens. "You think you're in control, but you're not. Every cry, every plea, the way you fall apart—it's all mine."

His words sink into my skin, stirring something raw and visceral inside me.

I force my eyes open to check the time. But when he flicks my clit, my world tilts and a wave of bliss crashes over me.

"Thirty seconds left," he purrs, his voice like silk. "Plenty of time to ruin you."

Thirty seconds feels like a fucking eternity right now.

His stare burns with barely contained lust. At least I'm not the only one losing it.

Sensing he has me where he wants me, he doubles down, his rough palm kneading against my clit as his fingers plunge deep, setting a steady, mind-numbing rhythm that has my pussy walls quivering. My eyes roll back in my head. What is he doing? He's not playing fair—this must be cheating.

"My tattoo will look good on you. I can't wait to see my mark on your skin." His voice drops, a rough edge creeping in.

"Nope. Never," I barely manage to choke out, even as my restraint threatens to shatter.

He thrusts deeper, and his mouth claims mine in a kiss that's raw and all-consuming. His fingers circle my clit, coaxing me to fall apart for him.

It's maddening, how he can reduce me to this—a trembling mess at his mercy. My core contracts, responding to every stroke of his fingers, every flick of his thumb. I clench, desperate to hold back, but no amount of willpower can stop the wave threatening to drag me under.

One hard flick against my clit is all it takes—everything inside me detonates… Shit.

My thighs clamp around his hand, and my head falls back as the orgasm tears through me. I bite down on his shoulder to muffle the cry building in my throat, but it doesn't matter.

He knows I came. He can feel it.

Nikolai's fingers curl one last time, drawing out the final spasms. He withdraws his hand, bringing his fingers to his mouth, and sucks them clean, his blue eyes never leaving mine.

"God, you're fucking gorgeous when you lose yourself," he says, his voice thick. The words land like a weight between us. As I collapse against him, breathless and spent, his praise wraps around me like a warm flame.

For a moment, I stay there, soaking it all in. The steady rhythm of his breathing, his fingers combing through my hair, and his presence anchoring me.

And then, as if on cue, Nikolai opens his mouth and ruins everything.

"Fifty-eight and a half seconds," he whispers in my ear.

Heat floods my face as reality sinks in. I pull away, my mind racing. He can't be serious—not after what just happened.

With a cocky grin, Nikolai laces his fingers behind his head. He looks like a man who knows he's won, and I hate it.

I climb off his lap, desperate for space. "Are you sure that's accurate?" I gesture to the clock on the wall.

"Completely." His tone drips with amusement. "It's military-grade."

Goddammit.

My mouth goes dry as I grasp at straws. "Fifty-eight and a half seconds is basically a minute. I don't think that's a reliable number based on the margin of error."

His brow arches, the look in his eyes downright sinful. "Are you suggesting we try again? I'd be more than willing. Although this time, I'd like to make you come with my tongue."

Desire shoots through me, but I shove it aside. It's a terrible idea. Clearly, this man has some kind of sexual superpower I overlooked. "I wasn't suggesting that at all."

He shrugs, unbothered. "A deal is a deal. And you don't strike me as the kind of woman who goes back on her word."

When he reaches for the tattoo machine, my stomach drops, and panic lodges in my throat. His symbol—his mark—will be on my skin forever. Tears well in my eyes, blurring my vision before spilling over. But I won't break my word. My parents never followed through on theirs, and I swore a long time ago I'd never be like them.

I lift my chin. "Have you done this before?"

"Many times."

"A symbol and your initials. That's it?"

"That's it," he says softly. He steps closer, wiping the tears from my cheeks with a gentle touch. "Don't be scared. It'll be quick."

"I'm not afraid of the pain. I'm crying because, once again, you've left me with no choice."

He cups my cheek, his thumb grazing my lips. "Choice is overrated."

"Your mark won't change how I feel about you or this marriage. I'll never submit to you. I'll never sleep with you. It will mean nothing to me."

"Again. You mean you'll never sleep with me again." He brushes a wisp of my hair behind my ears, his hand lingering on my cheek.

I squeeze my eyes shut, fighting the way his slightest touch ignites a fire under my skin.

"Do it," I say, my voice brittle, because if this continues, I'll lose more than my dignity.

CHAPTER FIFTEEN

NIKOLAI

WITH A FINAL STROKE OF BLACK INK, THE HUM OF THE TATTOO machine cuts out, and I set it aside, taking a moment to admire my work. My initials, entwined with the Zhukov Bratva's crown, now permanently mark Sofiya's pale skin. A reminder of whom she belongs to.

"Are you done?" she asks, her eyes still squeezed shut, not wanting to watch me tattoo her.

"One more minute." Her skin is red and tender, the lines slightly raised. I need to apply the antibiotic cream and bandage it, but there's something else I need to do first.

Beside her hand, I lay a folded newspaper, the date printed clearly at the top. I snap a quick photo with my phone —the proof of life Roman asked for, with a side of fuck you. A reminder that every day he drags his feet, Sofiya is the one to suffer.

Though it seems I'm the one currently in pain. I've had a case of blue balls since I made her come all over my hand. But it was worth it—not only to win the bet but because watching her shatter for me was the sweetest fucking thing I've ever seen.

"You can open your eyes. We're done here," I say, tucking the newspaper out of sight.

Her lashes lift slowly, and she meets my stare for one long second before her attention shifts to her finger. She examines the ink. "What does it symbolize?" she asks, her voice steady. I expect tears or anger, but she surprises me with her composure. Maybe she's all out of tears.

"The crown stands for strength, loyalty, and the unbreakable bonds of brotherhood," I explain. My thumb grazes the edge of the tattoo lightly. "And my initials… because you're mine."

I expect her defiance, but not the way her hazel eyes meet mine with a calm that throws me off balance. "A tattoo doesn't make me yours. Neither does a piece of paper."

Her words slide under my skin, sharp and unwelcome. I didn't mark her only for Roman's benefit or to keep the Syndicate in line. I marked her because I wanted to and because the thought of her belonging to anyone else is like a stab to the gut.

"In my world, it does." She's my wife, and the tattoo makes it indisputable. Everyone who sees that mark will know I've claimed her. She's untouchable. "And Roman will agree when he sees a picture of your hand."

"Are you serious?" she growls. "Why? Isn't stealing me away enough? Do you know what this is doing to my sister? She's trying to get pregnant after years of trying. Her stress level is probably through the roof."

A muscle in my jaw ticks, but I focus on gently cleaning the tattoo. "Roman will control the information she's getting. This is not about your sister. This is about getting the Syndicate to fall in line and agree to a deal. A reminder that pissing me off has consequences."

She shakes her head, her mouth falling into a straight line. "Tell yourself whatever you need to, Nikolai."

We're both quiet as I smooth a thin layer of ointment over the ink and then wrap it in a protective layer of gauze. "You surprise me," I say finally. "I didn't think you'd see our deal through."

"I must have a talent for making bad decisions," she says tightly. "And what would you do if I didn't hold up my end of the bargain?"

My lips thin out. I'd probably rather not think about that. Holding her down and forcing ink on her doesn't appeal to me, but on some level, I knew she wouldn't back down. Maybe because she's stubborn as hell, and she'd rather grit her teeth than give me the satisfaction of breaking her word.

After a moment, she huffs out a breath. "Anyhow, it doesn't matter. I don't go back on my word. My parents did that enough to me as a child, and every broken promise taught me who I didn't want to be."

I tilt her chin upward with a finger, forcing her gaze to meet mine. "Your parents never deserved you."

Sofiya's parents sold her to my brother and Anatoly when she was underage. They will never be anything but the lowest of the low in my eyes. Maybe that's ironic considering everything I've done, but I've never pretended to be anything other than what I am.

The vulnerability flickering in her eyes sparks something unfamiliar inside me. Before I can stop myself, I lean in, brushing a finger over the corner of her lips. I have the strangest impulse to give her a soft kiss on the lips, but now that the bet is over, I don't think my touch would be welcome.

Maybe she senses my intention because her hazel-green eyes widen, searching mine like she's looking for an explanation I don't have. Her pink tongue darts out, wetting her lips, and she slowly withdraws her hand from mine. "Are we done here?"

I'm far from done with her, but as her lids droop with exhaustion, I exhale and release her. "Keep it wrapped for a few hours, and moisturize twice a day. No getting it wet until it's healed."

"Fine," she whispers, clutching her hand to her chest like it's a shield.

"Now go to sleep, moya sladost," I murmur, leaning in close enough to catch her scent. "Because I still have the smell of you on my fingers and the taste of you on my lips. And in those flimsy pajamas... What's the expression? Don't tempt the tempted."

Her pulse jumps at the base of her throat. She hesitates, her gaze dipping to my mouth before darting back up to meet mine.

I turn to face the window, gripping the edge of the frame to anchor myself as she leaves the room. It's the only way to stop myself from dragging her back here and giving her another reason to hate me.

An hour later, I'm at my desk, finishing paperwork, when Roman's reply to the picture of Sofiya's finger comes through. I'm not surprised he's awake at this early hour—men like us don't sleep, chained to our positions.

> Roman: There's a special place in hell for men like you, Zhukov.

I put down my pen, a sardonic laugh rumbling in my chest.

> Me: I'm sure I have reserved seating. But it's your reluctance to accept the deal that is costing Sofiya.

He can think I'm the monster here, that I marked her against her will. But I don't need violence to claim her. She can try to fight this pull between us, but her body betrays her. If Roman knew how she came apart on my fingers earlier, he'd understand that she's already mine.

Roman: I can't make this decision alone. There are others who need to weigh in.

Me: Help them understand the urgency. I'm sure your wife doesn't appreciate the delay.

Roman: Never mention my wife again. You have no idea what you've done to her.

Me: I do. That's the point.

I know where to hit to make Roman bleed. The Syndicate wouldn't flinch at business pressures—they're too insulated, too powerful for that. But when it's personal? When the stakes involve the people they love? That's when they move. Roman's weakness is Liza, and Liza loves her sister. Something their shitty parents never did.

That's the edge I have over him. I have no vulnerable connections like he does. No one that can be used against me. I value my brotherhood—Vadim and Eva, especially—but even their lives wouldn't compromise my decisions.

Going to jail for Sergey ended up costing me everything—that's why I make decisions with my head, not my heart. Leading with your heart gets you killed.

Roman: No one has ever come against the Syndicate and won, and you are no exception. One day, I will gut you alive and enjoy every minute of it.

I lean back in my chair, resting my head in my hands with

a faint smile curling my lips. Roman's words are the taunt of a man grasping for power he no longer has. It's true—the Syndicate hasn't lost to an enemy, yet. Still, the strongest empires crumble when they underestimate their opponents.

Two years in prison taught me patience. It taught me that control wins wars, not brute force. I can smell Roman's desperation from here, and it only proves I have him where I want him.

Me: Enough idle threats. I want action. Every day you drag your feet, Sofiya pays.

I turn off the phone, tucking it into my pocket, the last line hanging in the air like a fuse waiting to ignite. I imagine Roman's fury—the way he'll hurl the phone, maybe even stomp it to pieces. Satisfaction courses through me. I've planted a bomb in his mind, and it's only a matter of time before it detonates.

Morning light spills into my office, illuminating the papers scattered across my desk. I stretch, rolling the tension from my neck, when someone knocks at the door.

"Come in," I say, expecting Yelena with my morning tea. Instead, Emil steps through the door.

"Got a minute?" he asks.

I gesture to the chair across from me. "Of course. Have a seat."

Emil sinks down, trying to seem confident, but I can see a flicker of hesitation. Back when he first joined my bratva, we butted heads—his temper and pride made it hard for him to take orders from me since I'm only a few years older than he is. I gave him more room to screw up because of our history, but that only went so far.

He clears his throat, finally meeting my eyes. "I'm sick of house duty, Niko. Hanging around the estate, playing babysitter—I'm ready for more."

I lean forward, resting my elbows on the desk. "You think keeping my wife safe and my estate secure isn't important?"

Emil's jaw tightens, his fingers curling into loose fists on his thighs. "It's not that. It's—I'm ready for more responsibility. I've been loyal to you for years. I deserve a chance to enforce for the bratva, do something exciting."

I sit back, my hand dragging down my jaw, the stubble rough against my palm. When I look at Emil, I still see the hotheaded kid who acts first and thinks later.

I remember the day he charged into an alley, fists flying, because some assholes made a comment about his girlfriend's tits. He didn't wait for backup or think two steps ahead. It was three against one, and he didn't stand a chance. When I pulled him out, his face was a mess, his ribs bruised so badly he could hardly breathe. I get his need to stand up for his girlfriend, but blind anger like that is a fast way to get yourself killed.

"If you want more, show me you can handle it. Show me you can keep your head on straight when it matters. That you can think before you act."

His mouth sets in a hard line, his nostrils flaring. "How can I prove anything when I'm stuck here all the time?"

I slam my palm on the desk, cutting him off. "Prove you can handle the responsibilities you already have. Do your job, and do it well."

Emil's shoulders stiffen, but he doesn't break eye contact. "Fine," he mutters, shoving his chair back with a scrape and striding toward the door.

My chest expands as I rake my fingers through my hair. "Emil, wait."

I don't want to discourage him, but he needs to understand that climbing the bratva ladder takes more than big balls and quick fists.

He stops in the doorway, turning slowly, and I soften my tone. He's young and eager—I understand the need to do more. But right now, too much is at stake. "When this shit with the Syndicate is behind us, we can talk about another role for you. But until then, remember that a fuck-up puts my wife in danger. And that's not a risk I'm willing to take."

"Understood." He nods and squares his shoulders before disappearing into the hallway.

I watch him leave, my gaze drifting to the papers on my desk. The casino contract with Igor's signature stares back at me—a reminder that a war is still ahead of me.

CHAPTER SIXTEEN

SOFIYA

THE COOL WATER ENVELOPS ME, MUFFLING THE WORLD ABOVE AS I glide beneath the pool's surface.

When I come up for air, the gentle night breeze soothes my overheated skin. I swim to the edge, resting my forearms on the rough concrete while I catch my breath.

I've only been here a week, but days blur together without anything meaningful to fill them. No plans, no purpose, no way to communicate with the outside world. Sure, movies and television are options, but I can only stare at a screen for so many hours. I've also spent time reading, exploring, and picking up the piano again—something I haven't touched in years, not since my mother forced lessons on me.

My fingers are rusty, but it's something to do—a way to distract myself from my churning thoughts. I've spent countless hours concerned about Liza, for Daria and Alex unknowingly being watched by Nikolai's men, but all that has gotten me nowhere. I'm no closer to a plan or finding a way to escape.

Every day that passes, my old life feels like it's slipping

away, and Nikolai is taking up more and more space in my brain. I've tried to keep my distance from him, which hasn't been too hard, considering he's barely been around lately. I thought time away would help, but it hasn't.

I sigh and push off to float on my back, staring up at the stars. The sound of shuffling feet jolts me from my thoughts. I stand to find my guard, Emil, at the edge of the pool.

"Why didn't you invite me for a swim?" There's an amused look on his face, something I'm not entirely used to. I blink, caught off guard by this smiling version of him. Since I got here, he's kept his distance—and when I do see him, he's scrolling on his phone or smoking with the other guards. He seems pretty uninterested in the job, and I can't blame him. There's not much happening at the estate.

"Swim?" I let out a laugh, trying to lighten the mood. "Aren't you supposed to be on duty?"

I drop my feet beneath me, submerging myself deeper. I feel exposed. The only swimsuit Eva lent me is a tiny white bikini that leaves little to the imagination.

His lips tip up at the corners. "No reason I can't enjoy a swim while I'm on duty."

Without Nikolai around, Emil doesn't seem as tense. There's almost something boyish about him when he's not trying to appear so tough.

I must look confused because he gives a dry laugh, his fingers combing through his short hair. "I'm messing with you. But you should tell me when you leave the house."

"Sorry, I didn't know I was supposed to."

"Your husband's rules." He shrugs. "I really don't think there's much of a chance of anything happening to you here."

He drags a sun chair closer to the pool and sinks into it, pulling out a pack of cigarettes. He lights one with a flick of his lighter, exhaling a thin stream of smoke. Is he supposed to hang out for a chat? Samuil or any of my other guards would never do that. But maybe this is an opportunity to learn something about this place.

"You must be bored as shit, huh?" he says, taking a slow drag.

"I'm not sure if bored is the word." I tread water. My arms move in slow, steady strokes. "It's more like I feel stuck. Everyone else I went to school with is moving on to the next phase of their life, and I'm here… as collateral, without any real purpose."

My thoughts drift to Alex and Daria. I wonder if Alex has moved to London yet, auditioning for West End shows, or if Daria has found a cozy little apartment in the Hollywood Hills. Does she have a sleek mini-convertible to zip around town, landing auditions for the next big production?

I want those things for my friends—I really do. But I can't help feeling a pang of jealousy. They're moving forward, chasing their dreams, while once again, my ties to the Syndicate keep me stuck in place, unable to live a normal life.

Then again, I'm the reason they have a guard shadowing their every move, ready to pounce if I step out of line. Maybe envy isn't fair.

He watches me carefully, his expression unreadable. "I get it," he says.

I pause, feeling like I've said too much to my guard. Damn. I must be lonelier here than I realized.

When I glance up at him, he's still looking at me. He takes another slow drag from his cigarette, the smoke curling around him.

"I guess guard duty isn't your idea of a good time?"

"It's being stuck at the estate I'm not crazy about." He rests an ankle on his opposite knee. "When Niko asked me to join his bratva, I was hoping to see some real action. Get my hands dirty, not sit around here. But orders are orders."

I swim to the pool's edge, propping my arms on the tiles. I didn't expect Emil to be so forthcoming, but since he is, I might as well take advantage. "Wait—he brought you in? I thought most people worked their way up."

His mouth flattens. "It was different for me. Niko and I grew up together. We lived in this rundown apartment block that smelled like piss and desperation. You learned to fight quickly, or you didn't survive. Niko was the oldest and he fought for all of us. He wasn't afraid of anyone—not the bigger kids, not the drunk adults, not even the gangsters hanging around outside. He stepped in, even if it meant getting knocked down himself. Especially by his mother."

"What do you mean?" I ask.

His jaw tightens, and he flicks ash into the air. "We came from a rough world, Sofiya. Different from anything you've probably seen. And trust me, we didn't grow up in a palace like this." He holds his arms out wide, gesturing around us. "Their mom—like all our parents—was barely getting by, always drinking and using drugs. She was really rough on the boys, especially when she was high. Niko shielded Sergey from the worst of it. That's who he's always been. Hell, he even went to jail for that fucker."

Shock slams into me. "He did?"

"He took the blame for some bogus drug charges. Prison is brutal, and he knew Sergey wouldn't have lasted a month. Those years behind bars, combined with the crap Sergey pulled afterward, changed Niko. It hardened him."

Imagining Nikolai as his younger brother's protector tugs at something inside. Liza did the same for me, shielding me from the worst of our parents' neglect and keeping me safe when everything around us was falling apart. Maybe that's what older siblings do.

My fingers tighten on the ledge as I try to reconcile the boy Emil described with the cold, sharp man he is today.

A little voice reminds me that he protected me too, in that chapel in Greece.

I'd nearly forgotten about that—the past was eclipsed by more recent events like the tattoo, making my finger throb.

Emil stubs out his cigarette underfoot and pushes himself to his feet. "I should go."

"If you're ready for more responsibility, why not tell Nikolai? He should get it, especially since you guys go way back." I smile, hoping to lighten the mood. "I promise not to take it personally that guard duty isn't your thing."

The humor drains from Emil's face. "We've already had that talk." His mouth opens like he's about to say more, but then his eyes flick past me, and his whole body goes rigid.

I don't turn right away. A strange heat prickles at the back of my neck as the air around me feels heavier. I don't have to look to know who's behind me. I feel him, his presence unmistakable.

When I finally glance back, Nikolai is standing poolside, his attention locked on me. His massive frame is backlit by the glow from the house. His suit jacket is gone, shirt collar open, the tie hanging loosely around his neck. His dark hair is tousled, sleeves rolled up, tattoos snaking down his forearms. Electricity sparks down my spine.

"Hope I'm not interrupting anything," he says, his voice deceptively light.

Emil straightens. "I was checking in. Making sure Sofiya was okay."

Nikolai's lips curl into something that isn't quite a smile. "Good to know you're so thorough."

Emil slides his hands into his pockets like he's trying to appear casual. "Just doing my job."

I glance between them, feeling like I've stumbled into the middle of something I don't fully understand.

"If you need me, I'll be inside." Shoulders tight, Emil retreats toward the house.

When it's only us, Nikolai's attention locks on me. He's tense, like a storm waiting to break, and I'm not sure why, though it might have something to do with what I'm wearing. But that's his problem, not mine.

Just to needle him, I let myself float on my back, the cool water lapping at my skin. I can feel his eyes on me, lingering where the wet fabric clings.

"How's the water?" His voice is low with an edge.

I glance over, keeping my expression neutral despite the shiver his tone sends through me. "Perfect," I reply.

"In that case, I'll join you."

Before I can process what he means, his hands move to his collar. With a sharp tug, he yanks his shirt open, sending buttons flying as the fabric peels off him in one rough motion. My breath catches as the full expanse of his chest comes into view, all muscle and ink, like every part of him was carved by the gods.

His muscles shift as he unbuckles his belt and kicks his shoes aside. My mouth goes bone dry as he sheds his pants, leaving him in nothing but a pair of black boxer briefs. But then those are gone, too. Holy shit. I've felt his cock, but I've never had the chance to see it. That's a shame because it's perfect—thick, long, and right now, it's at half-mast and growing.

"It's customary to wear a swimsuit when others are in the pool," I grumble.

"Well, it's my pool, and I prefer to swim naked."

I quickly spin around, my cheeks burning. "I'm not looking!" I blurt, my back to him even though I already enjoyed a generous eyeful. "What's up with you and stripping whenever you feel like it?" First was the kitchen, and now this. I'm beginning to think he likes to see me blush.

"My house, my rules. And it's nothing you haven't seen before." His voice drips with amusement.

"And nothing I plan on seeing again."

He laughs, a deep, rich sound. There's a soft splash of

water as he jumps into the pool. "You can look now. I'm fully covered so as not to offend your modest sensibilities."

A flush creeps up my neck when I turn around and see the ripples trailing his broad frame. He's heading my way, and I instinctively back up, trying to create distance.

His eyes narrow. "Are you running from me?"

"I'm not running… I-I'm swimming."

I just happen to be swimming in the opposite direction of him. But I don't make it very far. The second my back brushes against the pool's wall, he's in front of me. His grip tightens around my waist, pulling me against him. His bare chest is slick and warm, and I'm keenly aware of how close his naked body is to mine.

He catches my wrist, holding it firmly as he stares at the tattoo. "You know you weren't supposed to get your tattoo wet until it's healed."

"As you can see, I covered it with a waterproof bandage. For the record, I only did it because I don't want an infection."

He tilts his head. "Is this the first time you've gone swimming here?"

I hesitate before answering, my palms lightly pressed against his shoulders to create space between us. "Yeah," I admit. "I was getting restless."

His brow arches. "What do you normally do at home to keep busy?"

"I've been a student for the last four years. All I've done is dance. I had no time for anything else."

"You can dance here, too. There's plenty of room in my house. But what else would you like to do?" He studies me closely. "What have you dreamed of doing that you haven't had time for?"

His question takes me by surprise. I'm not used to thinking about what I want, what I'd do if I had the freedom to choose. My entire focus has been on dance and school for so long that everything else feels like a blank slate.

"I don't know," I say slowly, the honesty of it making me feel exposed. "I've been so focused on one goal for so long that I haven't thought about anything else but graduating and moving to Berlin."

"Maybe it's time to start thinking about it."

I scoff, trying to conceal the vulnerability creeping in. "What, you're my life coach now?"

He chuckles, his hand still secure at my waist. "No one would ever accuse me of being that."

I roll my eyes. "And what do you suggest, oh wise one?"

He tilts his head. "Cooking. Painting. Horseback riding. Hell, even skydiving, if you want to mix it up. Either way, I'm not stopping you from dancing."

"I don't only want to dance. I want to perform. I want to dance onstage and live my life on my terms."

He's quiet for a moment. The cool water licks at my shoulders, a sharp contrast to the heat radiating off Nikolai. With his wet hair slicked back and the shadows on his face more pronounced in the dark, my heart skips a beat. He's overwhelmingly, undeniably all man.

"Why Berlin? Why did you want to go there?"

"I thought I could start fresh in a new city. It has a vibrant arts scene, and it's far enough from Moscow that nobody would know my ties to the Syndicate. I could finally live without the weight of all this baggage." I release a bitter laugh. "I was even going to try to convince Liza and Roman that I don't need to take a bodyguard with me. I guess that'll never happen."

His thumb shifts, a subtle movement against the exposed skin of my belly. "You've been so focused on one thing you've forgotten how to just live. Maybe you should figure out what you enjoy when you're not chasing a goal," he says, his lips hovering inches from mine.

His words settle into a part of me I've tried to ignore. He might be right, and it frustrates me that he can see it so clearly. I try to push away from him, but he doesn't let me go. "Says the man holding me captive."

"I'm not any man. I'm your husband."

I glare up at Nikolai, my throat tightening. "I never asked for a husband."

His expression remains infuriatingly calm. "Yet here we are," he replies. "Life doesn't care about what we ask for."

"It's easy for you to tell me not to be so ambitious when you're prepared to go up against the Syndicate, for what? Money?"

His lips press into a thin line, but he doesn't hesitate. "Power," he says bluntly. "That's all that matters. After rebuilding from nothing, I know what it takes to survive."

I shake my head. "I've always wondered something. Why did you help Roman all those years ago? After you killed Sergey, you had no reason to risk your life to save me and my sister."

He shrugs. "For fun."

"Come on. That was fun for you?"

"I'll admit, aligning myself with the Syndicate was part of my reason, but I was fresh out of jail, and a little shoot-me-up action didn't sound all that bad. I also wanted to make Anatoly Petrovich pay for all the shit he'd done."

"I thought of you for years afterward."

The words are out before I can stop them, hanging in the air between us. Nikolai stills, his grip firm and his gaze sharp. I immediately wish I could take it back.

"Did you?" His voice is laced with an edge I can't place.

"It's not what you think."

He doesn't speak right away, but I feel the intensity of his focus like a physical weight. "Then explain it to me."

I exhale, my tongue darting out to wet my lips. "It was the

scariest thing I've ever been through, but I survived it because of you. And you made me feel safe," I admit. "Even if everything you've done since then has been totally fucked up."

His grin returns, wicked and self-assured. "And after?" he prompts. "You fantasized about me, didn't you?"

Flustered, I splash water at him. "I didn't say that!"

"You didn't deny it, either."

I groan, trying to twist away, but he holds me in place. "Fine! But it wasn't by choice… it just happened sometimes."

Like when I touched myself.

How could I have admitted all this to Nikolai? I didn't even have a drink tonight, but it feels like my lips are extra loose. It must have something to do with being relaxed in the water.

"I'm flattered, moya sladost." His fingertips skim along my waist again, dipping beneath the edge of my bikini, sending a shiver through me. "You've got my attention. Now, what are you going to do with it?"

I inhale sharply, trying to ignore the flutter low in my stomach. "I didn't ask for your attention."

"No? Then what's this?" His finger slides under the side strap of the bikini bottom and, with a flick, snaps it against my skin.

Need pulses between my legs like a fever, and I release a little moan that I try to disguise with a cough. "It's your girlfriend's bikini. I had no other options."

He shakes his head, his gaze heavy on me. "I'm going to let you in on a little secret…" He leans forward to whisper in my ear. "Eva's not my girlfriend."

I wave a hand in front of me. "Fuck buddy, whatever. Same thing."

He exhales with a short laugh as if I'm trying to be funny. "I didn't like Emil's eyes on you in this excuse for a swimsuit."

To make his point, he slips his finger beneath the thin band of my bottoms again, his palm brushing along the curve of my ass. A sharp hiss escapes me, and I struggle to hold on to my thoughts, but his touch makes it impossible.

"You're the one who assigned him to watch me," I hiss, clinging to whatever control I can muster. "Don't get angry when he's doing his job."

His rough palm curls over my hip, firm and possessive. If steam could rise from the pool, it would. My blood feels like it's on fire, my pulse hammering in my ears as he leans in close. His breath ghosts over my skin as he murmurs, "It didn't look like he was doing his job to me. Seemed like he was enjoying the view."

"Would you listen to yourself? You sound like a caveman."

"I'm possessive of you. Is that so wrong?"

I should say yes, or better yet, I should push him away. While I debate with myself, his fingers trace over my hip, lingering along the edge of my bikini bottoms, the deliberate caress leaving my mind blank.

"You don't own me," I whisper, but the words lack the conviction I want them to have.

He leans in, his lips close to my ear. "No, I don't own you, but I want you." His hand skims up my side.

Need coils low in my belly. I know I have to stop this before I lose myself. Before I let myself fall under his spell again. Every time I do, it ends with me feeling weak and ashamed.

I step back, breaking free from his hold, the water rippling around us as I put space between us. "I'm going to bed," I say, brushing past him.

"Good night, Sofiya," he calls after me, but I don't bother looking back. "Make sure to clean the tattoo and put some cream on it. I guess you forgot when I warned you not to get it wet?"

As I climb out of the water, I grab a towel and wrap it tightly around myself, flipping both middle fingers behind my back. I don't stop until I'm in my room.

CHAPTER SEVENTEEN

SOFIYA

THE NEXT MORNING, I STEP INTO THE KITCHEN TO FIND YELENA alone, her hands dusted with flour as she works a lump of dough on a big wooden cutting board.

She smiles when she sees me. "Good morning. How did you sleep?"

"Not bad," I lie. The truth is, I spent the night tossing and turning, my body aching with need. I refused to touch myself, determined not to give in to thoughts of my captor, but by the early hours of the morning, I broke. My fingers slid between my thighs, and I came harder than I ever have, Nikolai's name silently on my lips.

She moves to get me a cup of coffee, but I wave her away. "I can get my own," I assure her. In the short time I've been here, I've settled into a routine, and that, too, is dangerous.

As soon as I sit down with a steaming cup of coffee, she pulls out a platter of food meant for a small army. There are baked goods, fruit, a selection of cheeses and jams, hard-boiled eggs, and yogurt.

"Yelena, you fuss too much over me. I am happy with fruit and yogurt most mornings."

"Please." She dismisses me with a wave of her hand. "I haven't had anyone to spoil for so long. And you're Nikolai's wife. You need to eat a good meal to start your day, especially when you get pregnant."

I nearly choke on my coffee. "Pregnant? No. I'm not getting pregnant."

Yelena gives me a patient smile. "Of course, you will have a baby. When the time is right."

My misguided Cupid hasn't given up yet. If she only knew. "Do you see this?" I point to the stupid tattoo on my finger. "This is my so-called wedding ring. Do you think I want to have anything to do with the man who forced this on me?" Forced is relative, but I'd like to scrub my brain of the pact I made with him. "And this." I point to the gold cuff around my angle. "That is actually a tracking device, so he knows where I am at all times."

"He is… unconventional," she concedes, unbothered.

I can see I'm not getting through to her, so I smile and pop a grape into my mouth. "Let's agree to disagree on this one."

Yelena hums to herself, content as she kneads the dough, her movements practiced. I sip my coffee, watching her out of the corner of my eye. She seems harmless, though a little too eager to see me settled into Nikolai's life, but she might also be a good source of information.

I decide to test the waters. "Do you live here, too?" I ask, keeping my tone casual as I pick at a piece of toast.

She nods with pride. "Oh, yes. I have my own cottage in the back that Nikolai had renovated for me when he bought the estate. I even have my own little garden. They say Catherine the Great's niece used to tend to the roses there."

I blink, taken aback. "Catherine the Great? As in the former empress?"

Yelena waves a flour-dusted hand through the air. "Yes.

It's said the empress gifted her niece this estate. A piece of history, yes?" She looks around the kitchen with a small smile. "Nikolai has done a fine job modernizing it while keeping its original charm."

I nod as if this is nothing more than an interesting tidbit, but inside, I'm filing away every word. Knowing its history might help me figure out where this estate is located.

I take another sip of coffee. "That's… impressive. I wouldn't have guessed."

Yelena gives me a pointed look. "This house is too big to leave empty, don't you think? Did I mention there's a nursery on the third floor?"

"No chance in hell of me getting pregnant," I reiterate.

"Pregnant? Who's pregnant?" Eva walks through the entrance and settles beside me.

"No one," I'm quick to say. This is how rumors get started.

Her eyes drop to my stomach, and she gives a little wink. "If you say so."

Eva is once again chugging one of her gross green smoothies, dressed in workout gear: tight black leggings, a cropped tank top that shows off her abs, and an unzipped jacket hanging loosely from her shoulders. She looks like she just stepped off the cover of a magazine.

Considering how early it was, she probably spent the night with Nikolai. Something sour curdles in my stomach, realizing he spent the night with Eva—the woman he actually wants. She might not be his girlfriend, or at least that's what Nikolai claimed, but imagining them together still bugs me. Not that it should. I have bigger issues than worrying about whom Nikolai is sleeping with.

And in truth, I kind of like her.

Eva grins, making a show of inspecting my dress—or rather, her dress. "Oh, look at you. Showing less boob today. I had to dig to the back of my closet to find that dress."

I glance down at the simple navy dress Eva left for me. It's actually a bit loose around the chest. "Gee, thanks. This high collar should meet Nikolai's approval."

"Don't mention it. I figure it's better to keep the peace around here. You wearing one of my usual dresses would probably make him combust—and not in a fun way."

Despite myself, I chuckle. "Good workout?" I ask between bites of Yelena's delicious cheese pastry.

When Eva reaches to take one, Yelena slides the tray out of her reach. "One does not sip that disgusting green slime while enjoying my fine vatrushka."

Eva's face falls. "But I need something delicious after all this green slime."

Yelena sniffs at her before turning back to whatever delicacy she's in the middle of making. I can't help but laugh—these two have a funny dynamic. Eva frowns and takes another sip of the concoction.

"It was a good workout," she admits. "Lucky for me, Niko was distracted this morning, so I got in a few more hits than usual."

Something about her words gives me pause. "Hits?"

"Oh, we spar all the time. You should join us. It's always smart to know how to fight. And I bet you wouldn't mind getting a few hits in on your husband."

I raise an eyebrow. They spar? Either they're the least romantic couple imaginable, or sparring serves as their version of foreplay. Whatever the case, I'm not about to think about it.

"I'll pass. I have no desire to spend any more time with Nikolai than necessary."

"My ears are burning."

I turn to see Nikolai stride into the kitchen, wearing nothing but gray sweatpants. Dammit. My mouth goes dry, and I quickly spin back around, afraid my reaction will give away what I'm thinking—which is that he looks mind-meltingly hot. Again. You'd think seeing him naked last night would've been more than enough, but somehow, I'm still mesmerized by Nikolai without a shirt. Judging by his lack of effort to cover up, he seems to feel the same way.

"Good morning, Sofiya," he says, coming up to my side. I quickly brush the pastry crumbs from my mouth. His eyes sweep over me, and my skin tingles under his stare. "What a beautiful and demure dress you're wearing."

I roll my eyes.

Eva leans forward with a little smile. "You can thank me for that."

"Why, thank you, Eva," he drawls sarcastically, then turns back to me.

"I want to introduce you to someone," he says. I finally take off the blinders I wear when Nikolai is around and realize someone else is in the room. A man with dark curly hair and deep, soulful eyes steps up to me and holds out his hand in greeting. He also looks like he's been working out with Eva and Nikolai.

"I'm Vadim," he says. "I work for this guy here." He points toward Nikolai with his thumb.

I return his warm smile when I shake his hand. "How unfortunate for you."

He huffs a laugh. "I like her," he tells Nikolai. And then, to me, he says, "He does have his moments. Even if he can be a cranky son of a bi—"

"Yeah, thanks for the ringing endorsement." He runs a hand through his hair. I can't help but notice that Vadim seems at ease around his pakhan, which is a good sign. It reminds me of Roman and his partner, Pavel. Their men were relaxed around them but also knew when it was time to be serious. They ruled by respect, not fear, which is powerful.

Not that I want to give Nikolai too much credit. He certainly doesn't deserve a medal or anything like that.

"I'm going to go shower," Nikolai tells Vadim. "I'll be ready to go in ten."

As soon as Nikolai disappears upstairs, Vadim grabs a box from the counter, shakes it, and sits down across from me with a bowl. I glance at the colorful rings tumbling out. "Are those... Froot Loops?"

Eva stares at him like he's grown a second head. "You're eating that after our workout? Seriously?"

Vadim shrugs, spoon halfway to his mouth. "What? It's delicious."

Eva leans on the counter, her expression mock-stern. "We did two hours of cardio and strength training, and now you're going to undo it all with sugar-coated cardboard?"

Yelena chimes in from the stove, barely glancing back. "Let the man eat. He works hard. Besides, it's better than that green sludge you call a drink."

"Thank you, Yelena," Vadim says, pointing his spoon at Eva. "At least someone gets me."

Eva rolls her eyes, crossing her arms. "You do realize this is why you'll never have abs like me, right?"

Vadim snorts. "I don't need abs like you. I have a personality. Besides, you're only jealous of my beautiful face."

I laugh at their ridiculous bickering.

"As if," Eva shoots back before glancing at her watch. "Anyhow, I have a meeting with the Orlovs to get to." She claps me on the back. "See you later, Sofiya. I'll remind Niko to take you shopping."

"Yeah, I'd really like my own underwear, too," I admit.

Vadim's brows rise in surprise, but he hides his grin by focusing intently on his cereal.

"I'm sure you would," Eva calls over her shoulder before disappearing through the doorway.

Her comment about meeting with the committee surprised me. I didn't expect Eva to have a job. Most women tied to men like Nikolai don't, though my sister is an exception. Then again, her relationship with Roman isn't exactly traditional.

I sigh, guilt bubbling up. Every time I'm not utterly miserable here, I feel like I'm betraying Liza, Roman, the Syndicate, my friends, and everyone who's affected by this. I know it's ridiculous because me feeling like crap won't fix a thing.

"Whoa, what's with that frown?" Vadim asks, grabbing the cereal box and giving it a shake. "You know what could turn that upside down?"

I laugh, shaking my head. "I'm sorry, I can't imagine you working for Nikolai Zhukov. You're way too—"

"Fun? I get that a lot. But we're like yin and yang. We balance each other out."

I grab a handful of cereal and toss it into my mouth because why not? I swear Yelena shoots me a dirty look from across the kitchen where she's kneading dough. "And how did you two meet?" I ask.

"In prison."

I nearly choke. "I didn't expect that… not sure why."

"Yeah, most people don't, especially because of my military background." He shrugs. "But life has a way of throwing curveballs."

I lean my head into my hands. "Tell me about it."

Vadim's eyes soften as he rests his elbows on the table. "You're tougher than you look, you know," he says, his tone unexpectedly sincere.

I huff out a laugh. "I don't feel tough."

"Trust me. Most people wouldn't have lasted this long. And they wouldn't be laughing while eating cereal with me."

Before I can respond, Nikolai strides into the room, his presence commanding as always. His dress shirt is unbuttoned at the collar, revealing a hint of inked skin. His suit jacket hangs loosely over his arm, and the faint shadow of stubble adds to his rugged edge.

Vadim grins, gesturing toward me with his spoon. "Your wife has a pressing request. She'd like her own underwear."

My eyes widen, and heat rushes to my cheeks. "Vadim!" I hiss, mortified.

Nikolai's brow arches slightly, but his expression remains composed. "Noted," he says, his gaze sweeping over me briefly before shifting back to Vadim. "You ready?"

"Born ready," Vadim replies, rising with a grin. As they head for the door, he calls back, "I'll make sure he gets you the good stuff, Sofiya."

I drop my head into my hands, groaning.

Yelena chuckles from across the kitchen. "Don't let them get to you." She pauses, wiping her hands on her apron. "But if you want to take your mind off things, I could teach you how to make cabbage rolls. Every good Russian wife should know how."

I laugh, shaking my head. "Maybe. Although not because I want to be a good Russian wife, but because I might as well learn how to cook while I'm here."

I sit cross-legged on the bed, staring at the pile of DVDs like they're alien artifacts. The huge TV in the corner of the room has a built-in player, and while I figured out how to turn it on, getting it to actually play anything is a whole other challenge.

I guess streaming services are not allowed, so I'm stuck with this relic. But I'm so damn bored, I'll take anything as a distraction.

The remote is bulky and old, its buttons faded and hard to read. I press one, and the screen flickers to the DVD menu. Success? Maybe. I hit "play," but the screen goes black.

"Seriously?" I mutter, flopping back onto the bed.

After a day spent wandering the house, playing a little piano, reading in the library, and trying to shake off the nagging feeling of being out of place, all I want is to watch a movie—just one normal thing to make me feel like myself again.

I'm glaring at the remote, debating my next move, when a knock at the door cuts through the quiet.

"Come in," I call, too frustrated to care who it is.

The door creaks open, and Nikolai leans against the frame, one brow raised. "What the hell are you doing?"

I gesture at the TV. "Trying to watch a movie. Do you know how to use this thing? It's ancient."

He crosses his arms, the sides of his mouth twitching. "You don't know how to work a DVD player?"

"No! I've never had to use one. Because I grew up in the modern era, where we have something called streaming."

"Jesus. You're making me feel old."

I grin. "Well, you are."

"Move over. Let me show you how it's done before you break it."

I shift to the side, handing him the remote. He takes it, his fingers brushing mine briefly, and crouches by the TV, muttering something under his breath about "kids these days."

"How old are you, anyway?" I ask, leaning back against the headboard. I'm aware that I'm dressed in an old pair of Eva's sweats, but if he finds it weird, he doesn't mention it.

"Thirty-four," he says without looking up.

I whistle, long and exaggerated.

He glances over his shoulder, one brow raised. "At least I'm old enough to know how to work this thing."

I laugh, watching as he expertly navigates the buttons. The TV flickers, and the menu appears on-screen. He hands the remote back to me. "There. That's play. That's pause. That's stop. Think you can manage, or should I write it down for you?"

"Very funny." I roll my eyes. "So, what brings you to my door this evening?"

He leans casually against the dresser. "I thought you might be interested in going shopping tomorrow. Seeing as you're not too fond of borrowing underwear."

My cheeks warm, but a smile spreads across my face. "That actually sounds like a good idea."

I notice he's not in one of his signature suits. Instead, he's wearing jeans and a plain black T-shirt that stretches perfectly across his chest and shoulders. It's such a stark contrast, seeing him like this—casual, almost approachable—but it doesn't make him any less intimidating. If anything, it's worse. He's stupidly sexy even when he's dressed down.

"What are you watching, anyway?" he asks, nodding toward the screen.

I glance at the DVD case on the bed and hold it up. "*Scream*. Classic '90s horror. It's the golden age, you know."

"Never seen it. You complain about '90s tech, but you're all in for '90s movies?"

I shrug, grinning. "Different rules. Movies are timeless. Tech… not so much."

"Fair enough." He folds his arms, watching me with a mix of amusement and curiosity.

"Wait—you've never seen *Scream*?" I ask, sitting up straighter.

"Never."

My jaw drops. "What the hell? You're missing out. It's iconic!"

He chuckles. "Maybe I'm not much of a horror guy."

"It's a parody of the horror genre, actually. It's kind of funny." I bite my lip. "You can't live like this. You can watch it with me." I feel awkward as soon as the words are out of my mouth. I invited Nikolai fucking Zhukov to Netflix and chill with me. Then again, I really think he's missing out if he doesn't see it.

He raises an eyebrow, looking genuinely surprised. "You want me to watch it with you?"

"Yeah." I nod, trying to seem casual. "It's a classic. A cultural touchstone. You should at least see it once."

He tilts his head, considering. "I've got work to—"

"Of course," I'm quick to jump in, feeling silly for even offering.

His eyes flick to me, catching the faint disappointment I didn't mean to reveal.

"Fuck it. Yeah, let's watch the damn movie."

"Really?" I can't hide the excitement that creeps into my voice.

"Yeah," he says with a shrug. "But if we're doing this, we're doing it right. Popcorn. Coke. The full '90s cinema experience."

I grin, the tension in my chest easing. "Popcorn and Coke? You're a man of taste, Zhukov."

"You have no idea." He glances toward the door. "Stay here. I'll be back."

Not long after, we're sitting side by side on the small couch in my room, the lights low, popcorn in a bowl between us, and two cans of Coke on the table. On the screen, Drew Barrymore's Casey Becker character answers the phone while making popcorn, her blond bob adorable as she flirts on the phone with the mysterious caller.

I glance sideways at Nikolai. His posture is casual—leaning back, one arm draped along the back of the couch—but his eyes are locked on the screen, his jaw tight. He has no idea what's about to happen.

I watch him rather than the screen when Casey is forced into a terrifying game of horror movie trivia with her boyfriend Steve's life on the line. When she answers wrong and hears Steve's agonized screams, Nikolai's hand twitches against his leg. I bite back a smile, waiting for what's coming next.

Then it happens—Ghostface appears outside the glass

doors, and Casey's piercing scream fills the air. Nikolai flinches. Just barely, but enough to tell me he's freaked out.

"Are you scared?" I whisper, smirking as I take a sip of Coke.

He cuts me a glance. "Hardly."

"You look a little tense."

He narrows his eyes. "I don't get scared. I get… alert. And I don't like horror movies."

I laugh, the sound muffled by the next dramatic high-pitch wail from the TV. "So what do you like?"

"Heat. Die Hard. The Godfather."

"Don't you get enough adrenaline in your day job?"

He leans back, a piece of popcorn halfway to his mouth. "Movies don't come with consequences. I can enjoy the chaos without worrying about cleanup."

I sneak glances at him, my eyes drawn to the flicker of emotions playing across his face. His jaw tightens, and his brows knit together as poor Casey gets killed off.

He takes a sip of his drink. "So many stupid choices. Who would flirt with a creepy stranger on the phone like that?"

"It's a horror movie. People do stupid things. That's the point."

The harsh angles of his face seem softer in the glow of the TV. I let my gaze linger for a moment too long, and suddenly, his head turns, his deep, blue eyes meeting mine.

"You're staring," he says.

I flush and look back at the screen. "You're very into this movie for someone who called it stupid five minutes ago. You're enjoying this."

"Maybe." He settles back into the couch. "So are you."

"Maybe," I parrot him.

If I'm honest, I am enjoying this—sitting here with him, not just the movie—more than I expected. Watching his reactions is more fun than the film. And being in someone else's company, even if he is my captor, helps with the loneliness.

His hand shifts and comes to rest lightly on my leg, his warmth seeping through the fabric of my sweatpants. It catches me off guard, and for a second, I freeze.

I glance at him, unsure what to say.

"What?" he asks, his attention still fixed on the TV. "It's a scary movie. I'm scared."

"Right." I let out a quiet snort, shaking my head. "Whatever makes you feel better."

He keeps his hand where it is, and to my surprise, it feels... comforting. Maybe, just for tonight, I can wave the white flag between us.

Movement stirs me from sleep. I feel warmth around me—strong, steady warmth—and blink slowly, realizing the movie is over and I'm now in his arms.

"Seriously?" I murmur, my eyes still half-closed. "What is it with you and carrying me around like a sack of potatoes? Is this some weird fetish—like your love of stripping?"

He makes an amused noise. "Less scary than waking you up."

"Are you scared of me?"

"Terrified," he says dryly as he crosses the short distance to the bed.

I let my head loll against his shoulder, too comfortable to protest. "You should be. I'm a force to be reckoned with.

"I have no doubt," he mutters, lowering me onto the bed with surprising care. He pulls the blanket over me. This moment should feel weird, but it doesn't. Tomorrow, I'll go back to hating him.

"Did you like the movie?" I don't know why I care, but I do. Probably because I feel like he sacrificed his night to spend it with me.

"Other than the idiotic choices every character made and the absurd amount of screaming, I found it... acceptable. Maybe even better than acceptable."

I prop myself up on one elbow, giving him a look. "Better than acceptable? High praise coming from you."

He shrugs, his expression as serious as if we were discussing an international arms deal. "It had its moments. The commentary on horror clichés was clever. And the killer's reveal? Predictable, but it worked."

"You're seriously analyzing *Scream*?" I huff. "You know it's only a slasher movie, right?" When he lifts a shoulder, I say, "Next time, we'll do a deep dive into *Clueless* and its commentary on society."

"Clue-what? No idea what you're talking about."

"God, you're impossible." I flop back onto the pillow, but I'm smiling.

CHAPTER EIGHTEEN

NIKOLAI

Vadim's voice comes through the Bluetooth speaker, tight with irritation, as I roll the Bugatti out of the garage and stop in front of the house. "Seriously? You're ditching the meeting with Igor?"

I roll my eyes. "I've worked nonstop for days, trying to clean up the fallout from the Colombian shipment. I think I deserve a day off."

"Sure, but you've never taken one before."

"I have something important to deal with."

He scoffs. "And this meeting isn't important?"

Igor and I meet every week to discuss our various business ventures, and I've never missed one of those sit-downs. But today, I don't have anything new to report. I haven't heard from Roman since I sent him the picture of Sofiya's finger, but I expected as much. The Syndicate was never going to come to heel easily. Roman needs time to consider his options and then realize they all suck.

But Igor won't see it that way; he's like a dog with a bone. He'll grill me with questions about Sofiya, and I don't want to discuss her with him. I'd rather he forgot that she's in my life.

"I trust you and Eva to handle it." I lean back in the seat, watching the house through the windshield. After a beat, I add, "And Emil. He's been itching to get out of the house. Let him sit in, get a feel for how we operate."

I'm trying to meet Emil halfway. He's told me he wants more responsibility. Getting involved in the day-to-day operations will keep him focused and allow me to see how he handles himself. I can't deny that I have my own selfish reasons for wanting to keep Emil busy, especially since I didn't like coming home to find his attention on Sofiya.

Vadim laughs, the kind that says he doesn't believe me for a second. "Fuck, now I'm worried. Are you dying? Tell me the truth. I can handle it."

"Not today." I pause for effect, then add, "I'm taking my wife shopping."

The silence on the other end is thick. I imagine him blinking at the phone, his brain short-circuiting.

"You're taking Sofiya shopping," he repeats. "This is what you're ditching the meeting for?"

I understand his shock. I've never once missed work for anything personal, especially not for a woman. Then again, Sofiya isn't just any woman. She's my wife, my responsibility. That's what I tell myself, anyway.

Last night, I had a pile of work waiting for me, but when I saw how lonely she looked, I couldn't walk away. So I stayed with her and did something I hadn't done in years—I watched a fucking movie. A horror movie at that. But I didn't hate *Scream*. And more than that, I didn't hate spending my night with her.

"Careful," I warn. "You realize you're talking about my wife, right?"

"Words I never thought I'd hear you say."

Words I never thought I'd say either, but here we are.

"This is a duty, nothing more," I tell him, but his skeptical laugh makes it clear he doesn't buy it.

"I have to go. I'll touch base later." I hang up before he can continue giving me shit.

Killing the engine, I step out of the car and into the thick morning heat. Yelena let Sofiya know to be ready early, that she's going shopping today. I find her exactly where I'd expect to—seated in the kitchen while Yelena spoils her with a spread of her favorite foods.

"More blini?" Yelena asks, setting down a fresh platter of pancakes in front of Sofiya.

"I'm stuffed," Sofiya says, resting a hand on her lower belly before breaking into a grin. "Well, maybe one more."

When I walk in, all eyes land on me. "How come you never make me a feast like this?" I needle Yelena. She knows I'm not serious. I rarely eat breakfast, but it's obvious that Sofiya has become Yelena's favorite member of the household.

Yelena is more than my housekeeper. I met her years ago when she was working as a waitress at a restaurant I frequented. The bruises she tried to hide told me all I needed to know about her marriage. When I heard she'd been hospitalized with a broken bone and wouldn't be returning to her job, I stepped in, putting her mudak husband six feet under where he belongs.

After that, I offered her a job as a maid in my household. It didn't take her long to advance through the ranks. Within a year she was running my estate, but for some reason, she still insists on doing the cooking.

Yelena swats at me with a dishrag. "I'd spoil you more if you actually ate breakfast. With you, it's always coffee and go." She shakes her head, sighing like I'm a lost cause. "Sofiya here sits and enjoys the food I make. When you're ready to stop running yourself into the ground, I'll make you your favorites."

I laugh because she's right, but I know the real reason she pampers Sofiya is because she wants her to feel at home. Despite her own history with a shitty marriage, Yelena believes I'd be better off with the love of a good woman, and she's not shy about making it clear she wants a baby in the house, either. Her little matchmaking efforts aren't subtle. I've told her it won't work, but Yelena doesn't give up easily.

I grab a cup of coffee and turn my attention to my wife. "Good morning, moya sladost." My gaze flicks over her. She's wearing a tank top and denim shorts. Her hair is in loose waves around her shoulders. She's stunning, even without much effort. "Are you ready to go?"

She tilts her head, scrutinizing me. "With you?"

I lean my forearms on the counter. "Yes, with me."

She can tell herself she hates me all she wants, but I don't think her feelings toward me are that simple. I think she needs to cling to that hate like a shield because, without it, she's scared of what she'd do or how she'd feel. But if she wants to play this game, I'll indulge her.

Yelena looks up from the sink, a grin lighting up her face. She puts down the plate and dries her hands. "What a fantastic idea," she says, beaming at Sofiya.

Sofiya lifts her chin and looks at me like this is some kind of trick. "When you mentioned shopping, I assumed it would be one of your minions taking me, not you."

"I'm sorry to disappoint. Would you prefer I send a minion instead?"

"Nonsense," Yelena interjects, bustling over and practically ushering Sofiya from her seat. "You must go with your husband."

"Husband." Sofiya makes a face. She turns to me, planting a hand on her hip. "I'll go to see the look on your face as I spend as much of your money as I can."

I chuckle at her threat. "Watching you try will really turn me on."

With a mock huff, Sofiya brushes past me out of the kitchen. Before I can follow, Yelena stops me with a hand on my arm.

"Be good to her," she says quietly.

My muscles clench, but I don't argue. Yelena's earned her place in my life, and I know she means well.

I catch up with Sofiya as she heads down the stairs. The guards stationed outside quickly look away when she nods and offers a polite smile. Good. They know better than to let their eyes linger.

I lead her to the sports car, opening her door and gesturing for her to get in. Her eyes narrow with suspicion, like she doesn't trust my intentions. Last night felt like a step forward, as if we'd called an unspoken truce, even if only for a little while. But judging by her cool demeanor today, it seems that moment's passed.

When she slides into the passenger seat, I lean down to grab her seat belt and pull it across her upper body. My fingers graze her breasts, and she exhales shakily as I click the buckle into place.

"You're ridiculous," she mutters, a blush creeping into her cheeks. I'm struck by her beauty. Her bright hazel eyes lock on mine, neither of us willing to look away.

"When you see how I drive, you'll understand."

Sliding in beside her, I start the engine, shift into gear, and pull away from the house.

The roads around my estate are empty, as they always are, because it's private land. I bought much of the surrounding area to ensure my privacy and safety.

I push the car faster, the engine growling as I accelerate. Sofiya stays silent, but when I glance over, she looks like she's fighting a grin. When I take a sharp turn, the tires gripping the road tightly, a smile finally breaks free.

Fuck, she's even more beautiful when her face lights up

like this. It's a sight I don't get to see often—not that I deserve to, after everything I've done.

I tap play on my phone, scrolling until I find a gritty rock track that blasts through the car's speakers. Sofiya settles back in her seat, the wind tousling her hair.

This is the first time she's seemed relaxed around me, so I keep my mouth shut, knowing whatever I'd say would probably ruin the moment.

When the road snakes on a downward curve, I shift down and accelerate, drinking in her thrilled laughter.

"Jesus, maybe you missed your calling as a race car driver," she offers.

I blow out a breath. "Maybe, but where I'm from, that wasn't exactly an option."

She's quiet for a moment as if weighing her words. "I didn't know you grew up with Eva and Emil."

Irritation spikes through me. "Was Emil telling you stories last night?"

"Not stories, but it came up in conversation." She angles her head toward me. "He also said you went to jail for Sergey."

Fucking Emil. To this day, I feel like an idiot. I didn't see Sergey for what he'd become until it was too late. Eva used to warn me that he didn't have my back the way I had his, but I refused to believe it. I'll never be blindly loyal to anyone again.

Sofiya swallows, the little tendons in her neck working. "Why did you take the fall for him?"

I hate talking about my past, but I feel I owe her an explanation. She wants to know how I became this way—hardened, a monster in her eyes—and the answer is simple.

Heartbreak.

Killing Sergey broke something inside me.

"I grew up protecting Sergey. From my mother, her

boyfriends, the shitty world we grew up in. He was my younger brother. If I didn't look out for him, who would? It was minor drug charges, but they were going to throw him into one of the roughest prisons in the country. Sergey was tough in his own way, but he was never much of a fighter. Fine if he had a gun, but useless with his hands. That's a sure way to get killed in prison." My shoulders knot with tension. The hurt is still raw and always will be. "It's not uncommon for the pakhan to run things from jail. Sergey was supposed to handle things on the outside while I called the shots from inside." A knot forms in my throat as my eyes flick to hers. "I trusted my brother. Turned out to be the biggest mistake of my life."

Her voice is soft when she asks, "Is that why you killed him? Because he turned against you?"

I shake my head, glancing briefly at her before focusing on the road. "No. I killed him because he was going to kill me."

Her fingers curl in her lap, playing with the hem of her shorts. "You protected your brother. There's nothing wrong with that. Liza always looked out for me." She hesitates, then adds, "Sometimes I wish she didn't. Maybe then I wouldn't have been so blindsided when I learned what Anatoly was really like and how twisted my parents actually were."

"Have you had contact with your parents since Greece?"

She shakes her head. "And I never will. Liza and Roman are my only family."

A kernel of guilt worms its way inside, but I push it down. "I'm your husband. Technically, that makes us family."

She looks at me for a long time, like she's trying to peel back my layers.

I adjust my collar.

"I'm trying to figure out if you're delusional enough to believe these lies."

I raise a shoulder. "There's nothing delusional about it. I could show you the marriage certificate."

"A piece of paper or a tattoo marking me as your property

doesn't make us family. Don't you get it?" Her tone softens. "Has there ever been someone in your life who took care of you? Loved you just because—not because you pay them or owe them, or whatever?"

My grip on the wheel tightens. "Before my mother got messed up by drugs and alcohol, she tried." I pause, the words dragging up a memory I haven't thought about in years. "The Christmas right after my father left, she stayed clean for a few weeks and saved up enough money to actually do something. I didn't give a shit at that point, but Sergey was only four. He still cared. She got us each a toy car, identical except for the color. We played with those damn things for hours, running them up and down the hall. She cooked a roast chicken and made those horrible powdered mashed potatoes, but it was the best meal we'd had in months. But, fuck, at least she tried."

The memory stirs something deep inside me, and I fix my attention on the road ahead. Sofiya is also quiet, but when I look over at her a few minutes later, her gaze meets mine, and her expression softens. Not with pity, but with something else. When she turns back to the window, the knot in my chest begins to unravel.

CHAPTER NINETEEN

SOFIYA

My first thought when I got into Nikolai's car was to pay attention to where he was taking me, so that if I ever had a chance to escape or communicate with the outside world to get help, I'd have a sense of where we are.

That plan lasted about thirty seconds.

The second we hit the road, all those thoughts flew right out the window. Nikolai is distracting—in the way he reached over to buckle me in, his tattooed hands flexing on the gearshift, veins rippling over his forearms. It's how he blasted rock music and drove with one hand, like a professional driver.

Apparently, I have a thing for that.

He's been letting pieces of himself slip. Talking about his brother, his mother, and his time in jail. It's strange; hearing these things about his past makes him more human, less like the devil I've painted him to be.

Maybe we're not so different after all. Both raised by people who should've loved us but didn't. The difference is I didn't let it ruin me. Nikolai let it twist him into someone who takes whatever he wants, no matter the cost.

Why am I so drawn to him? Over the last few days, my self-control has been hanging on by a thread. Starting with the pool—his big, tattooed, naked body, slick and wet, so close I could feel the warmth radiating off him. The way he snapped the bikini string against my overheated skin. Watching the movie with me last night.

When I need to remind myself of who he truly is, I stare at the "wedding ring" tattooed on my finger—a reminder of the brutal man who put it there.

I'm lost in thought when a faded billboard catches my eye: Koporye Fortress – one mile. My pulse quickens. Koporye Fortress is a historic ruin not far from St. Petersburg. It's not much, but it's a clue. It helps narrow down our location.

Minutes later, we pull up to a modest but well-maintained two-story house at the end of a gravel road. It's definitely not what I expected for a shopping trip.

"Where are we?" I ask.

"A private boutique," Nikolai says, slipping off his sunglasses and tossing them onto the dashboard. "The owner is an Italian woman named Valeria. She caters to people like me."

"Assholes?"

His lips twitch. "People with refined tastes who value discretion."

Like a perfect gentleman, Nikolai opens my door and then leads me inside. The interior couldn't be more different from the plain exterior. It's elegant and inviting, with plush velvet chairs and crystal chandeliers.

Within seconds, two women glide toward us, their faces lit up as though they've spotted royalty.

"Niko. What a pleasant surprise. I wasn't expecting you." A petite woman in her forties, with a heart-shaped face and friendly eyes, steps forward and kisses him on the cheek.

"Sofiya, this is Valeria, the owner of the boutique. And, Valeria, this is Sofiya, my wife."

Her eyes widen, and she blinks rapidly. "Wife?"

"It's new," Nikolai offers.

"Of course," she says, recovering quickly. "Congratulations to you both."

"It's not really a congratulations situation," I clarify. "More like condolences."

Nikolai barks out a laugh while Valeria looks momentarily stunned. "My wife has an interesting sense of humor," he says, swatting my ass in warning. I flash him a sugary-sweet smile.

"We're here for Sofiya today, not me."

Valeria releases a nervous titter and then shifts her attention to me. "All right, Sofiya. What are you looking for?"

I shrug. "I only need a few things. The basics." What do I need to look good for? I don't leave the estate. As confident as Nikolai seems that Roman will cave to his deal, I know better. The Syndicate will find a way to get me out. Somehow. I hope.

Nikolai runs a finger down the center of his lips. "I thought you wanted to bankrupt me?"

I give a half shrug. "Can't be bothered."

"Oh, come on. Are you honestly going to give up that easily?" He cups my chin, meeting my gaze. "Go wild. Whatever you want—it's all yours. And trust me, nothing in here is cheap. Hell, buy two of everything just to piss me off."

I raise a brow. If he feels so strongly, I'm game.

"In that case." I cross my arms and glance at Valeria. "I need a whole new wardrobe. Head to toe. Your most luxurious pieces—cashmere, silk, suede. If it doesn't have a string of zeros on the price tag, don't bother showing it to me."

"Very good." Valeria reacts as though this is the most normal request she's ever heard. She steps back and gives me a thorough once-over as if taking my measurements by sight alone. With a bright smile, she claps her hands. "Why don't you head to the back fitting room? My staff and I will bring everything to you."

"That's fine. I'm happy to go through the racks on my own."

Valeria holds up a palm. "Absolutely not. You relax. It's my job to find you beautiful clothes."

"Thank you, Valeria. I'll show my wife to the fitting area," Nikolai says.

With a possessive hand on my lower back, he leads me through the luxurious store to a fitting area, where the walls are adorned with velvet wallpaper. The air is scented with expensive perfume, and one section is entirely covered in mirrors.

One of Valeria's assistants enters the room with snacks and champagne, offering both to us, but I wave her off, having eaten breakfast recently. They are obviously pulling out all the stops for Nikolai and his deep pockets.

I sink onto a cushioned bench, chewing on my thumbnail —a nervous habit I've never been able to kick. Nikolai, of course, notices. He leans in, gently pulls my nail from my mouth, and traps my hand in his. I try to tug it free, but his grip is firm and warm. God, his hands are so big.

"Such a bad habit," he scolds softly. "What's wrong?"

"Nothing."

He gives me a pointed look, the kind that says *don't bullshit me.*

"Fine. It's just… I don't want to be beholden to you. That's all. Don't get me wrong, I'd love to drain your bank account, but I'd rather do it by donating the money to charity or something."

He tilts his head, studying me. "I'll make you a deal. However much you spend here, I'll match it and donate the same amount to a charity of your choice."

"You're saying the more of your money I spend, the more good I'll be doing?"

"That's what I'm saying." His blue eyes gleam, and I hate how easily I lose focus when he looks at me like that. For once, he's not brooding or angry. He almost seems relaxed. Maybe that's why Yelena was so eager for him to take the day off.

"Fine," I tell him, stealing my hand back because it's a generous offer, and I'd be a jerk to turn it down. "Hope you don't come to regret that promise."

"I'm going to enjoy watching you spend my money more than you know." He grazes his fingertips along the side of my neck, letting them linger at my collarbone. Tingles explode at his touch. No matter how much I think I hate him, I don't hate his touch. "What cause would you like to donate to?"

I take a breath and try to focus, even though it's hard with his leg pressed firmly against mine. "Back in Moscow, I used to volunteer at this small dance school for underprivileged kids. The place was underfunded, understaffed, and barely holding on. The kids were so talented and so eager to learn—it broke my heart. Without that school, they'd never have had the chance to dance. It's an important cause. That's where I want the money to go."

He dips his chin. "Consider it done."

"Seriously?"

My pulse stumbles. With no hesitation or questions, he's willing to give money to a cause I care about. I look down at my hands, suddenly unsure of what to do with them.

I'm sure he only agreed because he wants me to spend freely, but the gesture still means something.

"Seriously," he repeats. "Now I want to know how come you haven't been dancing? There's plenty of room in my home."

"How do you know what I have or haven't been doing? Does Emil report everything I do to you?"

He shrugs and reaches for the champagne, pouring us each a glass. "I watch you sometimes through the security cameras."

My head snaps up. "You do what?"

"Don't play ignorant. You've been around bratvas long enough to know most homes have cameras everywhere."

"Yeah, but…" The words die out. He has a point, but the fact that he admitted to watching me is all kinds of fucked up. "Do you watch me in my bedroom? When I change? When I sleep?" My voice rises with every question that tumbles from my mouth.

"As tempting as that is, no." His fingers trail idly along the rim of his champagne glass. "Even men like me have limits. I respect your privacy in your room. But when you're in the library, the music room, or other common areas, it's fair game."

My fingers press against my temples. "What do you think I'm going to do? You have security everywhere, and I'm wearing an ankle monitor."

He chuckles, the sound a low ripple over my skin. "It's not about security. I like watching you. And if I'm honest, I was hoping to see you dance again."

"Again?"

"I was at your final recital. That's how I knew you were going to the club afterward."

"Oh my God. You were there?" Shock steals the air from my lungs. I don't know why I'm surprised. It actually makes sense.

His eyes soften. "Your dancing was… I don't have the right words for it. Beautiful, yes, but more than that. It was powerful. You were born to dance, moya sladost."

A sharp ache spreads through me, and I have to look away. His words unlock something fragile. But at the same time, he's the reason my career is nothing more than a shattered dream. "I don't dance in your home because it reminds me of everything I've lost. Of the future you stole from me."

Like Hades, he dragged me down into his world without warning. It's almost funny that the dance I choreographed turned out to be a preview of my own life.

A shadow crosses his expression. "You are my wife, Sofiya. I'll give you whatever you want. I'll fly in the best dance instructors in Russia or build you a studio worthy of the Bolshoi. Whatever you want, I'll make it happen."

I laugh softly, shaking my head. "Anything except freedom."

A muscle twitches in his cheek, but that's the only response I get before Valeria enters the room with two of her assistants, wheeling in rack after rack of designer clothes. But my brain is stuck on everything he just said. Does he truly care if I'm happy or is he trying to ease his own guilt?

Maybe this is his way of making peace with the fact that he stole my life. But why should I let him feel better about it? The idea of him building me a studio or flying in instructors is so absurd it almost makes me laugh. He's offering me the world, but not the one I wanted. The one I worked so hard for. And yet, there's a messed-up part of me that wants to believe he cares. Even a little.

"So, what do you think?" Valeria asks, pulling my attention toward her. She motions to everything laid out in front of me. It's not a few items like I imagined, but a ton of clothes. Dresses, evening gowns, casual clothes, coats, boots, blazers, heels, and accessories, including silk pajamas.

My eyes go wide. "I don't think I'll have time to try everything on."

Nikolai flicks his wrist toward the racks, his eyes glued to the phone in front of him. "Choose what you like, and we'll take it."

I like dressing up as much as the next girl, but I've always been on a budget. Even when my parents were trying to pretend we were still rich, I'd shop at the sample sales that designers held. Despite Roman and Liza's wealth, I never wanted to take advantage. A fashionable wardrobe was never high on my list of things to spend money on anyway.

But right now, it seems I have no choice. Oh well, it's for a good cause.

Four hours and a catered lunch later, I've tried on more clothes than I thought humanly possible. Valeria and her assistants have been tireless in their efforts to dress me, head to toe, for every occasion imaginable.

Each time I thought we were done, Valeria would waltz in with yet another must-have item I needed to consider. Everything is gorgeous, but I'm still holding out hope that I won't be around long enough to wear half of it.

Whenever I start to say it's too much, Nikolai casually reminds me how much money I'm raising for the dance school. He knows how to motivate me.

I thought he'd spend the day glued to his phone, doing whatever bratva bosses do, but instead, his focus has been entirely on me. It should have gotten under my skin, but it didn't. Every time he zipped up my dress or knelt to adjust the strap on my heel, I liked how his touch lingered. I like how he looks at me with unapologetic admiration and tells me when I look beautiful or sexy.

When was the last time any man other than Alex paid me a real compliment? It's been ages, and with Nikolai, I know he's not saying it to be polite. He means it.

And that realization terrifies me because hate and anger are all I have to keep him at arm's length. If I lose that armor, I'm in trouble.

I've tried on one last item, a slinky cocktail dress that caught my eye earlier. It's completely unnecessary—just like the silk lingerie sets, riding boots, and faux fur coats I know will probably end up collecting dust in the back of a closet.

I step out from behind the privacy screen and stand in front of the full-length mirror. The dress is stunning—it hugs my curves beautifully and is made from a sheer, emerald-green fabric. The plunging neckline and thigh-high slit practically dare anyone to look away. Nikolai will hate it because it shows a lot of skin, which makes it worth every penny.

Plus, it's for a good cause.

Nikolai stepped out of the fitting room a minute ago to take a call. I pop my head around the corner to find him pacing at the far end of the boutique, phone pressed to his ear. At the front of the store, Valeria and her assistants are busy packing up everything I'm buying, and given how generous I'm being with myself, it's a hell of a lot. Everything they didn't have on hand will be delivered to the estate later on.

I'm about to step back behind the privacy screen when something catches my eye on a side table tucked against the wall.

A phone.

Valeria's cell phone. My heart thumps wildly. She must have forgotten it here after she called one of her suppliers to ask about a pair of suede boots I was interested in.

I bite my lip, considering my options. The phone is probably locked, and Valeria is bound to notice it's missing, but she might not realize it was me who took it. And this could be my one and only chance to reach out to Liza and let her know I'm okay.

Screw it.

I dash across the room, and my fingers curl around the phone, lifting it off the table before I dart behind the privacy screen. Heat creeps up my neck. I don't even want to think about what Nikolai will do if he finds out what I've done, but I have to take the risk.

I shimmy out of the dress and pull on my jean shorts and

a floaty blouse I chose that I planned to wear home. Powering down the phone, I tuck it into the back of my waistband, right where Nikolai's men holster their guns. It's a snug fit, but the high-waisted shorts keep it secure.

"Did you want to take the dress?" Valeria's voice causes me to freeze in place. "We're all packed up at the front."

"Uh, yeah, that sounds great. I'll be out in a sec." I smooth down my clothes, praying there's no telltale bulge showing. As long as I'm careful to keep the blouse loose around me, it shouldn't be visible.

I'm on edge as I step out from behind the screen, clutching the dress. Please, God, don't let this be the moment she realizes her phone is gone. When I face her, she's smiling, dangling a pair of sparkly gold heels from her fingers.

"I thought these might work well with the last dress you tried on," she says, giving me a little wink.

"They sure will." I force a smile. "I'll take them."

"Perfect," Valeria chirps, clearly thrilled. "You're going to knock your husband's socks off, pairing that stunning gown with these sexy heels."

"Oh really," Nikolai's smoky voice cuts through the room. Both Valeria and I look up to find him leaning casually against the doorframe, his tattooed knuckles brushing along the edge of his jawline. His gaze is fixed on me. "Not so fast, wife."

What the hell does he know? A cold sweat breaks out along my spine. As I hold my breath, waiting for what he's going to say, Nikolai's lips curve into a slow, dangerous smile. "I think I'm going to need my own private fashion show at home for that dress and those heels."

Valeria laughs lightly while it feels like my throat is closing up. "In that case," she remarks, "please excuse me while I get the staff started on loading your car."

My nerves feel like live wires under my skin as Nikolai stalks toward me, slowly tucking a strand of hair behind my ears. "You have no idea what a tease it's been watching you try on clothes all day."

Instinctually, I step out of his reach. One wrong move, and he'd feel the phone stuffed into the waistband of my jean shorts. "I didn't mean for it to be," I say robotically.

His eyebrows pull together. "Everything okay?"

"Of course." I rub at my temples. "Only a headache. It's been a long day."

He tilts his head. "You did raise over three hundred thousand dollars for your efforts." When I don't respond, a shadow passes over his expression. "Let's go. I have painkillers in the car."

I nod and follow him out of the changing area. As I thank Valeria and the staff on the way out, my thoughts are already miles away. If I pull this off, I could be talking to Liza sooner than I ever imagined possible.

CHAPTER TWENTY

SOFIYA

THE CAR RIDE BACK TO THE ESTATE IS QUIET. NIKOLAI DOESN'T push me to talk. He offers me a painkiller, water, and his crumpled jacket, telling me to use it as a pillow.

I lean against the window, my eyes closed, inhaling the faint scent of his cologne, all the while wondering why I'm starting to feel safe with the man who could destroy me.

As soon as we get back to the estate, I tell Nikolai I'm going to lie down and dash to my bedroom, shutting the door behind me. I'm well aware that there are cameras in here, so I head into the bathroom instead and lock the door behind me.

Stepping into the shower, I huddle in the corner, trying to convince myself that even Nikolai wouldn't stoop to putting security cameras in here.

I pull the phone out of my shorts and stare at it. It's password-protected, but I'll find a way to break in, even if it takes all night. Once Valeria realizes it's gone, chances are she'll cut off service to her phone.

I tilt the phone under the light, searching for clues. Smudges on the screen catch my eye, hinting at the most-used areas. Carefully, I try a few combinations, tracing the patterns left behind. I hold my breath with each attempt, but none work. On the third try, the screen freezes. "Too many failed attempts. Locked for one minute."

"Shit," I mutter under my breath, pacing the room.

When the timer resets, I try the next obvious thing—generic PINs. "0000." Nothing. "1234." Still locked. I press my palms to my temples, frustration building.

I need another plan. A memory sparks, something I'd seen in a movie: a glitch involving emergency calls. It's a long shot, but at this point, I've got nothing to lose.

I tap the "Emergency Call" button and hold the power button, my pulse pounding in my ears. For a second, nothing happens. Then, the screen flickers, and the lock screen disappears.

My mouth falls open as the home screen loads.

I stare, breathless. "No way."

Blood pounds in my ears as I dial Liza's number. It hasn't been that long since I last saw her, and yet it feels like the Earth has shifted on its axis. Everything in my world has changed.

"*Privet*," she answers on the second ring, her voice cautious, maybe because of the unfamiliar number.

Hearing her voice stirs something inside me. "Liza, it's me."

"Sofiya!" A sob rips from her throat. "Oh my God, are you all right? Has he hurt you? The tattoo…" Her voice breaks.

Shit. Nikolai told them about the tattoo! A wave of heat rushes through me, chased by guilt because, if I'm honest, he didn't force it on me. Not that I wanted his mark, but I willingly played his game. Still, that's not a story she needs to hear.

"I'm okay. I promise it's not that bad," I assure her. I inhale, forcing the next words out. "And he hasn't hurt me... physically, at least."

What would Liza think if she saw me today, shopping with Nikolai? He insisted I buy half the store while promising to match every dollar in a donation to a charity of my choice. He's not a good man, but he might not be the monster I once thought either. He's lived through more than his fair share of pain and suffering, and there's nothing more human than that.

I don't know how to explain any of this to her because I can barely make sense of it myself. How would it sound if I defended Nikolai and told her he's not what he seems? Nikolai has caused her so much pain, but he's not the only one to blame. If I'd made different choices that night, maybe none of this would be happening.

"I'm so sorry," Liza gasps. "We should've protected you better. We should've… It doesn't matter now. The only thing that matters is getting you out of there. I need to get Roman. Please, don't go anywhere."

I press my back against the glass shower stall, gripping the phone tightly. Chaos erupts on the other end of the line. It sounds a lot like Roman shouting orders.

A second later, his husky voice comes through the phone. "Fuck, Sofiya. How are you holding up?"

He sounds as broken as my sister, and I hate that.

"I'm… I'm okay. I'm not locked up or anything. He doesn't bother me as long as I stay within the property limits."

"I'm going to get you out of there. My team is tracking your location through the signal from this call. Give it a few minutes, and we'll have your exact position."

"How are you calling us?" Liza asks, her voice tight with worry. "Is this safe?"

"I think so." I hope so.

"Don't worry. By tonight, I can have a team on-site to get you out of there."

Alarm races through me. "No, that's not a good idea! His

estate is heavily guarded. It would be a suicide mission even to try."

"And Sofiya could get hurt," Liza insists. "We can't take that chance."

Roman releases a deep sigh. "We have to try something. Sofiya, have you been able to explore? Is there anywhere on the property that isn't well monitored? Somewhere out of sight of the cameras and guards. I know it seems like a big deal, but we'll extract you quickly and get the fuck out of there."

"I—I don't know. Maybe. I'd have to look around more to figure that out for sure." I shake my head even though he can't see me. "Also, I have an ankle monitor. If I step off the property, he'll know immediately."

Roman's low curse is barely audible, but I can feel his frustration radiating through the line.

"It's not just me," I add quickly. "He's watching my friends, Alex and Daria. If I try anything, he'll go after them."

I feel terrible that this phone call alone could be putting my friends at risk if Nikolai discovers what I've done, but it's too late to dwell on that now.

"Don't stress about that. I'll keep your friends safe."

His assurance does little to ease the knot in my stomach. I'm willing to take risks with my life, but Alex and Daria don't deserve to be caught in the crossfire.

"Give me a minute," Roman says. I can't make out what's being said, but it sounds like there's some sort of argument. It takes a little while, but Roman finally comes back on the line. "We can't triangulate your location. He must have some kind of signal jammer."

My heart should sink, but instead, I feel an odd sense of relief.

"We need more time to figure this out. Can you call us back?"

"I'm not sure, but I'll try. Don't call or text this number."

Liza doesn't need to know I stole this phone or how risky it was. She has enough to worry about.

Roman cuts in. "Have you learned anything that might help us figure out where you are?"

I hesitate, but then share what I learned today. "Nikolai's estate is about half an hour from Koporye Fortress. I don't know in which direction. It used to belong to Catherine the Great's niece. The whole property is surrounded by woods, and I haven't seen any obvious landmarks."

"That's good. Leave it with us—we'll dig into it. In the meantime, look for a spot without cameras or heavy guard activity."

"Only if it's safe," Liza cuts in. "Don't put yourself in danger by sneaking around, Sofiya. Swear you won't."

It's a promise I can't keep, but I try to sound convincing to put Liza's mind at ease. "I won't, I swear." I swallow past a lump in my throat. "If I hadn't ditched Samuil to go to that club, things might have ended differently."

"You were trying to live a normal life. No one can hold that against you," Liza says gently.

I clutch the phone tighter. "Promise me you'll focus on your health and getting pregnant. Don't let this destroy your dreams. I want a baby for you and Roman."

Her tone carries a note of weariness. "I can't focus on anything else until you're safe and back with us."

I squeeze my eyes shut and tip my head back against the wall, searching for the right words.

"Nikolai isn't what you think. He hasn't abused me. He hasn't been cruel. I don't want to be here, but I'm not being tortured or anything. There's a music room with a fantastic old piano and a beautiful library. His housekeeper has been stuffing me with treats and—"

I stop myself.

Liza and Roman are silent for a beat, and I wonder what's happening on the other end of the line. They're probably exchanging a look, worried I have Stockholm Syndrome and I've lost touch with reality, and honestly, maybe I have. Do I sound crazy coming to the defense of my kidnapper? But I've seen another side of Nikolai, and it's confusing. He doesn't fit into the neat villain box I had ready for him.

It's Liza who finally speaks. "I'm glad to hear that. It does make me feel a little better."

"Roman, what if you gave in to Nikolai's demands? I'm sure if you negotiated with him, he'd let me go and grant me a divorce. Then we can all go back to living our normal life."

"Fuck, Sofiya, I wish it were that simple. What he's asking for is impossible. He wants access to our territory, and more than that, he wants the Zhukov Bratva to hold the same power and influence as the Syndicate. It would be like handing him a weapon to use against us."

"Of course. I understand," I murmur, and I do, but I feel a strange pull to defend Nikolai, even though I shouldn't.

"Focus on surviving. Stay on his good side and leave the rest to us," Roman assures me.

A sharp knock on my bedroom door freezes me in place. Oh shit!

"Someone is here," I whisper hurriedly. "I-I have to go."

"Be careful," Liza begs. "Only call when it's safe. We're here for you. We won't give up no matter what."

"I know, and I love you," I add, before hanging up.

Another hard knock has me scrambling to my feet. I shove the phone in the bathroom cabinet, hiding it behind a loofah scrub, before splashing water on my overheated face. "Give me a second," I call out.

Steeling myself, I take a deep breath in front of my bedroom door. This is it. Nikolai probably knows what I've done. My nails make little half-moons in my palms as I prepare to be dragged kicking and screaming to the dungeon.

CHAPTER TWENTY-ONE

NIKOLAI

The moment she opens the door, I know something's wrong. Sofiya stands there, pale and tense, her arms wrapped tightly around herself like they're the only thing holding her together.

"What happened? Are you okay?" My voice comes out hoarse, my chest tightening with worry. I step forward, reaching for her as she breaks into tears and I pull her into a protective hold.

Behind me, my men shift uncomfortably, their arms full of boutique bags. I glance over my shoulder, and with one hard glare, they get the picture and scatter without a word.

Inside, I guide her to the bed and sit her down before crouching in front of her. Her tear-streaked face is turned away, and I gently tilt her chin toward me with two fingers. "Sofiya. Are you sick? Is it the headache from earlier? I can call a doctor—"

"No." Her voice is hoarse. "It's not that. I was, uh… watching a sad movie."

I raise a brow. "A sad movie?"

She nods quickly, her eyes avoiding mine. She's lying—I can feel it in my gut. What I don't know is why.

"Something's bothering you. What is it?"

A shadow moves across her face. "I… I miss my sister."

I have an instinctive urge to close the distance between us. To take away her pain and sadness, comfort her, even though I'm the reason she was upset in the first place.

What did I expect? That she'd be thrilled to live here? That I could drag her into my world, and she'd simply accept it? I knew the moment I watched her dance that solo that there was a fire in her, a fighter who wouldn't give up easily.

Sofiya is a thorn lodged under my skin, impossible to ignore, no matter how much I try. Here I am ordering her the finest leotards, donating a ridiculous sum to her favorite charity.

What the hell am I doing? I've let myself soften. I've let her distract me, and it has to stop.

I stand, hardening my expression. "If the headache comes back, tell Yelena to call the doctor."

As I turn to leave, her eyes drop to the bag in my hand.

"Is that from Yumiko?"

No point denying it now. I pass her the bag without a word.

Before we left the boutique, I made Valeria track down the best dancewear money could buy. Somehow, she managed to source it all within hours, and one of my men picked it up.

Sofiya looks up at me, her eyes glassy, as she pulls each leotard from the bag one by one. She lays them carefully on the bed beside her—black with mesh panels, deep burgundy with delicate straps, and a shimmering dark green that catches the light. A pair of contemporary dance half-soles fall out next. Not that I know anything about dance shoes. Valeria thought they'd be helpful for Sofiya to have. Her fingers brush over the fabrics.

"I don't know what to say." Her gaze remains fixed on the leotards, and I can't read her expression.

I shrug, keeping my tone flat. "It's nothing."

As my sharp tone lingers in the quiet between us, I know my actions reveal way more than I'd like them to.

Her eyes shutter. "I'm not exactly going to take the dance world by storm while I'm held prisoner here."

"Whether you dance or not is not my concern. You have the leotards. Use them if you want to."

I storm from the room—annoyed at her but even more annoyed at myself for letting her get under my skin in the first place.

An hour later, I'm in my office, neck-deep in the endless shitstorm of paperwork that comes with running my empire, when there's a knock at the door.

"Come in," I say, still staring at my computer screen.

Emil steps inside, hesitating in the doorway. "Sorry to interrupt," he says. "Thought you'd want to know that Igor showed up unannounced. He just passed through the front gates."

My teeth clench as I sit back in my chair. My phone's been on silent all afternoon, and when I glance at it now, Igor's name flashes on the missed calls screen. He's the last person I want to see right now, and I'm irritated by how I left things with Sofiya earlier, but he's here, and I can't blow him off.

"I appreciate the heads-up." I nod at Emil in dismissal, but he doesn't step back.

"By the way, I meant to say thanks for letting me join the meeting with Igor earlier," Emil adds, shifting his weight. "It was valuable."

"Good," I say, distracted by Igor's surprise appearance. "Any idea what he's doing here right now?"

Emil shrugs. "I get the feeling he likes dealing with you directly."

I lean back in my chair, dragging a hand down my face. It's standard for my second-in-command to handle meetings I skip, but Igor is old school. He doesn't trust secondhand updates.

Heavy footsteps echo down the hallway. Emil straightens up as Igor's frame fills the doorway. He's built like a tank, his tailored gray suit doing nothing to soften the sharp lines of his shoulders.

"That'll be all, Emil," I say, standing to greet Igor. The two men exchange a brief, unreadable look before Emil nods and slips out, the door clicking shut behind him.

Igor strides toward me, unbuttoning his jacket with a deliberate tug as he crosses the room.

I round the desk and extend a hand. "I didn't realize you'd be stopping by tonight."

"A business matter has come up that requires an in-person discussion," Igor says, his tone edged. "And since I missed you earlier, I thought I'd drop by. Hope you don't mind."

"Not at all," I say, gesturing to a chair. "Sit. I'll pour us a drink."

Igor's calculating stare tracks me as I cross to the bar. "Busy day?"

I don't know what he's getting at, but I won't give him the satisfaction of riling me. "It was productive."

He sneers. "I was surprised to hear that you missed our meeting to take your wife on a shopping spree. Very unlike you."

Fucking Vadim and his big mouth.

I hold his stare, forcing a calm I don't feel. "Sofiya is an extension of me and my bratva. She's expected to look a certain way." My jaw tightens. "What's the business we need to discuss?" I ask, steering the conversation back on track.

I pass him a glass of brandy as we settle into the wingback

chairs in front of the fireplace. Igor raises the glass to his lips; his gaze is locked on mine as he takes a measured sip. "Our timeline has been moved up."

"What do you mean?"

"It means the minister wants to award the casino contract sooner than expected," he explains. "In the next three weeks."

"Well, that's fucking inconvenient," I snap, a wave of irritation building.

He leans back in his chair, his fingers drumming on the armrest. "It's been well over a week, and we've heard little from the Syndicate. It's time to apply more pressure on Roman to accept the deal. He's dragging his fucking feet because he thinks he can. We need to show him there are consequences for his inaction."

I swirl my drink, a bad feeling brewing. Igor hasn't spelled out how he expects us to bring the Syndicate to heel, but I know where this conversation is heading.

"Roman's not a man who admits defeat easily," I say, keeping my tone measured. "Don't forget, I know how the Syndicate operates. They need time to realize they're out of options and come to us. Trust me, I'll make sure they feel the pressure."

"How?"

My spine stiffens at the challenge in his voice. Igor may be powerful, but I'm the pakhan, and I don't take orders from anyone. I slam my palm on the table between us, making his whiskey glass rattle.

"You don't need to worry about the how," I bite out. "I said I'd handle it, and I will."

Igor's face hardens. "Will you? Because skipping meetings to take your wife shopping makes it seem like your focus is slipping."

"My focus isn't slipping," I grit out. "We just have different methods for getting results. You believe in the stick, but I see value in the carrot. Don't mistake that for weakness."

Igor reaches for his drink as he stares into the roaring fire. "I think we both know that sticks are more effective in the world we operate in. The Syndicate needs to see how brutal you can be. How much Sofiya is suffering at your hands. They need to be desperate—willing to do anything to end her misery."

Tension lines my shoulders, lodging at the base of my neck. Roman blew a gasket when I sent him the pictures of Sofiya marked with my tattoo, and that was child's play. Igor is right. Hurting her would set things in motion, but it would also have far-reaching consequences. More than that, the thought of causing her pain makes my stomach churn with disgust.

I grip the glass so tightly I'm surprised it doesn't crack under the pressure. "We need to be fucking smart about this. We're proposing a partnership with the Syndicate. If we abuse Sofiya more than we already have, when the time comes, they'll seek revenge."

"It won't matter. By the time they make their move, we will be untouchable." His tone goes cold. "If you can't do it, I will."

"You will not fucking touch her," I growl.

My eyes scan the room, looking for anything I could turn into a weapon. If he so much as looks at Sofiya the wrong way, I'll make him regret it. He doesn't deserve to breathe the same air as her.

A knock at the door interrupts the standoff. No one on my staff would dare disturb me during a meeting.

"Nikolai? Are you in there?"

Fuck. It's Sofiya. The universe must be laughing at me right now.

Unease anchors itself in my chest. The last thing I wanted

is for Igor to see how protective I've become of her, but I've done a shitty job hiding it.

"This is a bad time," I snap, hoping she'll scurry off.

Igor's fingers drum lazily against the armrest, his expression smug. "Not at all. Please invite her in. I'd like to meet your wife."

"Come in, Sofiya," I say eventually.

The door creaks open, and she steps inside, wearing the black leotard with mesh panels and a low scooped neckline that shows off her round breasts. I drag a full breath into my lungs to keep my reaction in check.

Sofiya's eyes widen as she realizes I'm not alone. She hesitates, looking to me for reassurance. "Oh, I'm sorry to interrupt. I wanted to say thank you for the leotard. It fits perfectly. I'll be on my wa—"

"It's no problem. We're finished here," Igor cuts in, rising from his seat. His gaze sweeps over her, lingering far too long. The way he drinks her in from head to toe sets my nerves on fire. "Are you going to introduce me, Nikolai?"

My blood turns cold. I clear my throat and force a mask of disinterest. "Sofiya, this is Igor Bocharov, the senior advisor to the minister of finance and an associate of mine."

Sofiya offers him a reserved smile. "Nice to meet you, Mr. Bocharov."

She extends her hand, and Igor seizes the opportunity. Instead of a quick shake, he lifts her hand to his lips and presses a slow, deliberate kiss to the back of it.

Her body stiffens at the contact. Not for the first time tonight, I regret not having a gun tucked into my waistband.

"Please, call me Igor. We've actually met before. In Moscow a few years ago. I was having dinner with some associates, and you were at the next table with your sister, her husband, and the mighty Maxim Belov and his wife, Kira."

Sofiya frowns, shaking her head. "I'm sorry, I don't remember that."

Igor chuckles, the sound predatory to my ears. "It was a brief encounter. I only stopped by to say hello to Maxim. You were very young then. I'm sure an old man like me wouldn't have left much of an impression."

I can't take it anymore. My patience snaps. "Go upstairs, Sofiya. I'm in a meeting."

Her eyes flick to mine, a hint of hurt in her expression, but this is for her own good.

"Good night, Sofiya," Igor purrs. "I look forward to seeing you again."

"Uh, you too." Sofiya licks her lips nervously as she backs out of the room. My molars press together. I wish like hell she hadn't come down here at all, and most definitely not wearing that.

The door clicks shut, and Igor turns to me, his face tight with disdain. "Buying her clothes to dance in, letting her roam freely around your house. Is that the kind of carrot you prefer to use?"

The weight in the room feels like a live wire, humming with unspoken threats. Igor and I have always agreed on one thing—you do what's necessary to secure money and power. You annihilate anyone standing in your way.

Right now, I don't give a shit about any of that. Primal need thrums through me to protect Sofiya, making me want to tear Igor limb from limb.

He places a hand on my shoulder, squeezing hard enough to make his point. "Use her," he insists. "Bring the Syndicate to its knees. You should be the most powerful pakhan in Russia—not Maxim Belov or Roman Vasiliev."

With that, he walks out of the room, a suffocating silence taking his place.

After Igor leaves, I grab the keys to the Bugatti and go for a long drive.

Pushing the car through tight bends at breakneck speeds is the only way to ease the weight crushing my chest. Igor's words won't stop echoing in my head—his accusation that the Syndicate isn't coming to heel fast enough, that I've gone soft because of Sofiya.

The worst part is he's not wrong.

She's fucked with my head, and it's up to me to screw it back on straight.

I might feel a scrap of something for my wife, but it doesn't change a damn thing. At the end of the day, I know all too well what happens when you care about someone so deeply that you give them everything—your freedom, your trust, your love, and your protection. They stab you in the back, leaving you bleeding and broken.

I won't make that mistake again.

I'll do whatever is necessary to bring the Syndicate in line. I have to prove to myself that I still have the edge and that I can be ruthless when I need to be.

Sofiya is a pawn, and I'll use her as one if that's what it takes to win.

I pull up in front of the house, slamming the car door behind me. Inside, I take the stairs two at a time. A voice in the back of my mind warns me that I can't be trusted right now. That I'm only going to do something I will regret later.

It's the middle of the night, and I'm not in a good place. I should go to the strip club and find someone to fuck, to take out all this dark, churning energy inside me.

But no one else will do.

CHAPTER TWENTY-TWO

SOFIYA

"Wake up, Sofiya."

Nikolai's harsh tone slices through the fog of sleep, yanking me awake.

Not this shit again.

I stare up at him, taking in his disheveled appearance. He's still dressed in today's clothes, his hair mussed, shadows under his eyes.

What could this be about? Does he know about the phone call to Roman and Liza? A sick knot forms in my stomach.

I push myself into a sitting position, my whole body tense. "What do you want?" I ask warily. "Have you been drinking?"

Nikolai exhales and rakes a hand through his hair. "I haven't had a drink in hours. This is about lighting a fire under your brother-in-law's ass. He has to see what his indecision is costing you."

His words send a chill through me. "Why… why now?" I whisper, my throat tightening.

He grabs my chin and angles my face to meet his stony

one. "Because I am sick of waiting, Sofiya. If using you is the only way to get a message to the Syndicate, so be it."

The edge in his voice sends a tremor through me. Something triggered this, but at least he hasn't mentioned Valeria's cell phone. If he knew I stole it, he'd say so.

My thoughts drift back to Igor Bocharov's visit earlier tonight. Nikolai seemed so tense. Could this have to do with me interrupting his meeting? It was stupid of me to go down to Nikolai's office wearing a leotard. I only wanted to thank him for the gifts. Roman told me to stay on his good side, after all.

"I'm sorry I interrupted your meeti—"

He shakes his head. "I'm not looking for apologies. I'm looking for you to come with me."

His eyes stay locked on mine as he yanks the covers off me. I perch at the edge of the bed but refuse to rise and join him. If he's going to act like this, he at least has to tell me my fate.

I hug myself tightly, acutely aware of how exposed I am in just a thin nightgown. "What are you going to do to me?"

He doesn't respond but continues to stand over me, his expression flat. For all he's trying to block me out, I see his hesitation. It's like he's forcing himself to play a role, and all I can do is try to get through to him before he does something terrible.

I push myself onto my knees and trail my fingers over the smattering of dark hair on his chest. His eyes squeeze shut, his body rigid under my touch. "Look at me… Look at me!" I demand, and he does, his eyes wary. "I don't think you want to hurt me, Nikolai."

Anyone from the outside might call me insane, but I mean every word. He's trying to prove something to himself, but it's costing him. His eyes drop to where my hand lingers, his breath faltering.

Then he blinks, and his expression goes flat once again. He grabs my wrist, pushing my hand away.

"I can carry you downstairs, or you can walk, but either way, you're coming with me."

"Don't do this," I plead. "It won't make a difference. The Syndicate will do what's best for the Syndicate. Roman isn't the only voice that matters."

He shakes his head, brushing me off, and moves to pick me up, but I hold up a hand to stop him. Been there, done that, and I'd rather walk on my own, my head held high. Some part of me still hopes I can reach him. He hasn't crossed a line—yet.

I don't fight. Sliding off the bed, I follow him down the stairs to the basement. The air feels heavier here, wrapping around me like a warning. Goosebumps ripple over my arms, though I'm not sure whether it's from the temperature or my nerves.

At the end of a hallway, he pushes open a heavy metal door to reveal a dank, dimly lit room with a single chair in the center, chains dangling from its arms. When he gestures to it, a heavy knot forms in my gut.

Maybe I was wrong. Maybe I misjudged what he's capable of.

I start to tremble and back away from him until I hit the wall. I scan the room for a weapon, anything to fight him off, but I come up empty, and there's no way I can overpower him.

"Sit," he orders.

I swallow hard, my throat like sandpaper, as I shake my head.

"I said sit." His voice is lower this time, and he wraps a hand around my arm and forces me into the chair. Saying nothing, he crouches before me, his warm fingers brushing over my wrists.

"Please don't," I whisper, tears pooling in my eyes. I look

up at the ceiling, trying to prepare myself for the cold bite of chains. But instead, I feel something soft and smooth wrapping around my wrists. When I glance down, I see he's tying my forearms to the chair with silk rope.

I barely have time to wonder why before Nikolai steps back, his hooded eyes sweeping over me like he's savoring every detail. His tongue grazes his bottom lip, and a slow smile curves across his face.

Without breaking eye contact, he shrugs out of his shirt, letting it fall carelessly to the floor. Reluctantly, I take in his sculpted shoulders, chiseled pecs, and a light trail of hair that disappears into fitted black pants that hang low on his hips. With his black hair and light eyes, he reminds me of Hades come to life.

"Bound and ready for me," he drawls. "I think I like you like this, Sofiya."

I ignore the implication in his words as he moves behind me. Metal gleams in the periphery of my vision. My stomach knots, and I press back against the chair, frozen as the blade comes into view.

The knife grazes my throat, my pulse thundering beneath it. His hand is steady as it trails lower, skimming over my collarbone before sliding down between the swell of my cleavage. I tense, and a small cry escapes between my lips.

What is he willing to do to me? How far is he willing to go?

The weapon only brushes against me, a whisper of threat, but I know he wants my family to see this. To see my fear and imagine my pain.

Somewhere in this room, I bet a camera is capturing everything, and I refuse to give him the satisfaction of breaking.

The blade lingers at the curve of my breast, its sharp edge pressing into me. With deliberate precision, he drags it upward, teasing my nipple until a whimper catches in my throat.

He lets the metal travel down again, following the rapid rise and fall of my breath, tracing over the dip of my waist and teasing the edge of my hip before gliding back between my breasts. Each calculated touch is an exercise in control, like he's soaking up my reaction, and no matter how much I try, I can't hide the trembling of my body.

The air grows heavier, and I can't tell where my fear ends and this unwanted desire begins. My body betrays me—a subtle arch, a sharp inhale, goosebumps rising in the knife's wake. His eyes flick down and darken, noticing everything.

"You like the danger," he murmurs, the sharp edge grazing my breast again. "It excites you."

"You're wrong," I gasp.

"Am I?" His eyes glint with challenge before he leans in, his tongue blazing a path along my throat—a contrast to the sharp edge tracing my flesh. He lingers, tasting me as though he has all the time in the world.

My nipples tighten into aching peaks, and I squeeze my legs together to ease the need building between my thighs. It's useless. Nikolai knows what he's doing; knows exactly how to make my body burn for him.

The point of the knife catches the neckline of my nightgown, slowly dragging the fabric down. My breath catches as the cool metal teases my skin, exposing me inch by inch. My nipples are impossibly hard, aching under his gaze. His tongue darts out, wetting his lips, and his low hum of approval sends heat pooling deep in my core.

"Shit. I think I need a taste of you," he grits out.

He lowers his head, and his mouth closes over one of my stiff peaks. My thoughts dissolve, the feel of his hot mouth all-consuming. My head falls back, the silk bindings biting into my forearms, each rough scrape against my skin only heightening my need. I'm drowning in sensation, powerless against the pull of him.

A little voice breaks through. I can't let this go further. I can't lose myself to him, not when he's using me to send a message to my family.

"Nikolai," I say shakily, my body at war with my mind. "Stop."

He stills, studying me.

I don't know where I find the courage to test him, but I do.

Slowly, I tilt my chin up, baring my throat. "If this is the only way for you to get your message across, then hurt me. I'd rather they see my pain than my pleasure."

With a glower, he slides his hand into my hair, twisting it tight until my neck bows, leaving me utterly vulnerable to him. I brace myself, expecting the sharp kiss of steel against my throat. Instead, his warm lips trace a path down my neck.

"Do you really think I could hurt you, moya sladost?" he asks, his warm breath ghosting across my sensitive skin.

"I don't know what you're capable of right now."

"Then let me show you."

In one fluid motion, the blade slices through the front of my nightgown. He yanks the fabric apart, exposing my bare breasts and the wet heat between my thighs to the room's chill.

Dropping to his knees, he pushes my legs apart and presses the handle of the knife inside me, sliding it deep and filling me completely.

CHAPTER TWENTY-THREE

NIKOLAI

Her body surrenders to me as I slip the handle of the knife inside her tight cunt, dragging it along a sensitive spot that makes her gasp. Slick with need, she clenches around it. I press my thumb against her clit, rubbing it in tight circles, relishing the way she squirms, her hips rocking forward. A sound between a sob and a moan escapes her.

I knew I'd never be able to go through with it. The idea of making her scream, of causing her any kind of pain, makes me feel physically ill.

When she put her small hand on my chest and said, "I don't think you want to hurt me," I knew she could see through my lies.

She was right.

But I still have a job to do. If I can't show Roman the real thing, I'll give him something that looks just as convincing.

Right now, Roman, the Syndicate, and the casinos are far from my mind. The only thing I care about is making her come so hard she sees stars.

Her head is thrown back, and from my vantage point

between her legs, I can see her beautiful pussy flutter around the handle with every stroke inside her. When she starts to lose herself, I pull it out, leaving her empty.

She whimpers, her lips parting in protest, but I don't give her what she wants. Instead, I run my tongue over the length of the ivory handle, teasing her, watching as her chest heaves with frustration and need.

"God, you taste good," I rasp. Leaning forward, I graze my teeth over the soft curve of her neck. Her breath hitches as I trail my lips up to her ear. "I love having you at my mercy. Desperate to come."

The sight of Sofiya, bound and exposed, her flushed skin glowing under the dim light, is more intoxicating than I could've dreamed. Her dusky nipples are tight, begging for my attention. I carefully work the knife's handle back inside her, moving with slow, deliberate strokes as my mouth trails along her collarbone, savoring the warmth of her skin beneath my lips.

"Nikolai." Her voice is hoarse, a warning, but I don't stop. I thrust the handle into her pussy again and again, watching the way she reacts, entirely at my mercy.

"You've been such a good girl, playing along so beautifully. I think you've earned a reward."

Her wide eyes meet mine as I spread her thighs wider, enjoying the way she gasps, every inch of her exposed to me. Her sex glistens, the intoxicating scent of her arousal filling my nostrils. It makes me fucking light-headed.

"You're perfect, Sofiya," I murmur, my voice thick with lust. "And you're mine."

"Nikolai," Sofiya whimpers. "Please…"

"Please, what?" I blow against her slick folds, my lips brushing close enough to make her thighs quiver.

She lets out a broken moan, her hips lifting in silent desperation. A low chuckle escapes me as I press a teasing kiss to her inner thigh. "Use those pretty lips to tell me what you need, or I'll have to find another way to occupy that mouth."

"I-I need your tongue on me."

My fingers curl carefully around the flat side of the blade, avoiding the sharp edge as I ease the ivory handle back into her slick pussy. Her wetness coats it, each slow thrust making her moan louder.

A groan escapes me as I lower my head, my lips finding her swollen clit. Her musky flavor explodes on my tongue, consuming me completely. I feast on her like I'll never get enough, her cries only spurring me on.

Her body tightens as I pull the knife free, replacing it with my tongue, plunging deep into her soaked heat. My hands grip her thighs, holding her steady as she bucks against my face.

"You taste like fucking heaven," I growl, my lips wet with her arousal. "So sweet. So perfect." Sofiya's head thrashes, incoherent pleas spilling from her lips. Her nails dig into the arms of the chair, and her legs quiver with need as her hips move wildly, chasing her release.

The sight of her coming apart makes my cock ache. I press my palm against the bulge, rubbing myself through the fabric to relieve the pressure, but it's not enough. Nothing will be enough until I bury myself inside her again.

I slide the handle back into her tight cunt, pumping it in rhythm with the circles of my tongue. Her cries grow louder, her thighs quaking as I tease her. There's a sick satisfaction in knowing that she's letting go despite herself, that I drive her so wild she can't resist.

"Oh God, oh fuck. Don't stop—I'm so close!"

She writhes, her wetness dripping down my chin as the sounds of her pleasure fill the room. Replacing the knife with my fingers, I curl them inside her, pressing into that perfect spot that makes her buck violently, turning her cries into screams.

"Let go for me," I order. "Come on my tongue, Sofiya. Soak me."

As if she's been waiting for permission, her climax crashes over her. She convulses with a broken sob, and her walls clamp down on my fingers as her release gushes over my hand and chin. I lap up every drop like it's the finest nectar, growling my approval against her sweet pussy.

Sofiya goes limp, and I place gentle kisses along her drenched seam, soothing her through the comedown. My blood burns, every inch of me on edge because I've never felt anything this fucking intense. I've had more women than I can count, but none of them ever made me burn like this—no one but her. Since she came back into my life, I haven't been able to touch anyone else. I don't even want to.

When the last spasm fades, I withdraw my fingers, bringing them to my lips. Holding her dazed stare, I lick them clean. My cock is iron-hard and leaking, but this moment isn't about me. Not yet.

She hesitates, her eyes darting around the room, lingering on the hard cement floor stained with the memories of blood and broken men. Then, her gaze shifts to the glowing red light of the camera mounted on the wall behind me.

Hurt flashes across her face. "What? You couldn't torture me, so you're going to send my family pictures of you seducing me?"

She's right. That was my plan, but something feral and possessive flares in my veins at the thought of anyone else seeing her naked, vulnerable, and losing control.

Crouched in front of her, I grip her chin firmly, forcing her to look at me. "Do you think I'd let anyone else see what's mine, moya sladost? Your pleasure, your pain, your body and soul—belong to me, your husband."

Her lashes lower, a war of emotions playing across her face. She's torn between the magnetic pull between us and resentment for how I'm blackmailing her family.

I trail a thumb across her bottom lip. "The only thing your family will see is images of the blade dragging along your clothed body," I add, because no one but me will ever see her naked again.

I'll choose a few stills from the video footage, one that captures just enough fear in her expression to leave them wondering what kind of hell I've put her through. But I won't think about that right now.

I crash my mouth onto hers, claiming her lips all over again. Her tongue tangles with mine in a dance that makes my blood surge.

My fingers slide back into her drenched pussy, her soft whimpers against my mouth feeding my obsession. I'm desperate to bury myself inside her, to feel her come apart for me again, but when she pulls back, I know the spell is broken.

Her eyes flutter open, and her expression cuts through me like a blade, vulnerable and filled with something close to regret. "Nikolai," she whispers, her voice thick. "Let me go… please."

Please. That one word slices through me, leaving me off balance. I fight the instinct to tighten my hold on her. Forcing her to stay would destroy what little remains of the fragile connection between us.

Gritting my teeth, I slash through the ropes binding her wrists, grab my discarded shirt from the floor, and give it to her. "Put this on and leave." My voice is rough with emotions I don't want to name.

Her fingers clutch the fabric as she hesitates, her gaze lingering on me for the briefest moment before she slips the shirt over her shoulders. With that, she turns and rushes out, her bare feet silent against the cold floor. She doesn't look back, and I don't stop her.

SOFIYA

I race back to my room, Nikolai's shirt clutched tight around me. My heart pounds like it's trying to escape my chest.

In the bathroom, I wash my face before staring into the mirror. My reflection looks the same, but everything feels different. What just happened, and why the hell did I like it so much?

Nikolai couldn't hurt me, but he's left something worse—marks on my soul. Shame clings to me every time I think about how I let him seduce me. I promised Roman and Liza I'd find a way out of this, but instead, I've done the opposite. I've fallen under his spell, his touch so damn addictive that it drowns out every warning in my mind.

I know he's using me to manipulate the Syndicate, but I still can't resist him. He's a craving I can't deny, no matter how much I hate myself for giving in.

What will Roman and Liza think when they see those images of a knife near my throat? They'll be distraught.

Sinking to my knees, I fish Valeria's phone out from its hiding spot. A wave of relief washes over me when the screen lights up and the battery is still over half full. The signal bars are steady, which means Valeria hasn't canceled her service yet. It doesn't make sense—surely she knows it's missing by now. Unless she assumes she misplaced it and is waiting for it to turn up. Either way, I'll count it as a lucky break.

Messages and missed calls from Valeria's contacts flood the screen, but there's nothing from Liza. I didn't expect there to be—she's smart enough to know the risk. Still, I need to let her know I'm okay. Quickly, I type out a message:

> Me: Any pictures Nikolai sends are staged. He never hurt or tortured me, but he wants you to think he did. I promise I'm OK. No updates yet, but I'm still looking. I'll reach out when the time is right. Turning off the phone now to save battery.

I stare at the words for a long time before hitting send. I hope she believes me, and I hope it gives her some peace.

With a sigh, I power the phone down and tuck it away. My relief fades quickly, drowned out by a wave of sorrow. Because what I didn't tell her is the worst of my lies: that I'm starting to fall for my captor.

I step into the shower, letting the hot spray cascade over my skin. Steam fogs the air, curling around me as the water streams over my body. I tilt my head back, closing my eyes, but there's no escaping the images playing behind my eyelids: Nikolai in the basement—his dominance, his control, the way he unraveled me so completely I could barely breathe.

My hand drifts down, brushing over my stomach and lower, chasing the heat building inside me. My fingers find the place he claimed, and I bite my lip as I circle my clit, teasing the sensitive bundle of nerves.

I press my forehead against the cool tile, my breath coming in shallow pants. I shouldn't be thinking about him, but the memory of his soft mouth and the hard drag of the knife's handle drives me closer to the edge.

My hips rock forward, and a whimper of need escapes my lips as my fingers slip inside my channel. I'm still a little tender from where the smooth ivory penetrated me, but it's a good sore—the kind that heightens sensation.

I work my fingers deeper, my thumb brushing my clit. I bite down on my lip, suppressing a cry as I replay everything that happened earlier. The feel of the blade's handle, the forbidden edge of what he did—it should have scared me, but it didn't. It thrilled me.

I always thought I was vanilla, boring even, but Nikolai makes me want things I never knew existed. Things I should hate. A shudder wracks my body, my hips grinding into my hand until I'm lost to the crashing waves of pleasure.

When it's over, I lean back against the wall, my chest heaving and my head spinning.

I hate that I let him consume me like this. More than that, I hate how much I want him to do it again.

CHAPTER TWENTY-FOUR

NIKOLAI

I've done many fucked-up things in my life. I've spilled blood, betrayed loyalties, and killed my own brother without a shred of regret. But somehow, using Sofiya like I did weighs on me like a sin I'll never be rid of.

After the basement, I sent Roman the pictures of her, the knife grazing the delicate skin of her throat, the curated terror etched into her features. Such a perfect lie. They'll light a fire under the Syndicate's ass as Igor said they would, but it comes at a cost.

I've been holed up in my office all day, haunted by the memory of how fucking good Sofiya tastes, how beautifully she came apart for me despite herself.

But when she looks at me like I'm breaking her, it feels like she's breaking me, too.

My phone buzzes, and Roman's name flashes across my screen. Fuck me. I knew this call was coming, but for some reason, I was dreading what he might say. The deal he might offer.

"Roman. Just the man I was looking forward to hearing from," I lie.

"You sick fuck," he growls, his tone deadly. "Do you think this is a fucking game? Do you know what I'm going to do to you the first chance I get?"

"Nothing because I have the power here. Now get to the point of this call because I have shit to do."

He huffs out a harsh breath. "This needs to end now. We are ready to make a deal."

The satisfaction I expected to feel at this moment is nowhere to be found. Instead, my pulse hammers, and something uneasy twists in my gut. I know where he's headed with this.

"The Syndicate will allow you to open a casino on our territory, but only on the condition that you give Sofiya back, grant her a divorce, annul the marriage—whatever it takes to erase your claim on her. Never fucking think of her again, never even say her name. She'll be dead to you."

I go still, my fingers digging into the leather of my chair. He's agreeing to my terms. It's what I wanted—except it's not what I want at all.

My eyes track to the clock on the wall, the same one Sofiya used to count the seconds to her orgasm. I'm in the room where I inked her ring finger. I know what I'm supposed to do, but the thought of losing her feels like losing the last shred of my soul.

"No."

There's silence on the other end. Angry silence.

"What the fuck do you mean, no?"

"I need a guarantee that you'll follow through. Words aren't enough. I won't give up Sofiya until I know you won't renege on the deal the second I hand her over."

"Are you fucking serious? I'm a man of my word. You're the one who's the goddamn traitor."

"Forgive me if trust isn't my strong suit. Call me when you've got proof you won't stab me in the back."

"Fu—"

I end the call and whip my phone at the wall, disgusted with myself.

Sofiya was never supposed to be my wife, never supposed to be mine forever. But she's etched into me like a brand, a fire that refuses to die, and until it does, I won't give her back.

I run my thumb across my lips. Everything I've worked for is hanging by a thread. But I can't find it in me to care right now. Not if it means I get to keep Sofiya for a little while longer.

I pull into the desolate lot, headlights slicing through the darkness. Igor is already waiting near his black SUV, the cherry of his cigarette glowing faintly in the night.

I sit for a moment, fingers drumming on the steering wheel, watching him. There's a tightness in my chest, a sense of foreboding I can't ignore. Reaching into the center console, I pull out my gun and slide it into my waistband. I've never needed one for our meetings before, but something tells me this conversation could go south.

I step out. The warm air feels heavy as I make my way across the cracked asphalt. His guards stand off to the side, chatting and puffing on their cigarettes as the stench of piss and stale beer wafts from the dumpster nearby.

With his pristine suit and shiny patent leather shoes, Igor looks out of place—too clean for the grime of the city's underbelly. Being seen with me wouldn't do his reputation any favors, so we meet far from prying eyes.

As I approach, the sharp angles of his face soften with a smile. He looks too pleased, and I'm sure it has something to do with the picture I sent to Roman.

"You did good," he says, clapping a hand on my shoulder. "You fucking showed the Syndicate what you're made of with those pictures. Roman and the rest of those bastards will be eating out of your hand in no time."

My stomach churns. He has no idea her pain in those pictures is fake, but it's the delight he seems to be taking in it that makes me want to pummel his face. It's like he wants to punish her for her family ties.

"Save your applause until I've told you the full story," I say, pulling back from his touch. "Roman called me earlier ready to make a deal, and I turned him down."

He pauses mid-drag, his expression tightening. "Why did you do that?"

I drag a hand over my jawline, forcing myself to hold his gaze. "Because I don't trust them to keep their word. Once Sofiya's back in their hands, there's nothing stopping them from turning on us. We need real fucking guarantees before we give her up."

Igor shrugs. "You're mobsters. Deals are settled with a gentleman's handshake, not a fucking legal document. What kind of guarantee are you expecting from them?"

"Something more binding than a handshake. Why should we trust their word and give up our leverage?"

My logic is sound, even if it's kind of bullshit.

Igor cracks his neck, a scowl settling on his face. "I understand, but we're running out of time," he growls. "I have the minister up my ass asking when we can lock this deal down. You need to make them desperate, willing to do anything. A video of a night in my cage should do the trick."

My hand moves before my brain can catch up, pulling the gun from my waistband and pressing the barrel firmly under Igor's jaw. His head tilts back, his mouth tightening, and the cigarette falls from his lips. It bounces once on the asphalt before rolling to a stop, the smoke curling faintly upward.

Igor's guards tense, their hands twitching toward their

holsters, but none of them actually do anything. They know me too well. They know I'm not bluffing.

My jaw tightens, every muscle in my body tense. I've never been more ready to pull the trigger.

"Not going to fucking happen," I hiss, my voice razor-sharp. "Let me set you straight. I'm the pakhan, and I decide what happens. There's no way in hell I'd let you touch a hair on her head. She's my wife. Mine. And I won't let anyone, including you, hurt her."

Igor's Adam's apple bobs as he tries to hold my gaze.

"C'mon, Niko," he pleads. He raises his hands, palms facing me, like he's trying to settle a spooked animal. "Look, you've grown attached to her. I get that. We all get that." He takes a half-step back, his eyes darting to my hand, still gripping the gun. "But everything you've worked for since Sergey is right there, ready for the taking. See this through, do what needs to be done, and the Syndicate will fall in line. We'll control all the casinos that matter in Russia. The money, the connections, the political sway—they'll all be ours. Don't you want that?"

I relax my grip on the pistol, slowly stepping back and lowering it into my waistband.

Do I want that? I've spent years clawing my way to the top of organized crime in Russia, convinced power was everything. I thought it would fill the hollow spaces inside me and make me untouchable, but it hasn't. The only thing that feels real and good, the only thing that might make life worth something, is Sofiya. But Igor's not the man to share this with.

"Of course, I do," I grit out. "I want all of it. But not if it means hurting her. I won't cross that line again."

Igor adjusts his collar, his hands dropping to his sides. "It's normal to feel something for a pretty girl, especially when she's been in your bed. But when Roman senses your weakness, he'll go for the jugular, and you'll lose a lot more than this deal." He steps forward, clapping a hand on my shoulder. "Think about what I said."

He turns and walks toward his vehicle, his guards trailing behind him.

That night, I'm sitting in my office, a bottle of whiskey half-empty on the desk, the room cloaked in shadows except for the faint glow of the desk lamp. I'm well on my way to getting drunk—the booze warming my throat but doing nothing to quiet my mind.

A rough laugh peals from my throat. Today was a fucking disaster. I turned down the Syndicate deal and threatened Igor with a gun for suggesting I use Sofiya for the pawn she was always intended to be.

But fuck, the way his words made me see red. He may not like it, but he'll have to deal with it. No one is laying a hand on her—not him, not me, not anyone.

A knock at the door cuts through the silence, and I sigh, dragging my hand over my face. The last thing I need right now is company.

"Not looking for a drinking buddy," I call out, hoping my sharp tone scares away whoever wants my attention.

The door creaks open, and Emil steps inside, his hands raised. "It's only me."

"Come in." I sigh. "Want a drink?"

He shakes his head. "Nah, I'm good. Eva wanted me to let you know the plane is scheduled to take off first thing tomorrow."

Fuck me. I nearly forgot about our trip to the Caucasus region to meet with the people we do business with—arms distributors, cartel representatives, mercenaries.

Emil steps forward, clearing his throat. "Would you consider letting me come along? I'd like to get experience dealing with arms negotiations and could back you up if things get tense."

I set the empty glass on the desk and meet his gaze. "No. I need you here keeping an eye on Sofiya."

His mouth tightens. "Can't Matvey or one of the others handle it? We've never had trouble at the estate, and I want to do something that matters—not just stand around waiting for nothing to happen."

"I said no," I grit out, tired of the pushback. "And you're not standing around. You're guarding my wife."

He opens his mouth, ready to fight me on this, but I pin him with a sharp glare. His expression tightens, and he nods. "Understood."

I let out a slow breath and even my tone. "Next time. I haven't forgotten what you've asked for."

"Sure," he says, already turning toward the door.

As he leaves, I roll my shoulders, trying to shake off the weight of too many demands and the nagging feeling that I'm losing control.

CHAPTER TWENTY-FIVE

SOFIYA

Days pass, and I don't see Nikolai. In fact, I don't see anyone because I stay in my room, feigning illness. Yelena checks on me regularly, bringing meals, doting on me like a worried mother hen. She's the one who mentions that Nikolai is out of town.

I didn't want to face him; my emotions were a tangled mess I couldn't begin to unravel. Knowing he's not in the house so I won't accidentally bump into him gives me the courage to finally leave my room.

After I shower and dress, I head down to the library, hoping to find something that will help me figure out where I am. If this estate was once owned by Catherine the Great's niece, it must have some sort of history recorded. If I can pinpoint its location, I can pass those details on to Roman.

The library is as grand as the rest of the estate, with shelves stretching high and packed with books that smell of leather and dust. I trail my fingers along the spines, reading the faded titles.

A collection of Russian historical volumes catches my eye,

their worn spines embossed with gold. I pull down a book on imperial estates and then another on notable Russian families. One by one, I gather a small stack and settle into a plush chair by the window.

Hours tick by as I sift through the books, cross-referencing passages and hunting for anything useful. All I uncover are vague mentions of grand estates—nothing concrete. Frustration bubbles over me as I toss the last book onto the floor and stretch out my back.

I wander to the window, needing a moment to clear my head. My gaze locks on to the woodlands stretching beyond the manicured grounds at the back of the property. A thought takes root: the woods are the only part of Nikolai's estate I haven't explored. If I'm going to find a meeting place for Roman to extract me when the time comes, it has to be there. If I can reach the boundary of the property, maybe I'll stumble onto a road or find a landmark, anything to help figure out where I am.

I glance down at the ankle monitor. Nikolai said it only triggers if I leave his property, and the woods should still fall within the estate's boundaries.

It's almost three in the afternoon. The guards usually change shifts around this time, lingering to chat or grab a smoke. This is my window.

I leave the books scattered on the floor and head toward the door. There's only enough time to run upstairs, swap this flimsy summer dress for something more practical, and put on better shoes than these slip-on sneakers.

As I rush from the library, I collide with Emil right outside the doorway.

"Whoa. Where are you running off to?" he asks, steadying me with a hand.

Emil already warned me that I'm supposed to let him know whenever I go outside, but I don't want his company for what I have planned. If he sees me outside, I'll need a good excuse.

I shrug. "Yelena's giving me cooking lessons again. Figured I'd grab some herbs from the garden before we start."

He leans against the doorframe, crossing his arms. "Cooking lessons, huh? I guess you're feeling better?"

"Yep, thanks. Just needed a couple days of rest."

He smirks. "Never thought the day would come that Yelena would allow anyone else in her kitchen to cook."

"She's trying to make me a proper wife. What about you? Do you cook?" Making small talk is the last thing I feel like doing, but I'm trying to put him at ease.

He chuckles. "Not if I can help it. House duty's already bad enough without adding chef to the list."

I nod, feigning sympathy. I'm running out of time to catch the shift change. "Well, I better not keep Yelena waiting." I say a silent prayer that Emil and Yelena don't bump into each other today and expose my lie.

He nods. "I'll be in the surveillance room if you need me."

I arch an eyebrow. "Where's that?"

"Right next to Nikolai's office. It's got a live feed from all over the house and property. Makes my job a little easier."

"Convenient." My stomach sinks. Of course, there's a surveillance room. Why didn't I think of that before? Cameras mean someone's always watching, even outside.

"We mostly play cards there. It's not like anyone's going to attack this place. Nobody even knows about it."

If Nikolai knew that, I think he'd have a conniption, but I can use it to my advantage right now. "True. Feels like we're really in the middle of nowhere."

"Yeah, you could say that." He runs a hand through his light hair. "Anyhow, you better not keep Yelena waiting. Oh, and don't go past the garden. Anything further, and I'll need to come with you."

"No problem." I watch him disappear down the hall before I take a quick glance at the clock. Crap, it's three. Too late to change my shoes or ditch this sundress for something more practical for exploring the woods. If I'm going to do this, it has to be now.

Steeling my nerves, I step out onto the back terrace. The wide stone expanse overlooks an immaculate garden, paths of neatly trimmed hedges winding around flower beds, and a bubbling fountain at the center. Beyond the manicured beauty lies my real goal—the edge of the woods.

I hope Emil's right that the guards watching the cameras spend most of their time playing cards.

Breathe. Don't panic. Don't rush.

The mantra steadies me as I walk along the garden path, keeping my pace calm.

Near the far corner of the garden, I spot two guards by a wrought iron bench. One smokes while the other gestures animatedly, caught up in conversation.

I crouch beside a large rosemary bush, pretending to study its leaves. Plucking a few sprigs, I roll them between my fingers, my gaze flicking toward the guards. Neither notices as I edge closer to the tree line, forcing myself to move slowly.

A branch cracks behind me, and my heart leaps into my throat as I whirl around, only to see a bird fluttering through the brush. God, I need to get a grip.

I keep going, staying close to the periphery as I slip into the woods. The moment I'm beneath the canopy of trees, I exhale. A few minutes later, when I look back, the estate is no longer visible, and it seems no one's followed me.

The deeper I go, the more obvious it is how unprepared I am. The woods are thicker than I expected, with underbrush clawing at my ankles.

My sundress catches on a thorny branch for the third time, and I stop to pull it free, tearing the fabric slightly. I glance back the way I came, but there's nothing—just trees. I've been trying to walk in a straight line, but at this point, who knows? Everything looks the same.

I press on, trying to keep my breathing steady, but nerves get the best of me. The longer I walk, the more it feels like I'm going in circles. Every tree looks like the last. Every shadow feels deeper. My pace falters as the weight of uncertainty settles over me.

How long have I been walking? It feels like an hour or two, but I can't be sure. My legs are aching, my feet are blistering in these awful shoes, and my stomach won't stop growling. I press a hand to it as if that will help. I was so focused on avoiding the guards earlier that I didn't think to bring water or food. Stupid.

I hug myself, shivering as the cold seeps into my skin. I thought I'd have reached the edge of the property by now, but all I see are trees, with no sign of a fence or road.

Overhead, the sky darkens. Thick clouds roll in, and the air smells faintly of rain. A summer shower would normally be refreshing, but getting caught in it now would only make things worse. I square my shoulders and keep moving.

Turning back isn't an option—not after coming this far.

CHAPTER TWENTY-SIX

NIKOLAI

THE BASS THUMPS THROUGH THE PRIVATE ROOM OF RED Cardinal, a deep, pulsing beat that rattles my bones. Strip clubs aren't my thing, and this one's no different, even with its marble floors, brass accents, and velvet couches adding an air of sophistication.

Tural Hasanov, head of an Azerbaijani cartel, sits across from me, his massive frame dwarfing the leather booth. The crystal tumbler in his hand looks absurdly small against his bear-paw hands. A half-naked dancer grinds in his lap while his men fan out behind him in designer suits, their slicked-back hair and gold watches a mobster cliché if there ever was one.

I don't need that show of force. I glance at Eva, relaxed by my side. Together, we're more than capable of taking down the room and have done so before.

Our arrangement with the Azerbaijanis has always been simple: they guarantee safe passage for my weapons shipments from Russia through their territory en route to Turkey, and I pay them generously for the service

Today's supposed to be our quarterly meeting, but the number of men Tural brought makes it obvious he's got something else on his mind. Still, he's spent the last half hour downing vodka and letting a stripper bounce in his lap instead of getting to the point.

Annoyance burns through me and I push the vodka bottle out of his reach and lean forward.

"I have a one-off arms shipment from Nigeria arriving at the port next week. Can you make sure authorities are busy with other shit that day?"

"So quick to talk business, Nikolai." Tural laughs and cups the obscenely fake tits of the stripper sitting on his thighs. She looks about as turned on as she would during a gynecological exam. "We're at a fucking strip club. You can have any woman in here or all of them at the same time. Business can wait until we've had some fun."

The look he gives Eva suggests he wouldn't mind taking a turn with her too, and I have to flick a look her way so she doesn't gut him right here. Not that I'd blame her.

Fun? Having a woman fuck me because it's her job is not my idea of fun. None of these women do it for me with their fake tits, puffy lips, and bored expressions.

The only woman who gets me hard is the one living under my roof, haunting my dreams, and fucking with my head.

I glance at my watch, letting my irritation bleed into my voice. "My jet's fueled and waiting. If you've got something to say, say it. I don't have time for this bullshit."

Tural's smirk deepens as the stripper disappears under the table. "What's the rush? Missing that new wife of yours already?"

My back stiffens. How does he know about Sofiya? I didn't announce it in the New York Times. I try to keep my tone casual. "Ah, I see word has spread."

His eyes roll back as the stripper's head bobs in his lap, and Eva doesn't bother hiding her look of disgust. "You know how it is. People talk. It's a big deal that the untouchable Nikolai Zhukov has taken a bride, especially one stolen from the Syndicate. Tell me, how long were you going to keep her a secret?"

"She's not a secret, just insignificant. A pawn. She's useful for one purpose, and when that's done, so is she." I keep my tone icy. I want everyone to believe Sofiya means nothing to me. Friend or foe, as soon as people discover something that makes me vulnerable, they exploit it.

But I'm starting to fear she truly is my weakness. Three days away from the estate, and she's constantly on my mind, consuming every thought. I haven't allowed myself to ask Emil for updates or check the cameras; the last thing I need is to fuel this obsession any further.

Tural regards me through a half-lidded gaze. "I hear your wife is a nice piece of ass. I hope you have had her on her knees sucking and fucking your cock every night."

My jaw tightens, and I exchange a look with Eva. I'm tempted to take out my gun and put a bullet in his head for how he's talking about Sofiya. More than that, I'm pissed that a scumbag like him even knows she exists.

My patience is wearing thin, unraveling further when he releases an aroused grunt and bucks his hips, thanks to the woman servicing him.

My hand slams onto the table, making the glasses clink together. "Enough. I don't have time for this bullshit, and I'm not looking for advice. You called me here for a reason, and I assume it's not so I can watch you get your dick sucked. What the fuck do you want?"

His guards come to attention, reaching for their pistols, but a single hard look from Eva has them freezing in place. They may not respect women, but they know that Eva is a trained killer. Tural reaches under the table and pushes the stripper away. I take a sip of my whiskey, the smooth burn a welcome distraction as she scurries off, looking for another rich asshole to service.

Tural zips up his pants and downs the rest of his drink. "The Turkish arms market is booming. Your military-grade weapons fetch triple what they did last year, yet my cut stays the same." He licks his lips. "Forty percent. That's my new rate for passage."

I've known this man for years; one of the first alliances I forged after taking power back from my brother. And in all this time, we've had a good working relationship. Trust is a dangerous thing in this business, and while I don't trust him more than I trust anyone else, I respect his ability to do his job. Still, I don't like being threatened.

I set my glass down, keeping my face blank. "I didn't realize we were renegotiating tonight. I'd think you'd want to save that for when you're sober."

He snorts. "I'm sober enough. You're clearing half a million per shipment while my men handle the borders, ensure security, and run the warehouses. I think it's only fair that I get a bigger slice of the pie."

I let the silence stretch, swirling the amber liquid in my glass as if I had all the time in the world. "Your risks are already factored in. Twenty percent is more than fair. But—" I glance at him, letting the tension build. "—since our arrangement has been mutually beneficial, I'll offer you a small increase. Consider it a show of goodwill."

I'm not feeling particularly generous toward him at the moment, but I'd rather not change up my arms operations right now. Setting up the casinos will take time, effort, and focus in the coming months. For now, keeping the status quo is worth swallowing a little irritation. That doesn't mean this bastard deserves another penny for what's essentially a glorified babysitting gig.

Tural's smile is flat. "Times change. You're not the only one with ambitions. Maybe I'll get into the gun-running business myself. The Turks would work with me directly if I provided the same product. We can cut you out entirely." He places his hands flat on the table, his rings catching the light. "I'm giving you the chance to stay in the game. Forty percent ensures our continued working relationship."

I laugh in his face. As if the Turks would seriously consider cutting me out in favor of this asshole. I've built my reputation on reliability and supplying only the best weapons, something Tural will never achieve. He's bluffing, but his threat is clear: pay up or lose access to the Turkish market through Azerbaijan. He thinks he has me cornered. What he doesn't know is that Eva has spent the last few months developing alternative routes through Armenia as a backup plan. It's more expensive, but every cent is worth avoiding this kind of extortion.

"And if I decline?" I say, leaning back in my chair, making it clear he doesn't scare me in the least.

"I think you know. Perhaps my new Turkish friends would be interested in other aspects of your operation. Your casino project, for instance. Or that lovely new Syndicate wife of yours."

The glass tumbler shatters against the wall before I even realize I've thrown it, fragments scattering across the floor. Eva's hand moves toward her weapon, and Tural's men do the same, tension crackling through the room.

My knuckles ache from clenching my fists, but it's nothing compared to the fury boiling inside me. So much for keeping my temper in check. There's no way I'm letting him think Sofiya is fair game.

I rise slowly, planting my fists on the table, dropping my voice to a lethal growl. "Let me make this crystal fucking clear for you. If you so much as mention my wife again, I'll flay the skin from your bones and hang it as a warning to anyone stupid enough to follow your example."

Tural's face tightens, and he holds his palms up. "Give me

a fucking break. You said yourself she's a pawn. Listen, we have history, and that means something, but at the end of the day, I'm still running the risks here. I'll honor the current terms until the end of the month, but after that, I need a forty-percent cut to keep things running smoothly."

My fist slams into his throat, the blow sending him crashing back into the leather booth. He gasps, clutching at his neck as the air is ripped from his lungs.

His men leap into action, weapons drawn. Eva steps forward, brushing her long leather coat aside to reveal a bulletproof vest, a sidearm tucked into a shoulder holster, and extra magazines lined across her belt. Tural signals his men to stand down, and one by one, their bravado crumbles, and they lower their guns.

"Come on, Niko. It's business. No need for this to turn ugly."

"That," I say quietly, adjusting my jacket, "was your only warning. Threaten me or my wife again, and there won't be enough of you left for an open casket."

No one says a word as we stride out of the club, but everything in me is coiled tight and won't relax until Sofiya is in my arms.

The car door shuts behind us, and Eva exhales, running a hand through her hair as she settles in beside me.

"That was a shitshow," she says bluntly. "You think Tural is trying to pull something?"

"He won't get the chance. But I don't like how he brought up Sofiya. That felt deliberate. Like he was baiting me."

Her eyes narrow. "Yeah, it didn't sit right with me either. You want me to start digging?"

I nod, rubbing a hand over my jaw. "Find out who he's

been talking to. If someone's feeding him information about her, I want to know who and why."

Eva leans back, crossing her arms as she studies me. "So... Sofiya, huh? You're going all in on this marriage thing."

I shoot her a warning look. "Careful, Eva."

She smirks, unfazed. "I'm just saying. I've known you for a good part of my life, Niko, and I've never seen you like this."

"Like what?"

She narrows her eyes in thought. "Like all touch-her-and-die and I'll-burn-down-the-world-for-my-woman alpha male."

"Jesus, you've been reading too many romance books."

My jaw tightens as I shift in my seat. I hate being called out, especially when it's true.

Sofiya's gotten under my skin in a way I didn't see coming. This feeling is dangerous. It's a vulnerability I can't afford. Caring about someone gives them power, and the last time I handed someone that power, I paid for it in blood.

Eva snorts. "Point taken, but you know… she looks at you the same way you look at her."

"You're meddling."

"I'm meddling as your oldest friend, not your second-in-command."

I fix her with a flat look. "Yeah, well, as a friend, you can kindly fuck off. As your pakhan, I'm sending you to Armenia tomorrow. I'm cutting ties with Tural, and I need you to secure a new deal to move our weapons into Turkey."

She gives me a mock salute. "Got it. But for the record? You're still not fooling anyone."

CHAPTER
TWENTY-SEVEN

SOFIYA

The wind cuts through the thin fabric of my dress, and I shiver, sinking onto a rock to rest my aching feet and face the very real possibility that I'm lost. Can you even call it being lost when you never knew where you were or where you were going?

It feels like I've been out here for hours, and now I'm not even sure which direction I came from. The woods stretch endlessly, trees blending into one another, and I'm no closer to finding a way out.

A scurrying sound from the bushes stops me in my tracks. A squirrel? Yeah, definitely a squirrel—maybe a fox at most. Bears don't live in this region. At least, I don't think so. The woods feel colder and creepier as the wind picks up, rustling the leaves in a way that makes the hair on the back of my neck stand on end.

A trickle of panic builds, but I force it down. Emil and the other guards must have realized I was missing by now. Well, maybe. I have been spending a lot of time in my room. They might assume I wasn't feeling well and went to lie down or something.

Best-case scenario: they saw me slip away on camera and are out looking for me right now. Sure, they'll be pissed, but I can handle their anger. Worst case scenario: Emil got caught up in a game of cards and is not thinking about me at all.

Maybe I should try and find my way back. At this point, with the sky darkening and a chill settling into my bones, it seems like the smartest choice. Standing, I brush off my dress and turn in a semicircle. I'm pretty sure I came in the direction of that oak tree, about ninety percent sure.

I stand and keep moving, my steps slower now. My flimsy shoes slip on the damp moss, and I catch myself on a nearby tree trunk. A few drops of rain splatter against my arm. I glance up as the skies open, unleashing a downpour that soaks me to the bone.

I scramble toward the nearest tree, hoping to find some shelter beneath its branches, but the wind picked up, and the rain is lashing sideways. My teeth chatter as cold seeps into my bones, and I wrap my arms around myself, trying to conserve the warmth I have left.

If things weren't so dire, maybe I'd laugh at the ridiculousness of it all.

Huddling under this tree is doing nothing to keep me dry. I might as well keep walking and pray that I'm heading in the right direction. I don't make it far before my foot catches on something. I stumble forward, my ankle twisting as I trip over something hidden beneath the mossy carpet. Pain flares up my leg.

I sink to the ground, clutching my ankle. I curse these damn shoes. I curse Nikolai, regretting the day he walked into the Greek chapel to save me. And while I'm at it, I curse Roman, the Syndicate, and any connections I have to the bratva.

But most of all, I curse myself for fucking up so badly. I

feel like a kid who always needs to be rescued—a burden to everyone in my life.

I lower my head onto my knees, my back pressed against the rough bark of the tree, and let all my emotions out. I've never felt so weak, so hopeless, so incredibly alone.

CHAPTER TWENTY-EIGHT

NIKOLAI

Hours later, I'm pulling up in front of the estate when my phone buzzes with a message from Emil.

Emil: Call me. There's a situation.

Every muscle in my body goes taut. I fire off a quick text:

Me: I'm here. Be in the security room in two minutes.

I slam the door behind me as I storm toward the house. When I reach their location, Emil and two guards are pacing, their faces pale as they watch the security monitors. "What the hell is going on?" I bark.

Emil exhales sharply, his words spilling out in a rush. "It's Sofiya. She's gone."

"What the fuck do you mean she's gone?" My blood turns to ice. "She couldn't have left the property without me being alerted."

Emil shoves his hand through his already disheveled hair. "She was last seen in the back garden, gathering herbs. She's not in her room, and we're reviewing all the security footage, but so far, there's nothing."

Panic grips me, and my voice rises to a roar. "Are you fucking serious? Get a team together to scour every inch of my property this fucking second. How long has she been missing?"

Emil gulps hard. "About four hours."

In an instant, my hand is around his throat, slamming him against the wall. "You didn't notice she was missing for four fucking hours?"

He chokes, clawing at my grip, but I don't loosen it.

One of the newer and clearly less intelligent guards rises from his seat. "She's usually in her room, but you said we couldn't look at that camera feed, so—"

Before he can finish, I spin and press the barrel of my gun to his forehead. "It's probably a good idea for you to shut the fuck up."

The color drains from his face, and I have to suck in a deep breath not to pull the trigger. "Let me make this clear. If something's happened to my wife, you're all dead."

I've wasted enough time talking with these idiots. Yanking my phone from my pocket, I frantically navigate to the tracking device app connected to her ankle monitor.

My stomach drops when I realize where she is. Deep in the woods at the far end of the property, and she isn't moving. Dread grips me, and I bolt outside, breaking into a run through the freezing rain.

My men will pay for their incompetence, but the person most to blame is me. She's mine to protect, and I failed her. The realization is a knife to the gut.

SOFIYA

My ankle throbs with pain, and my skin feels like ice, but all I can do to stay alive is huddle into myself. I'm so cold that I've stopped caring about what happens to me.

A deep, menacing growl tears through the stillness. My stomach clenches. Is this it? Am I about to die here, ripped apart by a hungry animal? I grab a broken branch nearby, ready to defend myself with what little energy I have left.

Then Nikolai emerges from the shadows like a man possessed. Relief crashes through me. His hair is disheveled, his chest heaving, and when his eyes find mine, they are filled with panic.

He drops to his knees beside me, his hands cradling my face. "Fuck, baby. Look at you."

I flinch, waiting for the anger, but it doesn't come. His thumb brushes my cheek gently.

"Are you hurt?" he asks, scanning me for injuries.

"My ankle. I don't think I can walk," I say, my teeth chattering.

He swears under his breath, his eyebrows pulling together as he scoops me into his arms, holding me close. "I'm so fucking sorry."

My exhausted brain can't figure out why he's apologizing. All I can focus on is his warmth chasing away the cold that had seeped into my bones. My fingers grip his shirt like he's the only thing keeping me grounded.

"I thought I was going to die out here, and it would be all my fault. I'm such an idiot."

"Don't say that," he insists, his voice strained. "You're safe now. I've got you, Sofiya. I swear, nothing's going to hurt you again."

His hold on me tightens, his heartbeat pounding against my ear as he moves through the trees with purposeful strides. A sob catches in my throat, and before I know it, I'm crying. I clutch at his shirt, clinging to him as if letting go would shatter me completely.

"Why do you care?" I gasp, the question slipping out between tears.

I raise my head to look at him through watery eyes. His face is hard, but his gaze is so tender it sends a pang through me. "You're my wife," he simply says, like it's the only explanation needed.

I bury my face in his neck and let it all out.

CHAPTER TWENTY-NINE

NIKOLAI

Sofiya is cradled in my arms as I climb the stairs, her cold, fragile body pressed tightly against mine. She's no longer shivering as violently as she was in the woods, but her skin still feels like ice.

The image of her crumpled form—her dress torn and muddy—is seared into my mind. It's something I won't be able to erase anytime soon.

She's wearing a flimsy sundress and slip-on shoes, the worst possible choice for venturing into the woods. I'd question her sanity if I didn't already understand her reasoning. She was trying to get away from me, looking for a way to escape. I don't blame her for that. She hates me for using her to hurt her family.

Husband or not, I'm the monster holding her against her will. But monsters aren't supposed to feel this way—destroyed by the sight of their captive in pain.

My staff shoot me alarmed looks as we pass, but I ignore them. Yelena rushes up to me, her face etched with worry. "What happened? Is Sofiya okay?"

"Call Dr. Safin," I order, not breaking stride. "Send her to my bedroom when she arrives."

My bedroom. Soon to be our bedroom because I'm not taking any fucking chances with her anymore. She is my wife and belongs in my bed. But we can have that discussion once she's healthy.

Yelena's eyes widen, but she nods and hurries off.

Sofiya shifts, her breath warm against my neck. "P-please don't make a big fuss. Honestly, I'm okay."

I hate how pale her face is and how weak her voice sounds. "You're not. Now, I'm going to take care of you."

Sofiya is silent as I carry her into my bedroom, her small frame quaking in my arms. It makes me so fucking mad to see her this way. I can still feel the cold radiating from her skin.

I head straight for the en suite and turn up the heat as high as it goes. When I release her onto a little stool in the corner of the room, I make sure to cover her shoulders with several thick, luxurious towels.

She continues to shake and stare at me as I focus on drawing her a bath, getting the water temperature just right. The tub is big enough for both of us, and I intend to get in with her.

As the water is running, I duck into my bedroom and grab a bottle of water from beside my bed. Striding back into the bathroom, I find her leaning against the wall, her eyes half-closed. "A b-bath isn't necessary. Wrap me in a blanket, and I'll be fine."

She stiffens as my hand trails down her cheek. "Jesus, Sofiya, we need to warm you up now. Either get in the bath, or we both get into my bed naked, and I use my body to warm you up."

Her jaw drops, but she doesn't realize how deadly serious I am. I open the bottle of water and cup the back of her head. She reaches for it, but I pull it out of her grasp.

"Drink," I say to her, unwilling to argue.

She does, gulping down the water like she's been stranded in the desert. When she puts the bottle down, she shoots me a defiant look. "You're very bossy, you know that?"

I can't help but smirk. "Comes with the territory. Now, clothes off and into the bath."

"I'll get in the bath once you leave."

"And risk a chance of you falling? I don't think so. And for the record, you're as stubborn as I'm bossy."

She sighs, her eyes glassy with pain and exhaustion. Fuck, I've wasted enough time arguing with her. If she's going to make this difficult, I'll have to take over. "Get undressed now, Sofiya. Your lips are blue."

"Turn around… please."

I do as she asks, but when I hear a quiet whimper, her modesty is the last thing on my mind.

I'm in front of her in a flash. "What happened? What is it?"

"My hands. They're so stiff. I can't undo the buttons." Her voice trembles, and the look on her face cracks something inside me.

"Fuck," I mutter, dropping to my knees. I reach for the top button of her soaked dress, my fingers brushing her skin.

The fabric clings to her curves as I peel it off her. Then I reach for the clasp of her bra. My pulse spikes as I unhook it and let the lace fall to the floor.

"Hold on to me," I say, steadying her as I kneel to slide her panties down her legs. My knuckles graze the curve of her thigh. I avert my eyes; the last thing I need is for her to notice me pitching a tent.

She steps out of the pile of clothes, her arms instinctively wrapping around her torso.

"It's okay," I murmur softly.

I slip my arms under her knees and around her back, lifting her easily. The tub is filled, steam curling in delicate swirls.

"This again," she quips softly, and I'm glad she's well enough to crack jokes.

I lower her into the water, her body sinking beneath the warm surface. A soft gasp escapes her lips, and her shivers subside as the heat works through her.

Taking care to prop her injured foot on the rim of the tub, I place a folded towel under her calf. Thankfully, it's the ankle without the tracking device. Her soft murmur of satisfaction stirs something primal in me, but fuck, I'm not going there right now.

I don't think twice before yanking my shirt over my head. My belt and pants follow, hitting the floor in a pile along with my shoes. Finally, I strip off my boxer briefs and step into the tub behind her. Days ago, she teased me about how often I got naked in front of her. Those other times, I was having fun. This time, I'm not.

The water laps against my skin as I pull her back against me. My arms wrap around her waist, her bare skin slick against mine.

"Better?" I murmur against her ear.

She nods faintly and relaxes against me. "So much better."

I hate how close of a call that was. Heads will roll. But first, I need to take care of my wife.

My wife.

Sofiya fits perfectly into the curve of my frame. I run my hands up and down her arms, trying to chase the last of the chill away and steady her nerves.

I bury my face in the crook of her neck, breathing in the clean scent of her skin. "When I couldn't find you, I almost lost it."

Sofiya looks back at me. Her lashes lower, but not before I catch a flicker of hurt. "Because I'm your bargaining chip?"

I shake my head, cupping her face with one hand. "No."

Her jaw tightens. "I don't believe you."

My lips crash against hers, the taste of salt and rain

lingering on her skin. Her breath mingles with mine, warm and uneven, setting my pulse racing. I'm supposed to be unbreakable, a man without a weakness. Yet here I am, fucking powerless to resist her.

A knock on the bathroom door is followed by a familiar voice. "Nikolai, it's Dr. Safin. Can I come in?"

"Yes."

The doctor swings the door open, surprise flickering in her expression at finding me and Sofiya in the bath—a look she quickly tries to mask.

With her hair pulled back into a no-nonsense bun and glasses perched on her nose, she looks as professional as she is. Dr. Safin doesn't bother with small talk—she's here because she's the best money can buy, and I pay her a fortune to be at my beck and call.

Her eyes settle on Sofiya, giving her a quick, clinical once-over. "What happened?"

"She was lost in the woods for hours. Hurt her ankle, and was freezing when I found her." The guilt still presses down on me.

The doctor nods and starts to unpack her equipment. "Can I have the room, Mr. Zhukov?"

"She's my wife. I'm not leaving," I say firmly.

Dr. Safin blinks rapidly, caught off guard. My marriage is obviously news to her.

Sofiya's hand finds mine under the water. "It's okay, Niko. I already feel better. Give us a few minutes. I need some privacy."

Fuck. I hate the idea of leaving her, but she called me 'Niko' for the first time—and with the look she's giving me, I can't say no.

I point a finger at the doctor. "You have twenty minutes. And she sleeps in my bed tonight."

"Of course," she responds as I rise from the water, taking care to be gentle. The doctor averts her eyes as I leave the bath and wrap a towel around my waist.

"I'm serious. I'm putting you on a timer," I say, holding up my phone.

I find Emil pacing in my office like a restless animal. The moment he sees me, he freezes, hands clenched at his sides.

"Sofiya's fine, right? Yelena said she didn't need to go to the hospi—"

I don't let him finish. Grabbing the front of his shirt, I slam my fist into his face.

"Fuck!" He presses a hand to his bloody nose. "I said I'm sorry."

Anger courses through me, and I press my fingers to my temples. "Keeping Sofiya safe was your only job. How the fuck did you screw it up?"

He glares at me. "She snuck off when I was distracted by Igor. I told her not to wander off outside without me, but she doesn't listen to instructions all that well."

"Watch your fucking mouth," I spit, my face inches from his. I suck in a deep breath and step back from him, attempting to calm my nerves. "And what the fuck do you mean you were distracted by Igor?"

"He stopped by with paperwork for you. What was I supposed to do, blow him off?"

Since when does Igor swing by to drop off paperwork? But I don't have time for this right now. I only have one priority, and she's waiting for me upstairs.

I shake my head. "You ask me for more responsibility but can't even handle the most basic fucking job."

He sneers. "I'm not a babysitter, Nikolai. If you wanted her under lock and key, you should've put her in a cage."

I grab him by the collar and shove him into the wall with enough force to rattle the frames nearby. "You think this is a joke? Say something like that again, and you'll find out just how expendable you really are."

I release him and take a step back, breathing hard. He doesn't know when to back down—he never has. I used to think that fire would make him invaluable once he matured, but now it feels more like a liability.

"I don't offer second chances, but I'm giving you one because of our history. If anything happens to Sofiya again on your watch—if she gets so much as a fucking paper cut—there won't be a next time. Do you understand?"

His gaze drops to the floor, a defiant curl to his lips. "Yes, pakhan."

I run a hand over my face, trying to tamp down the frustration simmering in my gut. "Don't make me regret the decision to trust you."

He glances away for a moment before forcing himself to meet my eyes again. "I won't."

I watch him leave, tension rolling off his back like steam. Emil is arrogant and headstrong—a lot like Sergey was.

I've killed one brother in this lifetime. I'd prefer not to kill another.

CHAPTER THIRTY

SOFIYA

My eyes flutter open, sunlight streaming through the window like an unwelcome guest. A pounding headache greets me, and my ankle throbs. But I notice something else unexpected and not entirely unpleasant: the heat of a body beside me.

I turn to be greeted by Nikolai's sleeping form. For a moment, I wonder why he's in my room before realizing I'm in his.

Memories trickle into my consciousness: getting lost in the woods, the cold rain cutting through me, the sharp pain in my ankle, and Nikolai, my unlikely savior, carrying me up the stairs into his room. And then the bath. Oh god, the bath.

Beyond Liza, Roman, Daria, and Alex, I can't think of the last time someone actually cared enough to fuss over me. But Nikolai did. He hovered like a mother hen, ignoring the doctor's reassurance that I'd be fine, ensuring I was comfortable and didn't need anything.

The doctor said it was nothing serious—a rolled ankle—and that I'd be fine with some rest and ice. But that didn't stop Nikolai from insisting I sleep in his bed as if keeping me close was the only way to make sure I stayed safe.

Now, in the light of day, I feel stupid. Running off was reckless, exactly what Roman and Liza wouldn't want me to do. But I was desperate to escape Nikolai's hold, knowing full well how much harder it was getting to resist him.

He's the cause of my family's misery, and yet I'm here, feeling all sorts of fucked-up things for him.

Nikolai Zhukov isn't just under my skin—he's in my veins.

And the scariest part is I'm done fighting it.

With Nikolai still sleeping beside me, I take in his unfairly chiseled jawline, the sexy stubble that shadows his face, and the way his dark hair falls across his forehead. It makes him look softer, less like a big bad mafia boss. It's a side of him I really, really like.

I'm frozen, unable to pull my eyes away. My heart races as my gaze drifts lower, tracing the hard planes of his chest, the ridges of his abs, and… fuck. The covers barely conceal the sculpted V-shaped muscles that angle downward. I'm pretty sure he's naked under there.

Okay, wow. I quickly reach down to confirm that I am not naked. Nope. Still wearing the sleep shorts and tank top that the doctor and Yelena helped me into last night. I don't even know why I thought I might not be. Maybe because waking up in his bed, feeling his presence so close, makes me hyper-aware of how vulnerable I was last night.

Taking care to move gingerly, I turn on my back and stare at the ceiling. Will it be weird for us to wake up together? Emotions were heightened yesterday, but yeah, it will probably be weird this morning. Maybe it's best if I show myself out.

I carefully slide one leg out from under the covers, the cool air hitting my skin. I pause, holding my breath, but he doesn't stir. Emboldened, I inch my other leg out, shifting my weight toward the edge. As I'm about to lift the sheet and make a break for it, an arm coils around my waist, and I'm yanked back, flush against Nikolai's very naked, very hard form.

"Where do you think you're going, moya sladost?" His voice is a low murmur in my ear, making my core clench.

"I'm going back to my room. I'm feeling better, thanks." I try to wiggle out of his arms, but he doesn't allow me to move a muscle. Being restrained in Nikolai's arms feels very familiar. Except this time, I don't totally mind it.

"You're not going anywhere." Am I imagining the huskiness of his voice? Maybe, but I'm definitely not imagining his thick length pressed against my ass.

"I think it's best if we... we, uh..." I stumble over my words. Okay, this isn't going well. I can't help but respond to his touch. "Niko—you're naked. We better not..."

His growl drowns out the rest of my sentence. "I like it when you call me Niko." I hadn't realized I'd called him that. I look up and find him watching me, his gaze uncharacteristically soft. "And, for the record, I'm not naked. I'm wearing underwear. Only for you, wife, because I usually do sleep naked."

I swallow hard. "Well, thank you again for everything yesterday. I'm feeling better... I, uh, can you let go?"

"Not yet." In one deft move, he rolls me onto my back and leans over me, one arm bracing beside my head while his other hand glides along my cheekbone. In this position, he's staring into my eyes, and I couldn't look away even if I wanted to. His fingers brush over my cheek. "Your color is much better. But you're not going anywhere until the doctor checks you again."

My eyes flick to his mouth and then back to his endless blue gaze. I'd never noticed the ring of yellow around his irises; it almost made him look predatory. I shake my head, trying to come back to my senses.

"She can look at me in my room." Realizing I need to make a move now if I'm going to get out of here unscathed, I inch my leg toward the edge of the bed in an attempt to wriggle out of his grasp.

Big mistake. His hips slide right between my thighs, and just like that, I've managed to trap myself in the worst way. A low groan slips out before I can stop it.

Nikolai's gaze turns molten. "Is that an invitation, wife?"

My cheeks burn. I should be putting space between us, not dragging him closer. But when he rocks against me, his erection dragging over my pulsing clit, all rational thought flies out of my head. Sensations take over, the blistering heat building between us threatening to consume me whole.

He makes an amused sound. Gathering my wrists above me in his huge hand, he lowers his lips until they're right beside my ear. "How are you feeling? Any pain?"

"No, no pain." My ankle was throbbing minutes ago, but now it's my clit throbbing in a rhythm that's impossible to ignore.

"That's my girl. How about you tell me what you want so that I can grant your every fucking wish."

The question hits harder than it should. Because what I want is simple and impossible all at once—I want him. This dangerous man who holds my world hostage. Who threatened everyone I love. Who's using me like a chess piece on his board. I'm not naive enough to believe he wouldn't follow through on every one of his threats. Yet here I am, craving his touch like oxygen. No one's ever made me feel what he makes me feel. It started in that little chapel in Greece, and no matter what I do, he's still here, impossible to shake.

But I can't admit that, just like I can't admit how the thought of him touching Eva, or anyone else, makes me want to scream.

"I want you to get off me."

He knows I'm lying. I can see it in the tilt of his lips. The way my hips move in needy circles against him gives me away.

He chuckles, the sound rich. "I don't think that's true. Your pussy is soaking my cock through your shorts and my boxers. I think you're aching for me, just like I'm aching for you." He punctuates his words with a slow, deliberate grind of his hips, and I practically convulse beneath him. I have to stop my eyes from rolling up in my head. "Now tell me. What. Do. You. Really. Want?"

I bite my lip, not trusting myself to say anything more.

Everything that's happened between us until now carried an undercurrent of hate. I told myself I had no choice. Not really. But this right here? I have a choice.

I squeeze my eyes shut, trying to hold on to the last fraying threads of my control. But it's no use. He's stripped me bare, peeling away all my defenses until only my desperate need for him remains.

He must see the longing in my eyes because another slow thrust is all it takes to shatter my resolve. I arch toward him, craving the spark of contact.

Nikolai's answering groan is pure male satisfaction. He drops his head into the curve of my neck. "Oh, sweet wife, you have no idea what you do to me. Your smell, your skin, the sound of your goddamn voice haunts me. It's like every sweet inch of you was made to drive me insane. Now I'm going to need you to hold on tight because I'm about to fuck you so hard, you'll feel me for days."

His mouth crushes mine, demanding and possessive, as our tongues tangle in a kiss full of need. He releases my wrists to explore my body, his rough palms sliding under my shirt to cup my breasts, his fingers plucking at my nipples until they're stiff and aching. I arch into his touch, silently begging for more.

I'm dimly aware that this is a mistake I can't come back from. After this, I won't have the strength to resist him.

Niko's hands on me, his mouth devouring mine, and his hard form pressing me into the mattress have reduced every coherent thought to ash.

"Tell me what you need."

"Keep doing what you're doing. Just like that."

Meeting his gaze, I spread my thighs wider, offering him better access. His dick presses against me through my sleep shorts. His eyes darken as I moan from the pressure against my clit.

"Good girl. Get this shirt out of the way so I can make you feel good."

I shift enough for him to lift my tank top over my head. The blanket slips down, and Nikolai—no, Niko—stops, his eyes heavy-lidded as they take me in.

"You're perfect," he murmurs, cupping my breasts. His mouth descends on my left nipple, sucking the areola into his mouth.

"Ohhh!" The sensation burns through me, racing to my toes before pooling low in my belly. My back arches, desperate for more contact.

His skilled mouth alternates between my breasts, his tongue swirling around each peak, teasing me while I'm pinned beneath his delicious weight. I want him to consume me whole.

I clutch his taut ass, bringing him closer, his hard cock pressing into me as I try to soothe the ache in my core.

"Yes, don't stop. Please, I'm almost—" The words escape me in a breathless whisper. The rhythm of his hips and the heat of his mouth on my breasts have me teetering on the brink of release.

Niko releases my nipple, his eyes dark with lust. "Ask me nicely to come, and I might let you."

"Let me?"

"Yes, let you. Now ask nicely, moya sladost."

My fingers dig into his shoulders as his tongue tangles

with mine. He releases my wrists to grip my ass, holding me firmly in place. I'm beyond rational thought—I need more than this teasing friction. I need to feel him deep inside me.

"Please, Niko, fuck me and make me come."

The plea escapes before I can think better of it, but I don't care. I need this. I need him to claim me like I need air to breathe.

"Christ," he groans, his eyes rolling back. "Extra points for calling me Niko. You better be damn sure because I'm about to spread these legs wide and fuck you senseless."

His words hit me like a physical force, and any lingering doubts dissolve. I want this. I want him with an intensity that should frighten me. Instead, it thrills me.

He shifts back onto his knees, dragging my sleep shorts down my thighs. I feel exposed under his intense stare, but the raw need in his eyes as he drinks in the sight of me makes me feel powerful. His rough hands glide between my inner thighs, urging them apart.

"Dripping wet," he growls, his thumb ghosting over my slit. The teasing touch makes me buck against his hand, a desperate sound torn from my throat.

"Please," is all I can manage.

Rising briefly, he pushes down his boxer briefs and kicks them free before settling back between my spread thighs.

He slides one leg over his hip, careful to avoid my bad ankle, his other hand cradling my head.

"This okay?" he murmurs, his voice hoarse with restraint. I nod, too far gone to speak. His dick notches at my entrance and then he sinks into me, inch by delicious inch, sending shock waves through my body. My breath catches, the stretch heightening every sensation.

When he's fully seated inside of me, he pauses, allowing me to adjust to his size. My inner walls pulse around him, and his jaw clenches with the effort of holding still.

"So full," I mumble.

He groans, his forehead dropping to mine. "You were made to take my cock."

He drives into me, slow but unrelenting, stealing what little control I have left. My nails bite into his shoulders as bliss pulses through me. I'm so close to shattering.

"Faster," I plead, rolling my hips to meet his.

With one hand gripping my ass, the other slides between us to circle my clit. With every stroke, I'm trembling on the edge.

"That's it," he breathes against my neck. "Come for me, moya sladost. Let me feel you milk all the cum out of my cock."

CHAPTER THIRTY-ONE

NIKOLAI

Sofiya is all I can feel—her skin warm beneath mine, her breath against my lips, her body trembling as she melts into me. It's overwhelming, this connection, this need to claim her in every way.

My fingers grip her ass, holding her steady as she moves with me, matching each thrust and pulling me deeper into her heat. Her breaths come faster, her body tightening as she gets closer. Then her palm slides between us, catching me off guard. I slow, letting her explore. Her fingers touch the place where we're joined, where my cock sinks into her slick heat.

Moving carefully so as not to hurt her ankle, I shift her leg higher. Her cry of pleasure makes me throb inside her. "That's it," I grunt. "Let me hear how good I make my wife feel."

Her lips part, but I capture her sounds with my mouth, kissing her deeply.

I increase my pace, gritting my teeth to maintain control as her hand stays between her legs, her fingers coated in our arousal.

"Do you like feeling my cock tunnel into that sweet pussy of yours? Do you like feeling how you stretch for me?"

"Yes," she gasps, her voice trembling with need. Her hand moves from between us, sliding up my chest before locking around the back of my neck, her nails scraping against my skin.

She surprises the hell out of me when she grabs my hand and guides my fingers to wrap around her throat. Shit. Never in a million years did I think Sofiya would ask for anything kinky. She's inexperienced, but there's no hesitation. With her head tilted back and her throat exposed, she gives herself to me.

"Please," she begs. "I need… this."

I still. "Do you know what you're asking for?"

"At the club, when I snuck up on you, you wrapped your hand around my throat and… I don't know. Something about it made me feel alive. I trust you, Niko, and I want to feel… restrained."

Her words undo me. This side of her is raw, beautiful, and completely unexpected. I let my palm rest lightly around her throat, my thumb brushing the line of her jaw. Her eyes flutter shut, a shiver coursing through her.

Slowly, I tighten my hold enough to let her feel the loss of control she craves.

"Put your hand around my wrist," I instruct her. "If it gets to be too much, pull me off you. Got it?"

"Okay," she agrees, eyes hazy with lust.

"I'll be careful," I promise. "I'll never cut off your airflow, but I need to know you feel safe with me."

Her fingers grip my wrist as I apply a bit more pressure, letting her feel the weight of my control. Her lips part in a soft moan, her trust evident.

"Such a good fucking girl for me, aren't you?" I grit out, my voice husky. "Look at you taking my cock like it was made for you."

Her head tilts back, exposing the curve of her throat to me, her lips parting with a sharp breath as I push deeper. Her nails rake against my skin, and I reward her with a deliberate stroke against her clit.

My free hand slides to her hip, anchoring her in place as I enter her pussy again, feeding her every inch. "You're mine, Sofiya," I growl. "Say it."

Her breath hitches, her body trembling under me as I thrust deep, my grip steady on her neck.

She shakes her head, not willing to admit what we both know.

I freeze, and she whimpers with frustration. A dark laugh escapes me. "Keep fighting, baby. I'll make you beg before this is over."

Her hips roll instinctively, seeking friction, but I stay maddeningly still. "You don't play fair," she pouts.

"This isn't a game, moya sladost," I say, pressing my palm against her hip to stop her from moving. My lips trail along her collarbone, nipping at the delicate skin, and I give her throat a slight squeeze. "Say it, and I'll make you come so hard you'll forget your own name."

She scowls up at me, and it's adorable. "Nikolai…" she whimpers, the sound drenched in desperation.

My smirk deepens, and I shift, angling myself to press against her G-spot. Her body trembles, her nails digging into my biceps as I take her to the brink. "We'll see if I can't convince you," I croon, swirling a digit over her clit in a steady rhythm.

She bucks, eager for more, but I slow my movements, teasing her with each shallow thrust before pulling out, leaving her empty.

"Please," she begs, her body taut with need.

I press against her clit again, just enough to keep her teetering on the edge. "Say it, or I'll leave you like this, desperate and begging."

"Jesus, you're impossible." She squirms beneath me, but I don't move a muscle. "Fine! I'm yours, would you just fuck me already." Her words spill out in a broken rush.

"Gladly." With a groan of satisfaction, I drive into her hard and deep, giving her everything she's been aching for. Bowing my back, I flick her nipple with my tongue, then draw it into my mouth with slow, deep sucks.

I grind my pubic bone into her clit, still feasting on her tits. Her eyes fly open, locking with mine.

"You feel so fucking good, your pussy strangling my cock like this."

That's all it takes for her climax to hit. My palm flexes around her neck, as her inner walls milk me. Her moan is raw and unrestrained as her release pulses through her.

I loosen my hold on her neck, letting her suck in air, her face flushed and radiant. With a guttural groan, I thrust deeper, locking our hips together. Her body grips me tight. My head falls back, muscles coiled as I shudder, and spill my load inside her.

Bracing my weight on my arms, I press a tender kiss to her forehead.

Her chest heaves, and I'm struck by the way she looks at me—like she trusts me, even after everything.

"Was that so hard to admit?" I murmur as I press my forehead to hers, savoring the connection. We're both sweaty and panting like we just crossed the finish line of a race. I have a sinking feeling the moment I pull away, reality will come flooding in, and she'll regret getting off on the dick of the husband she never wanted. The man holding her captive.

"Nikolai," she gasps. "I didn't really mean—"

"Niko," I say, keeping my eyes closed just for another moment. "It's Niko now."

She releases a shaky breath as I slide out of her tight cunt. When I roll to the side, her eyes dip between her legs. My cum is leaking out of her, and it's fucking hot. She looks so beautifully ruined with her dark hair messy and puffy lips. She attempts to close her legs, but I stop her.

"Don't you dare take this moment from me."

I crush my mouth against hers, fierce and possessive, before shifting lower, pressing kisses to the hollow of her throat. My fingertips trace her curves as I make my way down her body. Her chest heaves as I spread her legs wider, exposing her glistening cunt.

"What are you doing?" she asks in a hoarse voice.

"I want to see if we taste as good together as I imagine we do."

I trace her folds, my eyes glued to the spot where my seed is dripping out of her. I don't think I've ever seen something so perfect.

I dive in with a purpose, tasting our combined pleasure, savoring every drop. My tongue glides along her slit, reveling in the taste. I circle my lips around her clit, applying enough pressure to have her squirming with frustration.

Each sound she makes sends a rush of fire through my veins. Her fingers dig into my scalp, her breath coming in pants, as I hold her in place, licking out her cunt as if I'll never get enough.

When her cries grow louder, I nip at her sensitive bud, giving her what she wants. Her legs clamp around my head, her entire frame shuddering, coming apart under my mouth.

"Open up for me. You're going to take my cum." I seal my mouth over hers. My tongue slides between her lips, coaxing her to taste the mixture of us together. She hesitates for a moment before she deepens the kiss, her fingers weaving into my hair.

Her reaction is pure need, as raw and unfiltered as my own. When I pull back, her lips are swollen, her cheeks flushed. She's mine in every way, and I won't let her forget it.

My thumb brushes the corner of her lips. "See how good we taste?"

She nods, looking a little shy, and I pull her closer. For a moment, she melts against me, but it doesn't last. Soon, her body stiffens, tension creeping into her shoulders.

"I should go," she says quietly.

She makes a move to leave, but I slide a hand around her waist. "Go where? You belong in my bed. You're my wife."

A ragged breath slips from her. "This doesn't change anything between us."

"That's where you're wrong. This changes everything." I grab her chin and force her to look at me.

"Niko…" Her voice is barely a whisper, holding emotions I can't decipher.

I exhale, moving an auburn strand of hair from her face. "You scared the shit out of me. I hated finding you like that," I admit. My chest constricts, picturing her body, pale and shivering in the rain.

Fear gripped me in a way I haven't felt since I was ten years old, and I came home to find Sergey pinned against the living room wall. Our mother's latest boyfriend, a brute named Viktor, had Sergey by the throat, yelling about stolen money. I was too small to do anything but scream at him to stop, my voice cracking as I begged. I can still see the blood dripping from Sergey's nose, the bruise forming on his cheek.

That helplessness and panic. It all rushed back the moment I saw Sofiya slumped against a tree.

"It was a mistake," she admits. "I needed to get out of my head for a little while. To feel like I wasn't trapped here."

"Don't ever risk your life like that again," I say. "Emil has a broken nose because of it."

Her eyes widen. "Are you kidding me!"

"He failed at his only job—keeping you safe."

"It wasn't his fault. I ran off before he could have stopped me."

I shake my head. "That's not how this works. If you're under his watch, you're his responsibility. End of story."

Her mouth opens to argue again, but my phone buzzes on the nightstand. I glance at the screen. "I asked Dr. Safin to come back. I want her to look you over again this morning. She's here now."

Sofiya's cheeks flush as her gaze darts to the rumpled bed. "She can't come in here! It smells like… like…"

"Sex?" I offer, grinning.

She groans, covering her face with her hands. "I don't want her to see me like this!"

I laugh. "We're not doing anything wrong."

She rolls her eyes, muttering, "You're impossible," and moves to grab her clothes. But the moment she stretches, she winces.

"Ankle still sore?" I ask, softening my tone.

"A little."

"Let me help you." I scoop up her clothes and dress her carefully, pressing a soft kiss to her lips when I'm done. "I'll give you space for the doctor to look you over, but when she's finished, be ready for me to eat that beautiful pussy of yours for the rest of the day."

CHAPTER THIRTY-TWO

SOFIYA

Nikolai hasn't left my side in two days. He should be out running his empire—making deals, crushing rivals, and doing whatever it is bratva kings do. Instead, he's holed up in bed with me, bringing me food, icing my ankle, indulging me with '90s horror movies (and a few action flicks because I'm generous), and even climbing into the bath with me.

And then there's the sex. Honestly, I'm starting to think my ankle is the least of my problems. The way he keeps me pinned to the bed every chance he gets, it's a miracle I can walk at all.

We're living in a bubble, tangled in silk sheets and bad decisions, giving in to the attraction that's been simmering for so long. But bubbles pop. And when this one does, I'm not sure where we'll stand. He's still on one side, and I'm on the other.

I'm still lying in bed, wrapped in sheets that smell like Niko, when he walks in with a tray piled high with food.

My heart does a stupid flip at the sight of him. He's wearing nothing but gray sweatpants slung low on his hips, his dark tattoos stark against his skin, the muscles in his chest and arms flexing as he moves. He looks impossibly handsome for a man who was up most of the night with one hand buried in my hair and the other around my throat.

With a devious smile, he lowers himself onto the bed, the tray balanced in his hands. It's stacked with fruit, eggs, pancakes, a steaming mug of coffee, and a Russian cheese Danish perched on top like a cherry on a sundae.

"Is all this for me?" I ask as he sets the tray down beside me.

"Maybe I can convince you to share," he deadpans, sliding into bed beside me. "Although I already enjoyed the most delicious breakfast of all."

My cheeks redden. Oh yes, he certainly did.

"I bet Yelena was floating around the kitchen knowing that you were bringing me breakfast in bed." In truth, he's done this every morning, and Yelena is downright delighted.

"You can say that. She had the platter ready and waiting the moment I came downstairs. And see the pomegranate seeds." He holds one up to my mouth, and I open so that he can slide it between my lips. "Good for fertility, she pointed out."

"She's on that again? I hate to tell her, but I've had the birth control shot."

His eyes narrow playfully as he places the tray on the bed between us. "You did, did you?"

I can't help the laugh that escapes me. "Calm down. It helps with menstrual cramps. I'm not very experienced, as I'm sure you've figured out by now. Having sex with a stranger in the bathroom was a first for me."

"I know."

I arch a brow. "How do you know?"

"Because I've kept tabs on you over the years."

My jaw falls open. "Please explain 'keeping tabs'."

Niko's lips twitch into a faint smile, and he reaches for my hand. "Exactly what it sounds like. You were my wife, Sofiya, even if you didn't realize it. I had someone keeping an eye on you. Roman protected you well, but I still knew where you lived, your school, your teachers… and every boy who got too close."

I should be angry, but instead, it feels oddly comforting, like he was watching out for me, even from a distance. Jesus, is this a sign of Stockholm Syndrome?

"Then I'm sure you know none of those boys held my interest long enough for me to keep them around."

"That's the only reason they're still alive." He smiles, but I'm not entirely sure he's joking. "How come?" he asks.

"A long time ago, a man saved me from something terrible. I guess I never forgot him. Made everyone else seem like a boy in comparison."

His eyes flash with approval, and he picks up a strawberry and gently presses it to my lips. I take a bite, the sweetness bursting on my tongue.

"Good girl," he says, his voice thick as he stares at my mouth.

I chew slowly, narrowing my gaze. "You're enjoying this way too much."

"Of course I am." He leans in, his lips grazing my ear. "You taste better than anything on this tray."

My cheeks burn, and I fiddle with the edge of the sheet, trying not to look at him. But my mind can't let go of his words from earlier. "Did you… did you look into the hospital?" I blurt, cringing at how awkward I sound.

He pauses, his expression sharpening with curiosity. "Your medical records said it was appendicitis."

I lower my gaze to the floor. "Not exactly. It happened after everything in Greece. I didn't know how to cope. My world had collapsed, and I couldn't process what my parents were capable of doing to their own children just to save their reputation." My voice falters, and I grimace. "I felt like a burden to Liza and Roman, just lying around all day. I had no interests, no motivation. I knew they were worried about me, but—" I break off, swallowing hard. "It wasn't about ending things. I just wanted to feel numb for a while, to escape it all."

Niko's brows draw together, worry etched into his features as his hand slides over mine.

"It was a bad mix: sleeping pills and vodka. But waking up to see Liza and Roman so distraught was when I knew I had to change. That's when I found dance. It gave me a reason to keep going."

He stills, his voice rough with emotion. "I had no fucking idea. If I knew—"

"Would it have changed anything?"

He drags a hand down his face, exhaling hard. "I can't change the past." His intense gaze connects with mine. "What is it you want? Not what everyone else expects of you. Not what the world thinks you should do. What do you want? Is it to perform in front of a packed theater? Be in the spotlight?"

I open my mouth to say, "Yes, of course," but the words catch in my throat. Have I ever truly thought about what makes me happy? As much as I enjoyed choreographing and performing that solo for graduation, was it my true passion or just a way to escape Moscow, the Syndicate, and my past?

Niko stays silent, letting me sort through my thoughts before I speak.

"I don't know if that's what I want," I admit finally, my voice barely above a whisper.

"Dancing lets me lose myself, and I need that. I don't care about the spotlight—it was never about that. I think it was about proving that I'm worthy of something special after feeling unworthy for so long."

His hand gently cups my cheek. "You're not worthless. You're extraordinary, Sofiya. Talented, kind, and strong as hell. You've been worthy all along, moya sladost. It's the world that wasn't worthy of you."

My stomach flips. No one has ever said anything like that to me before, and I don't know if I believe it. But the conviction in his voice is undeniable. "You're giving me too much credit. I'm stubborn, but that doesn't make me special."

"Yes, you fucking are. And I'll prove it to you."

"Oh?"

"I have something for you. A gift."

I grin. "What kind of gift?"

"I bought you a dance school."

My eyes widen. Did I hear him correctly? "You did what now?"

He smiles, the lines around his eyes softening. "I saw how you lit up when you talked about the dance school you had me donate to. So, I thought, what's better than donating to one? Buying you your own school."

My eyebrows shoot up. Is he seriously gifting me a freaking school like it's nothing? "I don't get it, what's the catch?"

"There's no catch. A local dance school was struggling, about to shut down, so I bought it. Now it's yours to do whatever you like with. I'll fund it entirely. You can make it free, pick the staff and students yourself—all that's up to you."

My throat tightens. I can't believe he'd do something like this for me. It's overwhelming in the best way, but I'm not sure how to process it.

He must sense that, because his warm palm settles on my thigh. "Whatever your vision is, we'll make it happen."

Vision? I bite my lip, doubt gnawing at me. "I'm a dancer. I don't know the first thing about running a school."

He snags a blueberry off the platter, popping it in his mouth. "What did you admire about the school you had me donate to? You can model it after that or consider what you'd like to do differently. You'll figure it out, moya sladost." His lips graze mine, sending butterflies through my stomach. "You're meant for this. I know you'll be incredible because you're passionate about dance and care about this cause."

If I'm honest, the idea of building a school, of creating a space where dancers can thrive, is exciting. But starting something this big feels impossible when I don't even know what my future holds.

I squeeze my eyes shut, unable to look at him as I say the one thing we both know is true. "What happens with the school when this ends?"

By this, I mean us and the insulated world we're living in.

His hand ghosts over my cheek, forcing me to look at him. His blue gaze is unwavering. "It's yours no matter what. It's in your name, and I've already set up a trust to fund it. Even if you never want to see me again, it belongs to you."

I shake my head. Thinking about our end sends a dull ache through me. One way or another, I'll have to choose a side—Niko or the Syndicate. No matter which side I choose, or which side wins, it will leave me broken.

"Hey, what's with that face?" he asks, cupping my jaw.

My hand slides up his chest, tracing the hard lines of muscle and the ink etched into his skin before resting above the steady thrum of his heart. I swallow hard to find my courage.

"What if you made peace with the Syndicate? We can go to Roman together and negotiate a truce. He'll understand it if I tell him things have chan—"

Niko shakes his head before I can get the rest of my words out. "This is not a situation where I can just apologize, and we can be friends again. I made a mortal enemy out of them." He shrugs, lightly. "I'm pretty sure Roman would shoot me the first chance he got, no matter what you say."

A knot tightens in my throat. He's probably right, but I'd never forgive myself if I didn't do everything possible to protect the people I care about, including him. "But if I can put in a good word..."

"Hey," he says, rubbing my arm. "Don't think about all of that right now. I'll figure out something, I always do."

I want to believe him, to trust that he can make a plan that won't end in bloodshed. But I'm not sure that's even possible at this point.

He cups my face, his eyes smoldering, shadows flickering in their depths. "You're mine, Sofiya. You've been mine since the moment you stepped into that Greek chapel."

"Tell me there's no one else," I whisper. "That I'm the only one."

I feel so vulnerable asking him this, but I need to know if there are other women, like Eva, still in the picture.

"There's never been anyone else, and there never will be."

The raw truth in his tone steals my breath. No one has ever made me feel like this. Seen. Important. Cared for.

His fingers continue their descent, gliding over the curve of my breast and slipping between my legs to ease my shorts aside.

My thighs part, warmth igniting in my core. I can't resist him, and I'm not going to try anymore. The moment his fingertips brush over my slit, my mouth drops open.

His free hand tangles in my hair, pulling as his fingers slide inside me. The stretch is perfect, the pressure so intoxicating that a low moan escapes me.

"Promise you'll dance for me soon," he growls against my skin. "I want to see you just as you were onstage. Free."

My breath stutters as he teases my clit, giving it a small pinch. My hips jolt forward, but I meet his gaze with a challenge. "And what are you going to do for me?"

His mouth curves into a wicked smile. "Pretty please, moya sladost." He slides his hands beneath my ass, dragging my shorts off, spreading me wide like I'm his favorite meal.

"I'll eat your pussy as often as you like."

"You already do." I laugh softly, but it quickly dissolves into a sharp inhale as his tongue sweeps through my folds, slow and deliberate at first, before growing more insistent, each flick and stroke making my eyes roll back.

A whine slips from my lips as he tightens his grip on my ass and buries his tongue inside of me. Every nerve in my body sparks to life, tuned to the electricity of his touch.

"Niko." I draw in a ragged breath, my back arching off the bed. All I can do is clutch the sheet as he devours me. He knows exactly how to make me unravel.

Even if this is all we'll ever be. Even if this moment is fleeting, something we'll both look back on when everything falls apart. Even if the future holds nothing but heartbreak, I'll take this—this feeling of being wanted, of being his, even if it's temporary.

CHAPTER THIRTY-THREE

NIKOLAI

"This is it," I announce, removing the blindfold I insisted Sofiya wear, not wanting to ruin a moment of the surprise. I push the door open and step aside, allowing her to walk in first.

She crosses the threshold, her head turning this way and that, soaking up every detail of the studio space around her. It's pretty basic. A wall of mirrors, a worn wooden floor, and a barre lining the wall. When she turns to face me, her eyes shine, her smile stretching so wide it's impossible not to feel the pull of it.

"You're kidding," she says, shaking her head. "This is my dance school?"

I nod, leaning against the doorframe, as she spins on the spot. "All yours," I confirm.

She's wearing a sweet red polka-dotted dress that flutters around her milky thighs, her auburn hair tumbling down her back. But it's the awe in her expression that makes me feel something—something I didn't think I was capable of feeling anymore.

I never had Christmas mornings growing up. I didn't know the thrill of opening presents or watching someone else unwrap the perfect gift. Well, not entirely.

One year, I'd saved everything I had to buy Sergey a teddy bear from Moscow's most luxurious kid's toy store. The joy on his face when he opened it was enough to make me forget how much I had skimped and saved for months.

This moment feels like that—only more significant.

She grabs my shirt, her lips finding mine in a lingering kiss. When she pulls back, her voice is breathless. "Take me on the grand tour."

I chuckle, grazing my knuckles along her cheek. "Where do you want to start? There is a second floor with another small studio, changing rooms, a staff room and an office."

Objectively, the place is nothing special. The walls are a dull beige, and the wooden floors have seen better days, the varnish worn thin in spots. The mirrors, dull and streaked, look like they haven't been cleaned this decade, and the overhead lights flicker faintly.

But she doesn't seem to notice any of that. It's like she only sees its potential. Maybe it's the same way with me. She can see beyond my faults—and there are many.

It's been a week since she ran into the forest; nothing and everything is different. We've fallen into place like two pieces of a puzzle that were always meant to fit. It's new and familiar all at once.

As we tour the upstairs, her sharp eyes drink everything in, assessing. "New shower curtains and a fresh coat of paint on the lockers will go a long way in here," she notes as we step out of the changing rooms.

"Make a list. That's why we're here. I wanted you to have a good look before we plan the renovations."

She freezes, turning to me with wide eyes. "Renovations?"

"What did you think? That I'd leave it like this?"

"No, but... renovations take time." Her lips press into a

thin line, doubt creeping into her expression. She thinks we're on borrowed time, that all of this—the school, us—is temporary.

I don't agree.

"Not for me." I shrug. "People tend to move quickly when I tell them to."

She looks away, emotion getting the best of her. I let my fingers trail lightly over her shoulder, grounding her.

"What's wrong?"

Her shoulders rise and fall, and she brushes at her damp lashes, as if the tears embarrass her. "I'm fine. I don't even know why I'm crying."

"Yes, you do." I slip a finger beneath her chin, tipping it up so she can't avoid my gaze.

She swallows hard. "No one's ever done something so freakin' nice for me." A smile breaks through. "And of all people… it's you. My captor."

"Your husband," I'm quick to correct. Because we've moved past captor/captive long ago. What we are is something very different, even if it can't be easily named. "You deserve it all, moya sladost. The sun, the moon, and the stars. If I could give you the world on a fucking platter, I would."

She lets out a soft laugh, sweeping away the last of her tears with the back of her hand. "Who are you? You don't make sense."

I lower my forehead to hers, letting her feel the weight of my conviction. "Maybe we don't make sense, but I'm not sure if that matters. It's just right between us." She closes her eyes, our faces still pressed together. Both of us lost on this carousel of emotions. I pull back to meet her gaze. "Now that you've seen this place, what are you thinking?"

She pauses, biting her thumbnail. "Well, for starters, it needs a coat of paint, new floors, and real studio lighting. New barres as well, because those ones look like they're held together with duct tape. The storage space needs to be expanded, and I was hoping we could add a library—just a small one—with books on dance history, anatomy, things to get the kids excited."

I raise a brow, impressed. "A library? Look at you, thinking out of the box. I like it."

She smiles, shaking her head. "Don't make fun of me. These kids deserve more. They deserve to feel like they're part of something important."

"I'm not making fun," I say, running my knuckles lightly along her jawline. "I love that you already care about your students. It's more than I ever had growing up."

Her head tilts. "What did you have?"

"Not much. My mother wasn't a mother in any real sense. She was hooked on drugs, a prostitute. We had nothing. No stability, no safety. Just me trying to figure out how to keep Sergey and I alive."

Her eyes soften, but I press on before the pity can take root. "I didn't just look out for him. There were other kids in the neighborhood—ones like Emil—who needed someone too. I don't know why I did it, but it felt… necessary. Like if I didn't, no one would."

She swallows hard, her fingers curling into the fabric of my shirt. "That's a lot for a kid to carry."

"It was. But it made me who I am. Taught me how to fight, how to survive."

"Is that why you're so hard on Emil?"

"I never wanted this life for him, but he chose a life of crime anyhow. At least working for me, I can keep him out of trouble."

She purses her lips in thought. "That gives me an idea. Scholarships. For the kids who can't afford shoes or uniforms. An outreach program that connects with schools or other organizations so we can help the students who need it most."

"You've thought of all this after just one visit. I'm fucking impressed," I say, enjoying her eyes lighting up.

"There's also something else I've been thinking about." Her hazel eyes glint as she points to a lone chair in the corner of the studio. "Sit down, Nikolai."

"Back to Nikolai again?"

She crosses her arms, the tilt of her head playful. "Would you just listen for once? I'm in charge now, and I want you to sit."

I let out a low chuckle, raising my hands in mock surrender. "Yes, Mrs. Zhukov." The name suits her fucking perfectly. I cross the room and drop into the chair, leaning back with my hands behind my head.

"You wanted me to dance for you, remember? Well, my ankle's better." She arches a brow, her lips curving into a wicked smile. "Play something sexy."

My blood thrums at the suggestion in her tone. I scroll through my phone, landing on a track with a deep, pulsing rhythm that fills the room.

The look she gives me is dark with promise as her hands skim down her body, slow and sensuous, drawing my eyes to every curve. She turns, her back arching as she sways to the beat. The hem of her dress slides higher, flashing me glimpses of bare skin.

She's not just dancing. Each movement feels raw and intimate, meant for my eyes only.

Heat spreads through me with every sway of her body, every flick of her hair, every sultry glance she sends my way.

She steps closer, moving in time with the music. Her hands lift, fingers tangling in her hair, and I swear I feel every shift of her body like a physical touch.

My abs tighten when she sinks to her knees and crawls across the floor toward me. It's so fucking sexy how she doesn't break eye contact the whole time. My cock is hard and aching, every nerve alive with need.

Still on her knees, she settles between my legs and puts on a show. Her hands trace their way up her body, cupping her breasts and tugging at her nipples through the silky fabric of her dress. She leans in, her breath brushing against my lips, making me throb. I need to see those pretty lips wrapped around my cock.

She rises to her feet, undoing each button of her dress until it slips down, revealing every perfect inch of her. My gaze devours her—the glow of her skin in the soft light, the curve of her breasts, the tautness of her stomach.

She unhooks her bra, letting it fall away as she arches her back, unapologetic in her beauty. Next, her panties slide down her legs, and with a wicked smirk, she uses them to bind my hands behind my back.

"Jesus, what are you doing to me? A man of my age can only take so much."

"Torturing you." She gives me a saucy wink before doing her best to put me in cardiac arrest as she straddles one of my thighs, gripping my shoulders for balance. The friction from her bare pussy pressed against me, even through my pants, has me clenching my jaw to stay in control.

She starts to move, her hips undulating against me in time with the pounding bass. Her breath comes in soft pants, her body brushing mine with every shift.

"Fuck, baby, I'm going to come in my pants like a fucking teenager if you keep that up."

She blushes, eyes downcast, as her breath warms my neck. Her hands glide up my chest, nails dragging over the fabric of my shirt.

She moves faster, rocking against me, her fingers tangling in my hair with a gentle tug. My body tenses, every nerve on edge, and when she kneels before me, that tension shifts—morphing into a raw, consuming hunger.

Her fingers trace my length over my pants. My muscles tense beneath her touch, anticipating what comes next.

She takes her time working my belt free, sliding the leather through the loops. The sound echoes in my ears, mingling with the rush of my own blood. She pops the button of my fly and lowers the zipper.

Cool air brushes against my heated skin as she eases my dick free. I suck in a sharp breath, my hands fighting against their lace restraints. But all thought empties from my brain when she wraps her fingers around me and strokes. Pleasure surges through me, hot and electric.

The tip of her tongue flicks out, and a guttural sound escapes my throat. Her eyes meet mine, dark with lust, a wicked smile curving her lips as she licks a bead of pre-cum from the tip, relishing it like a forbidden treat.

When the wet heat of her mouth finally wraps around me, it's like I've died and gone to heaven. She takes me deeper than I thought she'd be able to. What Sofiya lacks in experience, she makes up for in enthusiasm.

When she's reached her limit, she swallows, pushing just a little further, and a strangled curse escapes me.

"Eyes on me, I want to see that elegant neck working."

One glance from beneath those lashes, and I unravel completely. Sofiya might be kneeling in front of me, but she has all the power. I grit my teeth, trying to hold back, but it's a challenge when she looks this good with her plump lips wrapped around my fat cock.

Her tongue swirls around my length as she bobs up and down. One hand grips me at the base, twisting perfectly in sync with her lips. A low hum escapes her, sending a shiver of pleasure through me.

Her nails scrape along the sensitive cut of muscle just below my abs. She inches higher, her palm pressing against my stomach, tracing the ridges there as if she's memorizing every dip and rise, testing my restraint.

My hips jerk involuntarily, pushing my cock to the back of her throat. Tears gather in her eyes, and she stills for a moment, breathing through her nose, adjusting to my size but not giving up.

"You're doing so good, moya sladost." My words sound tortured even to my own ears. "Are you going to swallow me down when I come for you?"

She gives a little nod of her head and widens her eyes. That's all it takes for my cock to jerk in her mouth and for a flood of cum to erupt down her throat. She puts in the effort, drinking me down, giving as much as she takes, and damn if I don't come undone right here.

She's ruined me, this woman. And I don't think there's any way to come back.

CHAPTER THIRTY-FOUR

NIKOLAI

The city rolls by in flashes of gold and stone as the sun starts to lower over St. Petersburg's ancient streets.

Sofiya leans her head against the window, her fingers pressed against the glass. We've just left the dance studio and are heading back to the estate.

"This city is beautiful." She sighs. "It's nice to see people out and about, enjoying themselves. Just living a normal life."

Her words hit me like a jab to the ribs. I've kept her locked away for so long that even the simplest sights feel like a revelation to her. She glances back at me, her expression genuine, and something in my chest tightens.

"One day, I'll give you a tour of the city." One day. The words sound empty, even to my own ears. But she doesn't push for reassurances or ask for a timeline. She just leans back against the seat and smiles softly.

"I'd like that."

I glance out the window, then back at her, watching as her face lights up, taking in the world outside. What's the point of ruling the city if I can't share it with her?

I signal to let the car behind us—the one carrying my guards—know there's been a change in plans. "Do you like ice cream?" I ask.

Her head tilts, a playful curve to her lips. "Doesn't everyone?"

"Want to try the best ice cream in the city?"

"Is it… safe? I mean, is it okay for us to be in public?"

Normally, I'd avoid crowded areas, but I have guards with me, and the look on her face is enough to make me take the risk. "It'll be fine."

I pull the car to a stop outside a tucked-away ice cream parlor with a bright green awning. It's not flashy, just a small window and a few café tables where people are clustered, holding cones piled high.

When I park, I type out a quick text to Matvey, explaining the plan and telling them to stay close but make themselves scarce.

I come around the car, open Sofiya's door, and help her out. I might be a criminal, but I'm still a gentleman in my own way. She smiles, bright and carefree, and whatever hesitation I felt fades immediately.

We step up to the counter, her eyes darting to the menu written in chalk on a board next to the window. "So many flavors. I don't know what to choose." Her teeth sink into her full bottom lip, drawing my attention. All I can think about is tugging it free and sucking it into my mouth.

"I've never had pistachio ice cream before," she exclaims.

"That's because pistachio ice cream is garbage."

She frowns, narrowing her eyes. "You said this place has the best ice cream in the city."

My lips quirk up. "It does. But that doesn't mean pistachio is a flavor that should exist."

She crosses her arms, tilting her head in mock offense. "I'll take my chances. And just because you were so grumpy, I won't be sharing with you."

The vendor glances at me, his movements stiff, like he's nervous. I tend to have that effect on people. "Give me a scoop of everything," I tell him.

He doesn't even blink, just nods and gets to work.

Sofiya places a hand on my arm, raising her brows. "What are you doing? We can't possibly eat all of that."

"You said you didn't like to share." I shrug. "I'm not risking you hogging all the good flavors."

She grins, unapologetic. "You are a madman."

We're sitting at a small table tucked against the side of the stone building, the remnants of what must've been ten scoops of ice cream between us. Sofiya leans back in her chair, licking the last bit of pistachio off her spoon with a satisfied sigh.

"I can't believe we ate all of that." Her tone is somewhere between impressed and horrified.

"We?" I arch a brow. "I had two bites."

"Liar," she shoots back, narrowing her eyes. "You were practically hoarding the pistachio."

"Because it was damn good," I tease. "I'm a believer."

She scoffs, a spark of laughter in her eyes. "Next time, I'm ordering. You've lost that privilege."

Will there even be a next time for us? The question claws at my chest—I know there won't be unless I make a change. The truth is, I'm done pushing away what I want. And what I want is Sofiya—not just for now, but forever.

Fuck. The realization sears through me like fire.

But keeping her means making peace with the Syndicate. She's already told me she won't choose between me and them. I need to make that choice for her before it's not a choice at all. Because a war always leaves losers.

"I have to tell you something." Her head tilts with curiosity, and I force my next words out even though she might not like them.

"After I sent Roman the pictures of you in the basement, he accepted my deal. Agreed to all my terms, but I turned him down."

Her brows shoot up, her expression blank, like I've spoken a foreign language. "Why? Wasn't that the point of taking me?"

"Because it meant sending you back, granting you a divorce, and never seeing you again." I let out a breath and tuck her hair behind her ear.

"I couldn't do it."

Her lips tremble, her eyes searching mine. "You're serious?"

"I've never been more serious about anything in my life."

She rises to her feet, her chair scraping against the ground, and launches herself into my arms, burying her face in my neck. "I stand by my words when I called you crazy earlier."

I brush a hand over my neck. "You're not mad?"

"I'm not mad. Maybe I should be, but it means you choose me. Even though it's costing you the casino deal. But…" Her brows knit together. "I can't be yours until there's peace."

"I know. I haven't forgotten."

I've been turning this over in my head for days, and there's only one way forward. If I'm going to prove to the Syndicate that I'm serious about making things right—and about being the husband Sofiya deserves—I have to walk away from the casino deal. Actions speak louder than words. I'll do everything I can, and then pray they don't decide to kill me anyway.

She scowls. "How do you know I want to stay with you? Were you going to ask me?"

I grab her wrist, tugging her forward. My voice drops to a low rumble. "No, my sweetness, I'm not going to ask. I think you know I'm a man who takes what I want."

I'm unsure if she's going to slap me or kiss me when she surges forward, her hands sliding around my neck. "Right answer, mudak."

She crushes her lips to mine. The kiss is hot and consuming, the kind that makes everything else fade away. When she finally pulls back, she's flushed and breathless.

"You make me a very happy man, moya sladost." I nuzzle her neck, inhaling her skin.

"Don't think you're off the hook," she says, poking a finger at my chest. "You've still got plenty of work ahead."

"Give me a few days to figure things out. I promise I'll make this right with your family."

Her eyes search mine. "Can I ask you a question?"

"Anything."

"What's the deal with that Igor guy? There were some seriously weird vibes when I interrupted the two of you in your office."

I sigh, pinching the bridge of my nose. "Igor Bocharov is… complicated. He's a crooked politician. One that's very handy to have in my pocket." I shake my head. "We've partnered on a number of projects, but the biggest one is this casino deal. Well, was the casino deal."

"You sure you're ready to give that up? Maybe there's a way you can keep it and make amends with the Syndicate."

I pause in thought. For a moment, there's nothing but the buzz of the city around us. Sofiya opens her mouth to say something, but the sound of a revving engine cuts through the air.

The sharp crack of gunfire follows.

Instinct takes over. I tighten my arms around Sofiya and drop us both to the ground, shielding her entirely as more shots ring out.

People scream, the street erupting into chaos. Tables overturn, glass shatters, and my guards move into position, guns drawn, scanning the area.

"Stay down," I growl, keeping my body pressed against hers.

She's trembling beneath me, her breathing rapid. "Niko—"

"I've got you," I promise her. My focus shifts to the street, catching a flash of black—someone on a motorcycle weaving through traffic.

I release Sofiya just enough to grab my weapon, aiming carefully. People are ducking under tables and scattering. There's chaos all around, but I hone my focus and fire twice. The shots are precise, but the rider swerves, disappearing down a side street.

"Fuck," I hiss, shoving the gun back into my holster. I turn to my guards. "One of you, follow him."

Dima nods while Matvey jumps behind the wheel of the car I drove.

I look down at Sofiya, who's still crouched on the ground, her face pale. "Are you hurt, moya sladost?" I run my hands over her body as my chest tightens with discomfort.

She shakes her head. "No. You?"

"No, but we need to get out of here now."

I help Sofiya to her feet, keeping her close with one hand, my weapon in the other, as I guide her toward the waiting car.

She climbs in, and I follow, pulling the door shut behind us. Matvey floors the gas, and we speed off. Fuck, I just wanted a normal afternoon with Sofiya, but chaos follows me everywhere.

Sofiya exhales shakily. "Do you know who attacked?"

"No. But I sure as hell am going to find out."

Her fingers twist in the fabric of her dress, her eyes searching mine. "Is this because of me?"

I run a hand down my face. "It doesn't matter," I say finally. "What matters is you're safe, and I won't let anything happen to you."

On the way back to the estate, I call Vadim to update him and arrange for him to meet me in my office. I also message Eva, still in Armenia, telling her to keep her phone close.

Sofiya is shaken, as expected, but she promises me she'll be fine and tells me to deal with what I need to. Leaving her alone is the last thing I want, but being attacked while I'm out with my wife is nothing short of a declaration of war.

I'm pacing my office when Vadim arrives. His grim expression mirrors my own.

He lowers himself into the chair across from me, his shoulders stiff, as I hit the speakerphone button and dial Eva. The phone rings twice before her worried voice breaks the silence. "Nikolai. What's going on?"

"You're on speaker with me and Vadim," I say, before detailing the attack from start to finish. My chest tightens as I speak, knowing how close of a call it was. If Sofiya had been hurt, I'd never forgive myself.

Vadim mutters a curse, dragging his palm down his face. "That wasn't random. Someone was following you. They knew where you'd be. This was deliberate—meant to send a message."

"Did you catch the guy on the bike?" Eva asks.

"Dima tried, but the motorcycle was long gone before he could close the distance."

Vadim rolls his shoulders. "You think it's the Syndicate?"

"No. They'd never put Sofiya's life in danger like that."

"We didn't leave things on good terms with the Azerbaijanis," Eva reminds me.

Fuck. She's right. "Tural?"

"My contacts tell me he's furious we dropped them," Eva continues. "He's stupid and reckless enough to seek revenge."

That motherfucker. My fists clench with the urge to smash

something. The bastard knows Sofiya is my weakness—I did a shitty job hiding it during our last meeting.

"We need eyes on Tural and his cartel—businesses, safe houses, contacts—everything. Let's find out what he's up to before we retaliate."

"Let me run point on this," Eva says. "I'm in the region."

"Fine. But be careful. We don't know what else he's planning."

"Always."

I release a tense breath. "I need to tell you both something. I've made a decision that will change everything." I lean forward, resting my elbows on my knees. "I'm pulling out of the casino deal."

Vadim's eyebrows hit his hairline. "That's a hell of a pivot."

Eva lets out a low whistle, but I can sense her smile from the other end of the line. "Any particular reason?"

"I think you can guess it's about Sofiya. This is the first step toward fixing things with the Syndicate—and proving I'm serious about her."

Today's attack was a reminder I can't put off making peace with the Syndicate. Sofiya is too important to risk, and the longer I keep them on ice, the more tense this situation becomes.

Vadim scowls. "Roman Vasiliev is not known to be a forgiving man."

"Maybe not, but he's a practical man, and peace makes more sense. If I show him I'm willing to sacrifice the deal to avoid war and protect Sofiya, he'll see reason."

"You're optimistic," Eva quips. "But love makes people do crazy things."

Love? I never said anything about love, but… Fuck. Is that what this is?

Vadim coughs to hide a smile. "When did we start using the L-word?"

"We didn't," I snap. Not yet, at least.

"For now, this stays between us. I haven't told Igor yet, but we need to be ready for the fallout. He's going to be livid."

Losing Igor's political support will hurt, but I'd be lying if I said I trusted him fully. Every instinct tells me to keep him away from Sofiya, no matter the cost.

Vadim gives me a pointed look. "This is everything we've spent the last year working for. Are you sure this is the right move?"

"Never been more sure of anything in my life."

CHAPTER THIRTY-FIVE

SOFIYA

I STAND AT THE COUNTER, MY HANDS STICKY WITH RICE AND ground meat, rolling the mixture into neat bundles as Yelena watches over me like a hawk. The kitchen is warm, the tang of tomato sauce mingling with the earthy smell of cabbage.

"Too loose," Yelena says, reaching over to prod one of my rolls with her finger. "It'll fall apart in the pot if you don't tighten it."

I glance down at the roll and frown. "Oh, come on, it's not that bad."

Yelena shakes her head. "But it can be better. The way to a man's heart is through his stomach."

I stifle a laugh, trying again with exaggerated care. I don't know how I let Yelena talk me into this cabbage roll lesson. Well, I do know—she's trying to distract me, and honestly, I need it.

It's been a tense few days since we were attacked in public. Still, it hasn't all been bad. We've fallen into a strangely domestic routine. Niko wakes up early, works out, brings me breakfast in bed, and then we shower together. It always ends the same way—with me on my knees, bent over the sink, or my legs wrapped around him against the wall.

Afterward, he disappears into his home office for a few hours. I know he's dealing with the fallout from the attack. He has reason to believe an Azerbaijani cartel is behind it, and he's working on taking them down. I was surprised he shared that with me, since we've never really discussed bratva business before. When I asked him for details, he opened up, which is something I appreciate.

I'd like to say the public attack was the scariest moment of my life, but it wasn't. Being taken and almost married off to Sergey was, but this came close. Once again, Niko saved my life.

Now, instead of fantasizing about him for the next five years, he could be mine.

My husband. My protector. Maybe even the father of my future children. I'm falling hard for him, which terrifies me because there's still so much up in the air. He promised to make things right with my family and the Syndicate, and I have to give him a chance to prove himself.

But he needs to deal with the immediate threat first.

I sigh, presenting my latest cabbage roll for Yelena's inspection.

She purses her lips, studying it like it's a masterpiece, then gives me a small nod. "Getting there," she declares.

I frown. "Well, if Niko complains about a cabbage roll falling apart, he's welcome to make his own dinner."

Yelena scoffs, wiping her hands on her apron. "You think that man would ever step foot in this kitchen to cook? Please. That's why you need to get it right."

"What is this about making my own dinner?" Niko's deep voice fills the room as he strides into the kitchen. He looks mouthwateringly good in his suit. The dark fabric is tailored perfectly to his broad shoulders and lean frame. Knowing what's underneath all that material leaves my mouth dry.

Before I can respond, he's behind me, his arms wrapping firmly around my waist, bringing my backside flush to his front. His lips brush against my neck, planting a lingering kiss that I feel down to my toes.

Yelena doesn't miss a beat. She smiles knowingly, then quietly excuses herself.

"Going somewhere?" I ask. This life has inherent risks, but I don't like the thought of him leaving the estate while his enemy is at large.

"Meetings. And I'll be careful," he murmurs, his breath warm against my skin as his fingers trace lazy patterns along my ribs. "What are your plans?"

"Isn't it obvious?" I close my eyes when he drags his nose down the side of my neck. "I'm learning to be a perfect Russian wife."

His chuckle vibrates against me. "You're making Yelena's dreams of domestic bliss come true."

I snort. "I doubt I can ever live up to her standards." I point and flex my healed ankle. "Might even put on one of those fancy leotards you got me and do a short warm-up sequence. I want to compile all the best practices the school instructors could use."

"Good idea." His palm slides lower, grazing my hip. "But don't wear yourself out, because I have plans for you tonight."

"Really?" I turn in his arms, meeting his gaze. "What kind of plans?" I whisper seductively.

He kisses my forehead. "We're going out, and the only clue I'll give you is to dress up."

My head snaps back in surprise. "We're leaving the estate?"

He smiles. "It's safe. We captured the Azerbaijani cartel leader behind the attack and all his top lieutenants. He's being transported to St. Petersburg today. So tonight, we celebrate."

The idea of going out with Niko, even for one night, fills me with excitement. "You're seriously not going to tell me anything else?"

"That's the fun of a surprise. Now, be good today," he teases, leaning in for a kiss. His mouth moves against mine, soft yet demanding, his hands on my hips, pulling me against him. It's so damn easy to lose myself in his scent, his touch, his drugging kisses.

The sound of footsteps brings me back to the present. I pull away, expecting to see Yelena, but it's not her. Emil stands frozen in the doorway, his eyes flicking between us.

Unfazed, Niko gives my ass a firm squeeze before stepping away. "Be ready by eight."

As he walks past Emil, he claps him on the back with a low murmur of something I can't hear, but the sharp look he throws him is unmistakable.

Emil crosses to the espresso machine in the far counter. He pours a mug, his back to me, the tension practically radiating off him.

I exhale slowly and grip the counter, working up the courage to say what I need to. "Emil, I need to apologize to you."

"For what?" he snaps, still not looking at me.

"For… the woods. For putting you in that position with Niko." The silence feels heavy as I search for the right words. "I never meant for you to get in trouble. I didn't choose to be here, and I was desperate for a sliver of freedom. You have to understand that."

He finally turns, his jaw tight, his expression hard. "Doesn't look like you're desperate to get away anymore. Seems to me you've settled in just fine. You and Niko are a happy little family, huh?"

I flinch at the bitterness in his voice. "I really am sorry. If I'd known it would get you in trouble…" My words trail off. The truth is, even if I had known, I'd probably still have done it. "The point is, I didn't mean for you to take any of the blame, and I'm sorry you did."

His eyes narrow as he takes a slow sip of coffee, leaning back against the counter, studying me. "You don't have to make excuses. You tricked me. Next time, I won't be so naive as to trust you."

"There won't be a next time," I say carefully. "Things are different now."

He lets out a humorless laugh. "Yeah, I noticed. We all have. He's distracted. Spending his days wrapped up in you instead of running his empire. He's taking his eyes off the ball, and it's going to get us all killed."

His words feel like a punch to the gut. Since Niko has been giving me so much of his time and attention, does that mean he's neglected his duties?

"That's not true," I say, my tone defensive. "He's handling his business."

"Is he?" His eyes bore into mine. "Because from where I'm sitting, that's not the case. First, the Azerbaijanis. Next, it'll be the Syndicate coming for him, for all of us. And when that happens, you'll only have yourself to blame."

I grip the counter to steady myself, an ache spreading through my chest.

"Don't say I didn't warn you," he says flatly before turning and walking away, leaving the room steeped in the weight of his warning.

After Emil leaves, my head is a mess. I can't think, focus, or even look at the cabbage rolls I'm supposed to be helping with. When Yelena returns, I mumble some sorry excuse about having a headache and needing to lie down, then slip away to the bedroom I occupied before moving into Niko's.

Now, I'm in the bathroom, sitting with my back against

the door, Valeria's cell phone clutched in my hands as I decide what to do.

Niko asked me to give him time to figure things out, but what if we don't have time? After he rejected Roman's deal, I can only imagine how tense things are back home.

What if they are planning something? The Syndicate has endless resources at their fingertips, and while I know Niko does too, maybe he's been too distracted to see them coming.

Emil might be bitter, but that doesn't mean he's wrong. I can't be the reason that Niko, or anyone for that matter, is killed.

Hands shaking, I make the call I've put off making for a long time. Liza picks up right away.

"Sofiya… Is that you?" Her voice is tight, on the edge of breaking.

"It's me," I assure her.

A deep exhale. "Are you okay? Tell me you're okay. Are you hurt? What did he do to you?" Her questions hit like rapid fire, leaving no space for answers. "Roman's in the other room, I'll get him—"

"No," I interrupt, the word coming out harsher than intended. "Liza, I need to talk to you alone. Please."

"Okay," she replies but I can hear the reluctance in her voice. "What's going on? Are you safe? Are you still…" She trails off as if she can't bring herself to say the words.

I close my eyes, shame washing over me in hot waves. How can I explain that somewhere along the way, in between the threats, the mind games, and the tattoos, I've fallen in love with my captor? My husband.

Wait… love? Is that what this is?

"I'm safe," I assure her, trying to keep this conversation on track. "But I need you to listen. Just let me talk because this is not easy to explain."

I swallow hard and grip the phone tight. "When this started, I was Niko's captive, yes, and I didn't want to be here. But he never hurt me—never abused me or treated me the way you think he did. He wanted everyone to believe I was being tortured, and miserable but that was never the case. In fact, it was the opposite."

She's quiet on the other end, but I can practically feel her disbelief. "Is he there with you right now? Is he making you say this?"

"No, he doesn't know I'm making this call. I stole this phone a while ago. He has no idea. But I need you to hear me out."

She lets out a sharp breath. "I don't understand. None of this makes sense."

I tip my head and look at the ceiling. "It doesn't make sense to me either, but things… changed between us. He's shown me parts of myself I didn't know existed, given me faith in myself I never had before."

"Do you even hear what you're saying?" she says, her voice breaking slightly, raw with emotion. "You're defending the man who abducted you and forced you into marriage. Tell me you see how insane this is?"

"What he did was wrong; it was savage. I get that," I say, the words catching in my throat. "But he's shown me a different side to him. He bought me a dance school for kids in need. Something I can run, that's mine to do with as I see fit. He's made me feel like I can do something good. I can be more than just someone who's been through hell."

"Roman offered him a deal. The Syndicate agreed to every one of his demands, and he still turned them down. This is the man you want to be with?"

"He had his reasons, Lizka. That doesn't change how I feel about him. I don't want him killed. I don't want anyone killed —or for this to spiral out of control."

When she speaks again, there's a note of desperation in her voice. "Sofiya, we know where you are. The information you gave us about Koporye Fortress and the estate of

Catherine the Great's niece checked out. Roman's tech guys pinpointed your location. If you can get to a safe place, Roman and his men can get you out."

My stomach drops, and my hands go clammy. I feel like I'm betraying my sister with what I'm about to say, but if I leave him, I'll regret it for the rest of my life.

"I'm so sorry, Lizka. I know how hard this must be for you to understand, but I want to be with him. I'm in love with Niko, and I think he feels the same." My voice cracks, and I swallow hard. I know he feels the same. "He's going to make amends with the Syndicate and show you how serious he is about me. About us. But for now, you have to promise me the Syndicate won't attack."

"This is crazy, Sofiya," she pleads. "I don't know what to tell you. The Syndicate isn't just Roman. Pavel and Maxim—Nikolai crossed them too. He betrayed their trust in a way he can't fix."

Tears prick at my eyes as I press my palm to my forehead, trying to clear the chaos in my head. "You don't understand… If something happens to you, Roman, or anyone I love, I'd be devastated, but…" My voice grows husky. "If something happens to him… I'd feel the same."

"I need to see you," she says after a beat. "I need to see for myself if this is real. If you're really okay, or if…" She trails off, but the unspoken words sit between us. *Or if he's broken you.*

I nod, even though she can't see me. "That's fair." I don't know how we'll manage it, but I owe her that.

"Give me a day. I'll talk to Roman and the others. But Sofiya, I can't make any guarantees."

"I know."

"I miss you so damn much," Liza says, voice thick. "And I just want you to come home."

"I miss you too," I breathe. "And I'm sorry for what this is doing to you. I know it's tearing you apart." I try to smile through the ache in my chest. "It's funny, isn't it? I wanted to escape bratva life, and now I'm more entrenched in it than ever."

A long pause stretches between us before Liza says, "I love you, Sofiya."

"Love you, Lizka," I reply, blinking back tears.

The line goes dead, and I sit there, the full weight of what I've set in motion crashing over me.

CHAPTER THIRTY-SIX

NIKOLAI

Igor crouches over one of his bushes, snipping at a stray stem with a pair of shears as I approach. He shades his eyes with one hand and looks up at me.

"Another unexpected visit. Maybe you're here to learn how to garden?"

Two of his guards linger nearby. I guess after you press a gun to the underside of a man's chin, people get jumpy.

"Not quite," I say, adjusting my cufflinks. "Gardening's not my thing."

Igor straightens, brushing dirt from his hands as he turns to face me. His smile doesn't reach his eyes. "Pity. It teaches patience and focus—two things you seem to be running short on."

I ignore the jab and reach into my jacket, pulling out the casino contract.

He gestures to the papers with a sharp nod. "Are those signed yet?"

I shake my head. There's no point dragging this out. "I'm pulling out of the casino deal."

His expression hardens, and he tosses the shears onto the ground. "I see. And what brought you to this brilliant decision?"

"The deal no longer aligns with my priorities. I'll make sure you're compensated. I know you're losing more than just money, and I'll do what I can to make it up to you."

Igor's laughter is harsh. "Ah, your priorities. Let me guess—your pretty little wife?"

My expression hardens. He has a right to be angry with me, but if he mentions Sofiya again, it won't end well. "That's right. Sofiya is my priority, and that means making things right with the Syndicate."

His lip curls in disdain. "You're either the dumbest bastard I've ever met, or you've got a death wish. There's no way in hell that the Syndicate will ever forgive you."

"Watch how you speak to me," I snap. His guards shift closer, but I don't give a shit. "I've got my priorities straight. I know what truly matters, and it's her and whatever future we share."

He shakes his head, his dark eyes drilling into mine. "I warned you not to fall under the spell of a beautiful woman, but you walked right into her trap. She tricked you, just like your own brother did."

The word "brother" hits like a punch to the gut. My vision narrows, and the old wound he's reopened burns fresh.

In two steps, I'm in his face, my voice low and cutting. "Say that again. I dare you."

I catch movement from the corner of my eye as his guards shift, reaching for their weapons. I feel the threat at my back, but I don't move, my focus locked on Igor. His smirk fades, as he glances back at his men.

"Sergey betrayed me, betrayed everything I built. Sofiya is nothing like my snake of a brother." My fists clench and unclench at my side. "You've been a trusted partner, and I'd prefer to keep it that way. But if you disrespect my wife again, I'll end you without a second thought."

Igor blinks, his cocky mask slipping back into place. "You're playing a dangerous game, Zhukov. You walk away from this, and you lose everything. And I won't be here to pick up the pieces."

I step back, rolling my shoulders. "Don't worry about me, Igor. I know exactly what I'm doing."

When I step inside the office, Vadim looks up from the couch, where he's sprawled with one foot resting on the coffee table. He sets his drink down, eyebrows lifting in question. "How'd it go?"

I loosen my tie, letting out a sharp breath. "About as well as I expected. Which means not well at all." Dropping into the chair behind my desk, I drum my fingers on the polished wood. I haven't been to this office above one of our nightclubs in over a week, preferring to work from home to stay close to Sofiya.

"Can you blame him? He lost money and political clout in one move."

"That's how the game is played. I don't make the rules." I shrug. "He definitely didn't like me choosing Sofiya over him."

Vadim snorts, stretching his arms over his head. "You think he'll retaliate?"

"He'll pull his political support, but he isn't stupid enough to come after me directly. He knows I'll bring a war he can't win." I pause in thought. "Still, Igor's not someone to underestimate."

"I'll have our men keep an eye on him," Vadim says. "Speaking of dangerous motherfuckers, what's your plan with the Syndicate?"

I lean back in the chair, staring at the ceiling. "Plan? I don't have one yet." There's no way I can call Roman and admit that everything I've said over the past few weeks is a lie. That I've never hurt Sofiya and never could. That I've fallen for her harder than I ever thought possible. Whatever my next move is, it has to be bold enough to convince him I'm serious about being with Sofiya. "Let's handle the Azerbaijanis first, and then I'll figure out how to deal with the Syndicate."

Vadim runs his thumb along the rim of his glass. "Have you heard from Roman since you turned down his offer?"

"No." I flex my fingers around a paperweight. "Not sure if that's a good thing or a bad thing. But it doesn't matter anymore."

Vadim lets out a quiet chuckle. "You're either brilliant or suicidal. Hard to tell sometimes."

I stand, crossing to perch on the edge of my desk. "What's the latest on Tural?"

"Eva's en route with him and a van full of his men. Last I heard, they're hogtied in the back like a delivery of Christmas hams."

I smirk, picturing it. "I'd like to know how she managed that." Then again, Eva is capable of some very creative solutions when it comes to getting what she wants. "And when do we expect this... delivery?"

"Later today. She'll tie them up at the warehouse so you can question Tural tomorrow."

It's not often that I'd prioritize a party over getting the answers I want, but tonight is the birthday party for one of my top lieutenants.

Most importantly, Sofiya will stand at my side tonight while my men pledge their allegiance to her. They need to understand that protecting her is no different from protecting me, and I expect them to lay down their lives for her.

I've kept her presence in my life quiet until now, knowing men like Tural would see her as a target. But what Sofiya and

I have is real, and it's time she stands at my side where she belongs.

I pick up the paperweight again, turning it over in my hands. "Good. I want Tural to look me in the eye and explain why targeting me and my wife was a smart fucking idea."

Vadim hums in agreement. "Do we have hard proof that Tural's behind the attack?"

I place the paperweight back on the desk, standing and adjusting the cuffs of my shirt. "By the night's end, we'll have everything we need. The pieces are finally falling into place."

CHAPTER THIRTY-SEVEN

SOFIYA

My call with Liza plays in my head for the rest of the day. I hope I haven't made a mistake by involving her, but it felt like my only choice.

Even if she thinks I've lost my mind, I know she has my best interests at heart and will do whatever it takes to keep me safe. Roman, on the other hand, won't be nearly as calm about any of this. That's why I had to talk to Liza first. If anyone can get through to him, it's her.

I don't know how she'll pull it off, but if she can manage to arrange a meeting where no one ends up dead, they'll see things aren't the same anymore. Niko is not who they think, at least not entirely.

Evening rolls around, and it's time to get ready for our mysterious date tonight. Niko didn't give me many details, but he did tell me to wear something special, and that's what I'm going to do.

Niko had all my clothes moved into his bedroom, but I haven't explored the walk-in yet since I've mostly worn yoga pants or summer dresses.

An idea pops into my head, and I can't help but grin. I rummage through the racks until I find what I'm looking for. It was the last piece I tried on, one of the many things I bought purely for the joy of spending Niko's money, but I never thought I'd have the opportunity to wear it.

I strip down to my underwear and slip the emerald dress over my head. The fabric is sheer and gauzy, clinging in all the right places, the deep V neckline showing just enough to tease, as does the dramatic slit up the side.

I stand in front of the mirror, biting my lip. Jesus, it's sexier than I remember. Niko never did see me try it on at the boutique, so this will be his first look. And it's one I hope he appreciates.

I step into the gold strappy heels Valeria suggested I pair with the dress, adding inches to my height and making my legs look longer than they are. I keep my makeup simple—a black lash and a bold red lip—a look my sister helped me perfect. That was always our thing, her doing my makeup while we gossiped. Hope flickers at the thought that we might do that together soon.

I leave my hair loose over my shoulders, the dark strands brushing against my back.

When I check my reflection in the mirror, I have to admit —I look good. The ankle monitor even adds a little edge to the whole look. But something pulls at my gut.

Niko is possessive, and this dress is bound to push his buttons, which is fine if we are alone, but just in case we're not, I reach for a shawl, wrapping it loosely around my shoulders. It softens the look and hides just enough cleavage to keep me from feeling completely exposed.

With one last glance in the mirror, I head downstairs.

"So, where exactly are we going?" My voice sounds high to my own ears as I glance at Emil's profile from the backseat. He's focused on the road, his expression tight.

"It's a surprise, remember," he says, shifting gears.

I let out a soft sigh, turning to the window. St. Petersburg sprawls before me, glittering under the streetlights.

My gaze drops to my lap, where my clutch sits, the ankle monitor visible beneath the hem of my dress. I smirk to myself. Only I could turn an accessory like this into part of an outfit.

Emil clears his throat, drawing my attention back to him. "Look, about what I said earlier, I was out of line." He sighs, his hands tightening on the wheel. "Things are tense with the Azerbaijanis breathing down our necks. I shouldn't have taken it out on you."

"It's fine," I say, not wanting to drag it out. "I understand. Things are complicated right now. I don't want to see anyone hurt either."

He glances at me in the rearview mirror. "I'm glad to hear that."

Before he can say more, his phone rings. He puts an earbud in to keep the conversation private and answers with a clipped, "Yeah, she is." A long pause. "Don't worry. It's all worked out."

I frown, glancing at Emil, but his expression is unreadable. Is it Niko on the phone? Is he asking about me? My heart races—part excitement, part nerves. I have no idea what tonight is about, and that only makes my anticipation sharper.

A few minutes later, we pull up behind a low-rise building. As soon as we park, the passenger door swings open, and Nikolai stands there, looking devastatingly handsome. Fitted black pants cling to his muscular thighs, and his dress shirt is unbuttoned just enough to hint at the ink covering his chest. His hair is tousled like he's been dragging his hands through it, and his jaw is dusted with stubble, but it's his eyes—those piercing, deep-blue eyes—that steal my breath.

He holds out his hand, and I take it, stepping out of the car. His gaze sweeps over me.

"You're beautiful, moya sladost," he murmurs.

A spark shoots through me at his words, and I grin. "You don't look too bad yourself."

I clear my throat and take a quick look around. We're in the back alley of what appears to be a club, music spilling from under the door. He offers me his arm, and I slip mine through his, as he leads me through the back entrance, down a long, dark hallway.

"Are you finally going to tell me where we are and what we're doing here?"

He smiles, his hand warm on my back, leading me through the halls. "This is one of the nightclubs I own. Tonight we're closed to the public for a birthday party for one of my men."

My head snaps toward him. "Does that mean I'm going to meet your people?"

"That's exactly what it means." His hand twines with mine. "I think it's time everyone meets the pakhan's wife, don't you? If anything should happen to me, my men need to know who to lay down their life for."

I shake my head, at a loss for words. "Are you sure? With the way things are going—"

In a flash, he has me pushed up against the wall, his thigh wedged between my legs. His gaze narrows as he tips my chin so I can't look elsewhere. "You. Are. My. Wife." He lifts my hand and drops a kiss onto his tattoo. "One day, I'd like it if you wore my ring. Not just my mark."

My heart takes off at a gallop in my chest, but I can't help giving him sass, anyhow. "Does that mean you plan on asking me like a proper gentleman? Not just a savage who takes what he wants?"

He smirks. "Both."

Then he crashes my lips against his, sucking my bottom lip between his teeth. My hands grip his shoulders as I pull him into me, kissing him back. My body is on autopilot, moving on instinct, fingers tunneling into his hair as his tongue plunges into my mouth, practically eating me alive.

When he pulls away from me, I'm gasping for air like a fish out of water, and he seems perfectly composed. "Now, we better join the party," he growls, "because if I have to spend another minute alone with you, I'm going to fuck you against this wall."

I bite my lip because that doesn't sound like a terrible idea.

With a possessive hand on my back, Niko leads me down a long hallway and up a flight of stairs. We stop in front of a door that, from the sounds of it, leads to the actual club. He pauses, taking in the shawl wrapped tightly around my shoulders. "Are you cold?"

Nerves settle in my gut. If I knew I'd be meeting his men, I wouldn't have worn this, but there's no point in calling attention to it now. I wrap it tighter around me.

"Uh, a little. Who is this party for?" I ask to change the subject.

"Stanislav. One of my lieutenants. You'll meet him soon." He stares into my eyes. "I told Igor I'm out of the casino deal today. Tomorrow, I'll reach out to Roman. Not that it'll be easy."

Warmth fills me, but it's tinged with the slightest bit of guilt. I should tell him about the stolen phone and the call to Liza. I will tomorrow. He may not be happy about it, but I owe him the truth.

I nod, and he grasps my hand, threading his fingers through mine, and leads me through the door into the main club. Subtle electronic music and the heat of a crowd greet us. The party is in full swing.

As we move through the room, the sea of people parts for

us. Well, for Niko. People greet him with nods and respectful gestures, but they keep their distance, giving him the space he clearly commands. Nikolai dips his chin, acknowledging the people we pass. Curious gazes follow us, particularly me, and I find myself grateful for the anchor of his hand in mine.

At the far end of the room, we approach a small table that appears to be reserved for a select few. Everyone stands, and I suddenly feel nervous with all eyes on me. Nikolai pulls me into his side. The only person I recognize is Vadim.

"You remember, Vadim?" Niko asks.

"How could I forget? The cereal lover, right?"

Vadim makes a move to kiss the back of my hand. It's about halfway to his lips when Niko scowls and clears his throat in warning.

"Nice to see you again," he says, with a mischievous grin, letting my hand go. Vadim then introduces me to his friends, a blonde woman named Tatiana, and her sister, a redhead named Galina.

"Why don't you take a seat? Vadim and I have a few people to talk business with first, but I'll have champagne brought over. Loosen you up a bit before I introduce you to everyone." He trails a hand down my arm, leaving little sparks in its wake.

As soon as we're alone, both women give me their full attention.

"Okay, I've got to ask about you and Nikolai," Galina says, leaning forward conspiratorially.

"Tell us everything. I mean, he's been a confirmed bachelor for years, and then suddenly, he shows up with a wife? The sister-in-law of Roman Vasiliev, no less." She rubs her hands together. "There's got to be a juicy tale there."

Tatiana shoots her sister a look as glasses of champagne appear at our table. "Don't be so nosy," she scolds.

Galina rolls her eyes. "Give me a break. You know that's all anyone here is talking about."

Tatiana turns toward me. "I mean, we are curious, but I don't want to pry into your business."

I laugh. At least they're being honest. "Let's start with what you do know."

"Not much," Tatiana admits. "Nikolai went to Moscow and came home married to you. Everyone's been tight-lipped, but I can assure you, all the single ladies in St. Petersburg had a good cry about it."

My eyebrows hit my hairline. I'm surprised that's all that's known about us, but I guess when the pakhan wants people to keep their mouths shut, they do.

Before I can say anything, Galina jumps in, resting her chin in her palm. "I bet it was a whirlwind romance. Love at first sight, swept off your feet, all that fairy tale stuff, right?"

I nearly choke on my champagne. If only they knew how far from a fairy tale this marriage started—more like a horror story, complete with a villain who's all too real—one whom I fell head over heels for.

"Not exactly," I say, taking a sip for liquid courage. "Niko and I started as an arrangement, of sorts. It's… complicated."

Galina's eyes widen as if I'm about to spill some juicy gossip. "Complicated how?"

I fiddle with the stem of my glass, choosing my words carefully. "Let's just say the marriage wasn't my choice." I peer across the room and see him standing, talking to a group of men. When his eyes catch mine, he gives me a little wink, and my stomach does a summersault. "I feel differently now."

Tatiana nods thoughtfully. "That's the case with most bratva marriages. You're just lucky that your husband's not some old fart twice your age and three times your weight." She makes a face. "Like my betrothed."

Galina smirks. "Well, Nikolai is three times your size… but in a good way."

We share a laugh, but when I look over at Tatiana, she looks down. "But aren't you here with Vadim?" I ask.

"He's just my older brother's best friend. That's the guy my parents promised me to." She nods toward an older man scolding a waiter, his face twisted in irritation as he waves an empty glass in the air.

"I'm sorry," I say, not even trying to sugarcoat it. "You guys come from a bratva family?"

Galina frowns. "Unfortunately. Once Tatiana is married off, I'm next. That's why I'm having as much fun as possible until my parents force me kicking and screaming into a wedding dress."

A warm hand skims down my back, stealing my attention. Nikolai leans in, his breath tickling my ear. "Ready for me to introduce you?"

I'm feeling nervous, but I agree, anyhow, and excuse myself, allowing Nikolai to lead me across the room.

"I'm going to introduce you to the birthday boy, Stanislav."

As we approach, Stanislav, a man in his early thirties with sharp cheekbones and a neatly trimmed beard, rises from his seat, as do a dozen or so of the men around him.

"Pakhan," they say nearly in unison and bow their heads in a sign of respect.

He allows them a moment, before he speaks again. "I want to introduce you to my wife," he says. Nikolai clears his throat, and the room falls dead silent. "This is Sofiya. From this moment on, her life is as valuable as mine. You will protect her, obey her, and, if necessary, die for her."

This isn't what I expected. Nikolai's hand tightens on my waist. "Any man who fails in this duty answers to me. You will treat her with the respect and care due to the wife of a pakhan, understood?"

A chorus of "Yes, boss" fills the air. They bow their heads, as they did for Nikolai a moment ago.

"Thank you," I say, trying not to fidget with the end of my shawl. These men barely know me, yet they've vowed to protect me like I matter. It's touching, but that kind of loyalty has its risks. If the Syndicate refuses to negotiate, if Nikolai and Roman can't reach an agreement, it could cost them their lives.

It's one more reason why I need to come clean with Niko tonight about my contact with Liza. I don't want anyone hurt because of me.

"Happy birthday." I direct that comment to Stanislav. "Quite a turn-out you have."

It's true. The party is in full swing, and it's nice to be out in the world, talking and drinking. A small dance floor is off to the side with a few people enjoying themselves.

Stanislav gives me a broad smile. "Thank you for attending. It's truly a pleasure to meet you. No man is more deserving of a beautiful woman by his side than our pakhan." Apparently, everyone else agrees, with heads nodding and men stepping forward to shake Nikolai's hand.

Nikolai wraps an arm around me. "I agree. My wife is very beautiful."

I flush with pleasure but have no time to respond because Tatiana and Galina are waving to me from the dance floor.

"Enjoy yourself," Niko whispers in my ear. "We still have some business to discuss."

"Oh, you men and your important mafia business," I tease, but I don't mind taking the opening he provided. It's been so long since I let loose.

Galina throws her arms around me as soon as I step onto the dance floor. I get the feeling she made quick work of that bottle of champagne.

"I love this song," she announces loudly in my ear. It is a good song—a massive pop hit from last year over a techno beat. "Take off that stupid wrap and dance with us."

Wrap? Right, the shawl hiding the super sexy dress I have

on underneath. The one that seemed like a good idea earlier, but with a roomful of his men, I get the feeling it won't be appreciated.

"No, that's okay. I find it a little breezy in here."

Tatiana laughs. "Breezy? Are you kidding, I'm dying." She lifts her thick mane of hair off her neck.

"I'm good, honestly." Both women shrug and continue to dance. It feels so good to let loose and move, to just enjoy myself like any other woman my age. I sway my hips to the beat, spinning slowly, letting the rhythm take over.

I glance at Nikolai, deep in conversation with Stanislav, but his eyes remain locked on me. His lips curve into a familiar smirk, and his raised brows remind me of the night we met at the club. Judging by the heat in his stare, he remembers, too.

"I've never seen the pakhan look at a woman the way he looks at you," Tatiana half-yells in my ear to be heard over the thumping music. I flush. I doubt that's true, but it still makes me feel good.

Out of the corner of my eye, I catch a flash of blonde hair and a supermodel-like figure—Eva. She looks stunning, as always, her skin-tight black pants and halter top drawing attention with every step. She walks up to Nikolai and leans in, kissing him on both cheeks.

I know there's nothing between them anymore—Niko told me as much—but I can't help the prick of jealousy that creeps in. I liked being the one to hold his attention, the one he couldn't look away from.

I realize I've stopped dancing when Tatiana touches my shoulder. "Everything okay? You need a drink or something?"

"I'm fine," I assure her. My voice is tight, but I force myself to smile. "But yeah, maybe a drink's a good idea."

"No! You can't leave yet. This is the best song." Galina

throws her head back and her arms in the air as the music shifts to a more sensual, hypnotic beat.

I glance at Nikolai, who's still smiling at whatever Eva just whispered in his ear. A spark of defiance ignites in me. If he's going to let himself get distracted, then I'll just have to remind him exactly where his attention belongs.

"You know… it is a little warm in here," I say, my tone light. With a flick of my wrist, I toss the shawl over a nearby chair.

Cool air glides over my skin, and I feel a rush of boldness. I sway to the music, rolling my hips in time with the beat.

Galina gives a low whistle. "Damn, you've been hiding that body all night. If I had a figure like yours, I'd live in that dress."

Tatiana spins me, and I stumble into her, laughing as I catch my balance. The heat of the room and the pulse of the music crackle like electricity under my skin.

Galina nudges me, smirking. "You're turning heads, you know that, right?"

I shrug, throwing her a mischievous smile. "Good."

I sense his stare first—a simmering heat that sends a shiver through me. When I finally glance at him, Nikolai's eyes are locked on me, dark with a dangerous edge. Welp. I've definitely got his attention.

I look away first, tossing my hair over my shoulder, my heart pounding as I keep dancing. I've poked the bear; now I have to see it through.

"Uh-oh." Galina's voice is barely above a whisper, but I don't miss the warning. My head snaps up just in time to catch Nikolai storming toward me, his jaw clenched, his arms rigid at his sides, and his fists curled tightly.

"Sorry," Tatiana whispers with a grimace as she and Galina quickly retreat. So much for girls sticking together. Not that I can blame them. Nikolai looks absolutely lethal.

The dancers step aside as he cuts straight through the

room, clearing a path to me. I keep swaying, pretending I don't notice him until he's right in front of me. My nose brushes against his solid chest, but I refuse to look up.

"What are you doing?" he asks with a lethal calm that sends a shiver of both fear and excitement through me.

I tilt my chin up, feigning innocence. "Dancing. What are you doing?"

"Wondering why my wife thought it was a good idea to wear that sexy little number," he says roughly. "Especially when she knows I don't like sharing." His gaze drags over me possessively. When his eyes linger on my breasts, my nipples tighten—and he notices.

Is it my imagination, or has the room gone completely silent? My hands land on my hips. "You didn't tell me where we were going. I thought tonight would be just us."

Before I can blink, his hand wraps around my arm, and he's leading me off the dance floor. The air feels charged, and I catch glimpses of men glancing away as Nikolai cuts through the room with me in tow.

"Where are we going?" I ask, unable to hide the tremor in my voice.

"To show you what happens when you act like a brat, wife."

CHAPTER THIRTY-EIGHT

NIKOLAI

Sofiya wanted my attention, and now she has it. My bratty little wife knew exactly what she was doing the moment she tossed that shawl aside and swayed those hips like she was on a stage.

She wants to play games? Fine. I'll play, but she should know by now I never lose.

"You're acting like a neanderthal. Let go of me." She tries to wrench her wrist from my grip, but I don't let go until we're in my office, the door shut behind us.

She was half naked in front of all my men, dancing seductively. They all had the brain power to look away, and for that, she must be taught a lesson.

Punished.

Fuck, that word alone gets my dick hard. "There are consequences to your actions, moya sladost." Pushing her down onto the couch, I stand above her making use of our power and age difference. "Now explain to me what you were thinking, showing everybody what's mine?"

She narrows her eyes, refusing to give up. "I can ask you

the same thing. Did anyone ever tell you it's bad taste to invite your former mistress to the same party as your wife?"

Jesus fucking Christ. Is this about Eva?

I lift her effortlessly, slide into her seat, and settle her onto my lap. She's playing with fire, but she doesn't seem to care. Her breaths come fast, our lips just a whisper apart. I can't tell where her anger ends and her arousal begins. My hand cups her chin, tilting her face toward me, forcing her to meet my eyes.

"I meant it when I said there's no one else. Eva isn't my lover and never has been. She's an old friend and a high-ranking member of my bratva. You're mistaken if you think she's anything more to me."

"Liar. You admitted she was your girlfriend the first day I got here."

"I never admitted anything. You assumed she was and I didn't correct you because I liked how jealous you got."

She bites her lip. "Was not."

Her body goes rigid, and I drag my nose up the side of her neck. "Now that I know what a brat you are, I think I need to show you who owns these gorgeous tits."

"How are you going to do that?" Instead of sounding scared, she sounds turned on.

I trace the edge of her panties, moving along the crease of her inner thigh. "I'm going to start by checking how wet you are for me." She licks her lips, her breath coming in short, hot pants. "What do you think I'm going to find? Are you soaked through for me, pretty girl? Does the thought of me teaching you a lesson make your pussy wet?"

"No," she rasps without conviction.

"Liar." I hook my fingers around the elastic of her panties and pull the strip of fabric to the side. That motion alone is enough for my knuckles to drag across her slit, covering me with her readiness. "I can feel how much you want your husband's cock. Your panties are fucking soaked."

She lets out a mewl, as I stroke one finger up the length of her slit, but I don't push in. Just tease her entrance, showing her what a little slut she is for me. For her husband. Try as she might to deny it. She can't.

My fingers continue to pet her but I don't give her the penetration she needs. I brush her clit with the barest of touches, not enough to relieve her need, just enough to make her desperate for more.

"On your knees in front of me," I command.

She complies, sliding off the couch and kneels between my spread thighs. I undo the button of my pants, pull down my fly, but leave my cock covered. Sofiya licks her lips. "Are you going to make me suck your cock?" The pure need in her voice makes me laugh.

"I said I would teach you a lesson, and I will. You flaunted these beautiful tits for everyone to see, and now, I'm claiming them as mine."

I reach forward and wrap my hands around each of her breasts, giving them a little squeeze over the material, before I pull down the bodice of her dress to find her braless.

I groan out my appreciation. "Perfect," I say almost to myself. "Now, pull my dick out of my pants."

She swallows hard and gazes up at me, eyes narrowed. Is she thinking of denying me? "You know I'm not here to play games." I move a strand of hair away from her face to have a clear view of her unblemished skin, and the flush of color adorning her cheeks. "Do it. Take me out."

She licks her lips, and reaches inside my pants, wrapping her warm fist around my length. Pure fucking bliss. I close my eyes, relishing her touch before shoving my pants and briefs down and maneuvering her toward my cock. I'm too far gone to wait. I need her touch now.

"Take my dick in your mouth and get it nice and wet."

She parts her lips, and I slide the head of my cock across her tongue, savoring the wet heat. "Deeper," I demand, my voice rough. She obeys, taking me inch by inch until I hit the back of her throat. Her cheeks hollow as she sucks me down, her eyes locked on mine.

"Good girl," I growl, tangling my fingers in her hair to guide her. I watch her struggle, a soft gag escaping when I push in too far. Drool spills down her chin, coating the length of me as she tries to keep up. I pull back, letting her catch her breath, but only for a moment.

"Again," I demand, sliding back between her lips. She moans around me, the vibration making my balls tighten. Her tongue works me perfectly, and when her hands move to cup my balls, I nearly lose it.

When I finally pull out, her lips are swollen, her chin slick with spit. She whimpers, reaching for me, but I'm not done yet. "You've had your fun. Now it's my turn," I say, smearing the wetness down my length with a satisfied groan.

I grip her breasts, pressing them around my cock as I thrust between the soft mounds. Her nipples pebble against my thumbs, begging for attention, but my focus is on the way her flesh cradles me, how perfectly she fits me.

"Look at you," I husk, my hips driving forward, my stomach tensing with each thrust. "Made for me. These tits are mine, aren't they, moya sladost?"

She gulps, her gaze locked on me, her cheeks flushed. "Say it," I demand, my voice dropping. "If you want to touch yourself, tell me who they belong to."

Her lips part, her voice hoarse. "They're yours," she whispers, a bratty spark in her eyes. "But don't get used to it."

I grin darkly. "We'll see about that. But you were a good girl. Reach down and make yourself come for me."

She doesn't need to be told twice. Her hands tremble as they slip between her thighs. I take over, squeezing her breasts together, my cock sliding faster as her fingers start to move.

I lean forward, my lips brushing against her ear as I whisper, "Harder. Make yourself come while I fuck these perfect tits."

I pinch her nipples, twisting just enough to draw a gasp from her lips. Her head falls back, her moans growing louder, and the sight of her so undone is enough to drive me to the edge.

Her rhythm picks up, her hips rocking against her hand, the slick sound of her arousal mixing with the wet glide of my cock between her breasts. When she cries out, bracing herself for release, I knock her hand away, plunging two fingers into her tight heat, grinding my palm against her clit.

"Come for me, Sofiya," I growl, my cock throbbing.

Her body jerks and trembles as her climax washes over her, soaking my hand with her release. I don't take my eyes off her face—her parted lips, the way her expression goes slack with pleasure, her breaths coming in shallow gasps.

Just fucking perfect.

I let her bask in the aftershocks, her body soft and pliant in my hands, completely undone. Meanwhile, my need for her burns hotter, my cock aching for relief. I'm done waiting.

With one arm around her waist, I haul her up, peel off her panties, and settle her onto my lap. Her dress rides up around her waist, her bare skin pressed against me. The contrast between us is intoxicating—her exposed and vulnerable, me mostly dressed and in control.

Holding her steady, I guide myself to her entrance, dragging the swollen tip through her slick folds.

Her head falls back, her voice tight as she murmurs, "What are you doing?"

I smirk, continuing to tease her soaked pussy. "Oh, moya sladost, did you think we were done?"

Her eyes flutter open, and I push forward enough to make her gasp. "No, sweetheart," I growl, gripping her hips. "Now you're going to take every inch of my cock."

CHAPTER THIRTY-NINE

SOFIYA

"Are you going to put me inside you, or should I do the honors?" Niko's voice is low and smooth, full of dark promise. It's not a question—it's a challenge, one I can't resist rising to.

My palm flattens against his chest as I sink down, inch by inch, his thick length stretching me in a way that makes me gasp. I have to force myself to breathe, my body straining to take him fully. His low, guttural curse makes my skin tingle. I can feel the restraint, but I want him to snap. I want him to lose control, just like I am.

His eyes are dark with lust as he leans in, kissing me as though he's starving and he'll never get enough. I suck on his bottom lip, my tongue swirling with his, the heat between us building fast. I've just had an intense orgasm, yet I'm aching for more. My body pulses with need, every nerve alive and begging for his touch.

"You're so fucking tight. This pussy was made for me. Do you see that, moya sladost? You were made to be my wife."

Before I can answer, he grabs both sides of my hips and thrusts up, filling me completely.

"That feels so good," I whisper, rocking into him. "What are you doing to me?"

His eyes darken, and a smile lifts his lips at my confession.

"The same thing you do to me." With one hand, he grabs my hair, tugging it to the side to expose my neck. His tongue drags across my skin before he nips and sucks, marking me. "Now ride me. Let me watch those gorgeous tits bounce."

Desire crashes through me, leaving me breathless and utterly at his mercy. I roll my hips, giving him the show he demanded, but when his teeth graze the sensitive spot on my neck—a wicked mix of pleasure and pain—I struggle to stay upright.

"You're my gorgeous slut, aren't you, wife? Only mine."

"Fuck, yes," I cry, unable to hold the words back. My thighs tremble, muscles locking as I teeter on the edge of another orgasm. Niko moves like it's his sole purpose to destroy me, pounding into me with a ferocity that leaves me shaking.

His hands are everywhere—tugging my hair, kneading my breasts, gripping my ass as he slams me down on his cock at a relentless pace.

"Listen to those sounds you make, Sofiya," he growls, his voice thick with hunger. "You're desperate, aren't you?"

I nod frantically, incapable of lying. He knows my body better than I do.

"Good. I want you to come on my cock. I want to feel every inch of you breaking for me."

He presses two fingers to my lips. "Suck," he orders. "Get them nice and wet for me."

My tongue swirls around his digits, pulling them deep into my mouth. His eyes burn into mine as I hollow my cheeks, and my heart races. Christ, this man is sinful.

He slides his fingers free, his smirk dark and knowing as

he moves them behind me. Then I feel it—a slow, deliberate circle at my entrance, one I've never allowed anyone to touch before.

"No," I gasp, jerking slightly. "I've never—"

"Shhh," he soothes, his voice a purr. "You'll like it. Trust me, moya sladost. I'll make you feel so fucking good."

Before I can protest, he applies gentle pressure, his finger teasing the tight ring of muscle. My body stiffens, but his free hand finds my clit, rubbing slow, deliberate circles until my resistance melts away.

The tip of his finger presses inside, and I gasp, my body tensing before slowly relaxing into the sensation. It's strange, not painful, but enough to steal my breath.

"You're taking it so good," he whispers against my neck, sucking my skin into his mouth as his palm grinds into my clit. A bolt of pleasure shoots through me, white-hot and blinding.

A few more thrusts and I shatter, my pussy clenching around him as he works his finger deeper, his thumb stroking my clit, the dual sensations overwhelming. I scream his name, my cries echoing through the space.

"Look at me," Niko growls, grabbing my chin and forcing my eyes to his. "That was the sexiest thing I've ever seen. Now keep looking at me as I fill you with my cum."

His hips slam into mine, fast and unrelenting. My walls grip him like a vice, responding to him with each deep, punishing thrust. I'm barely holding on as his breath stutters, his muscles tightening beneath my hands.

He groans low and guttural, his head dropping to the crook of my neck as he thrusts once more, burying himself deep. His cock thickens, and he shudders violently, his release spilling inside me as his body jerks.

For a moment, all I can focus on is the heavy press of his chest against mine as his hand cradles the back of my neck.

His lips brush over my shoulder, as if he's savoring the moment.

"You know," I say, my voice still breathy, "if this is what it takes to get your attention, I might have to act like a brat more often."

He pulls back enough to meet my gaze. "You're playing with fire, moya sladost. But if that's the game you want to play, I'll happily oblige."

I stand slowly, my legs trembling as I adjust my dress back into place and smooth down my hair. "What now?"

"Now we return to the party," he says, arching a brow. "With that wrap firmly in place."

I roll my eyes, and his hand comes down on my ass with a light slap. "Behave," he says, smirking.

Before either of us can move, a booming knock shakes the office door.

"We're busy!" he snaps.

"Get out here. We're under attack!" Vadim shouts from the other side. His words are cut off by the distinct crack of gunfire.

Fear barrels into me, as Niko pulls me close and pushes me beneath the solid oak desk.

"Stay down," he barks, yanking open his desk drawer and pulling out a gun and ammo.

I curl into myself, knees pressed to my chest, my hands shaking. Screams echo from somewhere outside the office, making my stomach churn.

Niko crouches in front of me, his hands finding my face, steadying me. "Sofiya, look at me. You stay under this desk, do you understand? I need you to stay safe so I can do what needs to be done."

"No!" I gasp, my voice cracking. "Don't go! It's too dangerous."

He leans in, pressing his lips to my forehead "I need to. But I can't do what's necessary unless I know you're safe. I'm going to lock the door from the inside. Don't open it unless it's me or one of my men."

Tears prick my eyes as I nod, my throat too tight to form words.

His thumb brushes my cheek—a fleeting moment of tenderness before he's gone.

I clamp my hands over my ears, trying to block out the chaos outside, but it's the thoughts in my head that are doing the worst damage.

Is this Roman and the Syndicate?

Liza warned me they knew where Niko's estate was. Did they track us here?

My chest tightens painfully as I picture Niko and Roman's men fighting, lives lost on both sides. The thought is suffocating. This is everything I've dreaded—and it's all my fault.

CHAPTER FORTY

NIKOLAI

I crack open the door of my office, my pistol gripped tightly in my hand. The sounds of chaos—shouting, gunfire, shattering glass—slam into me like a physical force. Every fiber of my being rebels against the idea of leaving Sofiya alone and unprotected, but I have no choice.

I slip into the hallway, keeping my back pressed to the wall. The muffled commotion of violence filtering through the building sets my teeth on edge as I move through the back corridors, my senses on high alert.

As I round a corner, a series of shots ring out, aimed directly at my head. I dive, but not fast enough—pain explodes through my shoulder. Fuck! Blood runs down my arm, but I push past the burning ache. Raising my gun, I fire back. The attacker crumples to the ground, motionless.

He's clad head to toe in black, a balaclava obscuring his face—no way to identify him. I'll search him as soon as I get the chance.

I pause, scanning my surroundings, then creep forward, my steps near-silent. At the entrance to the main room of the club, the conflict grows louder. I stop at the threshold, taking in the destruction: overturned tables, shattered bottles, and scattered debris littering the floor. My men are hunkered down on one side, locked in a fierce exchange with the attackers on the other.

There's no clue as to who these men are—Syndicate soldiers? Tural's cartel? Or someone unexpected?

Crouching low, I creep along the edge of the room, ignoring the searing pain in my shoulder. I make it to the bar, sliding over the top and dropping to the sticky floor behind it. Bullets rip through the shelves above me, showering me with glass and booze. Cursing under my breath, I crawl on my stomach to the end of the bar, my gun clutched tight.

Peeking around the edge, I spot one of the attackers, his back turned as he reloads behind an overturned table. I don't hesitate. I rise, aim, and fire. The bullet finds its mark, and he crumples to the ground.

One down. Who the fuck knows how many more to go.

I duck back behind the bar, my ears ringing. My men are holding their ground, taking cover behind toppled booths and shattered furniture, but the attackers are using the DJ booth as a shield. It's sturdy enough to absorb most of our rounds, giving them the upper hand.

I inch to the edge of the bar, trying to find a better angle. Just as I'm about to fire, I catch movement—one of the attackers raises his hand, motioning sharply to the others.

In unison, they break formation and sprint toward the shattered windows. Glass crunches beneath their boots as they vault over debris, disappearing into the night.

What the fuck?

For a moment, no one moves. The room is unnervingly quiet, the acrid scent of gunpowder thick in the air. I rise from my position, stepping into the middle of the room to take in the carnage.

Slowly, my men emerge. Vadim climbs out from behind an

overturned table, his gun still drawn. Others step out from behind shattered furniture and the cover of broken booths.

"What the hell was that?" Vadim mutters, raking a hand through his hair.

"An ambush. But they didn't stay to finish what they started."

In the far corner, one of my men lies near the entrance, his lifeless eyes fixed on the ceiling. Fuck. My stomach sinks, but as far as I can tell, he might be the only casualty—which feels like a minor miracle.

"Let's check the wounded," I say. "And get Dr. Safin here immediately."

Vadim is already moving, barking orders to the others as he pulls out his phone.

I instruct a few senior soldiers to sweep the building, making sure none of these black-clad bastards are lurking in the shadows.

Vadim is at my side when Eva bursts from the back room, pushing a group of trembling party guests into the main space. They're all affiliated with my bratva, but that doesn't mean they've ever experienced something like this before.

Eva takes one look at me and blanches. "Shit, Niko, your shoulder—"

"Will be fine," I cut her off. The nick is the least of my problems right now. "What the hell was that?"

Vadim shakes his head. "They came out of nowhere, like ninjas in all black, but retreated before the fight was finished."

"This doesn't add up," I grit out. "Why leave like that? Unless they were just trying to send a message. If so, it's lost on me."

Eva's eyes sweep the room. "Any idea who's responsible?"

"Not yet, but we need answers." I gesture at my shoulder with my chin. "I dropped the guy who did this to me in the hallway outside my office. Search him. And if any of them are still breathing, I want them interrogated."

"Understood."

"Vadim, check the security footage to see if we can ID any of them. I need to get Sofiya out of here. Call me when you have something."

CHAPTER FORTY-ONE

SOFIYA

I CLAMP MY HANDS OVER MY EARS AND SQUEEZE MY EYES SHUT, trying to block everything out. I feel powerless. Worse, I feel responsible—even though I'm not sure this is the Syndicate's doing.

I'd like to think Liza wouldn't let this happen—not after what I told her. But maybe she couldn't get Roman or the others to listen. Maybe they're here to "save" me, thinking I'm brainwashed or under Niko's spell.

The sound of fighting filters through the walls. The skirmish must be happening in the main room. I promised Niko I'd stay put, not move until someone came for me—but what if I could stop the fighting? If Roman's men realized I'm here, they'd put down their weapons. Wouldn't they?

I'm debating what to do when there's a sudden knock on the door.

My nerves spike. If it were Niko, he'd say so. Could it be Roman or one of his men?

"Sofiya, open up. I need to get you out of here." Relief floods me as I recognize Emil's voice.

I scramble to my feet and unlock the door. Emil steps inside, quickly shutting it behind him. "We need to move. Now," he says, his expression tense.

"Where's Niko? Is he okay?"

"He's fine. But his orders are clear—I'm to get you out of here. He'll meet us back at the house."

My stomach churns. "I don't want to go. If this is the Syndicate attacking, I can help stop it."

"We don't have time for this, Sofiya. Niko said to get you out of here no matter what."

"But—"

"No 'but.' Move." His grip is firm on my arm as he pulls me into a long, dark hallway. It's a different route from the one we came in through.

I consider breaking his grip, telling him I can help, but maybe I'm being reckless. Walking into the middle of a gunfight could be suicide.

All I can do is hope Niko and the others make it out safely. This isn't his first battle, and I have to trust he will make it out safely.

Emil shoves me into the backseat of a car—not the Land Rover we came in. The door slams, and I barely have time to click my seatbelt before the tires screech, and we speed off.

The car careens around a corner, throwing me against the door. I grab the handle to steady myself, glancing out the tinted windows. Unease drips down my spine. Is Emil worried we're being followed? Could we be a target?

I start to ask, but his phone rings, and he picks up immediately. Maybe it's Niko. I can't hear the words, but his biting tone cuts through the air. He keeps glancing at me in the rearview mirror, his expression tense. Does he think this is my fault? It wouldn't surprise me. Like he said, I distracted Niko, and now this.

When he hangs up, I lean forward between the seats. "Was that Niko? Is he all right?"

He doesn't answer. Doesn't even look at me.

"Emil?"

"Just shut up and let me do my job."

His harsh words sting, but I swallow my frustration. Everything is on edge right now, and pushing him won't help.

I chew on my nails, my thoughts racing. As soon as we're back at the estate, I'll call Liza. I need to know if the Syndicate is behind this. If they are, maybe it's not too late to stop whatever they have planned.

I'm so lost in my head, my mind looping through worst-case scenarios, that I don't notice the car has stopped until the door beside me swings open.

My head jerks up, and my stomach drops like a stone. Igor Bocharov. My whole body goes rigid.

He slides in beside me, slamming the door shut behind him.

"Hello, Sofiya," Igor drawls, his tone far too pleasant for the circumstances.

My throat tightens, and I press back against the seat. "What's going on? Why are you here?" I demand.

The car speeds off again, and I catch Emil's stony expression in the rearview mirror. This isn't good.

Igor leans back, his posture casual, like we're old friends catching up. "Don't look so scared. We're just going for a little drive."

I shake my head, my pulse pounding in my ears. "Emil, stop the car right now. I want to get out."

Emil ignores me. I lunge for the door handle, not caring that the car is moving.

Igor's hand clamps down on my wrist like a vise, twisting hard. I cry out in pain.

"You're not going anywhere, my beautiful little dancer. You and I have much to discuss."

"No we don't!" I scream, thrashing as Igor presses a cloth

over my mouth and nose. The chemical smell is overpowering, burning my throat. My vision blurs, and my limbs grow heavy as I fight against the darkness closing in.

The last thing I see is his smug face before everything fades to black.

CHAPTER FORTY-TWO

NIKOLAI

My shirt hangs open, the fabric slick with blood from the graze on my shoulder. With a grimace, I unscrew the vodka bottle, pour a shot, and toss it back.

Tilting the bottle, I let the alcohol spill over the wound. The sting is sharp enough to make my head swim for a moment.

"Fuck," I mutter, grabbing a fresh bandage and pressing it against the graze. It could have been worse. The pain is a welcome distraction, a reminder that I'm alive. It feels like the only thing keeping me from spinning out of control.

Sofiya could have been killed tonight. It would've been the second time her life was in danger under my watch, and that fact eats away at me. I've failed her again, and I fucking hate it.

Emil got her out while the fighting was still going on. I'm furious he didn't wait for my orders, but at least she's safe. He texted to say they're en route to the estate.

I still don't have a clue who's behind the attack—the

Syndicate, the goddamn Azerbaijanis, or some unknown enemy lurking in the shadows. In my world, anything is possible.

Eva and Vadim enter my office a moment later as I fumble with the bandage one-handed. Eva clicks her tongue and snatches it from me.

"You're going to make it worse," she mutters, taking over first-aid duty.

When she's done, Vadim presses a spare, clean shirt into my hands. "Try not to bleed through this one," he says dryly.

I rub at my temples. "What did you learn?"

Eva blows out a breath. "The men who attacked us arrived in an unmarked van. They were all wearing black, with no visible signs of affiliation. It's possible they were mercenaries hired for this job."

I nod, wiping the sweat from my face. "And the dead?"

Vadim shakes his head. "No tattoos, no scars, no identifiers. We're still running their images through facial recognition software to see if we get any hits."

I run a palm over my chin. "It feels like it was meant as a distraction more than an attack."

"The Belov Syndicate?" Vadim suggests. "Could they have been looking for Sofiya?"

My blood freezes. "How would they know she's here? Details of the party were kept secret until the last minute."

Eva clears her throat, drawing my attention. "About that. I was going to wait until tomorrow to show you this, but it might be relevant." She pulls a cell phone out of her back pocket. "This is Valeria's cell phone. It went missing the day you took Sofiya shopping at her boutique. Valeria was sure she had misplaced it, so she never cut off service. She didn't think much of it until she got her phone bill yesterday."

My eyebrows draw together. "What are you saying?"

"Valeria called me because she didn't want to accuse your wife of stealing. I hope you don't mind, but I did some digging. I found the phone hidden away in Sofiya's bathroom." Eva taps a few times on the screen before handing it to me. "It looks like she messaged and called her sister Liza a couple of times. The most recent call was today."

Everything inside me goes cold.

Vadim frowns. "You think Sofiya put this in motion?"

Eva grimaces. "We have to consider it as a possibility."

A sick feeling washes over me. Was Igor right? Is Sofiya using me the way my brother did? The thought feels like a knife to the gut.

"Fuck." I rub my temples, trying to make sense of everything. "But she didn't know where I was taking her tonight. I kept it a surprise until the last minute." I scroll through the call logs. "The last call she made was hours before she arrived here."

Vadim's lips twist as he lowers himself onto the edge of my desk. "Could she have overheard something? We shouldn't underestimate her." He gestures to the phone. "She's obviously more wily than any of us thought."

Anger flares hot through my veins. "She wouldn't do that."

"How do you know?" Eva asks gently.

I don't. I don't know fucking anything for sure. The only thing I have is a soul-deep conviction that she wouldn't betray me. But only an idiot would bet everything on that.

Vadim and Eva go quiet, giving me a moment to process.

"Listen," Eva continues. "She stole the phone before your relationship… changed. It's possible the Syndicate was able to override our jammers and trace the call today. It's also possible Sofiya didn't know they were coming."

I shake my head, the logic not adding up. "Why would they risk her getting hurt in the attack? And the Syndicate fights to win. If they made a move, none of us would be standing, and Sofiya would be long gone."

Vadim drums his fingers on the desk. "We still haven't

ruled out the Azerbaijanis. Tural might be locked in our warehouse, but someone who works for him could be behind this."

Of all the possibilities, this seems the most likely. "I'm going to the warehouse to question Tural." I crack my neck, my body vibrating with energy.

"Vadim, you stay here and deal with the clean-up. See if we get more details on who the dead guys are. Eva, you go back to the house and check on Sofiya. I want extra men protecting the estate tonight."

Vadim reaches for his gun, checking the chamber before holstering it. "And if the Syndicate was behind the attack? If Sofiya is working with them... What's our plan then?"

I grind my molars together so tightly it feels like I might chip a tooth. "I don't have a good answer for that."

A tense silence blankets the room, but I'm not here to discuss what-ifs. I motion for them to get on with it.

Tural hangs from a hook in the ceiling, his wrists bound, his feet barely brushing the concrete floor. Blood drips from his split lip onto his already ripped and stained shirt. Looks like Eva had a little head start.

He lifts his head when I enter, his swollen eyes narrowing. "Zhukov," he barks. "Come to finish the job yourself?"

"You look like hell," I say, rolling my sleeves up as I come to a stop in front of him.

"The same could be said about you," he rasps.

My fist connects with his face, a solid hit to the nose that makes him grunt in pain. I grab his face and force him to look at me.

"I don't have much time so I'm going to set out some ground rules. I'm going to ask you questions, and you're going to answer them truthfully and without hesitation." I raise my electric drill so he can see it. The message is clear. "You're dying tonight. How I kill you is still up in the air. So let's cut the bullshit. How about you tell me why you attacked my club tonight? Is it because the idiot you hired to take me and my wife out in the streets didn't do his job?"

I grab the drill and flick the switch. The motor hums, the bit spinning inches from his face. His bravado falters as the sound fills the room.

"The street hit was mine, but I had nothing to do with the party tonight. How could we? My men are all here, tied up like animals."

"Are you sure you don't have anyone left on the outside?" I snarl, pressing the tip of the drill under his chin just enough to make him feel the point. "You'd better think real hard about your answer because this is the part where I get creative."

Fear flickers in his eyes as he struggles against the restraints. "There's no one left!" he roars. "You got everyone who could help me. I swear it."

I lower the drill to hover over his abdomen. "How the hell did you know about my marriage to Sofiya? How did you know to threaten her? And don't feed me bullshit."

His head lolls forward, his breath coming in shallow pants. "You think I'm the villain here, Zhukov? You're blind. The real enemy is staring you in the fucking face, and you don't see who's playing you."

My vision blurs with rage as I shove the drill into his side, the bit piercing flesh. Tural screams, his body jerking violently, blood blooming like a dark flower on his shirt.

"Who?" I roar, yanking the drill back. "Tell me, or I'll go deeper."

"Who do you think?" he gasps, his face twisting in pain.

Igor.

Fuck me. Everything locks into place, the realization so sharp it feels like I've been gutted.

He was under my nose the whole time, and I didn't see it. My breathing slows, the drill suddenly heavy in my hand as Tural watches my expression.

"Figured it out, didn't you?" he wheezes.

I swallow hard, forcing the bile back down my throat. My mind races through every interaction, every warning sign I ignored. The uneasy feeling I've brushed off too many times.

I power up the drill and press it into his flesh, harder this time. His screams are raw and guttural. Blood spills, dripping onto the floor. So much for keeping this shirt clean.

"Why? What does Igor want from me?" I demand. Tural groans, his head slumping forward, but I yank his chin up. "Speak."

"How the fuck should I know? He didn't tell me his plan, he just tipped me off about your location the day of the attack. Said you'd lost sight of your priorities and needed help finding your way. All I wanted was getting a better cut on our deal, but you were too fucking stubborn."

His eyes roll back, lids fluttering. He's on the verge of passing out.

"Stay with me," I growl, slapping him across the face. His head jerks to the side.

"Igor has bigger plans for you," he taunts, his voice faint. "You have no idea what's coming. He's… he's working with s-someone powerful…"

His head slumps forward, the light in his eyes fading as he loses consciousness.

"Fuck!" I slap his face harder this time, but he's lost too much blood.

What does that mean… Bigger plans. Someone powerful? I've been blind, thinking I was always one step ahead. But Igor's been setting the board, and I've been playing right into his hands.

My phone vibrates, and I pull it from my pocket.

Eva's calling and I swipe to answer. "What is it?"

Her voice is tight with urgency. "Emil never came back to the estate. He's gone—and so is Sofiya."

The phone slips from my grasp, my pulse pounding in my ears. Everything inside me goes cold.

CHAPTER FORTY-THREE

SOFIYA

I COME TO SLOWLY, THE WORLD AROUND ME SWIMMING IN AND out of focus. My head throbs, and there's a bitter taste in my mouth that makes me gag.

A sharp ache in my shoulders pulls me back to reality, accompanied by the burning sting of the rope cutting into my wrists. My arms are pinned behind me, bound tightly to a wooden chair. I blink hard, trying to take in my surroundings. The room is small, with peeling paint, a cracked tile floor, and a single dim bulb swinging overhead.

My throat tightens as my eyes land on Emil crouching at my feet.

"Emil?" My voice is hoarse, my throat raw. "What are you doing? Where am I?"

"Shut up and don't move, or I'll cut into your skin," he threatens, not even looking up. Fear surges through me like a shot of adrenaline.

He's fiddling with the ankle monitor. Trying to cut it off, by the looks of it.

"Please, don't," I beg, tears stinging my eyes. "You don't have to do this."

He doesn't respond. He keeps his head down, carefully working on cutting through the cuff. My ankle monitor is the only chance Niko has of finding me.

"You're working with Igor, aren't you?" The answer is obvious, but I need him to admit it. I need to hear him say it.

Still nothing. My panic morphs into fury, and I rock back and forth in the chair, trying to knock him off balance. Emil plants a heavy hand on my knee, forcing me to stop.

"Sofiya." His voice is an irritated growl. "Do you want me to cut your fucking leg?"

"Answer me!" I shout, my voice cracking. "You're helping Igor betray Nikolai. Why?"

Emil finally meets my eyes, his expression dark. "Igor isn't a traitor. Nikolai's the one who let this happen. He's the one who needs a lesson in loyalty."

"What did he promise you? Money? Power? Do you honestly think anything in this world will protect you from Nikolai when he discovers what you've done?"

Emil snorts, his lips curling into a sneer. "You have no idea. This is bigger than money. You'll see soon enough."

He doesn't say anything more, just goes back to work. There's an unmistakable crunch as the gold splinters and the anklet comes free. A sick weight settles in my gut as he picks it up, turning it over in his hands before setting it on the ground.

"Don't!" I cry, but it's too late. The hammer comes down hard, shattering the tracking device—and with it, my only hope of being rescued.

"What do you want with me?" I whisper. "Are you going to hurt me? Kill me?"

The door creaks open, and my stomach turns to lead. Igor steps inside, his eyes gleaming as he takes in the scene.

He crouches to my level. With chilling gentleness, he

brushes a strand of hair behind my ear. My whole body recoils at his touch, my wrists straining against the ropes .

"Kill you?" he says, smiling coldly. "Oh no, my little dancer. You have no idea of your value. The most powerful men in the country would move heaven and earth for you. I'm going to use you. But first, we're going to have some fun."

The word fun sends ice dripping down my spine.

Desperation tightens every muscle in my body. "Emil, don't let him do this. Please. You don't want to hurt me. You can stop this—you can still make it right."

There's a flicker of something in his eyes, but it vanishes as quickly as it appeared.

Igor grips my chin roughly, jerking my face toward him. "Don't waste your breath on him," he sneers. "Look at me. I am the only one who matters. I determine your fate." My body trembles as his grip tightens. "Before we get to the fun, we must record a message for your husband and brother-in-law. That is, if they haven't killed each other yet." His smile widens. "I made sure Nikolai would believe the Syndicate was behind the attack. I can't wait to see how he retaliates."

"You orchestrated everything tonight?"

"It was the perfect time to take you while everyone was distracted."

Igor releases my chin, but the relief is short-lived. He steps behind me and yanks my hair, forcing my head back until I'm staring up at the cracked ceiling.

The lights snap on, bright and blinding, making me flinch. Emil steps forward, his phone raised, the lens pointed my way.

Terror claws at me as a knife presses against my neck. Igor leans in close, his breath vile as his lips brush against my ear. "Smile for the camera, little dancer. This is going to be fun."

CHAPTER FORTY-FOUR

NIKOLAI

The Bugatti tears through the night, headlights illuminating nothing but an empty road and darkness ahead. I grip the wheel, and press down on the accelerator as I near my estate.

The second I got off the phone with Eva, I opened the tracker linked to Sofiya's ankle monitor, but it showed nothing. My heart dropped when I remembered why: I disabled it earlier so she could leave the estate for the party without setting off an alarm.

Fuck!

I've called Emil repeatedly since leaving the warehouse, but each time, there's no answer.

The worst possibilities claw at me. Were they ambushed? Attacked on their way back to the estate? I can't prove it yet but all signs point to Igor being behind her disappearance.

I slam the wheel with my fist. I should've seen this coming. I should've known something was off with him. And now I'm paying the price.

I pull up in front of my house, barely stopping the car before I'm out and sprinting up the front steps.

Vadim and Eva are in the front hall. They turn toward me, their faces grim.

"What is it?" I demand.

Vadim's cheek twitches before he says, "It's Emil. He's compromised."

The words hit me like a physical blow. "What do you mean?"

"When I reviewed the security footage, I noticed Emil having a tense phone conversation. Turns out, he was standing near a bug I planted in the hall. I pieced together parts of what he was saying—he was talking with Igor about taking Sofiya."

The room spins. Emil. The man I trusted to protect Sofiya has turned on me. The betrayal cuts deeper than I ever imagined, dredging up old wounds.

Eva paces the foyer. "There's also footage of Emil leading Sofiya into a car—one that doesn't belong to the Zhukov Bratva." All of my vehicles have trackers, so this was a calculated move.

I grip the back of a chair, my knuckles white as I try to steady myself. "Igor," I say through clenched teeth. "Tural claimed Igor's been working against me, plotting something bigger. I didn't know how deep it went, but it sounds like he turned Emil."

Vadim curses under his breath. "What the hell does Igor want with Sofiya?"

"I don't know," I admit, my voice breaking with frustration. "Apparently, Igor's working with someone powerful. Tural passed out before I could get more information. I can't focus on that right now. Getting Sofiya back is the only thing that matters."

The tension in the room shatters with a rumbling sound, like thunder rolling over the estate.

"What the fuck is that?" Vadim mutters, reaching for his gun.

Eva draws hers as well, her gaze snapping toward the front doors. "Outside."

The three of us race out, bursting onto the lawn just as a helicopter descends. The deafening roar drowns out everything else.

If they were here to attack, we'd already be under fire. Still, I don't trust it. I keep my gun locked on the chopper, my finger hovering over the trigger, prepared for anything.

Eva and Vadim flank me, their weapons raised. The chopper touches down, and two figures step out into the night: Roman Vasiliev and Pavel Fedorov. Their hands are up, palms forward in a gesture of surrender.

"Don't shoot!" Pavel shouts, his voice cutting through the noise as they step onto the lawn.

Eva and Vadim glance at me for direction. I give a small shake of my head. We don't lower our guns, but we don't fire either. The two men, followed by a small contingent of their guards, make their way toward us.

They stop a few feet away. Roman's unflinching stare locks onto mine, his expression twisting when he takes in my blood-soaked shirt. "Sofiya asked for this meeting. If it were up to me, there'd be a bullet in your head right now."

It takes a moment for the pieces to fall into place: the phone call earlier today to her sister. Sofiya was trying to fix this, to negotiate peace between me and the Syndicate.

But peace might be impossible once he finds out what happened.

I lower my gun, dread settling in my chest.

"Let's go inside. We need to talk."

Roman and Pavel sit in the leather chairs in my office, their eyes drilling into me. Vadim leans against the far wall, his arms crossed, while Eva is seated on the couch.

I've told them everything from the beginning—about marrying Sofiya, my partnership with Igor, how I learned he's been working against me and likely turned Emil, and the events that unfolded tonight. The hardest part is explaining that she's missing.

When I finish speaking, Roman looks like he's seconds away from lunging across the desk and throttling me. Pavel's expression is cold, more measured, but no less lethal. They don't speak, and the silence is worse than if they were shouting.

I deserve their wrath for failing to protect Sofiya. I allowed someone to get close enough to betray me, and now she's in danger. I blame myself more than anyone. But blame won't bring her back. Nothing will except figuring out where she is.

"That's all we know right now. Igor's behind this, and Emil's working with him. That's where we start." I look at Vadim. "Have our hackers analyze CCTV footage and cross-reference it with traffic control systems to trace Emil's route after the club."

Vadim nods and fires off a text.

Roman tilts his head, his voice like ice. "This happened on your watch. The only reason we're still sitting here is because Sofiya begged Liza not to attack. Don't think for a moment that I trust you."

Eva crosses her arms and glares at Roman. "Well, you better learn some trust, because whether you like it or not, we're going to have to work together to find her."

Roman doesn't respond, but a muscle in his cheek twitches.

I clear my throat. "Sofiya wears a tracking monitor. I turned it off last night before we went out because I didn't want an alarm going off, but we need to find a way to activate it remotely."

"You had her wearing a fucking tracking monitor?" Roman growls.

I arch a brow. "Besides the point. Right now, it could be helpful."

Vadim straightens. "Let me see what I can do." He strides over to the computer at the side of the room, pulling the chair out and sitting. His fingers fly across the keyboard. "What kind of device is it? Did you encrypt the signal, or are we working with a default setup?"

I blow out a breath and hand him my phone with the tracking app turned on. "I don't fucking know, our tech guys set it up. Everything you need is right here."

Vadim nods, muttering to himself as he works. Roman watches him like a hawk, his tension palpable. Pavel rises to stand behind Vadim as he works.

I can feel Roman's eyes on me, and I meet his stare, refusing to look away. "Something you want to say to me, Vasiliev?"

"I'm trying to figure you out. If you've tricked or manipulated Sofiya into falling for you, I'll flay you alive."

I run a finger over the indent in my chin. "That's fair."

"What does that mean?"

I throw my hands wide. "It means I didn't trick or play or manipulate her. It means I fell just as hard for her. I'd burn the world to ashes to get her back. I'd trade every deal, every ounce of my power, for her happiness." My voice cracks, and I resist the urge to smash a fist through the wall.

Roman blinks, clearly caught off guard by my response.

I open my desk drawer and pull out the documents for the casino deal. Slapping them onto the desk, I push them toward him. "These are the papers Igor wanted me to sign. The deal I walked away from so I could show you how serious I am about her."

Roman picks up the papers, his expression hard as he flips through them. Finally, he sets them down and gives me a tight nod. "You're still an asshole, but I believe you."

It's not forgiveness, but I'll take it. However, nothing can erase the unease gnawing at me. Sofiya's still out there, and every second she's in Igor's hands feels like torture.

A moment later, Vadim curses and leans back in frustration. "There's no signal. They must've removed the monitor."

Pavel steps forward. "Mind if I try?"

Vadim looks at me, and I dip my chin. Pavel takes a seat and cracks his knuckles. "What kind of encryption am I dealing with?"

"Military grade," Vadim says flatly.

Pavel's lips twitch, the closest thing to amusement I've seen from him all night. "Let's see if it holds up."

The room goes quiet except for the rapid clicking of keys. Roman's eyes dart between Pavel and the screen, his hands curled into fists on the armrests of his chair.

After a tense stretch, Pavel straightens. "Got it. I've managed to pull up the last location where the monitor was active. It might not be current, but it's something."

Fuck. Finally, a break.

"What's the location?" I demand, stepping up to the monitor.

Pavel types quickly, and a map fills the screen. The area is an industrial zone on the edge of the port. Rusted warehouses and forgotten streets dot the grid.

"That place is a fucking wasteland. No surveillance, no foot traffic. But I know it. It's not far from an abandoned lot where Igor and I used to meet." My hands clench at my sides. "We can be there in under an hour."

"Do you want to use our chopper?" Roman offers.

I shake my head. "It'll be too loud, especially in an area like that. We need to be stealthy."

Eva is already halfway to the door. "I'll grab the tactical gear and prepare our men. Meet outside in five."

Roman claps me on the back. "You lead this. Whatever you need, my men and I will provide support."

It's not a full-on white flag, but it's as close as I'm going to get. "Appreciate it."

Before we can move out, my phone vibrates in my pocket. A second later, Roman's phone chimes, too.

We both freeze, exchanging a wary glance. My stomach tightens as I check the screen—a video message from an unknown number.

Roman swipes to open it, his expression tense. "What the fuck is this?"

I follow suit, dread curling in my gut. I hold my phone up so Roman can see. "Did you get the same video?"

He gives me a tight nod. The room falls silent as the video begins to play.

CHAPTER FORTY-FIVE

NIKOLAI

My stomach churns when I see the opening frame. It's my worst nightmare come true. Sofiya is tied to a chair, her wrists bound behind her. Her head is tilted back at an unnatural angle, Igor's hand twisted cruelly in her hair.

"Good evening, gentlemen." Igor's voice drips with mockery. He grins into the camera, a knife pressed against Sofiya's throat. She flinches, tears glistening in her eyes, but otherwise remains perfectly still. The rage inside me burns white-hot, but I can't tear my eyes from the screen. Sofiya looks terrified, but she's alive.

Vadim leans over my shoulder. "Fuck," he mutters under his breath.

There's no sign of Emil, but he could be behind the camera. That he might stand there, watching Igor do this to Sofiya and doing nothing, makes my blood boil.

"You left your precious little pawn unprotected, and now, she's mine. I thought you were smarter than this, Nikolai. I warned you about letting a woman make you weak, but you didn't listen, did you? You fell in love, and now you'll pay the price, and so will your pretty little dancer."

He gives a sharp tug to her hair as if to make his point. Beside me, Roman growls low in his throat.

Igor's voice darkens. "If you want to see Sofiya alive again, you'll play by my rules." Igor's smirk widens as he presses the knife closer to Sofiya's neck. She squeezes her eyes shut, trying to block him out, and every protective instinct in me roars to life. Every muscle in my body locks up, my heart pounding so hard I swear it might crack my ribs.

"Nikolai, you have 24 hours to sign over the casino deal and every asset tied to it. Roman, you'll give me and my new partners free rein in Moscow. Open borders, full access, no interference. And to ensure the Syndicate is sufficiently weakened, you'll also transfer 100 million dollars to an off-shore account.

"And in case you're under the illusion you can stop me, let me introduce my new partners: the Black Company. Roman, I'm sure that name rings a bell. You thought you erased them from the map. I'm here to tell you they've rebuilt and are out for revenge."

Roman's face darkens. The Black Company was a powerful Chinese triad that the Syndicate took down years ago. It sounds like they've risen from the ashes.

Igor's attention shifts back to Sofiya, and my blood turns to fire as he drags the flat of the knife down her cheek. "Oh, Nikolai. If only you listened to me when I warned you. Now Sofiya's mine, and trust me, the next 24 hours will be unforgettable—for both of us." She swallows hard, her throat working overtime. "If I get what I want, I'll drop her off at the old dockyards tomorrow at midnight. If not, well, I've already got buyers lined up who are very interested in her… talents."

The video ends, the screen goes black, and it feels like every cell in my body is vibrating, my blood roaring in my ears. The thought of Sofiya in Igor's hands, of what he's threatened to do, has me teetering on the edge of control.

For a second, the room is deathly silent, and then I drive my fist into the wall, the crack of impact breaking the quiet. Pain shoots up my arm, but I welcome it. My bleeding knuckles are the only thing anchoring me, keeping me from completely losing my grip.

All this time, Igor was playing me. How long had he been plotting against me? How long was I just a puppet in his carefully planned endgame—one I was too blind to see? Shame burns hot under my collar. He told me Sofiya would betray me, but it was him all along. The real snake. I draw in a ragged breath. I owe Sofiya so many apologies. Failing to see Igor and Emil for the traitors they are is something I'll never forgive myself for.

Vadim clamps a firm hand on the back of my neck, his grip steady. "Breathe," he says. "We'll figure this out, but now's not the time to lose it."

Across the room, Roman sinks into a chair, his head in his hands. Pavel stays silent, his face a mask of hard lines and tension.

"This shouldn't be possible," Roman mutters, his voice taut with frustration. "The Black Company was wiped out. We made sure of it."

"Obviously, we didn't." Pavel drags a hand through his hair. "We failed… I failed." I don't know what that means, but the two men exchange a heavy look.

The door creaks open, and Eva steps in cautiously. Her gaze sweeps the room, landing on me. "What's going on?"

"Igor sent a video. He's got Sofiya, and he's working with the Black Company Triad. They want everything—territory, money, the casino deal—and we have 24 hours to comply."

My phone dings, with a link to an encrypted server.

Roman looks up, his eyes shadowed. "We can't just give

them what they want. Even if we do, they'll just come back for more. They're playing us, they want to take us down."

"And if we don't?" I snap, my voice breaking. "What then? Do you think Igor's bluffing?"

Eva straightens from where she's leaning against the wall. "Let's not waste any more time. We have a possible location, thanks to the ankle monitor. Our men are geared up and ready. If we move now, we might have a shot at getting her back before the 24 hour deadline."

Pavel pushes off his chair, his expression grim. "What if the Black Company's soldiers are guarding the place? If we go in blind, we could be walking into an ambush."

Vadim drums his fingers on the desk. "I can get a drone above the location. It'll give us eyes on the ground so we know what we're walking into."

"That's our best option for now," I agree. "Let's fucking do this. I don't want to wait another minute."

The room bursts into motion, everyone filing out. I stay rooted in place, watching as Roman lingers by the door. He rubs his temples, exhaustion written in every line of his face.

I clear my throat. "Do you want to call Liza? Let her know what's going on?"

He drops his hands, shaking his head slowly. "No. There's no point in stressing her out until we know more. She's been through enough already. But I'll let Maxim Belov know what's happening. He needs to be looped in." Roman's eyes meet mine. "I can see how much this is costing you. How much you care for her."

"I fucking love her, and I'll stop at nothing to bring her home safely. And then I'll hunt them down, one by one, and make sure they suffer for this. It's going to be a bloody night in St. Petersburg."

Roman's lips twitch. "Alright, then. I've got your back every step of the way."

I exhale, steadying myself, before walking out the door and hope like hell I'm bringing my wife home tonight.

CHAPTER FORTY-SIX

SOFIYA

MY HEAD FEELS LIKE IT'S SPLITTING IN TWO, THE POUNDING behind my eyes making me groan. I blink, my vision clearing enough to see that I'm still tied to the chair, the horror still painfully real.

The ropes burn against my wrists as I flex them, my muscles stiff from hours of immobility. My mouth is dry, and my thoughts are sluggish. They must've drugged me. It's the only explanation for why I would've passed out sitting here.

After they filmed the video, I nearly had a panic attack, terrified of what Igor threatened. He's a twisted man, and I have no doubt he'll follow through on his threats.

I couldn't have slept for long because it's still night. Through the darkness, I see Emil sitting across from me, his chair tipped slightly back, one hand resting on the armrest, the other gripping a gun. His face is blank, his eyes cold as he watches me. Whatever Niko did to him, this can't be worth it —aligning with a psychopath.

My heart sinks as I imagine Niko and Roman watching

that video. It must have destroyed them both—though Roman might not even understand what it means.

I scan the room, confirming Igor isn't here. A ripple of hope stirs in me. If he's gone, I might still have a chance to reason with Emil.

I shift in the chair, flinching as the ropes dig into my wrists. "Emil," I croak, my voice barely above a whisper. His gaze flicks toward me but remains guarded.

"Igor's plan is insane. It'll never work. He's setting them up, and you know he won't let me go. You've seen what happens when people cross him. He's a monster. Whatever Niko did to you, it's not worth this betrayal."

Emil's lips curl in disdain. "You think he's so great? He never gave me the chance I deserved. I worked my ass off for him, proved myself over and over, and all I ever got were scraps. He underestimated me, Sofiya. Always has, even when we were kids. But Igor? He sees what I'm capable of. He's promised me second-in-command—something Nikolai would never give me."

"Igor's a liar, and he's aligning with a Chinese Triad that wants to take over Russian organized crime. Is that what you want? To help them destroy the Zhukov Bratva?"

His gaze shifts to the floor, and for the first time, he looks unsure. It's only a flicker, but it's enough to make me believe there's still a chance.

"You can fix this," I plead, leaning forward as much as the ropes allow. "Help me, Emil. We can leave this place together. Nikolai will forgive you, I promise. Make the right choice."

He looks away, his shoulders sagging. "It's too late. I've made my choice, and I'm sticking to it."

"You heard what he plans to do to me," I plead, my voice trembling. "Do you want that on your conscience? You could stop this."

Emil turns his back to me, running a hand over his face.

His fingers press against his temples, massaging as if trying to erase the thoughts I've just planted in his head. I know I've struck a nerve.

"Look at me. Please, look at me. If there's a shred of humanity left in you, don't let him hurt m—"

Approaching footsteps cut me off. Igor enters the room, his stern expression shifting into something darker, more predatory, as his eyes land on me. A chill races down my spine. He glances between us.

"Do we have a problem here?"

Emil shrugs. "No problem. Sofiya was running her mouth, and I was ignoring her."

Igor's gaze narrows on me. "Sounds like I should put that pretty mouth of hers to better use." My shoulders curl inward as if I can shield myself from him. He steps closer, hooking his thumb into my mouth and pulling my bottom lip down.

Every part of me recoils as Igor's thumb presses against my lip, his nail scraping the tender skin inside my mouth. His bitter taste makes my stomach churn, and I bite down hard. His skin splits beneath my teeth, the sharp tang of blood flooding my tongue.

"Fucking bitch!" Igor yells, jerking his hand back. His eyes blaze as he rears back and slaps me across the face. The force of the blow sends my head snapping to the side, the chair tilting dangerously before settling back. Tears spring to my eyes as my cheek burns with pain.

He shakes his hand and glares at the blood dripping from his thumb. Grabbing my jaw with bruising force, he lowers his face until it's inches from mine. "If you like playing rough, then let's play rough. You get to run, little dancer. Run an hide. But when I catch you—and I will—that's when the re fun starts."

The sadistic glee in his expression is terrifyi g. stomach heaves, and my mind screams at me to thin something, anything, but I'm frozen in terror as his words sink in. I look past Igor to Emil, but his eyes stay glued to the floor.

Fuck. I was so close to getting through to him.

Igor's hands are rough and impatient as he unties my legs. My arms remain bound behind me, looped around the back of the chair, but now I can stand. The cold floor feels rough under my bare feet as I rise, my legs trembling from fear and hours of sitting in the same position.

"Let's go," he snaps, yanking my arm hard enough to make me yelp as he drags me toward the back entrance.

We pass Emil sitting near the threshold, his posture rigid. "Black Company soldiers will be here soon. Keep watch until then," Igor instructs him.

I throw Emil a desperate look, silently begging him to meet my eyes, but he stares straight ahead, shutting me out. My body goes cold, hope slipping further from my grasp. I can't fathom what Niko ever saw in him; he has no soul.

Nikolai. The thought of him sends a wave of anguish through me. I know he's suffering right now. But I also know he'll do whatever it takes to bring me back. I just pray it doesn't cost him his life; whatever Igor has in store, it's far bigger than any of us could have imagined.

Igor forces me outside, the night chill slapping me like a physical blow. This area is littered with old shipping contain- rusted cranes, and the skeletons of derelict warehouses. ghost town, abandoned and forgotten, the perfect ground for someone like Igor.

breath is hot and rancid against my ear as he pulls ter. "Do your best to run and hide, little dancer. I r, and you are my prey." Nausea turns my words sink in. "You can fight me, hide from continues, his voice almost sing-song. "But ith my dick in all of your holes."

ess the horror of his words, he shoves me

forward. I stumble, barely catching myself on my unsteady legs.

"Run," he calls after me, his tone mocking. "I'll give you a one-minute head start."

My heart hammers as I take off, my bare feet slapping against the cold ground.

CHAPTER FORTY-SEVEN

NIKOLAI

We park the Humvee in the shadows of a crumbling overpass. Roman and I sit in the back, the drone monitor balanced on the center console between us. The live feed flickers to life as Vadim maneuvers the controls, the camera sweeping across the desolate area.

I take a swig of water, the tactical gear hot against my skin. My shoulder is throbbing, but that's the least of my concerns. I've never felt this restless or angry, this ready to do unthinkable violence. Maybe Roman senses my intensity because his look reminds me to stay calm. We can't lose our minds now.

The drone's camera pans slowly over the industrial wasteland. Rusted warehouses, stacks of shipping containers, and abandoned equipment fill the screen, their shadows stretching long under the moonlight. My fingers curl into my palms as I focus on the monitor showing another row of empty warehouses.

Roman exhales, breaking the quiet. "We're looking for a needle in a fucking haystack."

"We're looking for movement," Vadim says without turning around. "Anything that seems out of place."

I lean forward, gripping the back of the passenger seat. My eyes burn from staring at the feed, but I can't look away.

"If they're inside a building, we're shit out of luck," Pavel mumbles.

"Maybe, but in a place like this, any activity could be a sign," I tell him. "Footprints, vehicles, even a light turned on."

Eva's voice crackles over the radio from the vehicle behind us. "Anything?"

"Nothing yet," Vadim replies, his tone grim.

Vadim tilts the drone's camera over a cluster of shipping containers.

Every second we sit here, my mind whirrs with worst-case scenarios. Helplessness claws at me. She's with that fucking monster, and I know what he's capable of. It chills my blood.

Movement on the screen catches my attention. I blink. "Wait—what was that?"

Vadim glances back. "What?"

"I saw something, a flash of movement."

The others squint at the feed, but whatever I saw is gone. The drone hovers above an open stretch of cracked pavement between the maze of shipping containers.

Roman shakes his head after a minute. "I don't see anything."

I rub the back of my neck, a knot of tension growing. "Maybe it was my imagination," I mutter. Fuck, am I losing it?

I crack my knuckles, forcing myself to take steady breaths. If we don't find her soon, I'll have to do the unthinkable—sign the casino contract and hand over my legitimate businesses to Igor. It's everything I've built, my foothold in a world beyond the bratva, but for Sofiya, I would give it all up.

Still, Igor can't be trusted. Even if we give him what he wants, there's no guarantee he'll return her. But if we can't find her ourselves, what other option do I have?

Vadim tilts the drone to scan another angle, and then it happens again—I see a flicker of movement. Every muscle in my body tenses.

"There." I point at the screen.

This time, everyone sees it. Vadim narrows his eyes. "Hold on." He moves the drone lower, carefully maneuvering it toward the source. The night-vision camera isn't great, the grainy feed flickering as shadows stretch across the screen.

"Come on," Roman mutters, his voice tight.

When the image sharpens, I exhale, the blood draining from my face.

It's Sofiya.

Her arms are tied behind her back, and she's moving, running barefoot between the rows of containers. She darts around a corner, moving fast like her life depends on it. Shit. It probably does.

"What the fuck is going on?" Pavel mutters.

I don't take my eyes off the screen, my pulse hammering in my ears as the grim reality of what we're seeing sets in."

"She's running… Maybe she escaped him."

"Or maybe he's chasing her." Roman looks as disgusted as I feel.

"I lost her," Vadim husks, maneuvering the drone's camera. The screen flickers, but Sofiya is gone.

"We need to go in now. We can't wait," I insist, slipping in the comms earbud.

Vadim swivels in his seat. "I'll stay here and guide you. If we all move in, we'll tip them off. Igor and any Black Company soldiers with him will know we're here. You three go in. Eva and the others will hold the perimeter."

Roman, Pavel and I climb out of the Humvee and head to the rear compartment, where extra weapons and gear are stashed. I grab a tactical knife, sliding it into the holster strapped to my thigh, then take an extra magazine for my pistol and tuck it into my vest. Luckily, we had the sense to put on all-black tactical gear before we arrived here.

Pavel crosses his arms and rests a shoulder against the vehicle. "How do you want to do this?"

I lift my head and scan the surroundings. "I'll take the west side, Roman the east, Pavel up the middle. We close in and follow Vadim's instructions."

Roman pulls out a compact pistol, checking the chamber before sliding it into a holster strapped to his chest. "Just like old times, huh, Zhukov?"

I didn't expect Roman to crack a joke, but I appreciate the effort. I just wish it wasn't Sofiya's life in danger that keeps bringing us together.

We exchange a look, each of us silently acknowledging what's at stake. "How about next time we just catch up over a beer?"

"You got it." Roman clasps my arm briefly, his grip firm. "Good luck."

I wish the other two men luck as well, but I don't need it. Luck won't win this fight.

What's driving me tonight is pure vengeance, and I won't stop until Sofiya is back in my arms.

CHAPTER FORTY-EIGHT

SOFIYA

THE CONTAINERS STRETCH ENDLESSLY, THEIR TOWERING WALLS my only defense in this fucked up game of hide and seek. My chest heaves as I press myself into a corner, the metal cold against my bare skin. My feet are torn to shreds, and my wrists ache from pulling against the ropes, but I don't stop. Because every time I do, I hear Igor catching up.

"Where are you, little dancer? You can't hide from me forever," he taunts me from the shadows.

I clamp my lips shut, muffling the sob trying to break free. I don't know how long we've been out here, but I'm running out of energy. Fear gnaws at me, and exhaustion drags me down. Every step feels harder than the last.

The sound of his boots pounding closer sends my pulse racing. He's toying with me, dragging out this game of cat and mouse, and savoring every second of my terror.

"I can't wait to hear how sweet you sound when you scream." His voice carries in the still night. "And trust me, Sofiya, I'll make sure it lasts."

I wish I could cover my ears and block out his taunts. He's doing this to rattle me, and I won't let him win.

I wait, counting to ten in my head, then sweep around a corner. The rough ground tears at my feet, but I force myself to keep moving, weaving between the containers.

Without my hands free I stumble, almost falling, but manage to catch my balance just in time.

A faint buzzing sound pulls my focus upward. I squint into the dark. Something hovers above me, barely visible against the night sky.

My heart stutters wondering what it could be. A bird? Something else?

"I'm going to ruin that pussy so thoroughly no one else will ever want you."

Bile rises in my throat, but his ugly taunt only fuels my determination to keep going. I slip around another corner, but I trip over a loose pipe. My legs give out, and I slam into a container, collapsing to the ground. Before I can scramble back up, he's there, looming over me.

"Caught you." His voice drips with triumph as he grabs my arm and shoves me back down when I try to rise. My knees hit the concrete again, pain shooting up my legs. "Now, I get to break you."

He wraps an arm around my waist and hauls me to my feet. I thrash, kicking wildly. My foot connects with his shin. He grunts but doesn't let go.

"Bitch," he growls. I twist harder, driving my heel into his knee. He stumbles, and I slam my head back into his face.

There's a sickening crack, and hot blood sprays across my neck and shoulders. He curses, staggering back. I don't think —I just run, using everything I have to put as much distance between us as possible.

I round a corner and press into the shadows. It's quiet, but I know it won't last. I'm out of options. Running and hiding is only delaying the inevitable. Giving up crosses my mind, but no. Niko wouldn't want me to. He'd tell me to fight. He always said I was stubborn. Now I need to prove him right.

He's closing in, his heavy breaths getting louder. I push myself to run faster, but he's right behind me. Seconds later, he grabs my hair, yanking me back. I spin around before he slams me into the side of a container, pain ricocheting through my body.

His face is twisted with fury, blood running from his nose. "You're going to regret that, you stupid cunt. I'm done playing nice."

A scream bursts from my throat, the sound echoing around me.

If this is it, I won't go down without a fight.

CHAPTER FORTY-NINE

NIKOLAI

THE METALLIC TANG OF RUST FILLS MY NOSE AS I SLIDE BETWEEN two shipping containers, the narrow space cloaked in darkness. Sweat beads along my back, my body humming with adrenaline. My pistol is cocked and ready, my grip so tight it makes my knuckles ache.

Dark thoughts churn in my mind. Sofiya could be locked away in one of these containers, her screams muffled by steel walls. Or she could be out here, running for her life while Igor stalks her like prey. The thought makes me see red, but I push it aside to focus on what I need to do.

I grit my teeth and scan the next row. Again, nothing.

"Anything from the drone?" I whisper.

"Negative," Vadim replies. "There's a structure blocking my view in the west corner. Can't see a thing."

Roman's voice cuts in. "We're circling back. Nothing on our end."

Something shifts in the distance. My pulse spikes, and I freeze. It's quick—a shadow darting between two containers—but it's enough. I move forward, every nerve on edge as I close in, my focus trained on the faint sound of movement ahead.

Then I hear it—"You're going to regret that, you stupid cunt. I'm done playing nice." Igor's words are followed by a female scream.

My heart leaps into my throat and I take off running. The sounds echo through the rows of containers.

"I'm moving in!" I bark into the comms.

A gunshot rings out, knocking the air from my lungs. Shit, Sofiya!

I round a corner, my legs pumping, dread clawing at me. Then I see her—Sofiya slumped against a container, her whole body trembling as she sobs. Blood spreads beneath her, stark against the concrete.

My stomach drops. Am I too late?

I dash toward her, but my foot catches on something solid, nearly sending me sprawling. It's Igor's body. Blood seeps from his chest, pooling beneath him.

It takes me a second to realize it's his blood on the ground under Sofiya, not hers. Thank fuck. Igor deserved a far worse end, but right now, the only thing I care about is that Sofiya's alive.

I drop to my knees in front of her, gently cupping her tear-streaked face in my hands.

"Sofiya," I murmur. "It's me, Niko. You're safe now."

Her lips tremble, and a tearful smile appears. "You came for me."

"Always, moya sladost. I'll always come for you."

A sharp intake of breath pulls my attention. Emil stands a few feet away, a pistol in his hand. I'm guessing it's the one he just used to kill Igor. His haunted eyes meet mine, and I tense.

Emil might have saved Sofiya, but that doesn't mean he won't turn the gun on me.

Screw it. If he wants to kill me, so be it. I need to make sure my wife is okay.

I turn back to her. Her skin is cold, her eyes wide and glassy. Her dress is torn, knees scraped, and feet raw and blistered. A dried streak of blood stains the corner of her mouth, and a bruise marks her cheek.

Her arms are tied behind her back, and I quickly cut through the ropes. Her wrists are raw and red, the sight of them making my jaw clench. Darkness clouds my thoughts as I take in her condition.

Roman and Pavel appear at my side, and I give them a brief nod, confirming Sofiya is battered and bruised but otherwise unharmed. With a flick of my head, I signal for them to disarm and cuff Emil, who hasn't moved a muscle.

My wife is my priority; I'll deal with Emil later.

I gently press my forehead against hers. "I'm so sorry. So fucking sorry. I should've figured out how dangerous Igor was before you got involved. If I'd realized what he was capable of earlier, you wouldn't be in this mess."

She shakes her head weakly and rests a hand against my cheek. "It's not your fault Igor was a monster."

Pavel kneels beside Igor's lifeless body, checking his pulse. With a shake of his head, he confirms Igor is gone. Fury blazes through me at losing the chance to make him suffer for what he did, but at least he can't hurt her anymore. I spit on his corpse.

Carefully, I lift her into my arms. Her head falls against my shoulder, and I feel the soft puff of her breaths against my neck. "I'm going to get you out of here," I promise.

The screech of tires announces Vadim and Eva's arrival. Eva leaps out of her car, worry etched across her face. "Is she hurt? Do we need a hospital?"

"No hospital," Sofiya insists.

"Call Dr. Safin to meet us at the estate," I instruct Eva.

She's already pulling out her phone when Vadim approaches.

"We've got to move," he says. "Our men spotted activity nearby."

Emil looks up from where Roman has him in cuffs. "Black Company soldiers," he warns. "They're on the way."

Red colors my vision when I look at Emil. He made the right choice in the end, but there are certain betrayals you can't come back from.

Sofiya stirs in my arms as I cradle her closer. "You ready to go home?" I ask, my voice low enough for only her to hear.

She tilts her head up, her swollen lips curling into a small smile. "I'm ready. My home for a long time, I hope."

My lungs constrict, and I brush the hair from her face. "It was always yours, Sofiya. My home, my heart, my soul—they belong to you and always have. As long as I have you, I'll never need anything else."

She pulls my face to hers, gently pressing her lips to mine. I can't kiss her the way I want to because of her injuries, but even with the barest touch, the kiss is full of raw emotion.

When we pull apart, Roman and Pavel stand nearby, watching us.

"Roman? Wait—what are you guys doing here?" Sofiya shakes her head in disbelief.

Roman's expression softens as he leans in to press a kiss to the top of her head. "You think we'd miss out on all the fun?"

Pavel squeezes her arm. "It's good to see you safe, Sofiya."

"Let's wrap up this little reunion in the vehicles," Eva urges, scanning the area.

I carry Sofiya into the Humvee and strap her in. As I come around to the other side, I cast a final glance at Igor's lifeless body, his blood staining the ground beneath him. Vadim looks at me in question.

"Let him rot," I answer. "Right where his new partners can find him."

CHAPTER FIFTY

SOFIYA

I'M STARFISHED ON OUR BED, STARING AT THE CEILING, exhaustion tugging at my eyelids. I'm clean, warm, and fed, yet the events of the last twelve hours cling to me like a shadow. Nikolai hasn't left my side since we returned to the estate. I finally convinced him I could manage five minutes alone while he showers.

Earlier, I had a good cry, releasing some of the pent-up emotion. Now, lying here in the quiet, the weight of it all creeps back in. The only solace is that it's over, and I'm back with Niko. Somehow, this harrowing ordeal brought Nikolai and Roman together—the start of a fragile peace.

The bathroom door opens, and Niko steps into the room wearing only a robe. He looks exhausted, his face roughened with stubble. His eyes soften when they find me.

"Why don't you get into some cozy pajamas and join me," I suggest, patting the spot beside me in bed.

"I don't have cozy pajamas. I sleep naked, remember?"

"Oh, I remember," I say, smirking. "But don't knock it

until you try it. And for the record, I fully intend to buy us matching flannel Christmas PJs."

He gives me a faint smile. "For you, I'll make an exception to my no-clothes in bed rule. But only on special occasions."

When I stifle a yawn, he crosses the room, turns off the lamp, and pulls me into his arms. His warmth surrounds me, and I breathe him in, letting the steady rhythm of his heart calm me.

"Sofiya…" he says, with a note of hesitation. "Do you want to talk about what happened tonight?"

Dr. Safin asked me the same question, but the truth is, I'm not ready. "I need to forget about it for a while and process it on my own. Dr. Safin said she'd recommend a professional I can reach out to when I'm ready to talk."

"I understand, but I'm here for you. Anytime it gets to be too much."

"Are you okay?" I murmur, tilting my head to look at him in the low light. It must have been just as traumatic for him.

He lets out a soft breath, his fingers tangling in my hair. "That was terrifying. I didn't know fear like this until you. If I ever lost you…" He shakes his head and presses his lips to my temple. "Life wouldn't be worth living."

Tears prick my eyes. "I feel the same way. I love you."

"I love you too," he breathes. "More than I've ever loved anyone. I'll do whatever it takes to keep you safe. I promise you'll never be in danger again."

He blames himself for what happened, and I wish he didn't. I don't blame him. It was something out of his control, but no matter what I say, my abduction still weighs heavily on him.

I prop myself up on my elbows so I can look into his eyes. "I know you'll do your best, but that's an impossible promise. No matter what, living life by your side will always be worth it."

He holds my face and kisses me softly. It's the best feeling in the world.

"I wish it didn't have to be that way. If walking away from this world is what I need to do to keep you safe, you know I'll do it."

I shake my head. "We're married—that means accepting everything you are. I'm not looking for you to change."

He huffs a laugh. "You didn't choose to marry me the first time, but I'm going to give you a choice now." His hand coasts over my hair, stroking me gently. "Will you marry me, moya sladost? I'll give you the world, even your freedom."

"Yes, Niko. A thousand times yes. There's no one else for me." I cup his face, my smile breaking through the tears.

He clears his throat. "If you still want to move to Berlin and dance, I'll come with you."

"I've thought about it, and it feels like I'm exactly where I'm supposed to be, with the person I'm supposed to be with. But I'd like to open another school in Berlin."

"Another school?"

"I hope to make the school self-sufficient, separate from your funding. I can fundraise and bring in donors, maybe even host events. Eventually, I'd like to expand and open other schools."

"Why?" he grumbles. "I'll give you all the money you need to expand."

I smile at his grumpy tone. "It's important to me that I make this work on its own—expanding when the time is right." I brace myself on my forearm to look at him. "I want to live here, at the estate full-time, and travel as needed. How does that sound?"

He's quiet for a moment, wrapping a strand of my hair around his fingers. "If that's what you want, moya sladost. You know I'll never deny you a thing."

I lay back down and cuddle into him. We stay like that for

a while, wrapped in each other, until a thought occurs to me. "Can I see Roman before he leaves?"

He brushes a thumb across my cheek. "Roman and Pavel are staying a few days. Liza's coming, too. She'll be here tomorrow."

"Liza? Really?"

"Of course. She wants to be here for you."

Happiness unfurls inside me. It hasn't been that long since we've been apart, but I miss Liza like crazy. Then, another thought strikes me. "Can I call Daria and Alex? You know, my two friends that you threatened to kill if I didn't cooperate."

He stifles a laugh. "Of course."

How did you end up working with Roman and Pavel anyway? Did you call them for help when you realized I was missing?"

He makes an amused noise in the back of his throat. "That phone call you made to your sister. The stolen phone…"

I wince. "About that… I was going to tell you after the party."

"Yeah, well, it's lucky you did call them because they showed up here to talk and ended up helping to find you instead. The timing worked in our favor."

"You're not mad?"

"How could I be? You had every right to try and escape. I'm just glad you didn't manage to." His fingers draw lazy designs on my thigh. "Roman filled me in on all your phone calls and the clues you managed to piece together to help him figure out where we were."

"So, are you guys friends now or what?"

He strokes his chin. "We're not enemies. Not sure we're going to be drinking buddies anytime soon. I'm grateful, though. We couldn't have pulled this off without his help. Although, there's still plenty of work ahead of us."

I'm nearly drifting off. His touch more comforting than a

warm blanket. A final thought flits through my mind. "Emil," I mumble. "Please don't kill him."

I feel Niko stiffen beside me. "He betrayed me. He's the reason Igor was able to get to you."

"I know, but he also saved me. Igor had his hands wrapped around my neck when Emil shot him. He made the right choice in the end."

Niko clears his throat. "I'll take that into consideration."

I pat his arm, already halfway asleep. "Don't be a dick," I murmur before drifting off with his arms around me, soothing away every lingering fear.

CHAPTER FIFTY-ONE

NIKOLAI

Sofiya's soft, even breaths fill the room as I stand by the bed, watching her sleep. Her lashes flutter against her cheeks, her lips slightly parted, her body curled beneath the thick blanket. For the first time in too long, she looks peaceful.

But peace doesn't come for me. Not yet.

I tuck the blanket around her more securely, leaning down to press a kiss to her temple, before I straighten and turn toward the door.

I descend the stairs toward the basement to take care of the final task that needs my attention. It's one I've been dreading.

Emil.

He saved her life, but that doesn't cancel the sting of his betrayal. A festering wound that cuts deep. He was supposed to be loyal. I let him get close, gave him my trust and he used it against me, just like Sergey.

Roman and Pavel are waiting outside the room where Emil is being held. Roman leans against the wall, his arms crossed, while Pavel stands with his hands in his pockets, his head down. They both look as wrecked as I am after not nearly enough sleep. But this is the kind of relentless pace we're used to.

"He's ready for you," Roman says, tilting his head toward the cell door.

I nod grimly. But am I ready to do what I need to? I doubt it. I might be angry, but underneath, there is a potent sadness.

"Did you get answers?" Roman and Pavel spent the last few hours questioning Emil about the Black Company, needing to learn everything they could about the triad.

Roman's eyes narrow. "He didn't know as much as we'd have liked. The details he did know, he gave up easily. We didn't have to work him over too hard. We'll leave that to you."

I brush a hand down my face. "What's the story? I thought you dismantled the triad years ago." From what I understand, the Syndicate crushed the Black Company after fighting over control of the international wine fraud market.

Roman exhales slowly, his jaw tightening. "We thought we did when we attacked Lai King, the leader of the triad. Unfortunately, even ghosts can rise from the dead. We don't know who's running things now, but it's not the same operation we took down."

Pavel's lips press into a thin line. "It might be Hope King, Lai King's daughter, who was just a teenager when we destroyed the organization. We gave her a pass. Looks like that might've been a mistake."

Roman's voice carries a faint edge. "That was your call."

Tension ripples between the two men, their shared history surfacing like a crack in stone.

I glance between them but don't comment. Whatever this is, it's not my concern, at least not right now. I straighten and push the door open, giving them a final dip of my chin.

The cell is cold and dank, the concrete floor unforgiving beneath my feet. This is the same room I brought Sofiya to the night I needed pictures to push the Syndicate into action. The irony is dark and isn't lost on me.

Now, Emil sits strapped to the chair in the center of the room, his head bowed, trying to shut out the world. When I step closer, he lifts his gaze, his eyes bloodshot but steady.

I take a seat across from him, my hands curling into fists at my sides. Usually, I'd start a conversation like this with a few well-placed punches or a shallow knife to the gut, but I don't have it in me.

"You betrayed me," I say, dropping my elbows to my knees. "Why? What could Igor possibly offer you that made this worth it?"

"It's not what he gave me; it's what you didn't." The silence stretches, heavy and tense. "You never took me seriously. It was always Eva over me. Always her. Even when we were kids, she was the one you trusted and leaned on. I was just… there. When you finally asked me to join the Zhukov Bratva, it wasn't because you wanted me. It was because Sergey left a hole you needed to fill."

His words settle over me like a lead blanket. A storm of emotions churns inside me—anger, disappointment, but mostly a deep, hollow ache.

"I wanted to give you a chance to prove yourself," I say, my voice like gravel. "Even when you screwed up, I chose to believe in you. I wanted to believe in you. And you threw it back in my face."

He scoffs, shaking his head. "You brought me on because you had no one else. Don't pretend it was anything more than that."

I stand and take a step closer, my gaze burning into his. "What did Igor offer you? Tell me everything. I think I deserve to know, don't you?"

He hangs his head before meeting my gaze. His eyes are

weary. "Igor promised me I'd be his second-in-command. He understood me. He saw that I wanted more, that I was capable of more. Unlike you."

"You think Igor had any intention of keeping that promise? Of giving you power? He was using you, just like he used me."

Emil's lips press into a thin line, but he doesn't respond, probably because he realizes it's true.

"When did he turn you?"

"He first approached me when you were in the Caucasus region. He came by under the pretense of dropping off paperwork. That's when he asked me to spy on you. To see if you'd follow through with what needed to be done."

"What does that mean?" I growl, though I already have a sinking feeling in my gut.

Emil smirks bitterly. "Sofiya. He didn't think you could stomach hurting her, and he was right. You'd already fallen for her. Anyone could see it. I just confirmed what he already knew."

The words land like a punch to the gut, but I don't flinch. I won't show him that he got under my skin. "And overthrowing me using the Black Company—was that the plan all along?"

He exhales slowly, exhaustion slowing his movements. "I don't know. Igor didn't tell me everything.I do know they promised him control of the triad in Russia. All he had to do was deliver the casino deal with government backing and the Syndicate's promise to stand down. Taking Sofiya allowed him to kill two birds with one stone."

I inhale deeply, my hands curling into fists at my sides as the pieces click into place. I was played this entire time, blinded to the truth—and that's what put Sofiya in danger. The realization makes my blood burn like battery acid.

"Why?" I press. "Why would the Black Company care about the casino deal? I'm sure they can secure the same kind of deal elsewhere without the hassle of coming up against two powerful bratvas."

"Isn't it obvious? They want to crush the Syndicate. Get revenge for what happened in the past."

My jaw tightens, and wrath settles in my bones. If the Black Company is coming for revenge, I'll stand with the Syndicate.

"Give me one good reason why I shouldn't kill you right now."

He tilts his head, his lips curling into something that might have been a smile if it weren't so hollow. "I don't have one. Just kill me."

I tip my head back. Killing him would be easy, but would it feel like justice or leave me empty inside?

"It's too bad my wife begged me not to kill you."

He doesn't look relieved. He meets my stare without hesitation.

"Why did you step in? Why take out Igor when you knew this would be the end for you?"

He exhales, the sound heavy with something close to regret. "Maybe there's a shred of my soul left that hasn't turned black. She begged me not to let him hurt her, and I guess she got to me—like she got to you."

His words twist something inside me, but I shove the feeling down. Drawing my knife, I hold it so the blade catches the dim light. Emil's eyes widen slightly, but he doesn't resist as I grab his face and force him to meet my glare.

Before I can do any damage, the door creaks open. Eva steps inside, her hand landing on my shoulder. "Let me take it from here. I'll finish this for you. He betrayed both of us—all of us, actually." Eva shoots him a dark look.

I'm not a coward. I don't shirk my responsibilities. But maybe, just for today, I can let someone else carry the weight of retribution.

I pass her the knife. "An eye for an eye," I murmur.

Her lips tighten in understanding.

Emil's breath hitches, but he doesn't beg. He doesn't make excuses or try to bargain. He knows he's lost, and in some way, I can respect his acceptance.

"I'll let you live, but you'll never set foot in Russia again," is the last thing I say to him.

CHAPTER FIFTY-TWO

SOFIYA

Nikolai's hand is glued to my elbow as he helps me down the stairs, moving so slowly it feels like we're trying to sneak past a sleeping guard.

"Careful," he says, his brow furrowing. "Your feet—"

"—are fine," I interrupt. "You're driving me insane. I can handle a few stairs on my own."

He shoots me a look. "Maybe I should pick you up and throw you over my shoulder."

I roll my eyes, though I'm not totally against the idea. "I think you've carried me around enough for one lifetime."

"Never," he shoots back. "I like carrying you around."

By the time we reach the dining room, my smile is stretched wide. The room is buzzing with life—Vadim chatting with Roman, Pavel smirking at something Eva's said—and then my eyes land on my sister.

Liza stands as soon as she sees me, her chair pushed back hastily. A lump rises in my throat as she crosses the room in three quick steps and throws her arms around me.

"Sofiya," she whispers, holding me so tightly I can hardly

breathe. When she pulls back, her hands frame my face, her eyes sweeping over me like she's memorizing every inch. "I'm so relieved you're okay. When Roman told me what happened—" her voice breaks.

I grip her wrists gently, smiling through the tears spilling down my cheeks. "I'm okay because of everyone here. And because of you. You believed me enough to send Roman and Pavel to meet with Niko, and I'm so thankful you did."

Her thumb brushes a tear from my face. "I'm so sorry you had to go through that."

I shake my head. "It's behind us. That's all that matters." Although, from what Niko told me this morning, not everything is behind us. The Black Company is back on Russian soil, and they are targeting the Syndicate.

Before we can spill any more tears, Yelena sweeps into the room, directing the staff as they set the table with dish after dish—and, not surprisingly, many of my favorite foods. Then she crosses the room and wraps me in a hug that rivals my sister's chokehold.

"I'm so relieved," Yelena says softly. "It's over now."

And it is.

Niko pulls out my chair, his hand briefly brushing mine as he helps me settle into my seat. He kisses the top of my head before sitting beside me. Across the table, Liza's eyes are locked on us, wide and unblinking, as if she can't quite believe what she's seeing.

I arch an eyebrow. "Do you plan on staring at us through the whole meal?"

Liza blinks, caught off guard, her cheeks coloring. "Sorry! It's just… weird. You two—like this. I'm still trying to process it."

Niko smirks, leaning back in his chair. "You'll get used to it." His eyes dart to my finger. I'm wearing the ring he gave me weeks ago. I don't mind the tattoo so much now. It's not exactly a story for the grandkids, but it's one I'll cherish forever.

For now, his ring over the tattoo feels right.

Liza's smile is soft but not entirely free of tension. I can tell she's still struggling to reconcile the man who abducted me with the one I choose to call husband.

Roman notices it, too. He reaches out, his hand settling on the back of her neck. "If you saw what I saw last night, you'd understand."

Pavel leans forward and grabs his third cheese Danish while Yelena looks on with hearts in her eyes. "It's not exactly like these two were an obvious couple," he says, nodding toward Liza and Roman. "Weird shit happens all the time."

Eva clears her throat, her grin wicked. "It wouldn't be surprising to you if you'd been here from the start. Even when they were hating each other, they were still… not quite hating each other, if you catch my drift."

I roll my eyes but can't help the laugh that escapes me. "That says a lot, considering I thought you were his girlfriend."

Eva lets out a choked sound of disgust. "Even if I were into guys, it wouldn't be him. He's basically my brother."

"The day Niko skipped a day of meetings to take Sofiya shopping was when we all knew he was a goner," Vadim elbows my husband, who shoots him a glare. "Took him a while to figure it out, but we saw it plain as day."

Niko sighs, rubbing a hand over his face. "Do I need to leave so you can finish roasting me?"

Vadim grins. "No need. It's much more fun when you're here for it."

The teasing continues, but Niko turns toward me, a finger under my chin. "How do you explain falling in love with your captor, moya sladost?"

I release a huff of breath. "You're a complicated man, Nikolai Zhukov. Manipulative at times, controlling, maddening—but also loyal, protective, and brave in ways no one else is. You don't do anything halfway, including loving the people in your life. Even if that's scary after all you've been through."

He flinches, not quite believing me, but I press on. "You think you're too damaged, too dangerous, but I see the man who watched *Scream* with me because he knew I was bored and lonely. The man who bought me a dance school because he saw my real passion. You think you're hard to love, but you're wrong. I can't not love you."

His lips part, but no words come out. For once, Niko seems at a loss.

"I love you too, moya sladost, and that's never going to change," he declares, his voice unwavering. "You're mine, for as long as you'll have me. Even if the world burns to ash around us, I'll fight through the flames to keep you by my side."

My throat feels raw, and I have to hold back tears. He leans in, and the kiss he gives me makes it clear that he's forgotten we're at a table full of people. When we pull away, the room is still.

"Good," Yelena's voice reaches us across the table. "And now you have a baby."

I throw my head back and groan while laughter breaks out around the table. "Give us a year or two," I say as Niko grabs my hand under the table.

"It's never too early to start trying," he murmurs.

A few hours later, I'm curled up with Liza on a couch while everyone else talks Bratva business. A heavy blanket stretches across our laps as I carefully prop my feet up on the armrest.

Her head briefly rests on my shoulder, and she releases a weary sigh. "You look better than I thought you would."

I laugh quietly. "Thanks, sis."

"I'm serious." She turns to face me, her expression tight. "When Roman called last night and told me what happened —what could've happened—I thought I was going to lose my mind."

My heart contracts, and I grab her hand. "I know; I'd feel the same way if it was you. I'm sorry I've caused you so much stress these past few weeks."

"It's not your fault. It's that man of yours." She stares at me intently. "But fuck, the way he looks at you… I might have to forgive him, eventually." I know she's joking. Mostly. "Did you honestly think Eva was his girlfriend?"

"Yup. Well, more of a fuck buddy situation. She's gorgeous, was always around, and they're super close. It was a fair assumption. I also didn't know women could be that high up in the bratva."

Liza shrugs. "Maybe Niko is a feminist pioneer."

I burst out laughing. "Yeah, maybe."

"So tell me about this dance school he bought you?"

A grin spreads over my face. "It's for underprivileged kids who wouldn't get a chance to dance otherwise. I've already seen the space, and it needs work but we'll make it happen. Soon I can hire staff and start figuring out all the logistics. It's mine to do what I want with, even though Niko offered to fund it completely, I want it to stand on its own without relying on his money."

Liza frowns. Not quite the reaction I expected. "What about Berlin and your dreams of performing onstage? Is that something you're going to give up?"

I look down at my hands, clutching the blanket in my lap. "Not entirely, but dreams change. Maybe I'll get a chance to perform with the school. The school feels way more meaningful. And who knows, the next school I open could be in Berlin." We're both quiet for a moment. "I'd really like your help," I say to her. "If you're willing to, that is. I could use your business brain."

Liza smiles, brushing her hair behind her ear. "You know I'd love to help. Whatever you need." Her smile turns mischievous. "Better pick my brain now because I might be a little busy in nine months."

I blink, caught off guard. "Wait. Are you—Liza, are you pregnant?"

Her cheeks flush. "I think so. I'm late, and the home test was positive, but I want to confirm with the doctor before saying anything to Roman."

"That's amazing!" I hug her tightly, tears pricking my eyes.

"Don't get sappy on me. I'm still processing."

"Roman is going to freak out. In a good way, I mean." My eyebrows pull together. "How did this happen?"

"Well, Sofi, when two people love each other—"

I carefully elbow her in the ribs. "I meant, I thought you'd be too stressed to do the deed."

"Uh, I mean, I was stressed. It just turns out that my favorite method of stress relief is with my husband inside of me."

"Okay, TMI." I hold up a hand. "But this is the best fucking news in the world."

Her smile turns wistful. "It's still early, and I don't want to get my hopes up," she admits. "We still have a long road ahead of us."

She's not just talking about her pregnancy. There's also the Black Company threat to contend with. I haven't asked too many questions about them, and Niko hasn't volunteered any information, but I know it's what everyone is discussing now. Maybe the one silver lining is that the Syndicate and the Zhukov Bratva are allies again.

I wrap her in my arms because there's nothing more to

say. The idea that there could be a mini-Liza or Roman in the next year makes my heart feel so damn full.

"Think you and Nikolai will have kids someday?"

"Someday, sure. Right now, I just want to enjoy being an auntie and being with Niko. It feels like my whole life has been this race—trying to prove myself worthy of love. Even though you tried so hard to make up for our crappy parents, I guess it was easy to feel like I wasn't good enough for them." She's silent, but I know she feels the same. "But with Niko… he makes me feel like I'm enough, just as I am. It's the most incredible feeling, and I wouldn't trade it for anything."

She squeezes my hand, her voice gentle. "In the weirdest of ways, I'm glad you found him. You deserve every bit of happiness."

I smile, a riot of emotion playing in my chest.

I feel like I'm exactly where I'm supposed to be—with the man who sees me, loves me, and makes me whole.

EPILOGUE

One year later

NIKOLAI

The first thing I register is warmth. Soft lips drag along my skin, pulling me from the edge of sleep. A quiet sigh escapes my lips, my body instinctively responding to the wet heat wrapped around my cock.

My eyes blink open, and for a moment, I'm disoriented. The pale morning light filters through the windows of the Greek villa, painting the room in golden hues.

When I look down, I find Sofiya kneeling between my legs, her hair a wild tumble over her shoulders, her lips stretched around my cock, her hands braced against my thighs. She's a vision, her fluffy white robe slipping off one shoulder, revealing the curve of her collarbone.

"What are you doing?" My voice is hoarse with sleep, but I can't hold back a groan when she flicks her tongue over my morning wood.

She pulls back, her lips shiny and swollen, a teasing smile curving her mouth. "I couldn't wait. You said we couldn't see each other before the wedding, but you didn't say anything about not touching. So close your eyes and enjoy."

"It's the same thing, Sofiya," I rasp, but I don't stop her when she sinks back down, her mouth sliding over me again. I groan, my head falling back against the pillow. "You're a little minx."

She laughs softly, her hands tracing up my thighs. "It's been four days, Niko. Four fucking days. I need this, and I need you."

I do too, to be honest. Fuck this holding-out shit. Technically, we're already married anyway.

My hand tangles in her hair as her mouth keeps working me. I'm not sure how much longer I can last with how good she's making me feel. And if I'm going to fuck my wife on our wedding day, I want to make it count.

"Enough," I growl, tugging her hair gently. When she sits up, I pull her onto my lap. Her robe falls open, revealing smooth skin and curves that I haven't stopped thinking about. My hands slide up to cup her breasts, my thumbs brushing over her sensitive peaks. "If you're going to torture me, you're going to do it properly. With your pussy strangling my cock."

I position her above my length, her knees bracketing my thighs. "Show me how bad you want this," I breathe, my voice thick with need. "Bounce on my cock. I want to feel how much you've missed me."

She peels off her robe, her eyes heavy with lust as she lowers herself, inch by damn inch, the tight heat of her cunt making me groan.

"That's it," I breathe, gripping her hips when she's seated to the hilt. "Now move." I slap her ass so there's no question what I need her to do.

Her eyes darken, and with a quiet inhale, her hips rise up and slam down. Her hands grip my shoulders for balance as she rides me hard, her breathy moans filling the room.

"Fuck, Sofiya." I grip her hips, guiding her rhythm as my body arches beneath her. "I want to see your cunt swallowing my cock."

She knows exactly what to do. She leans back and shifts her weight to her hands, her dark hair cascading down her back. When she opens her legs wider for me, the view is better than the sunrise out the window.

The sight of her like this, on all fours, dripping wet and stuffed with my cock, pushes me close to the edge. I flick her clit just to watch her body jerk in response.

"I've been thinking about this for days," she whispers, breathless. "About how good you feel inside me."

I reach out and rub a finger across her slippery clit. "Then take what you need, baby. Use my cock however you want to."

She rides me harder, her movements growing more desperate and erratic. Her moans echo through the room, a symphony of raw need that fuels the fire burning between us.

"Don't stop," she begs. I couldn't even if I wanted to. I like her uninhibited and completely mine.

"You're so fucking beautiful like this. I can't wait to fill you up with my cum and put a baby inside you."

Her pussy squeezes me so hard I see stars. I guess she likes that, too. Sensing how close she is, I pull her forward and wrap my palm around her throat, giving her the extra nudge she needs to get there.

She trembles, her body tightening around me as her pussy convulses, milking the cum from my balls. Electricity races down my spine as I spill into her, holding her hips tight against me.

She collapses against my chest, both of us panting, and I press a kiss to her forehead. "You're going to be the death of me, Sofiya."

"But you love it," she murmurs. "You love me."

"So fucking much that I can't wait to marry you again."

Her lips brush my shoulder, and we stay as we are for a while, her warmth soothing every jagged edge inside me.

In a few hours, I'll marry her again, but this time, it's not about power or leverage. Marrying her where it all began feels fitting, like we're closing a circle. Our story has been wild, but it's ours.

Partnering with the Syndicate wasn't something I expected, but this time, it's different. Roman and I aren't just allies—we're brothers now.

"Do you know how proud I am of you?" I murmur, brushing a strand of hair from her face. "What you've built, what you've accomplished this year."

The dance school she created is changing lives. Hundreds of young people in need are finding hope through dance, and the first school was such a success that it's expanding into other regions.

Her sleepy smile feels like sunshine. "I couldn't have done it without you."

"You could have," I say, my voice thick with emotion. "But I'm damn glad you chose me."

I'll spend my life making sure she knows how much she's loved and how much she means to me.

She sighs, and I press a kiss to her forehead. "You mean everything to me."

Her voice trembles with emotion as she says, "Back at you."

I've spent so much of my life hardened by the world, but she's broken through and filled the emptiness inside me. She's made me whole in a way I never imagined possible.

Putting a ring on her finger for the second time feels like the start of forever.

SOFIYA

Your wedding day is supposed to be the happiest day of your life, and honestly, I can't think of a happier day than this.

The DJ switches tracks, and the beat picks up, drawing more people to the makeshift dance floor. Alex and Daria grab my hands and pull me into the center. We move without a care in the world—the moon above us and the sand beneath our feet.

"Seriously, Sofi," Alex says, breathless as he spins me around. "I'll never get over the fact that you married your bathroom hook-up. Technically, you still have never had a one-night stand."

"And I never will!"

"I'm still recovering," Daria jokes, smoothing her bob into place. "You disappeared, got kidnapped, and came out of it married and happier than I've ever seen you. My brain needs a moment to catch up."

I laugh, holding onto them for balance. "It's crazy, but we got our happily ever after."

I've come clean to my friends about most parts of Nikolai's and my story, but I left out the part where they were targets. No need to share that little detail now.

"Look at you," Alex says. "Dancing on the beach with your besties and family, married to the hottest man alive, and living your best life."

Daria tilts her head toward Nikolai, standing under the string lights, his suit jacket off, his tie loosened, talking to Roman as he holds my baby niece, Mila. "Seriously, Sofi. My ovaries will never recover after seeing Nikolai hold a baby. What are you waiting for? Get him to knock you up."

I roll my eyes, but a grin spreads across my face. "Okay, you two are officially banned from ogling my husband."

"Oh, please," Alex says, waving me off. "He only has eyes for you. It's nauseating."

I glance at my husband again, and he gives me a saucy wink. My heart flips, and the whole world fades away.

In the weirdest of ways, everything has worked out. Alex lives in London, waiting tables, but he's just landed a role in a major musical. Daria's in LA just as she dreamed, splitting her time between auditions and working as a dominatrix. It's unconventional, but it suits her.

"Excuse me, who is that?" Daria's attention is locked on Eva, who is taking a sensuous sip of her drink at the bar, returning my friend's interested gaze.

Well, tonight promises to end well. "Eva, Nikolai's right hand. Go and introduce yourself. She doesn't bite, but she can kick your ass."

"Clearly." Daria smooths down her dress. "I think I will."

Alex and I watch Daria saunter off, and I elbow him in the ribs. "What about you? Have you met Mr. Right yet?"

He sighs. "I've only met Mr. Right Now. But that's enough for me. Being single allows me time to jet back to Russia and support my bestie when she needs me."

I laugh as the sand shifts beneath my feet. "Speaking of which, I scheduled you to teach that choreography workshop next month."

Alex grins and throws an arm around my shoulder. "Wouldn't miss it for the world. What you've created is pretty special." He kisses the side of my head, then excuses himself to get a drink.

Barefoot, I stroll toward Niko and Roman, who've been joined by Liza. I pass Pavel and Vadim. From the sounds of it, they're engaged in some nerdy tech talk, and I smile and wave as I pass them.

Niko sways gently, rocking Mila in his arms. The sight of him, shirt sleeves rolled up, holding an infant like it's second nature, makes my knees weak.

"Careful, Niko," I tease. "You're setting ovaries on fire left and right."

Liza chuckles, leaning into Roman. "She's not wrong. That's a dangerous look."

Roman raises an eyebrow. "Let's not inflate his ego. It's big enough as it is."

"My turn," I say, reaching out for my niece. Niko passes Mila to me, and I cradle her closely, inhaling her sweet baby scent. For a moment, she snuggles against me, but then her face scrunches up, and she lets out a wail.

I bounce her gently, murmuring soothing words, but the cries only grow louder. Sighing, I pass her to Roman, who attempts to calm her, but Mila's not having it. Her little fists flail until Niko takes her back. Almost instantly, she quiets.

"Guess she's made her choice," I laugh.

Roman shakes his head, his voice deadpan. "You're doomed, Zhukov. Better start practicing bedtime stories now."

Niko looks down at Mila, his lips twitching into a soft smile. "Could be worse fates." When his eyes meet mine, I know exactly what he's thinking. Better practice again tonight.

Liza hugs me tightly, her voice warm and emotional. "Your wedding was perfect, Sofi. I'm so proud of you. Of both of you."

Roman nods, his expression softer than usual. "You've been through a lot, but you're stronger for it."

I think of everything I've overcome—the darkness I've left behind—and focus on this moment. On my future with Niko. On the life we're building together.

As I watch my husband cradle my baby niece, my chest swells. When his eyes meet mine, he says so much without speaking.

I love you.

You're mine.

This is forever.

Life isn't perfect, but at this moment, I can't imagine it being any better.

Thank you so much for reading!

Want more of Nikolai and Sofiya?
Download their **BONUS EPILOGUE** from my website:

https://monicakayne.com/bonuses

ACKNOWLEDGMENTS

Writing a book is never a solo endeavor, and I'm so grateful to the incredible people who've supported me along the way.

Nina, thank you for your excellent manuscript critique. You are literally the smartest person I know, and your feedback is always spot-on. You make me a better storyteller.

Deb, thank you for going above and beyond as a proofreader and as a fan.

Chanel, I appreciate you more than words can say.

Keanna, it's been such a pleasure working with you. Your marketing advice is *chef's kiss*, and I can't wait to see what 2025 brings.

Nana and Nana's boyfriend, thank you for suggesting 'moya sladost' as a pet name—it's perfection. I can't wait for you to help me pick the next name. ;)

Sasha, thanks for being an extra-big supporter and for catching those final typos!

To my writer friends and all the amazing readers I had the chance to meet at Sinners and Stardust in Boston in August 2024, thank you for making that such a special experience. Getting to connect with you in person is something I'll never forget.

Finally, thank you to everyone who has read my books and helped spread the word. I'm so lucky to do a job I love, and it's all because of you. I can't wait to bring you more filthy Bratva kings in the future!

With love and gratitude,

Monica xo

ALSO BY MONICA KAYNE

THE KOZLOV EMPIRE SERIES

Merciless Heir

Cruel Deception

Fierce Vow

Shattered Crown

BRATVA KINGS SERIES

Ruthless Reign

Savage Reign

All my books can be read as ***complete standalones****. There's no cheating, no cliffhangers, and a guaranteed happily ever after.*

ABOUT THE AUTHOR

Monica Kayne is a former documentary TV producer turned proud romance writer. She writes dark and swoony romance novels with a liberal dose of sass and humor. Her favorite characters to write are sweetly possessive bad boys and the feisty, smart-mouthed heroines they can't resist. When she's not dreaming up sexy plots, she can be found searching for the perfect Negroni and her next K-drama fix. She lives with her family in Toronto, Canada.

Connect with me!
www.monicakayne.com

TikTok
@monicakayneauthor

Instagram
@monicakayneauthor

Facebook reader group
Monica's Mafia Queens

Printed in Great Britain
by Amazon

61561723R00224